FOR OUR BRAVE, SENSITIVE MEN:
FLORENT, ARNAUD, FRED   I.A.
HIPPOLYTE, DARIUS, SAM   F.B.
BEN, KENT, JOËL   C.M. AND S.O.

# LOUIS UNDERCOVER

Copyright © 2016 by Fanny Britt and Isabelle Arsenault
Copyright © 2016 by Les Éditions de la Pastèque
First published in French as *Louis parmi les spectres* in 2016 by Les Éditions de la Pastèque, Montreal, Quebec
English translation copyright © 2017 by Christelle Morelli and Susan Ouriou
First published in English as *Louis Undercover* in Canada and the USA in 2017 by Groundwood Books

Song lyrics: "This is a man's world ..." by James Brown and Betty Jean Newsome from "It's a Man's Man's Man's World," 1966; "Feeeel-good" by James Brown from "I Got You (I Feel Good)," 1965; "Bye bye love ..." by Felice and Boudleaux Bryant from "Bye Bye Love," first recorded by the Everly Brothers, 1957; "For lovin' me ... gone" by Gordon Lightfoot from "For Lovin' Me," *Lightfoot!*, 1966.

Groundwood Books / House of Anansi Press
groundwoodbooks.com

We acknowledge for their financial support of our publishing program the Canada Council for the Arts, the Ontario Arts Council and the Government of Canada.

Canada Council     Conseil des Arts
for the Arts       du Canada

ONTARIO ARTS COUNCIL
CONSEIL DES ARTS DE L'ONTARIO
an Ontario government agency
un organisme du gouvernement de l'Ontario

With the participation of the Government of Canada
Avec la participation du gouvernement du Canada | Canadä

We acknowledge the financial support of the Government of Canada through the National Translation Program for Book Publishing, an initiative of the Roadmap for Canada's Official Languages 2013-2018: Education, Immigration, Communities, for our translation activities.

Library and Archives Canada Cataloguing in Publication
Britt, Fanny
[Louis parmi les spectres. English]
    Louis undercover / Fanny Britt, Isabelle Arsenault ; translated by Christelle Morelli and Susan Ouriou.
Translation of: Louis parmi les spectres.
Written by Fanny Britt ; illustrated by Isabelle Arsenault.
Issued in print and electronic formats.
ISBN 978-1-55498-859-4 (hardcover). — ISBN 978-1-55498-868-6 (Kindle). — ISBN 978-1-55498-860-0 (EPUB)
    1. Graphic novels. I. Arsenault, Isabelle, illustrator II. Morelli, Christelle, translator III. Ouriou, Susan, translator IV. Title. V. Title: Louis parmi les spectres. English.
PN6733.B75L6913 2017          j741.5'971          C2015-903778-6
C2015-903779-4

The illustrations were rendered in pencil and ink.
Printed and bound in China

*FANNY BRITT*
*ISABELLE ARSENAULT*

# LOUIS UNDERCOVER

TRANSLATED BY CHRISTELLE MORELLI AND SUSAN OURIOU

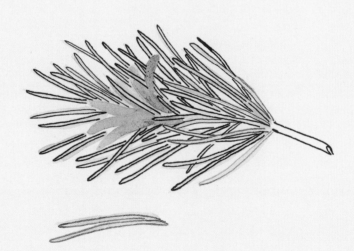

GROUNDWOOD BOOKS
HOUSE OF ANANSI PRESS
TORONTO   BERKELEY

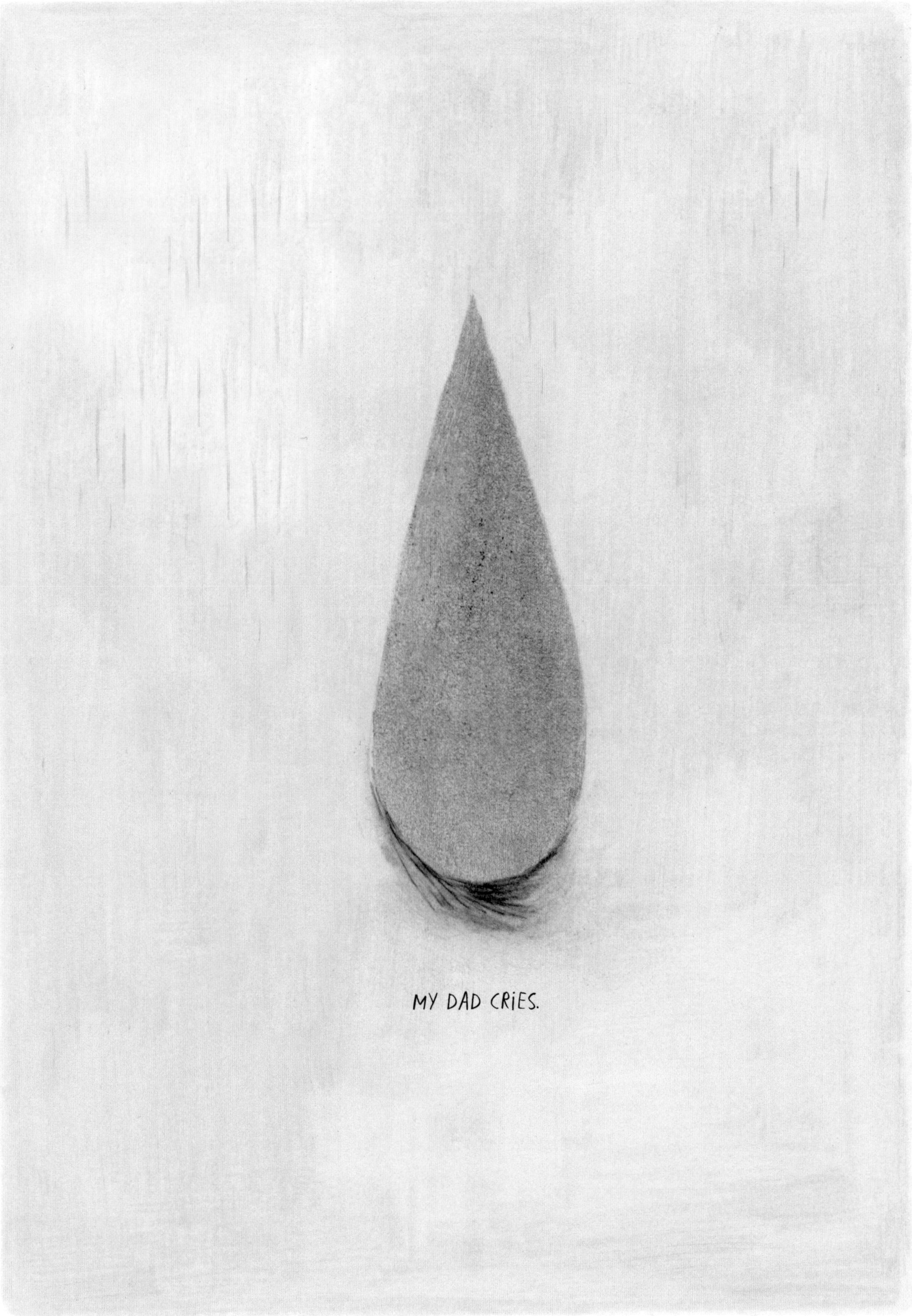
MY DAD CRiES.

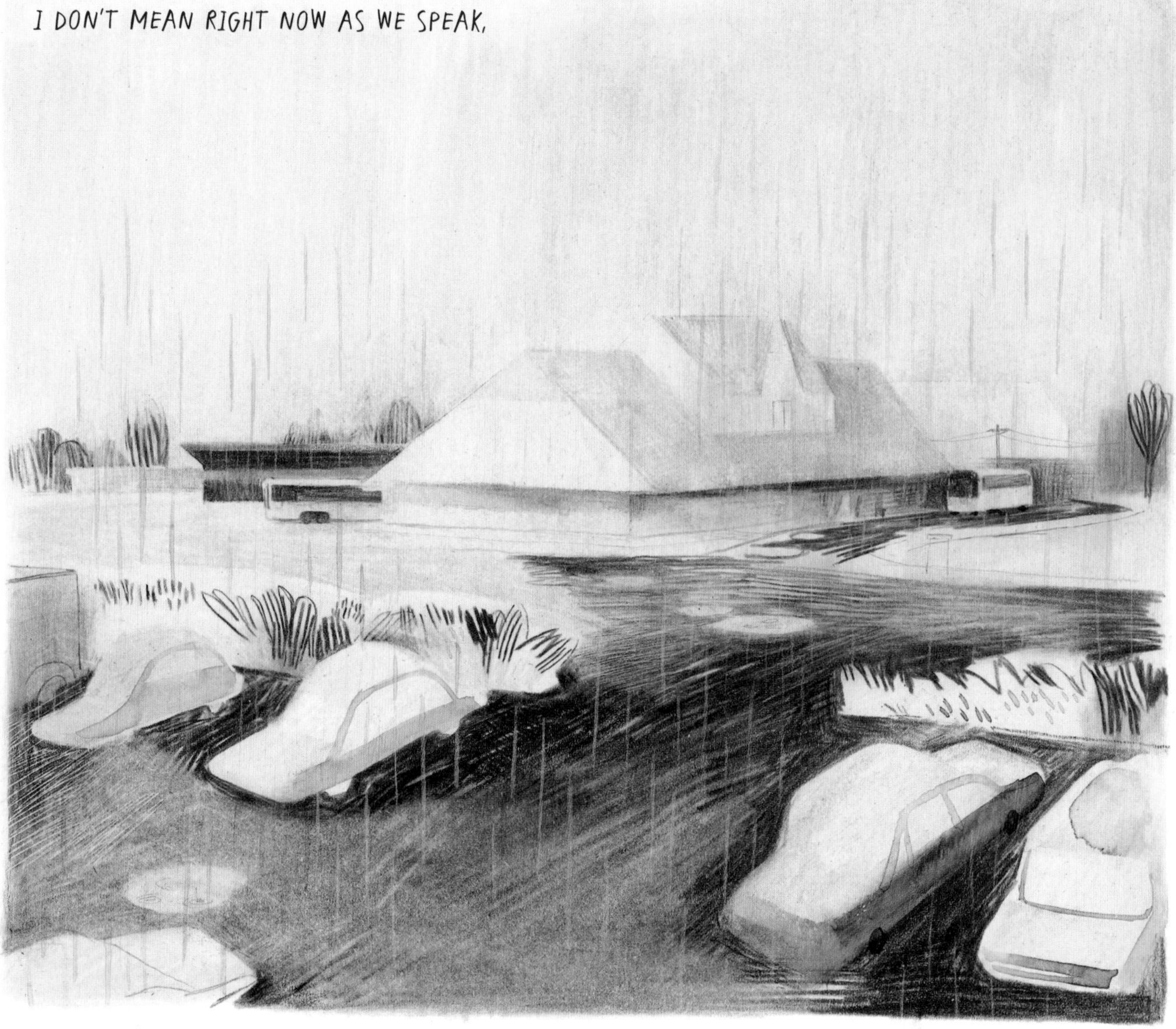
I DON'T MEAN RIGHT NOW AS WE SPEAK,

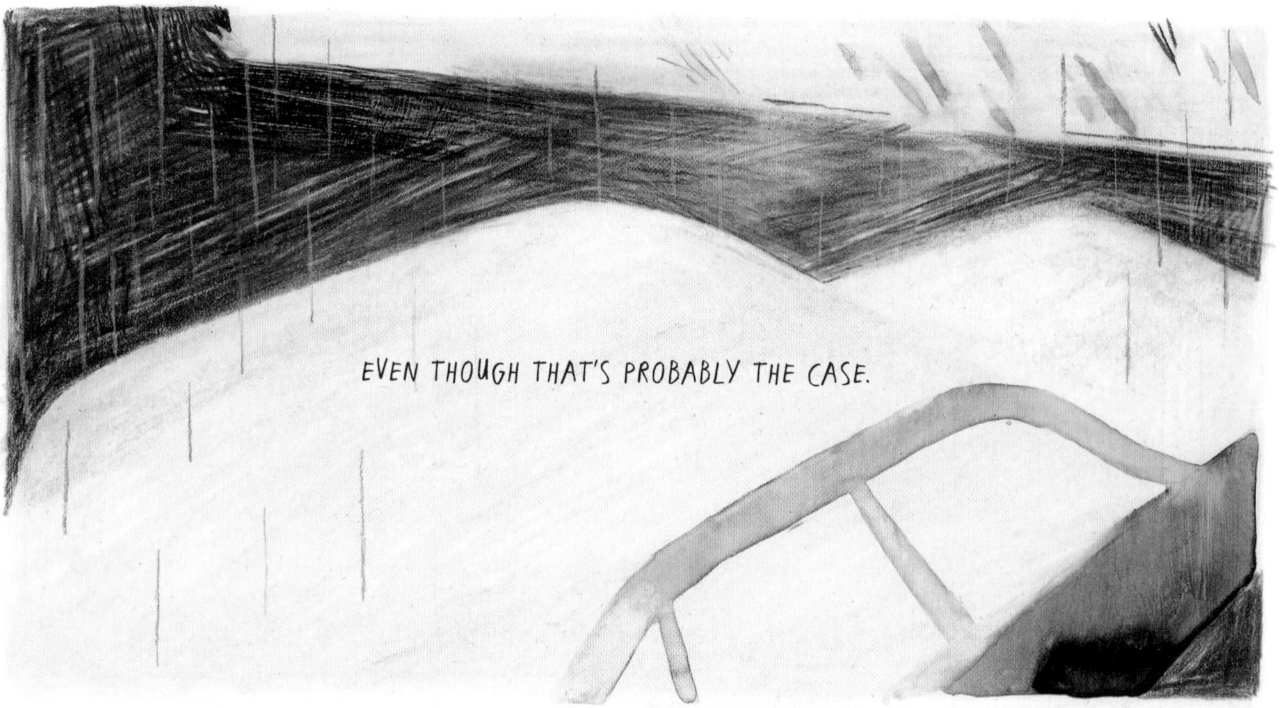
EVEN THOUGH THAT'S PROBABLY THE CASE.

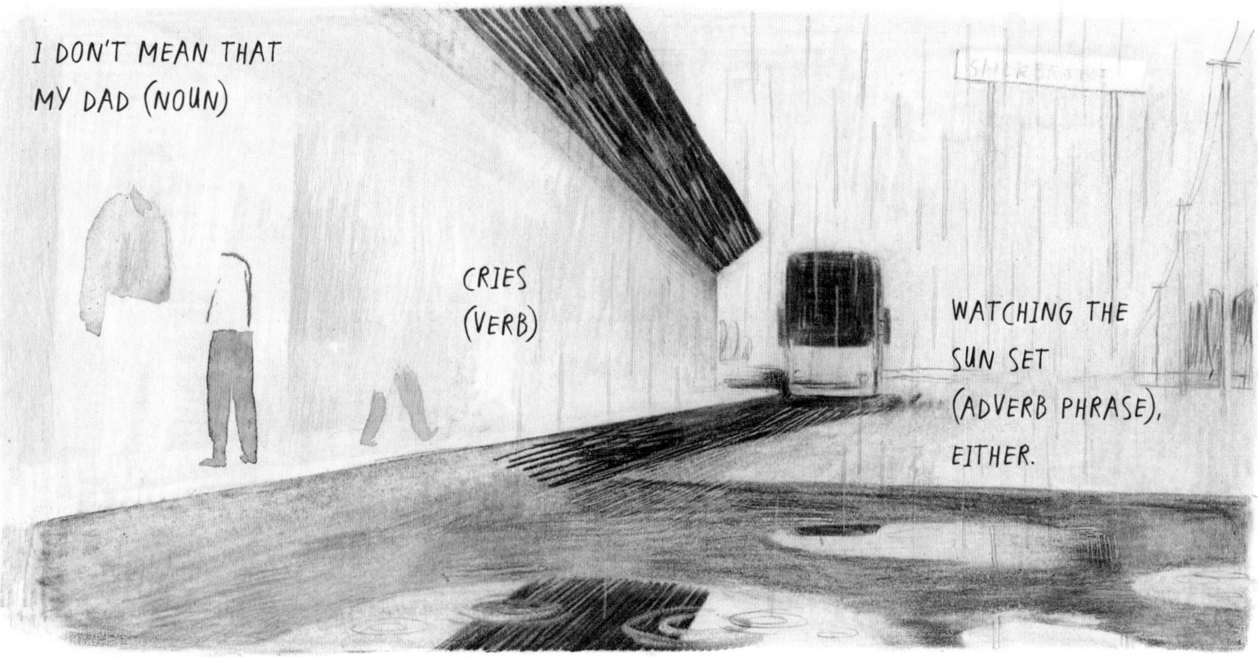
I DON'T MEAN THAT MY DAD (NOUN)
CRIES (VERB)
WATCHING THE SUN SET (ADVERB PHRASE), EITHER.

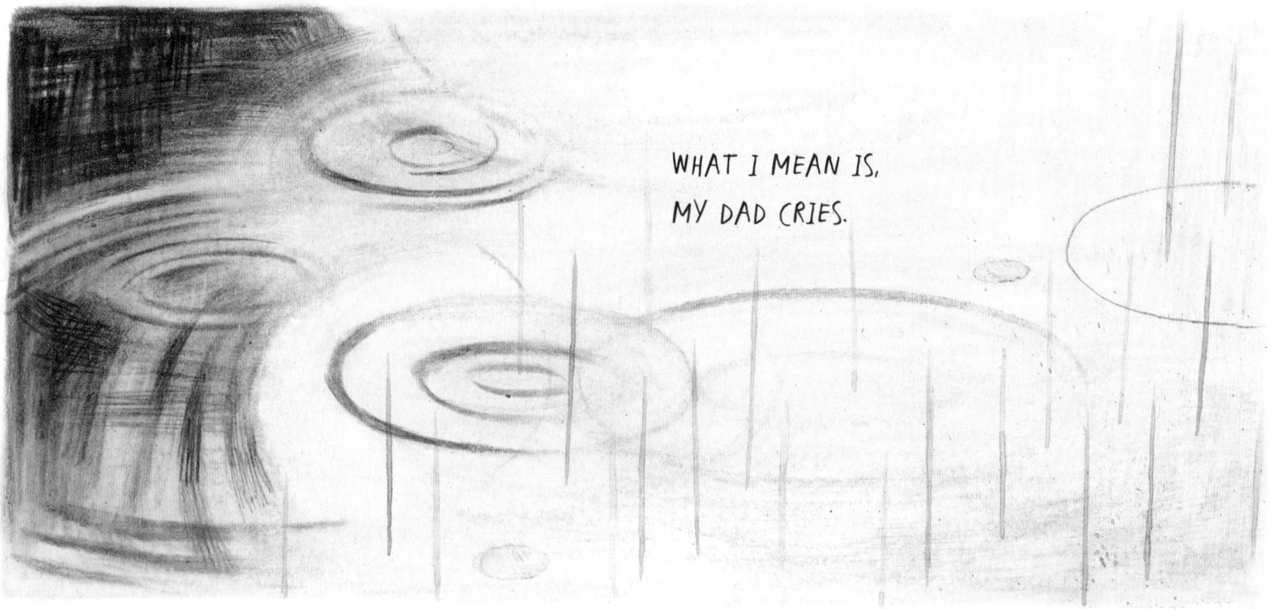
WHAT I MEAN IS, MY DAD CRIES.

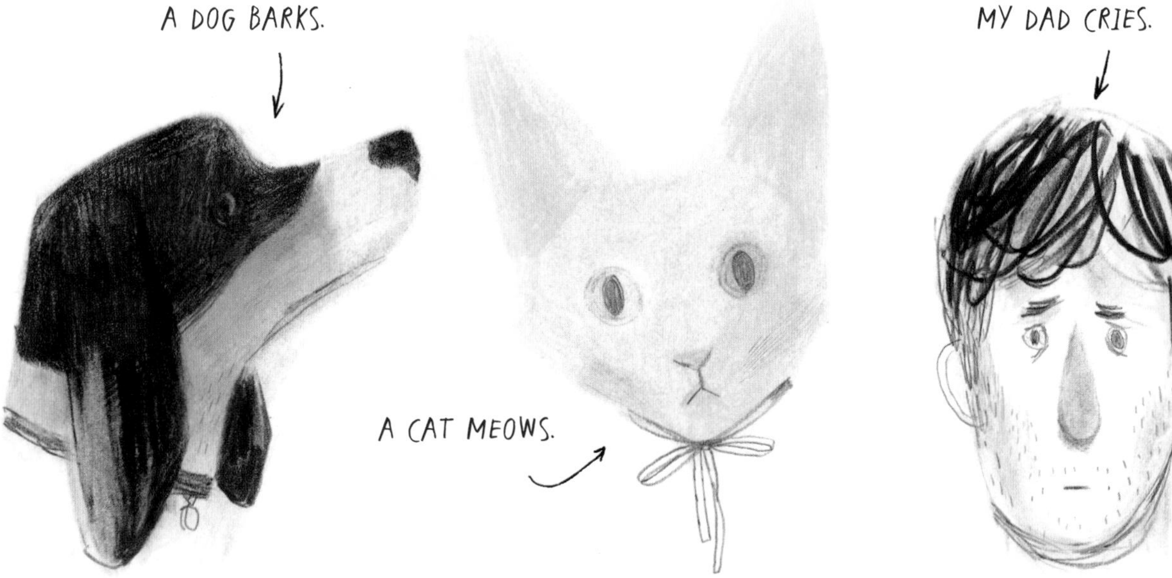
A DOG BARKS.
A CAT MEOWS.
MY DAD CRIES.

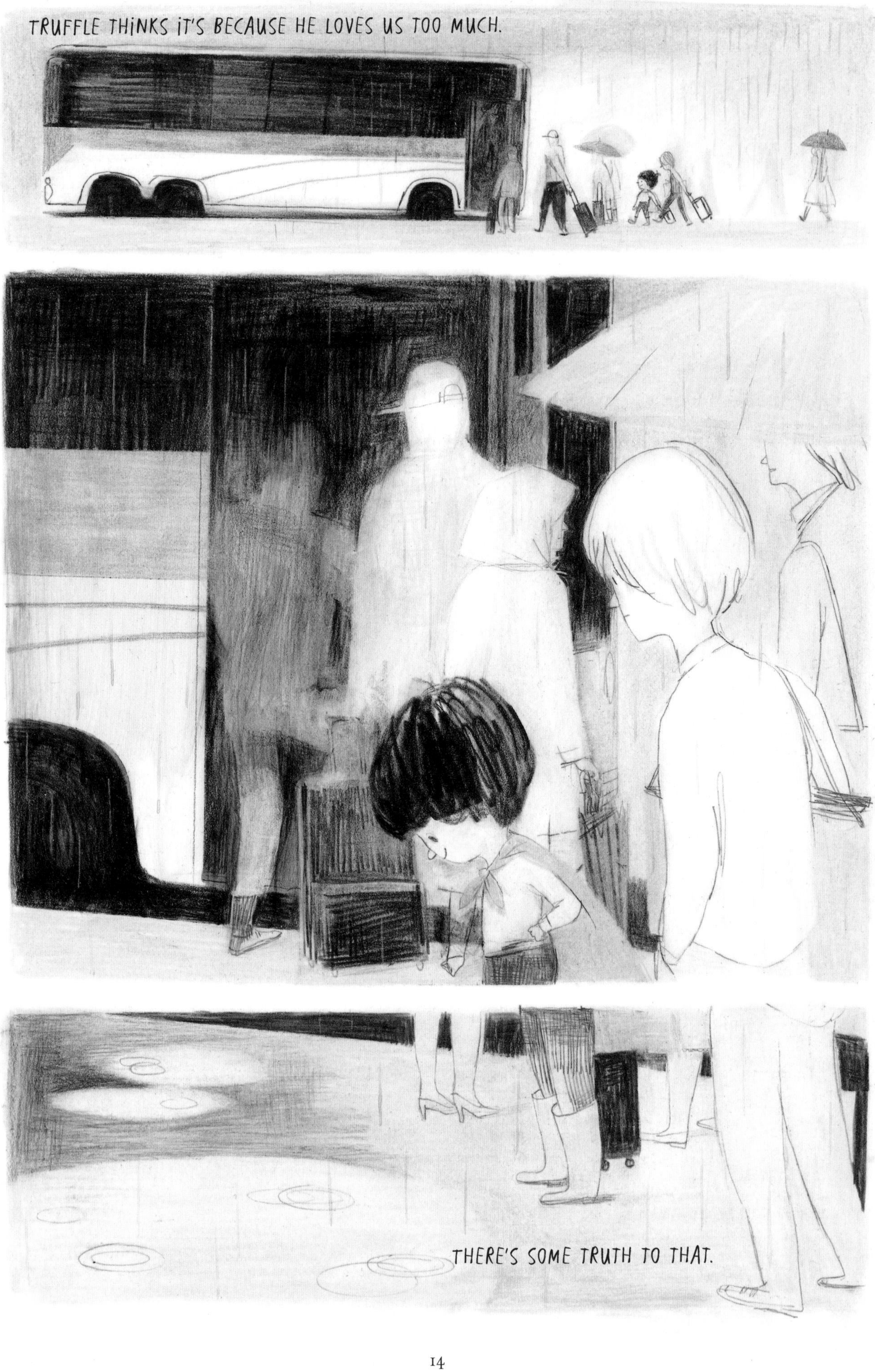
TRUFFLE THINKS IT'S BECAUSE HE LOVES US TOO MUCH.
THERE'S SOME TRUTH TO THAT.

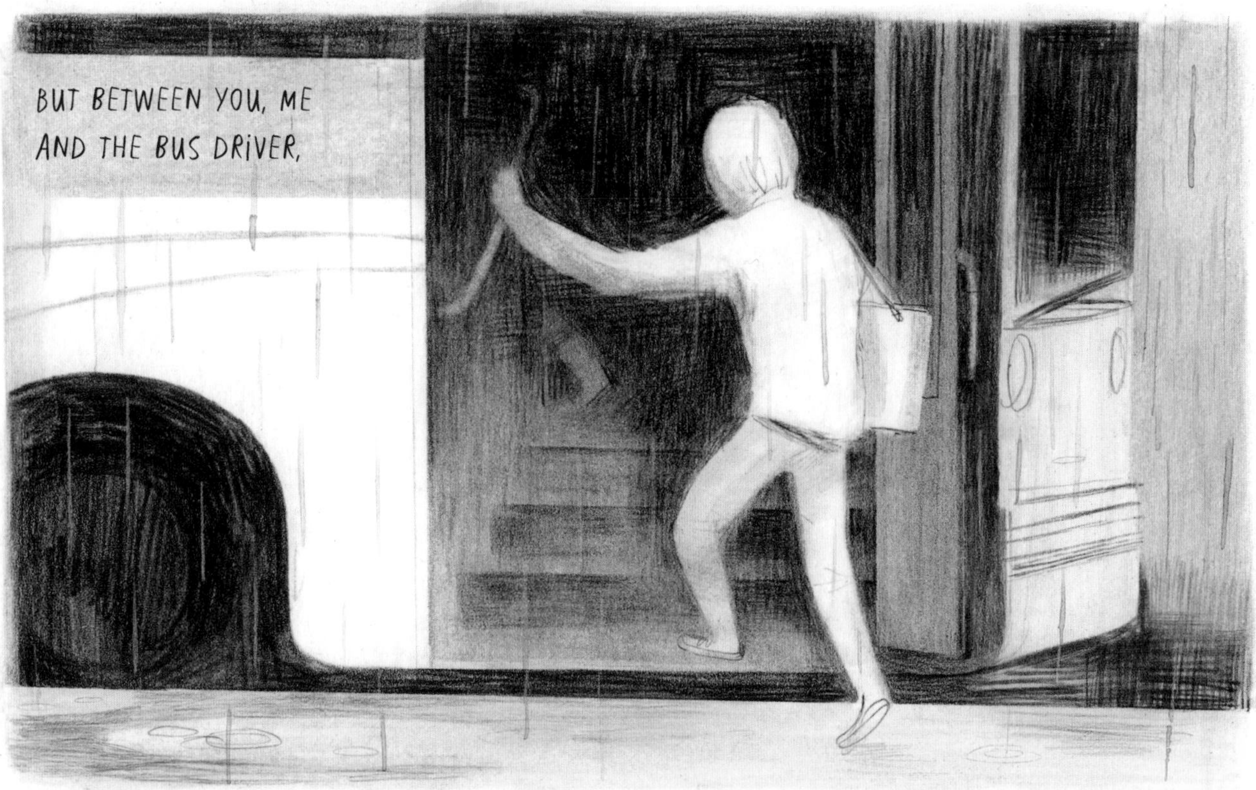
BUT BETWEEN YOU, ME
AND THE BUS DRIVER,

YOU DON'T NEED TO BE A ROCKET SCIENTIST TO KNOW THAT IF MY DAD CRIES,

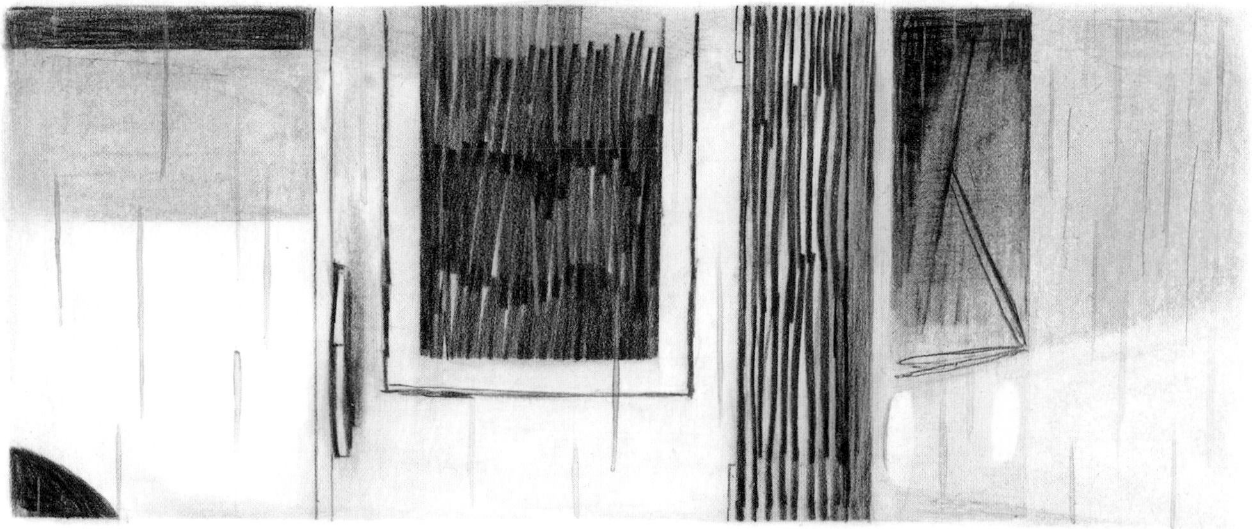

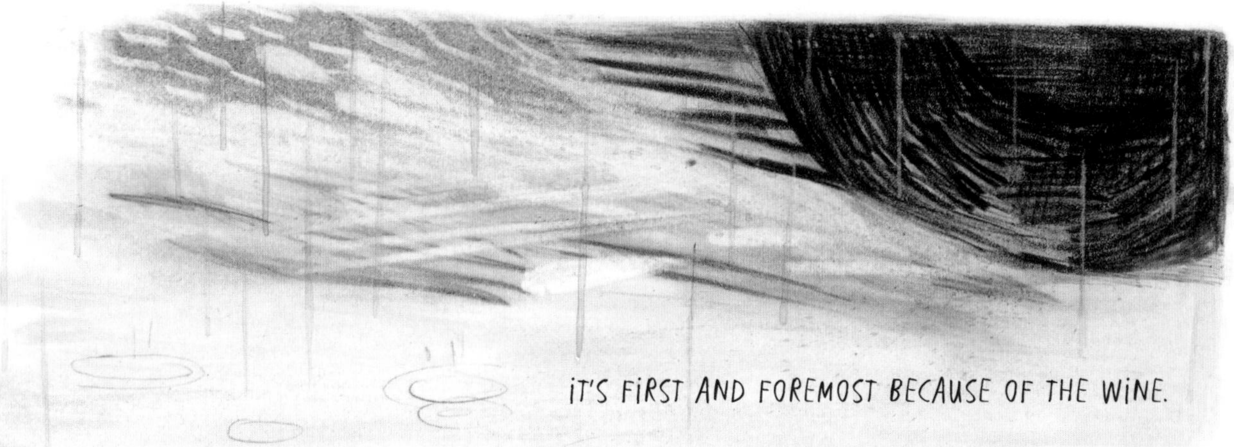
IT'S FIRST AND FOREMOST BECAUSE OF THE WINE.

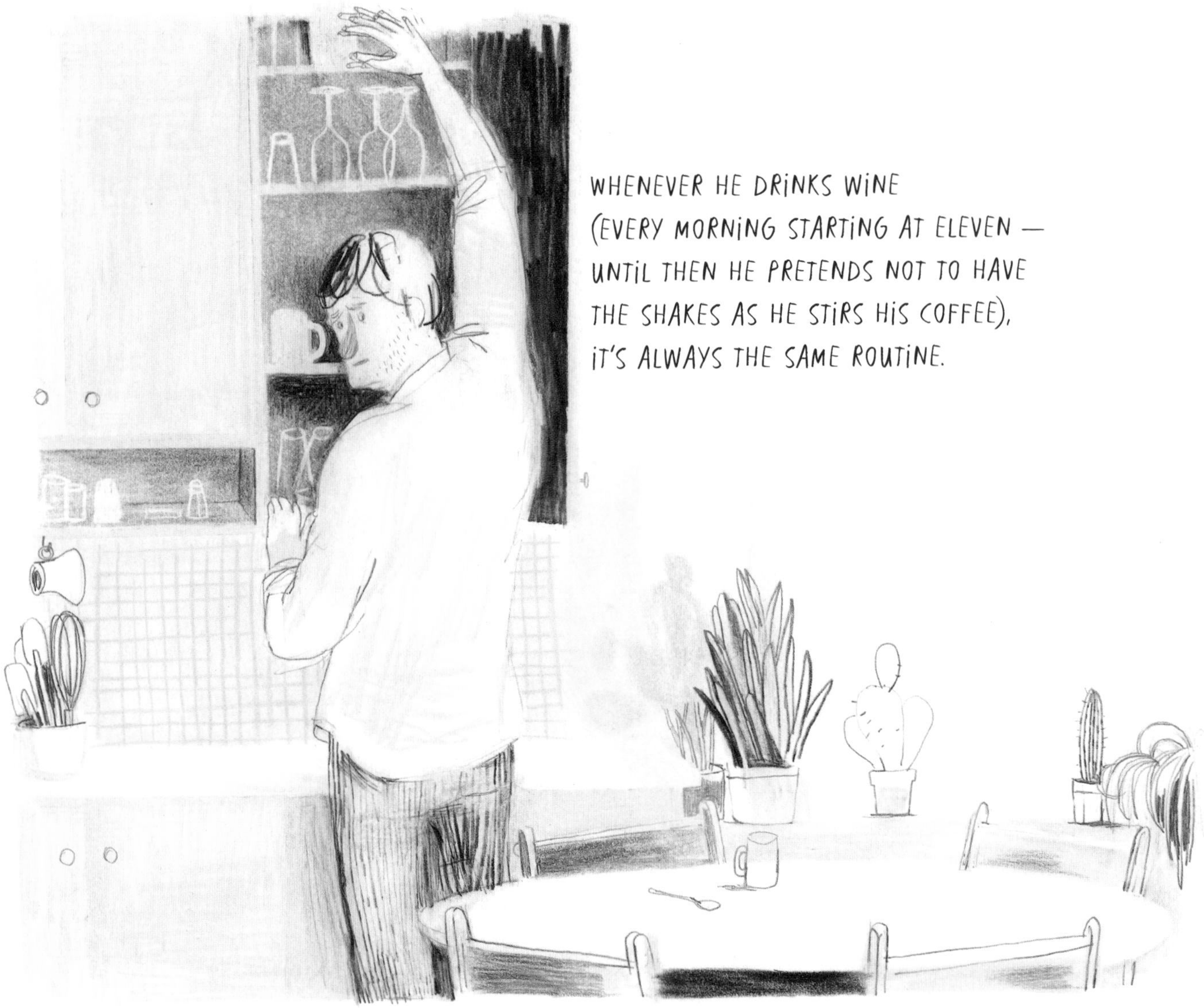
WHENEVER HE DRINKS WINE (EVERY MORNING STARTING AT ELEVEN — UNTIL THEN HE PRETENDS NOT TO HAVE THE SHAKES AS HE STIRS HIS COFFEE), IT'S ALWAYS THE SAME ROUTINE.

FIRST FEW SIPS, BOTH EYES CLOSE.

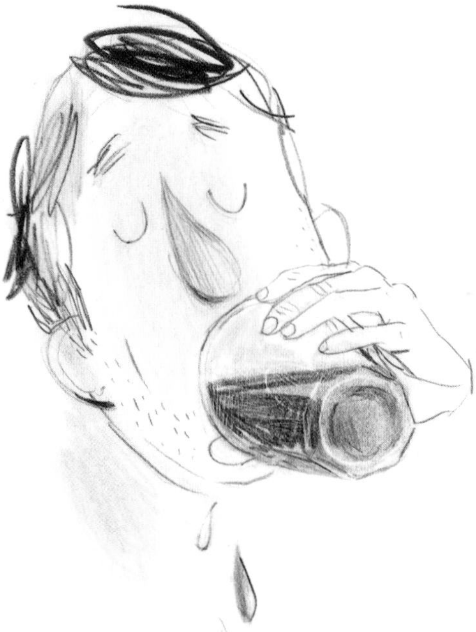

DEEP IN HIS CUPS, PLANS GALORE.

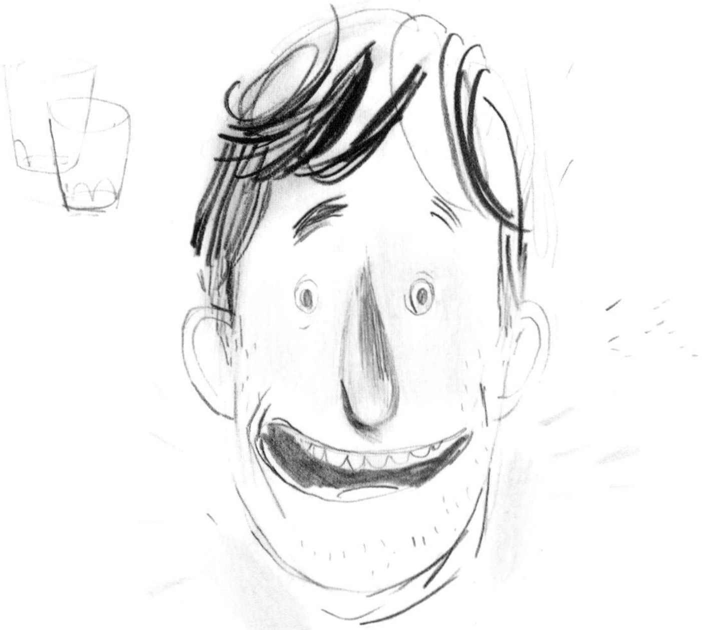

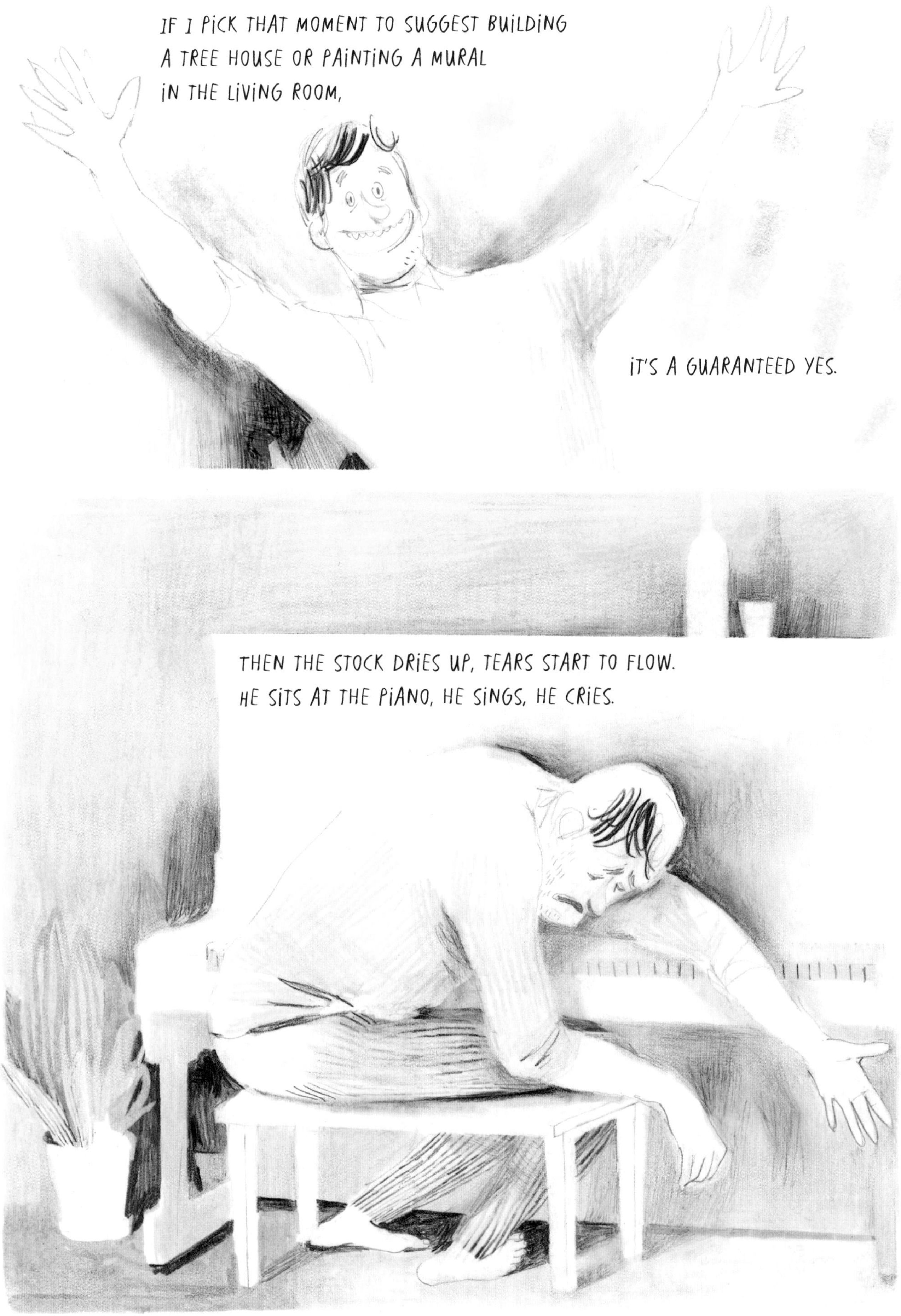
IF I PICK THAT MOMENT TO SUGGEST BUILDING A TREE HOUSE OR PAINTING A MURAL IN THE LIVING ROOM,
IT'S A GUARANTEED YES.
THEN THE STOCK DRIES UP, TEARS START TO FLOW. HE SITS AT THE PIANO, HE SINGS, HE CRIES.

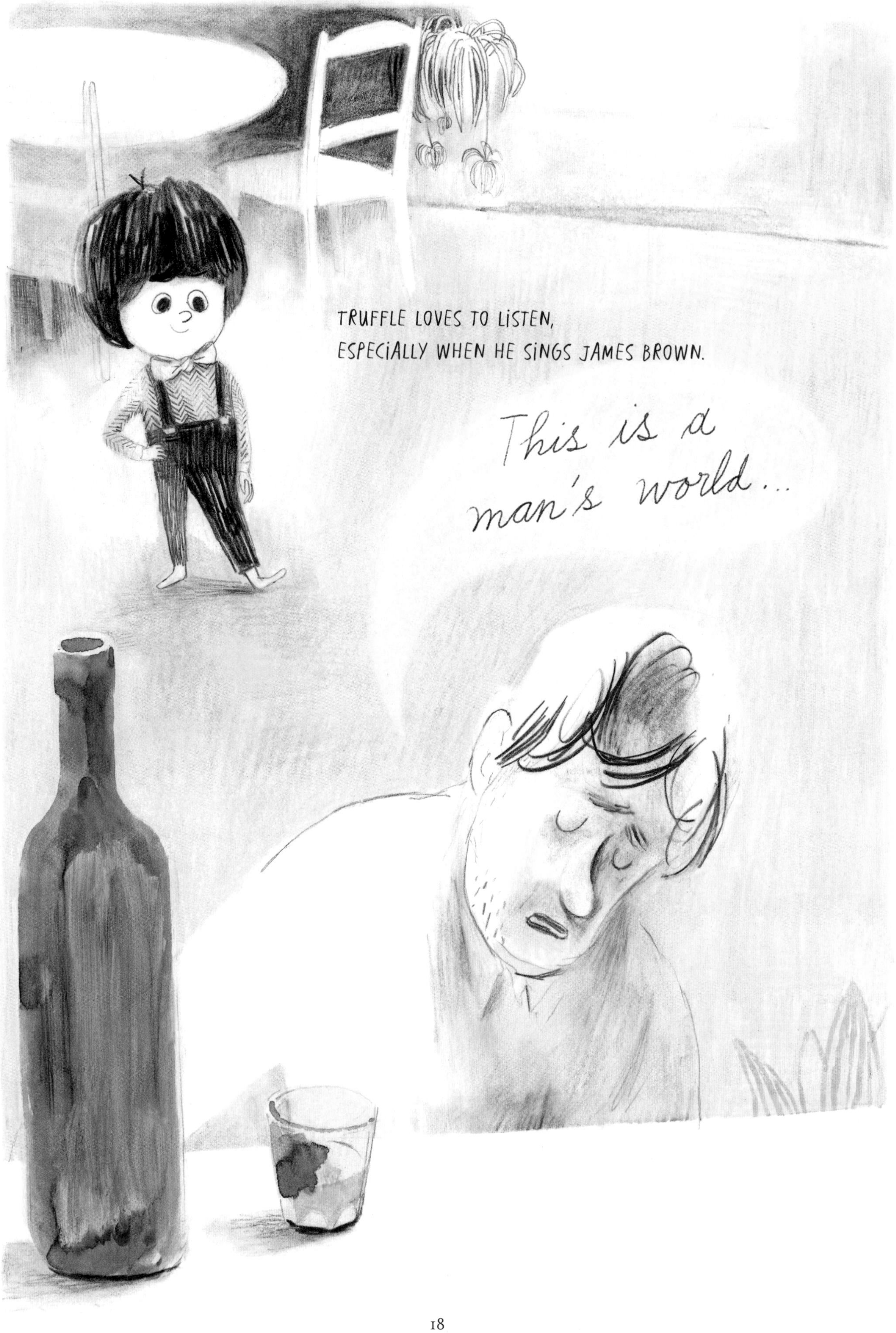
TRUFFLE LOVES TO LISTEN,
ESPECIALLY WHEN HE SINGS JAMES BROWN.
This is a man's world...

James Brown is looking for his love. That's why he's sad.

THEN MY DAD CRIES EVEN HARDER.

HE AND TRUFFLE ARE ALIKE THAT WAY.
THEY LOVE BIG, EXAGGERATED EMOTIONS.
THE ONLY DIFFERENCE IS THAT WITH TRUFFLE,
IT'S ALL MAKE-BELIEVE.

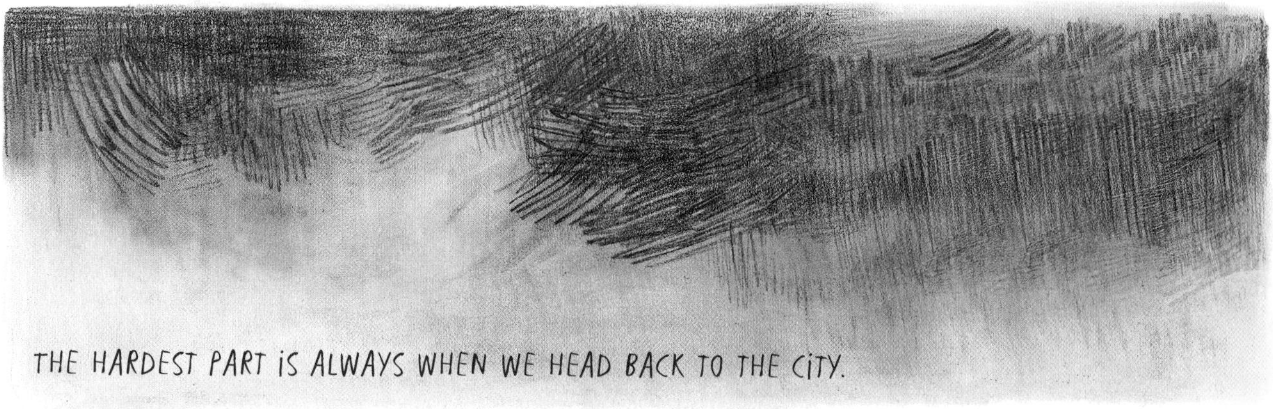
THE HARDEST PART IS ALWAYS WHEN WE HEAD BACK TO THE CITY.

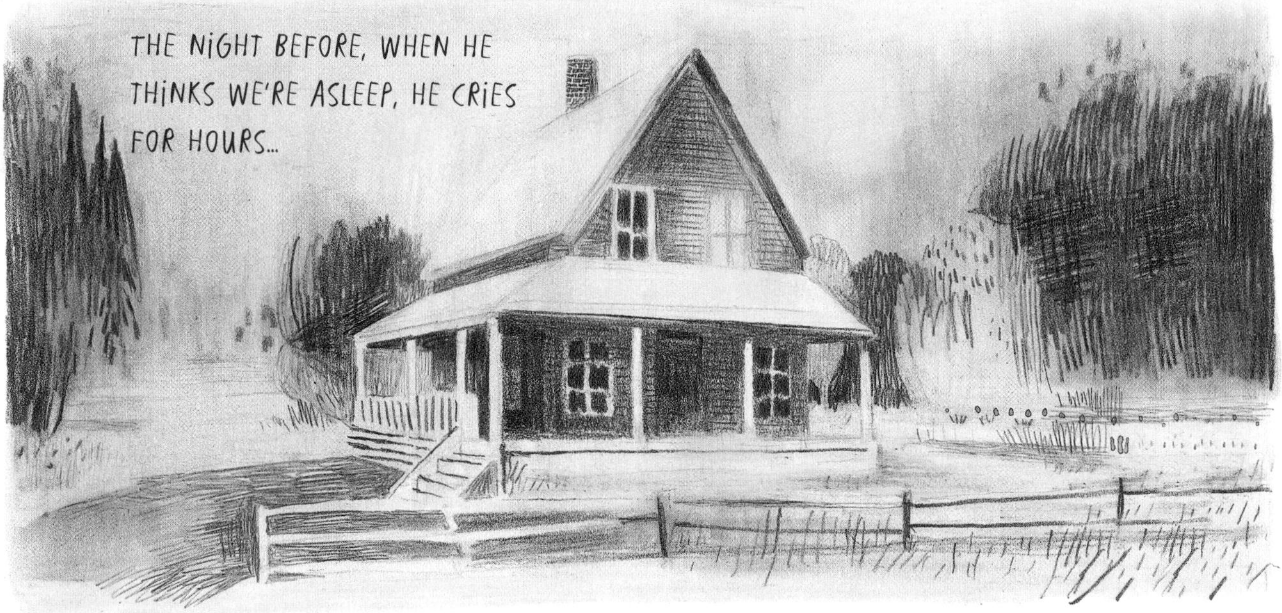
THE NIGHT BEFORE, WHEN HE THINKS WE'RE ASLEEP, HE CRIES FOR HOURS...

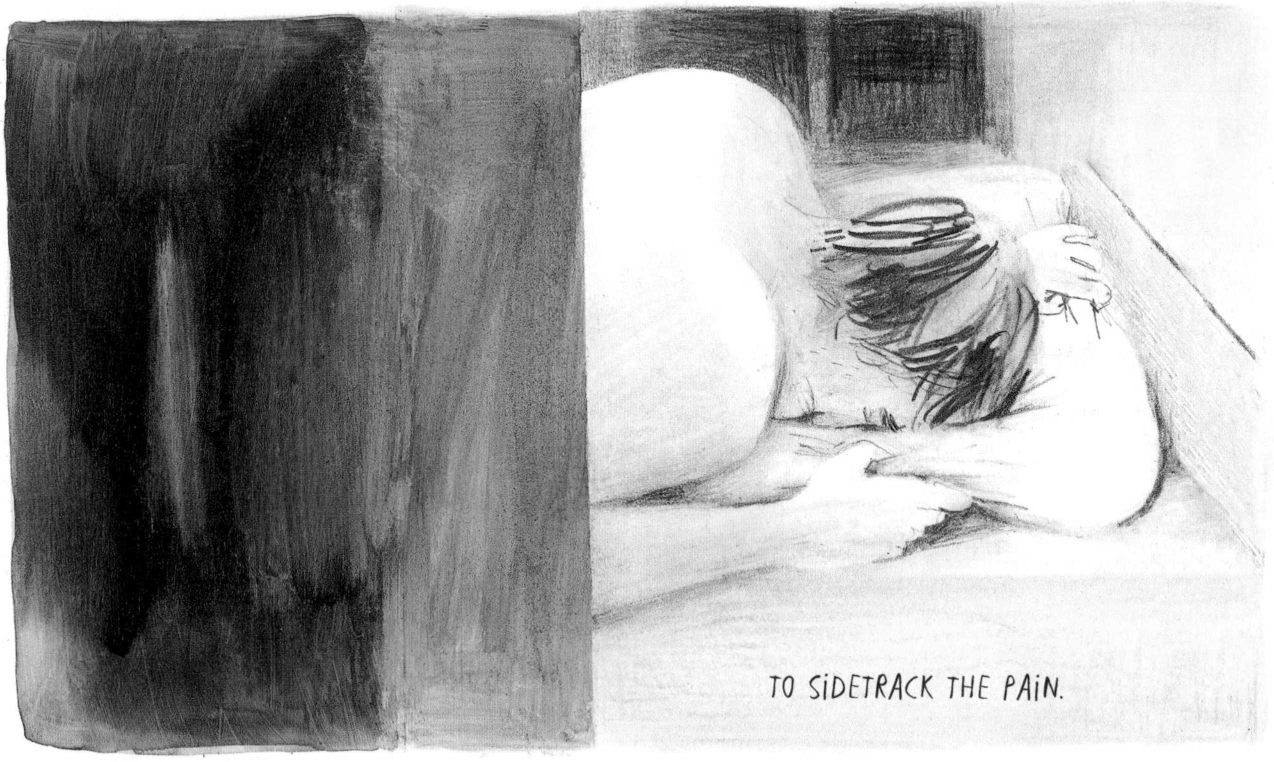
TO SIDETRACK THE PAIN.

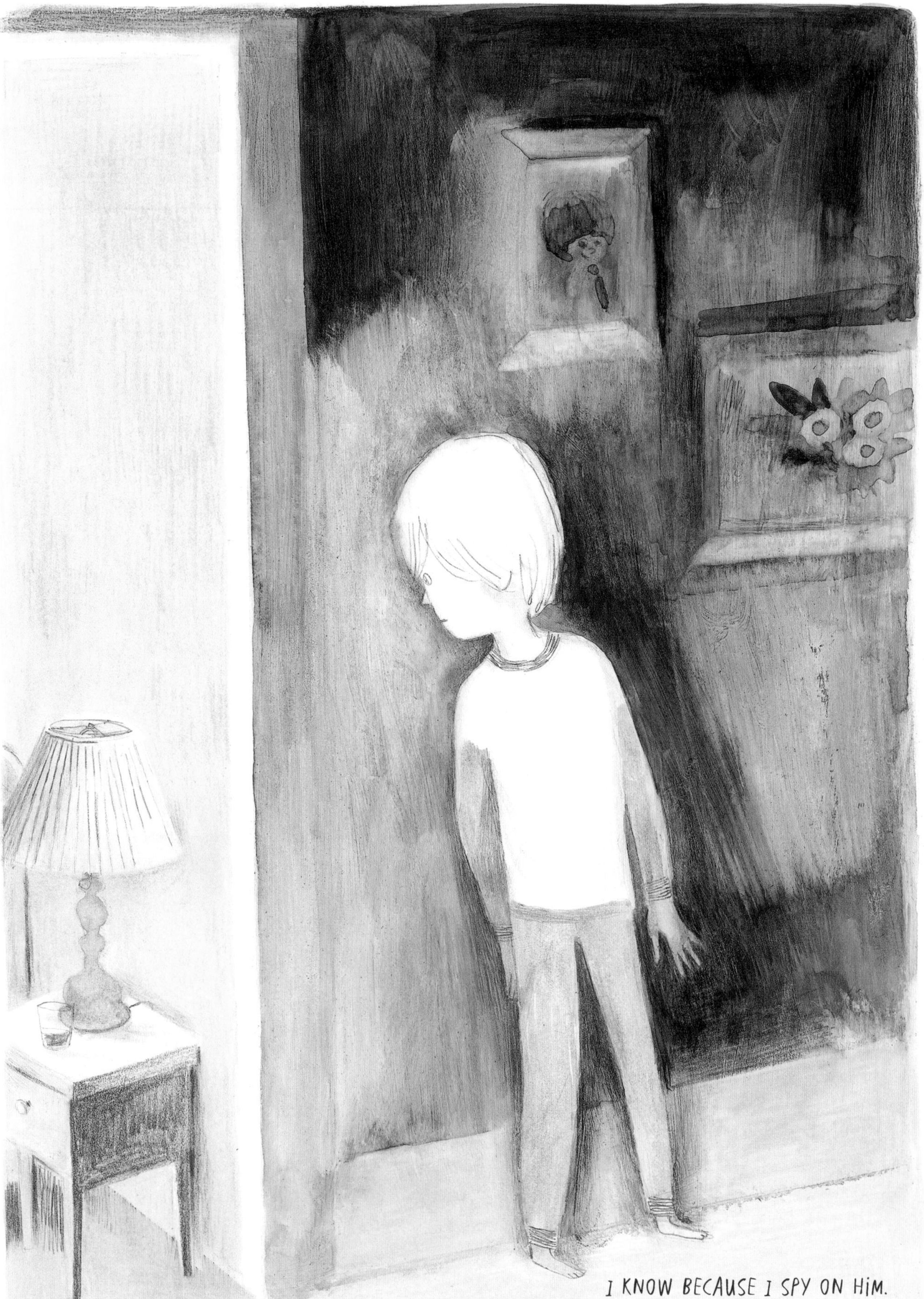
I KNOW BECAUSE I SPY ON HIM.

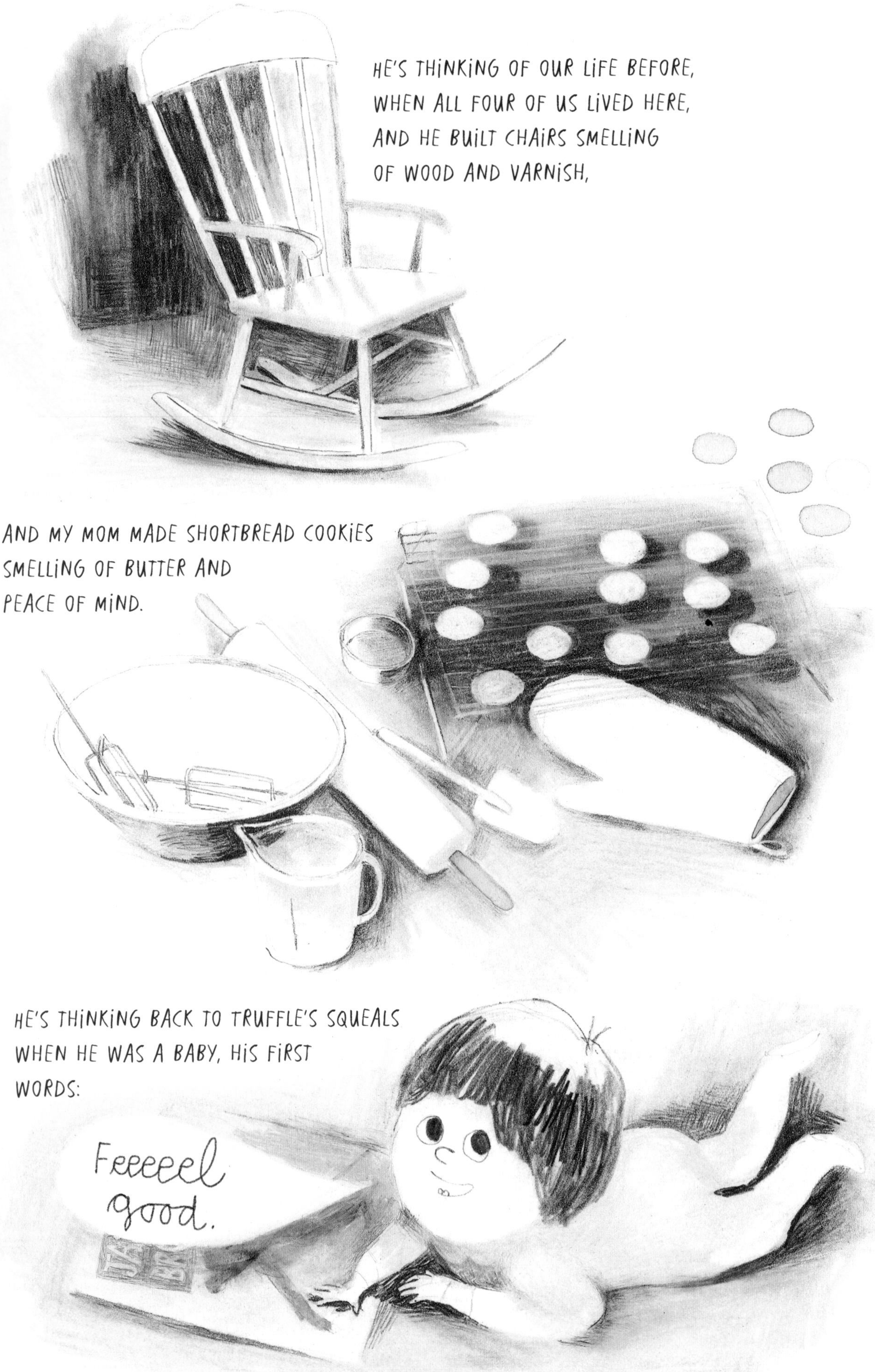
HE'S THINKING OF OUR LIFE BEFORE, WHEN ALL FOUR OF US LIVED HERE, AND HE BUILT CHAIRS SMELLING OF WOOD AND VARNISH,
AND MY MOM MADE SHORTBREAD COOKIES SMELLING OF BUTTER AND PEACE OF MIND.
HE'S THINKING BACK TO TRUFFLE'S SQUEALS WHEN HE WAS A BABY, HIS FIRST WORDS:
Feeeeel good.

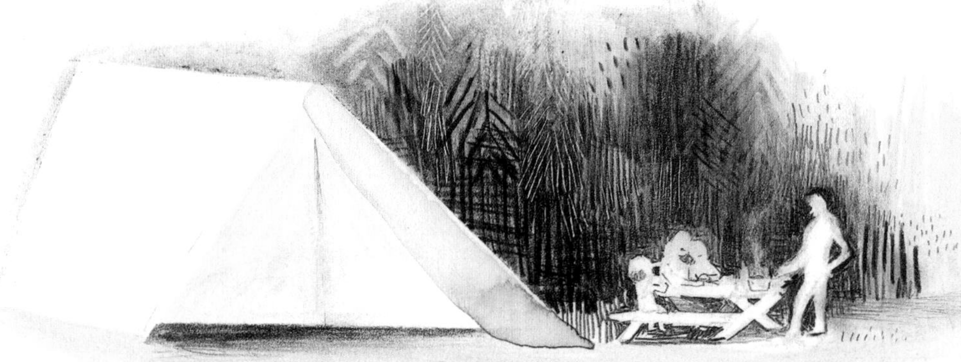

HE'S THINKING BACK TO OUR CAMPING TRIPS,

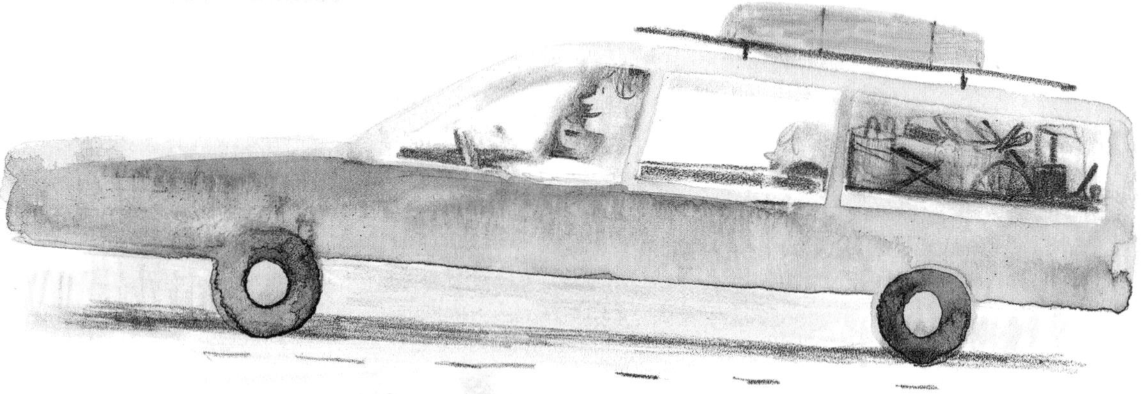

OUR GUESSING GAMES IN THE CAR,
OUR SNOWBALL FIGHTS.
HE'S THINKING OF MY MOM'S SMILE,
BACK WHEN SHE STILL SMILED.

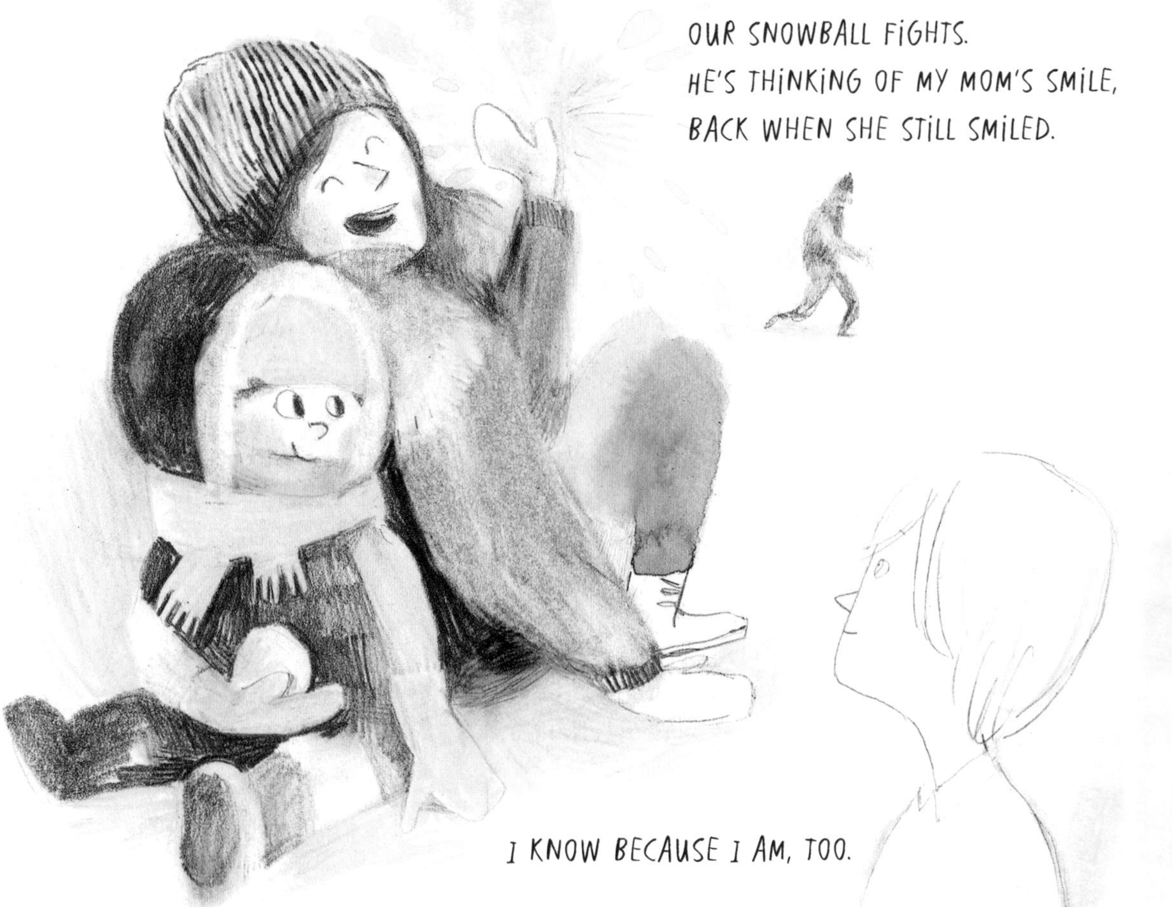

I KNOW BECAUSE I AM, TOO.

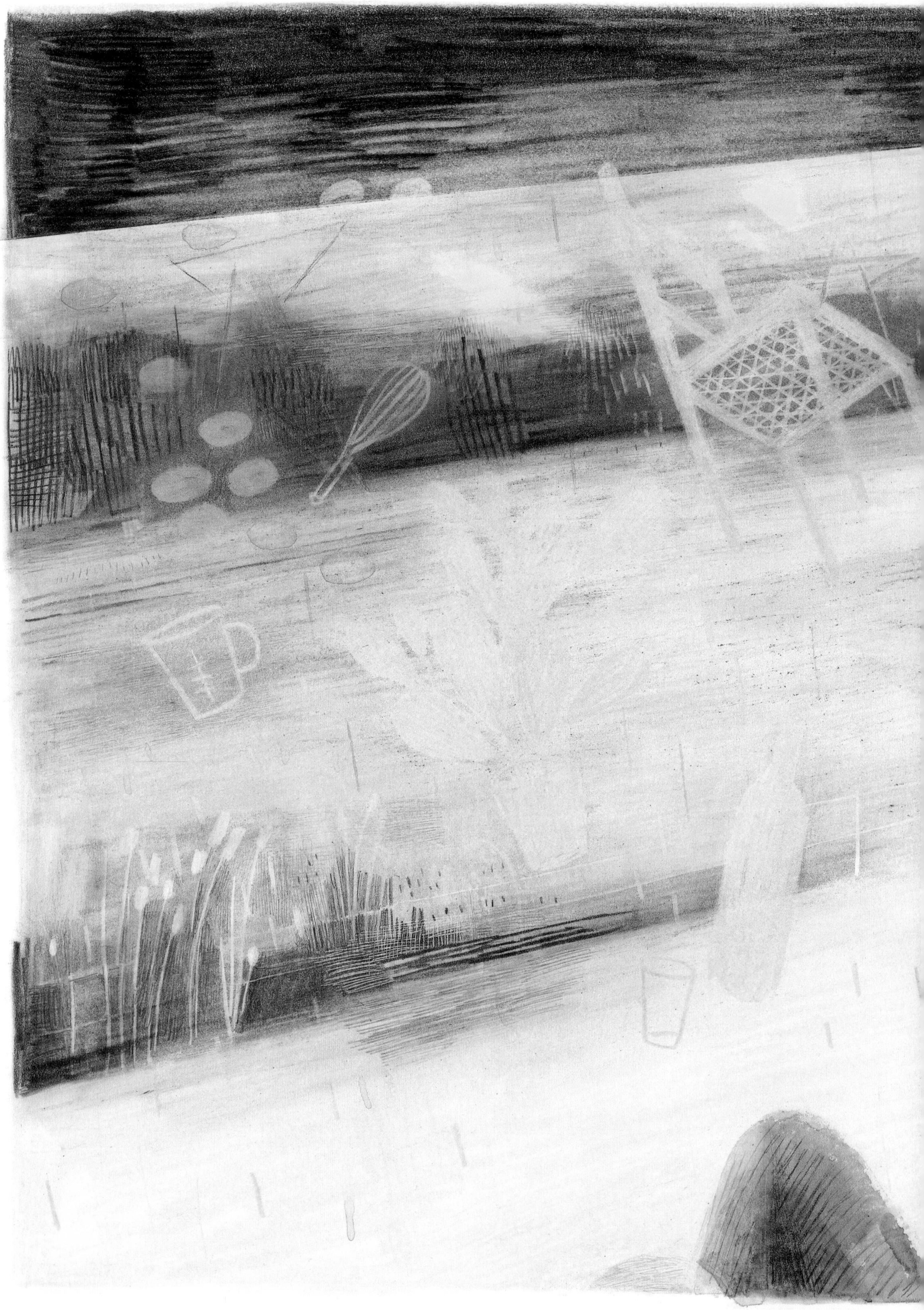

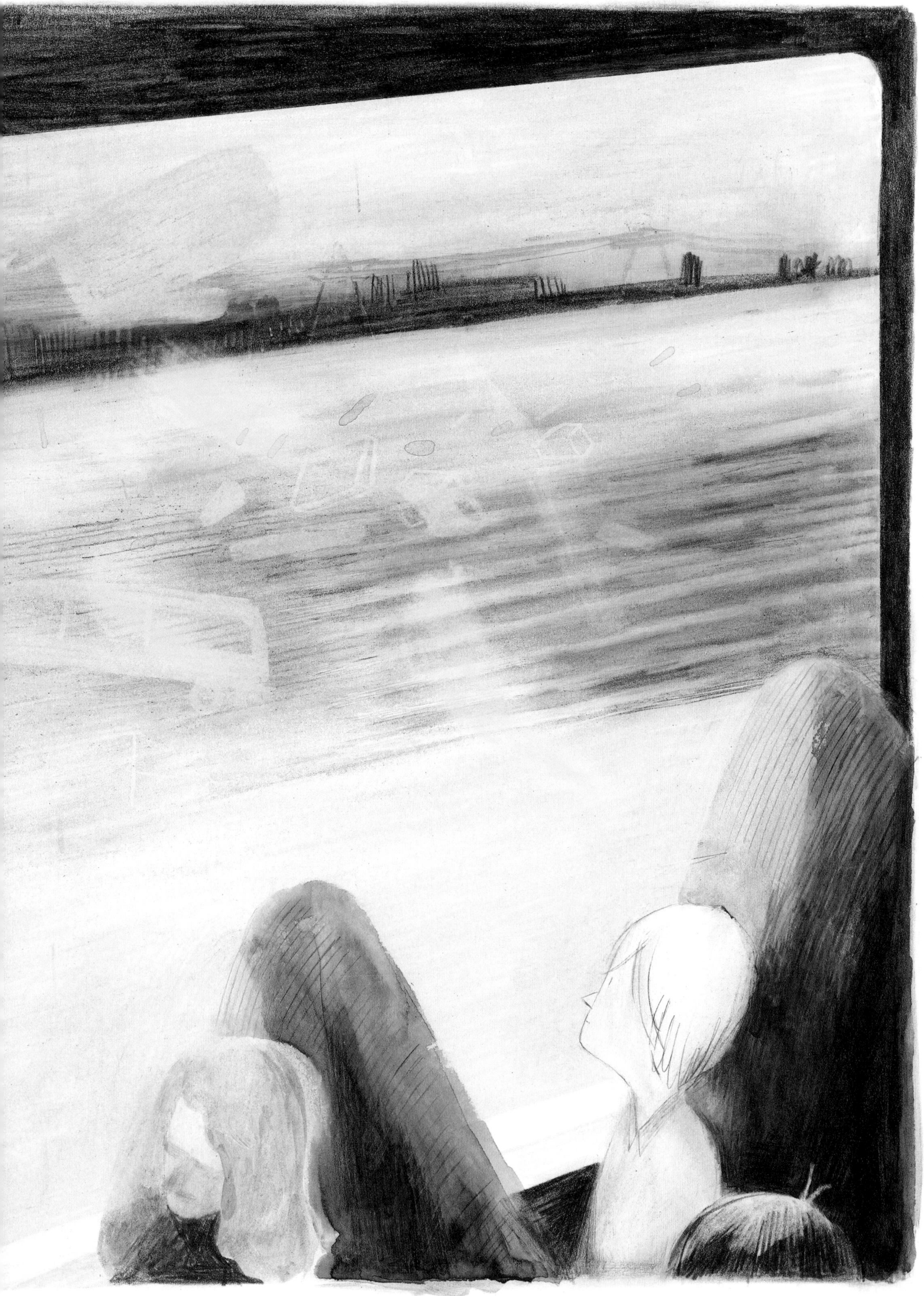

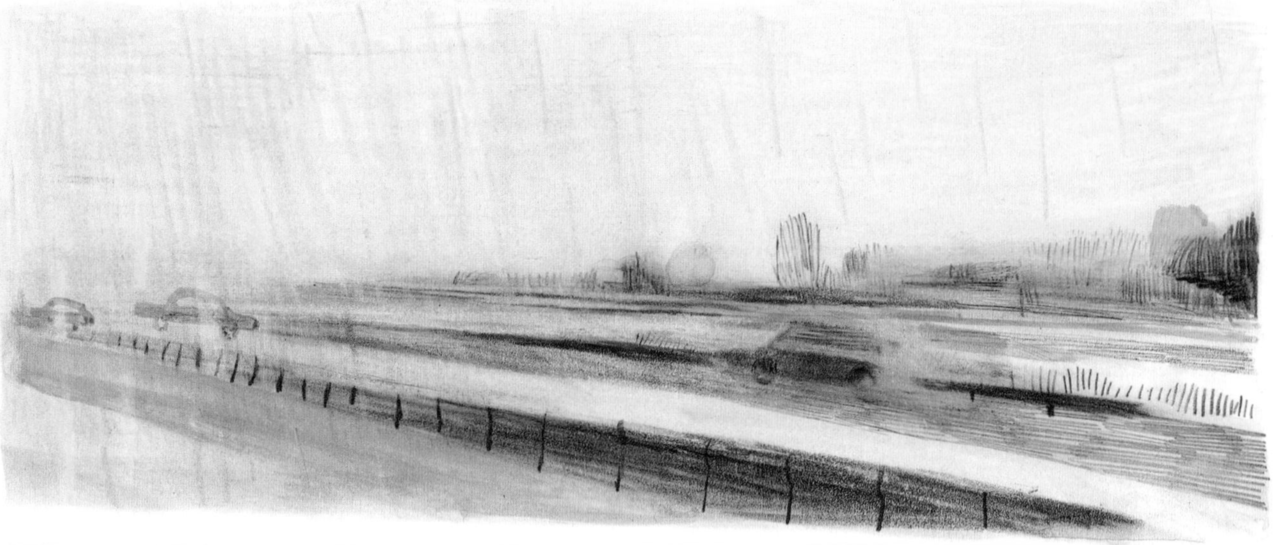

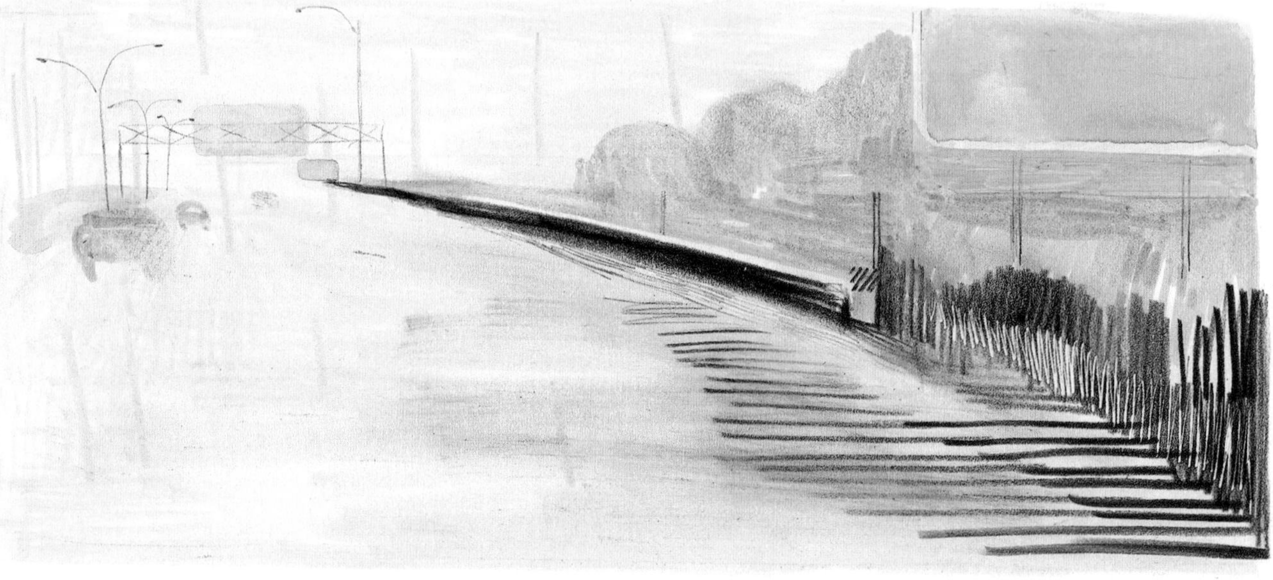

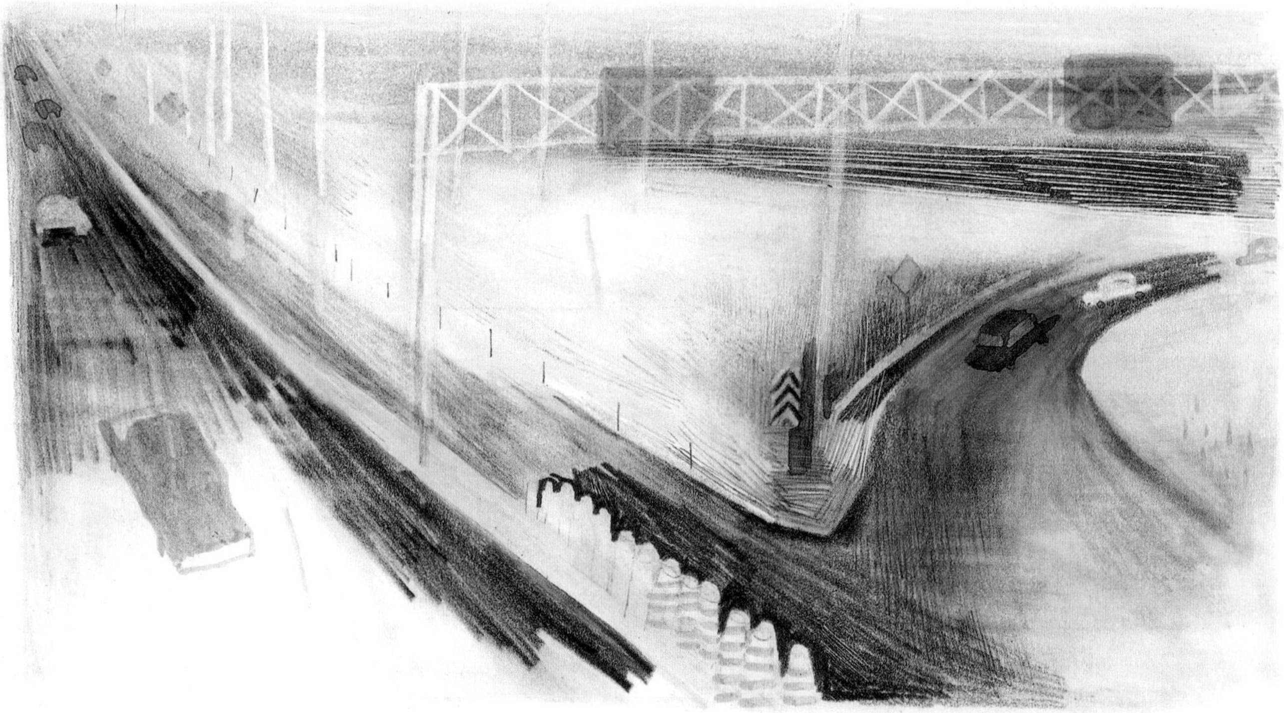

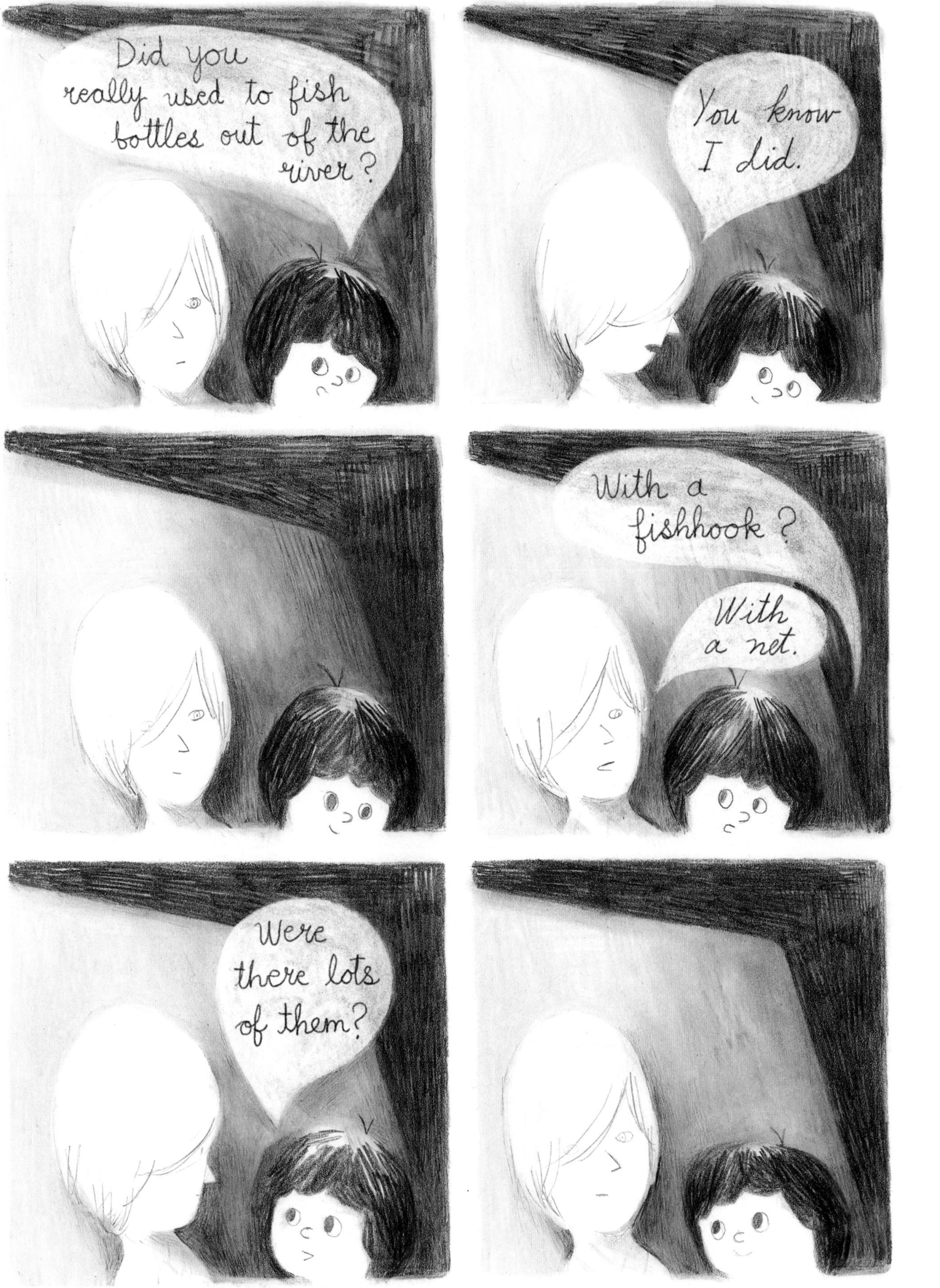
Did you really used to fish bottles out of the river?
You know I did.
With a fishhook?
With a net.
Were there lots of them?

Not at first.
You need to be
patient to fish.
Wait for the time
to be right.

When was
the best time of
year for it?

Probably the day after
Saint-Jean-Baptiste Day.
Especially behind the
Bergerons' lot.

Were there
tons then?

Tons.

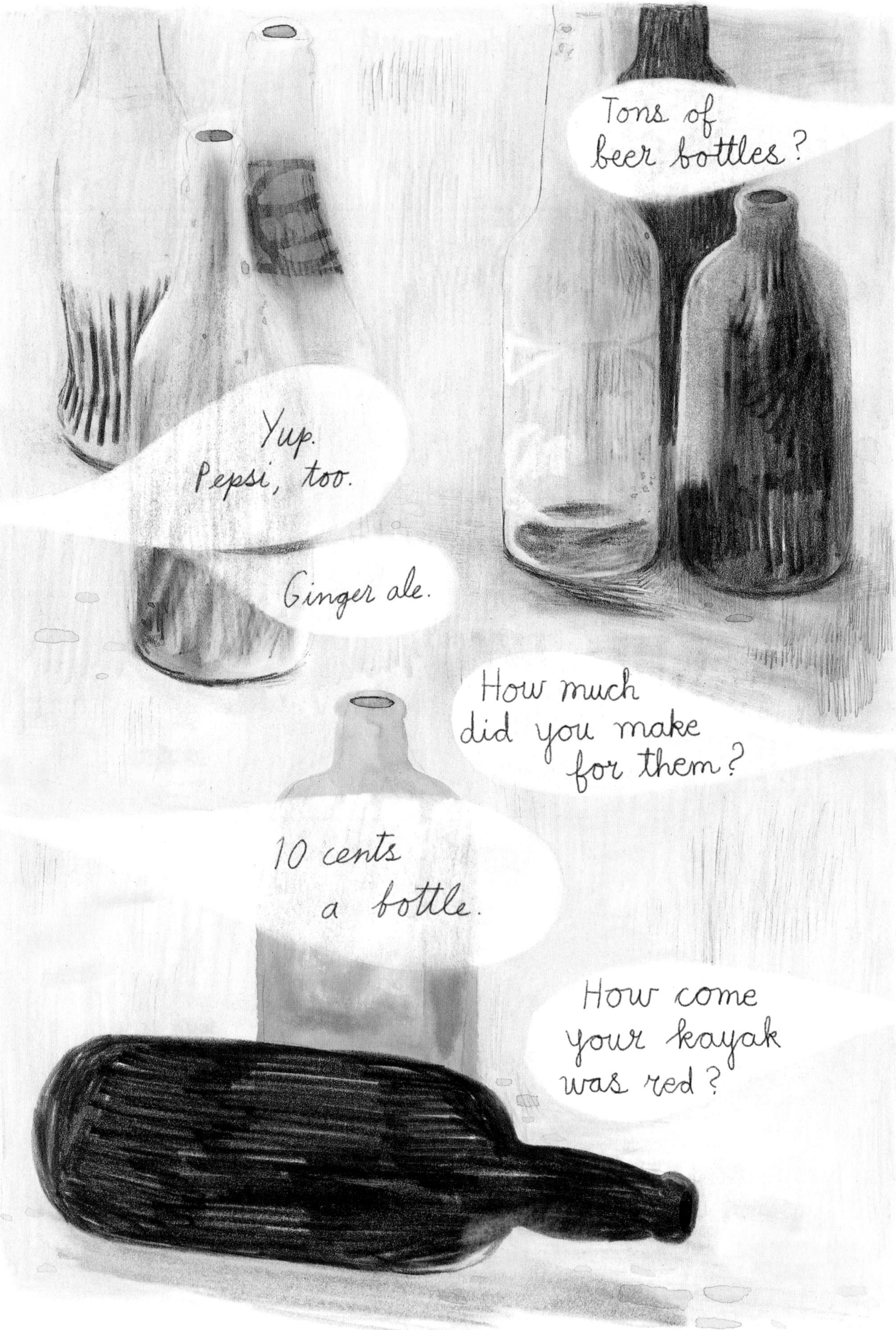
Tons of beer bottles?
Yup. Pepsi, too.
Ginger ale.
How much did you make for them?
10 cents a bottle.
How come your kayak was red?

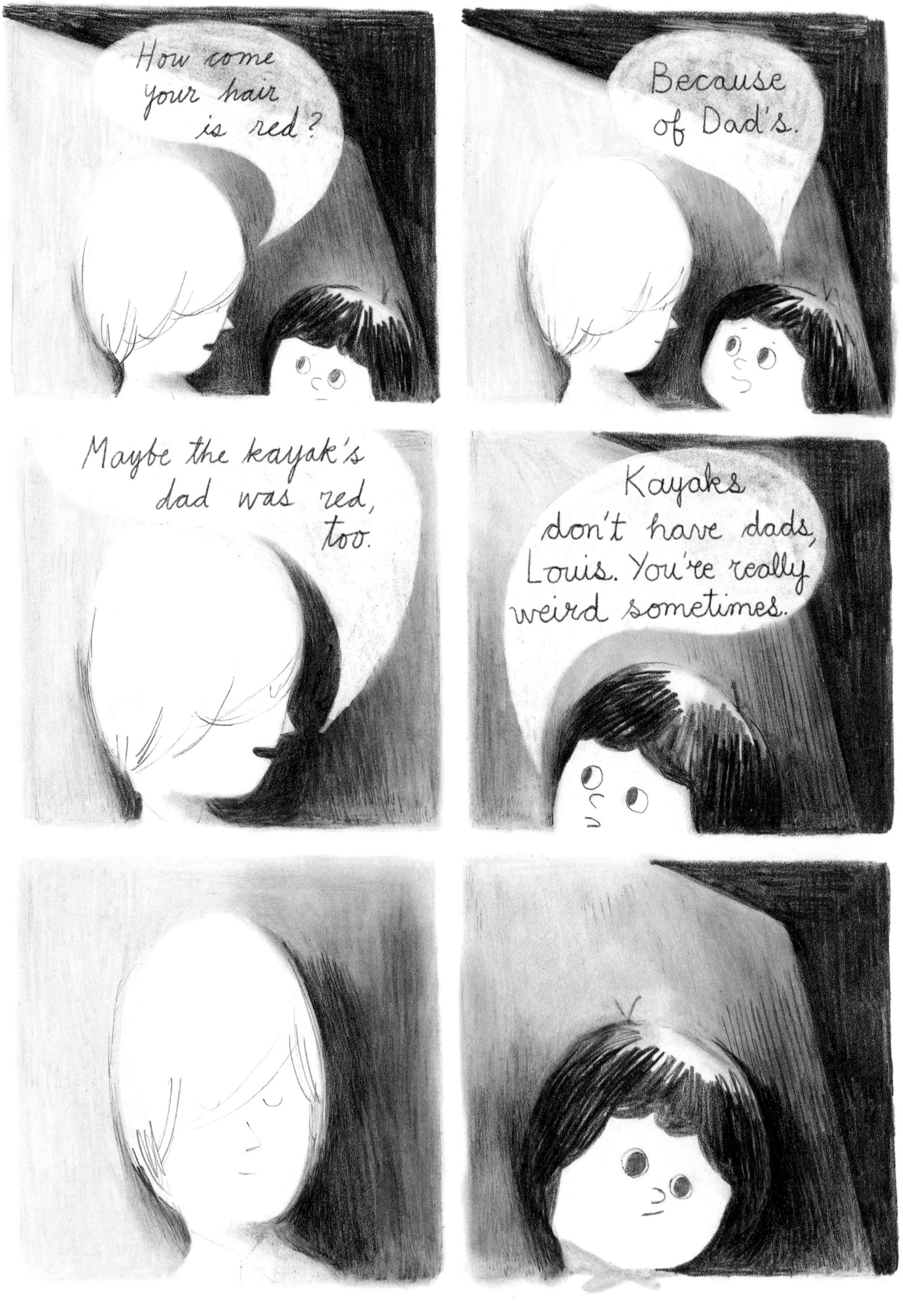
How come your hair is red?
Because of Dad's.
Maybe the kayak's dad was red, too.
Kayaks don't have dads, Louis. You're really weird sometimes.

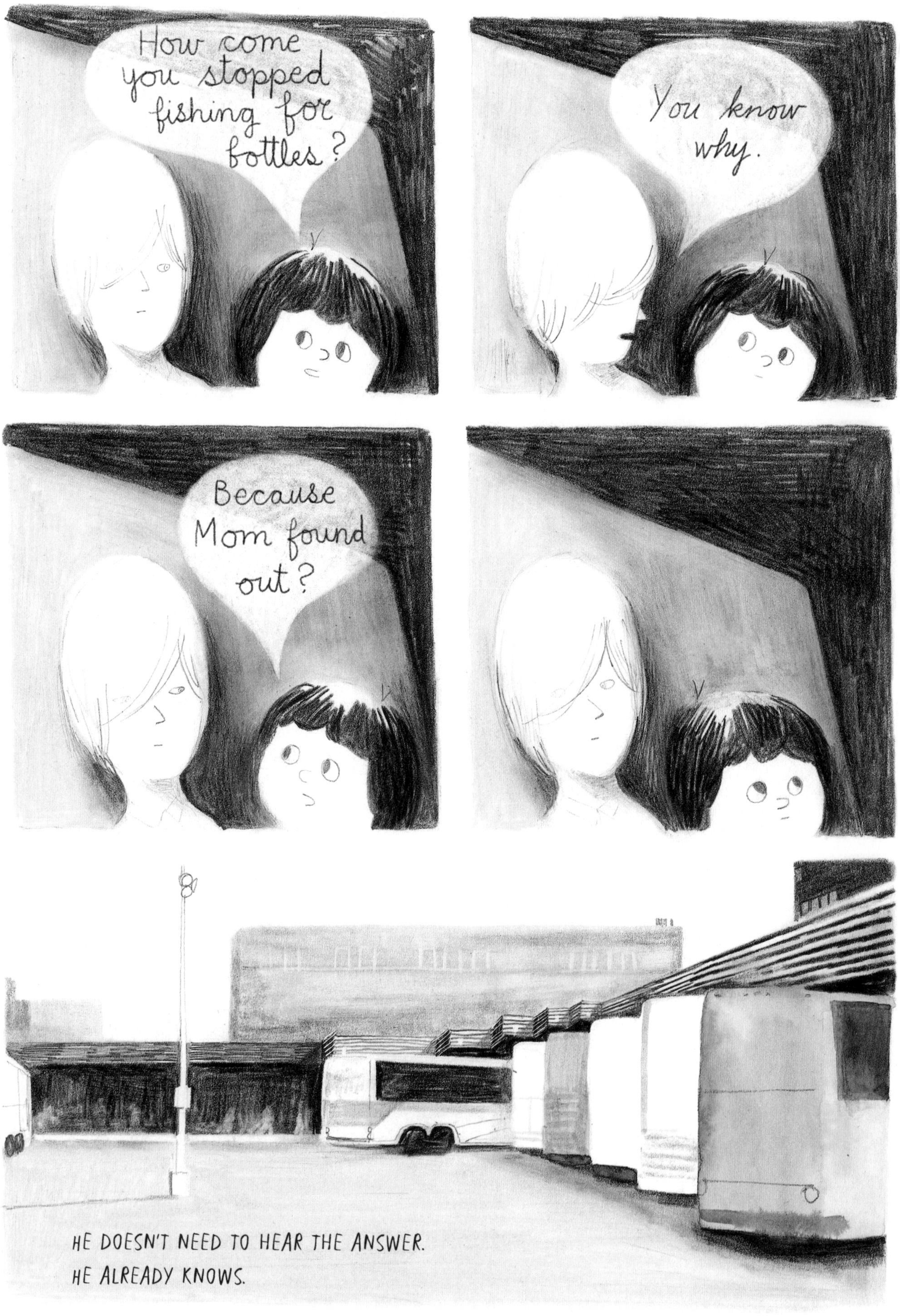
How come you stopped fishing for bottles?
You know why.
Because Mom found out?
HE DOESN'T NEED TO HEAR THE ANSWER.
HE ALREADY KNOWS.

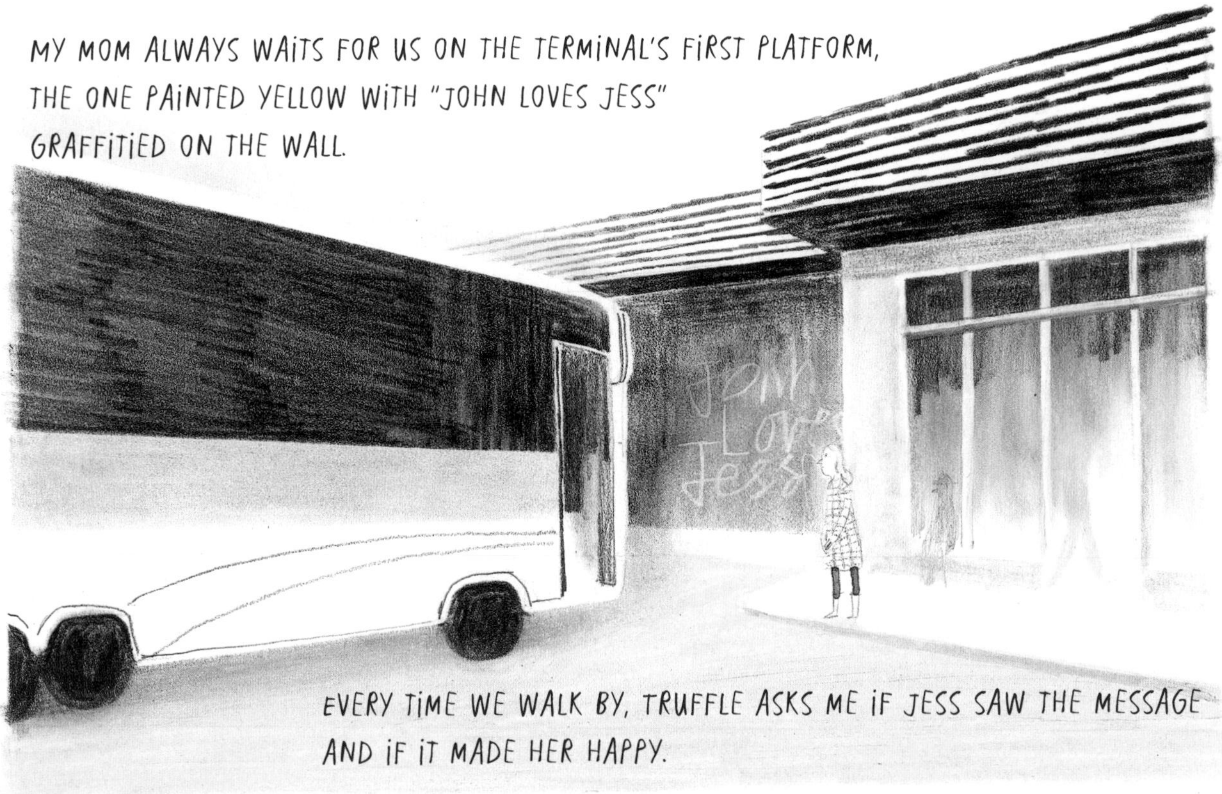
MY MOM ALWAYS WAITS FOR US ON THE TERMINAL'S FIRST PLATFORM, THE ONE PAINTED YELLOW WITH "JOHN LOVES JESS" GRAFFITIED ON THE WALL.
John Loves Jess
EVERY TIME WE WALK BY, TRUFFLE ASKS ME IF JESS SAW THE MESSAGE AND IF IT MADE HER HAPPY.

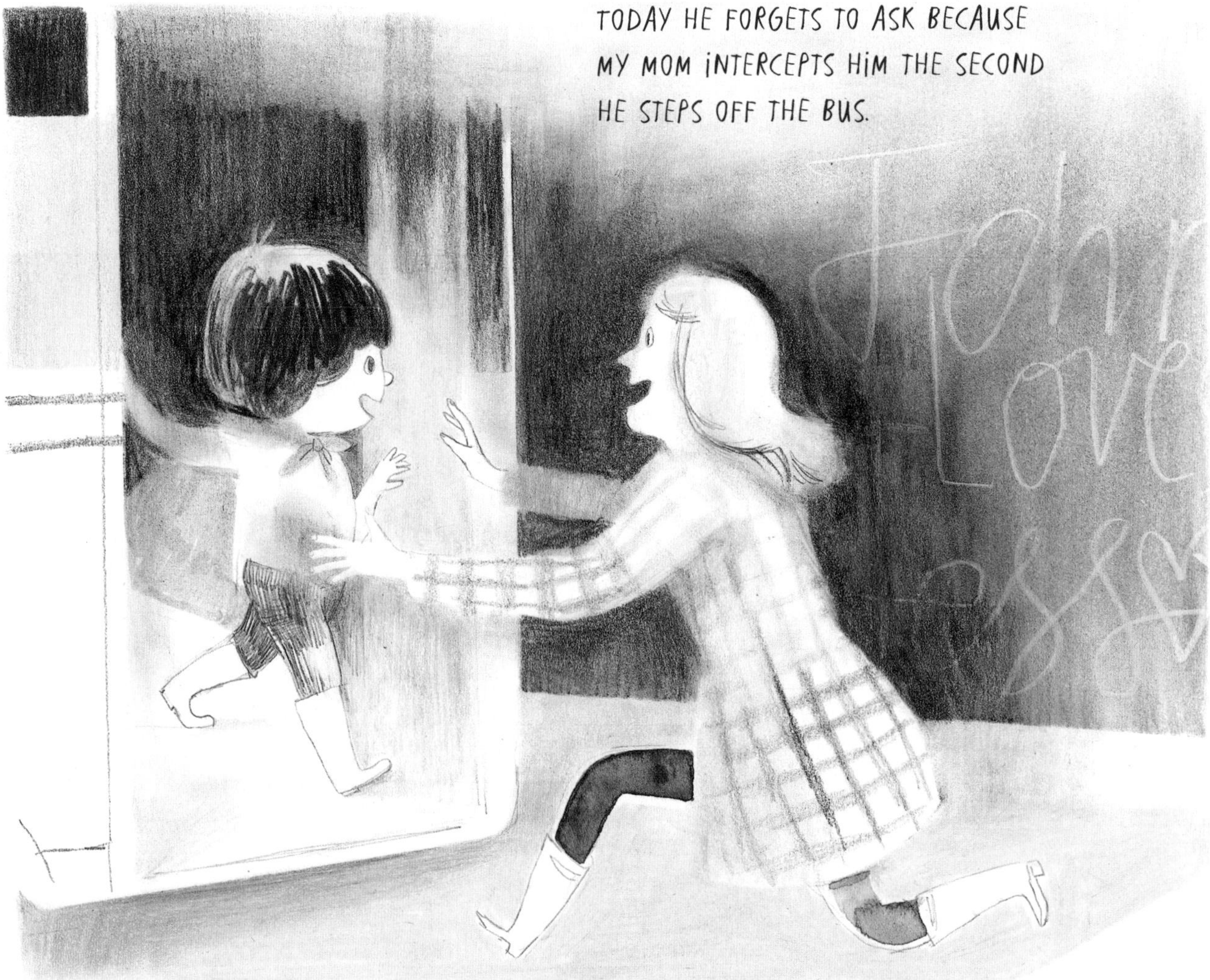
TODAY HE FORGETS TO ASK BECAUSE MY MOM INTERCEPTS HIM THE SECOND HE STEPS OFF THE BUS.

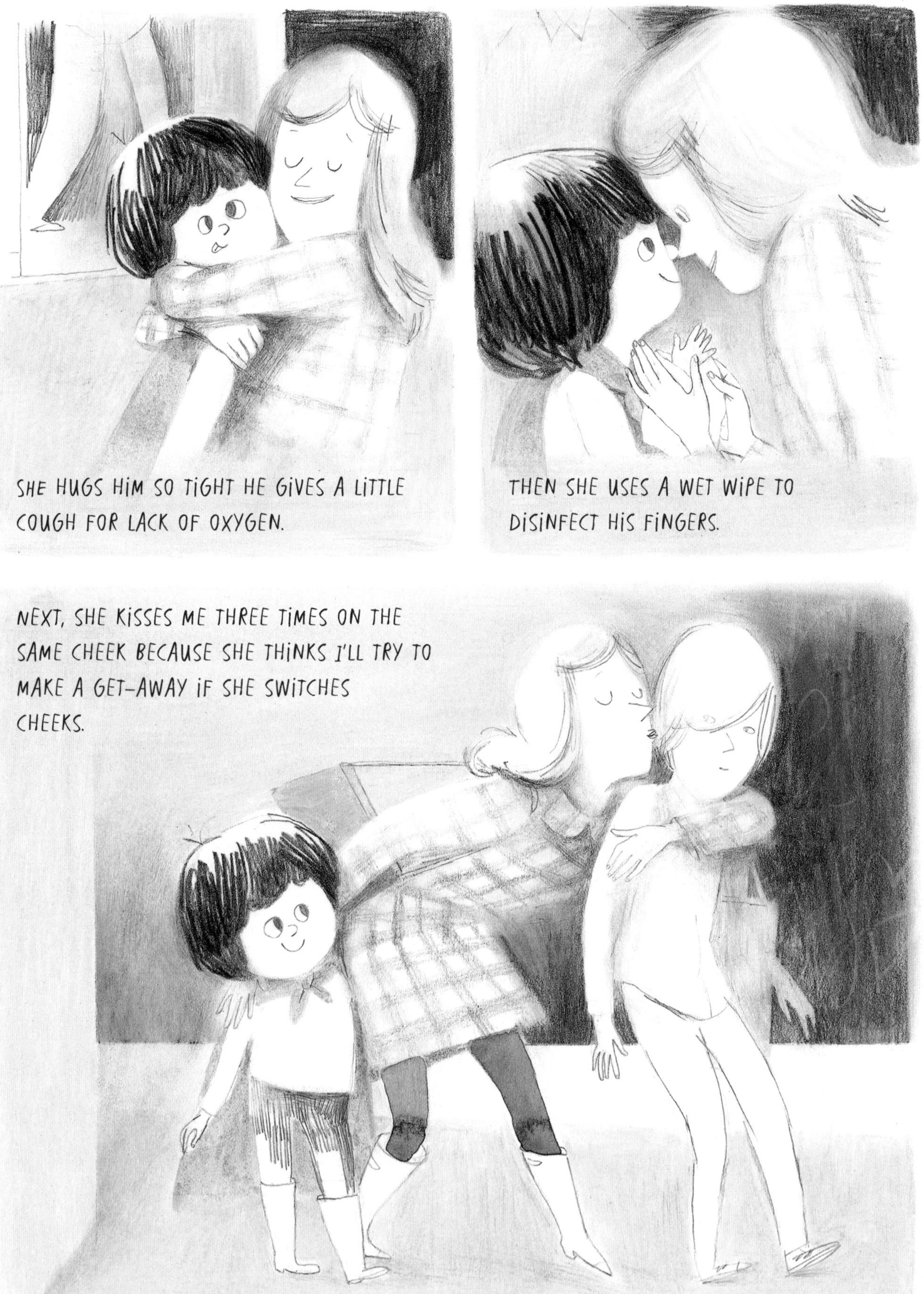
SHE HUGS HIM SO TIGHT HE GIVES A LITTLE COUGH FOR LACK OF OXYGEN.
THEN SHE USES A WET WIPE TO DISINFECT HIS FINGERS.
NEXT, SHE KISSES ME THREE TIMES ON THE SAME CHEEK BECAUSE SHE THINKS I'LL TRY TO MAKE A GET-AWAY IF SHE SWITCHES CHEEKS.
SHE'S PROBABLY RIGHT.

SHE TRIED TO USE THE WET WIPE ON ME FOR THE LONGEST TIME.
NOW SHE'S GIVEN UP.

SHE ALWAYS
PROMISES US TACOS, AND
WE RACE EACH OTHER TO THE CAR.

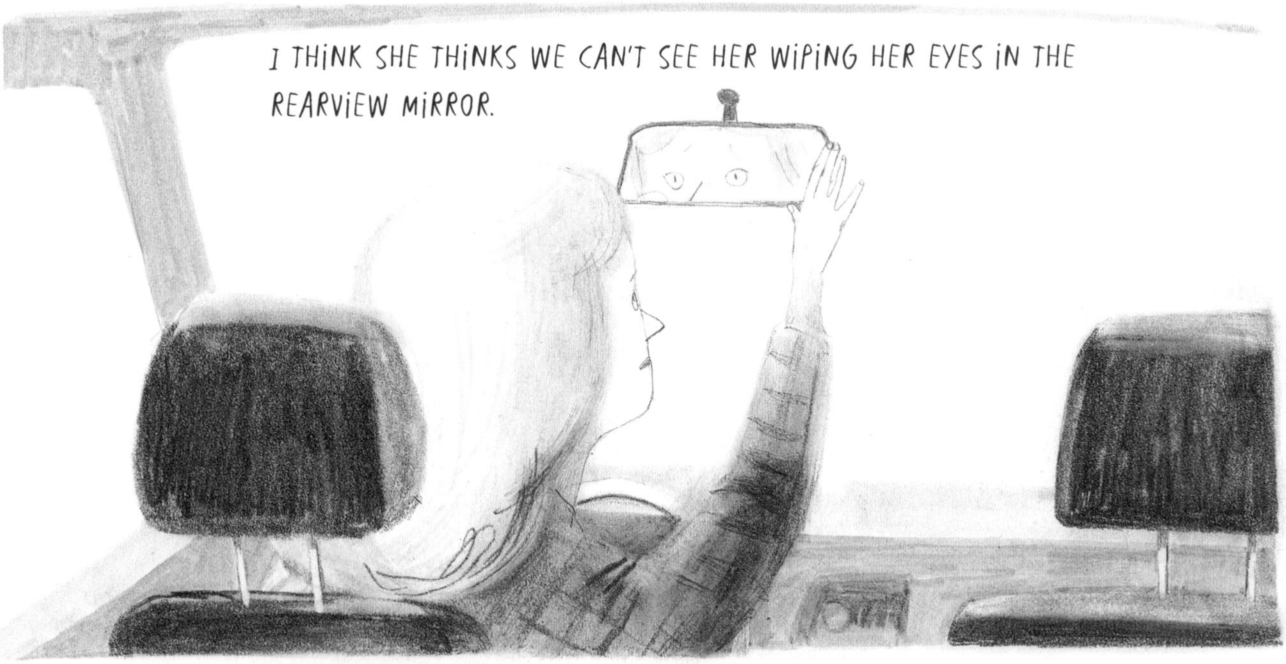
I THINK SHE THINKS WE CAN'T SEE HER WIPING HER EYES IN THE REARVIEW MIRROR.

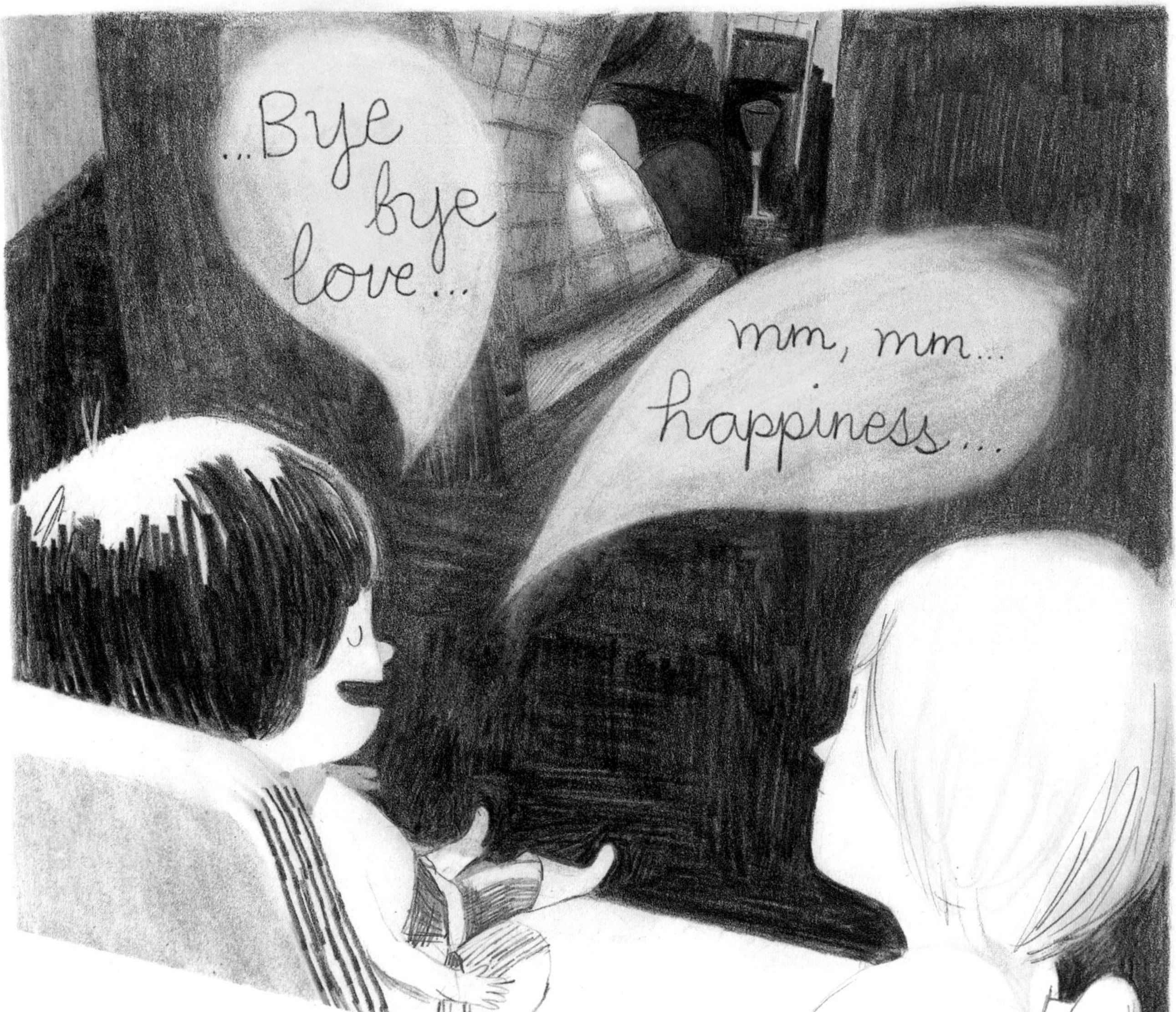
...Bye bye love...
mm, mm... happiness...

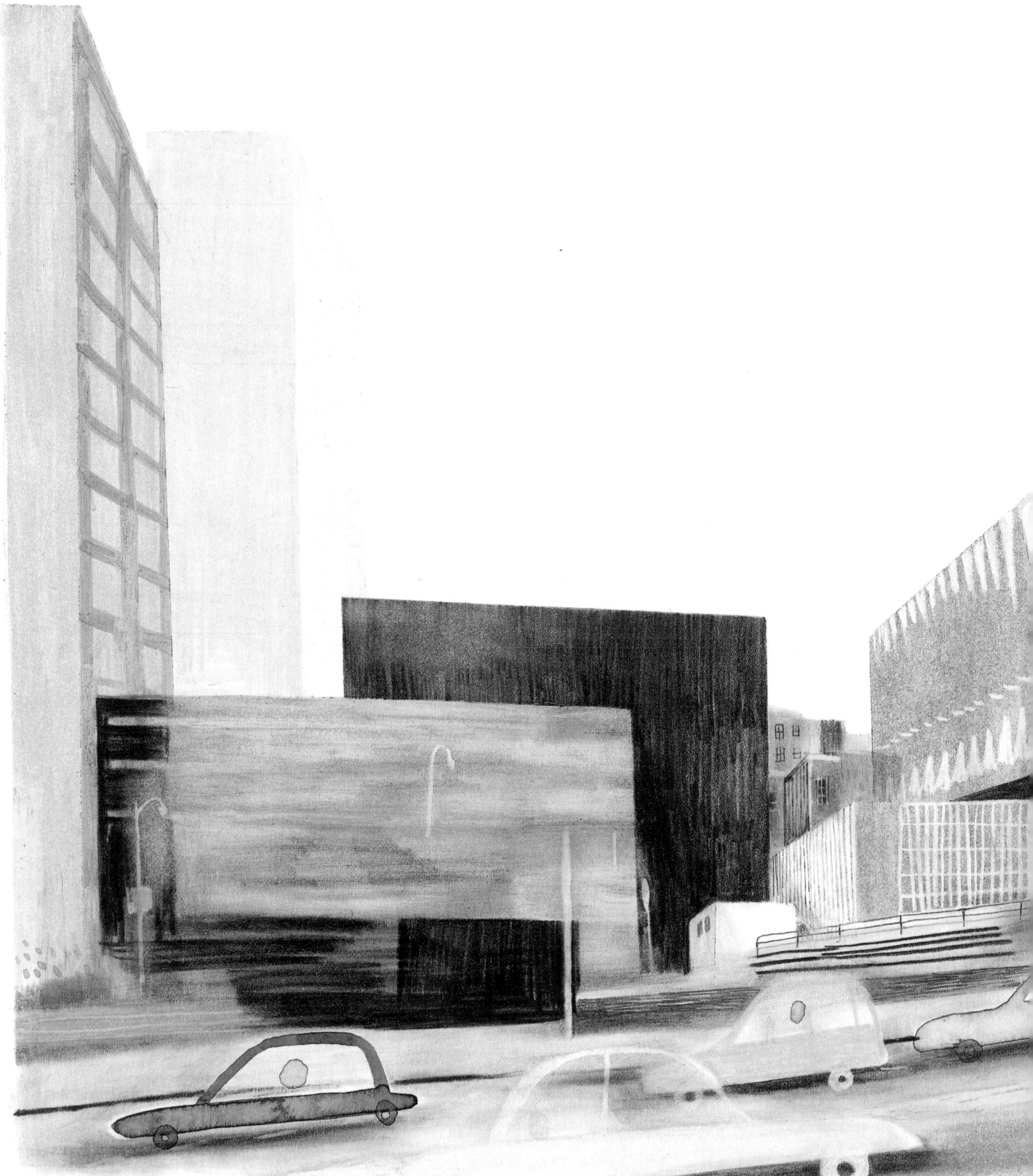

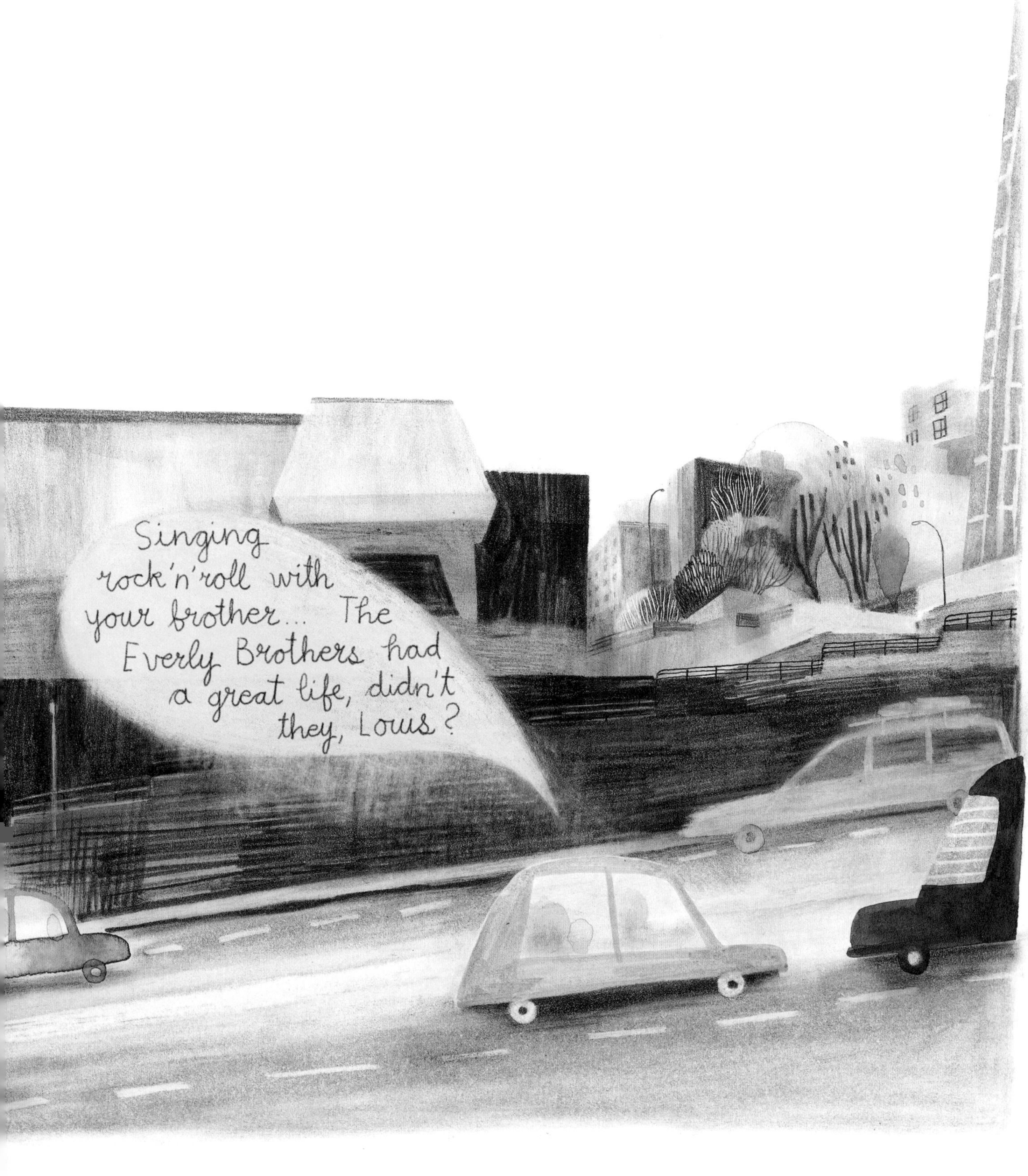
Singing rock'n'roll with your brother... The Everly Brothers had a great life, didn't they, Louis?

THE TREE HOUSE

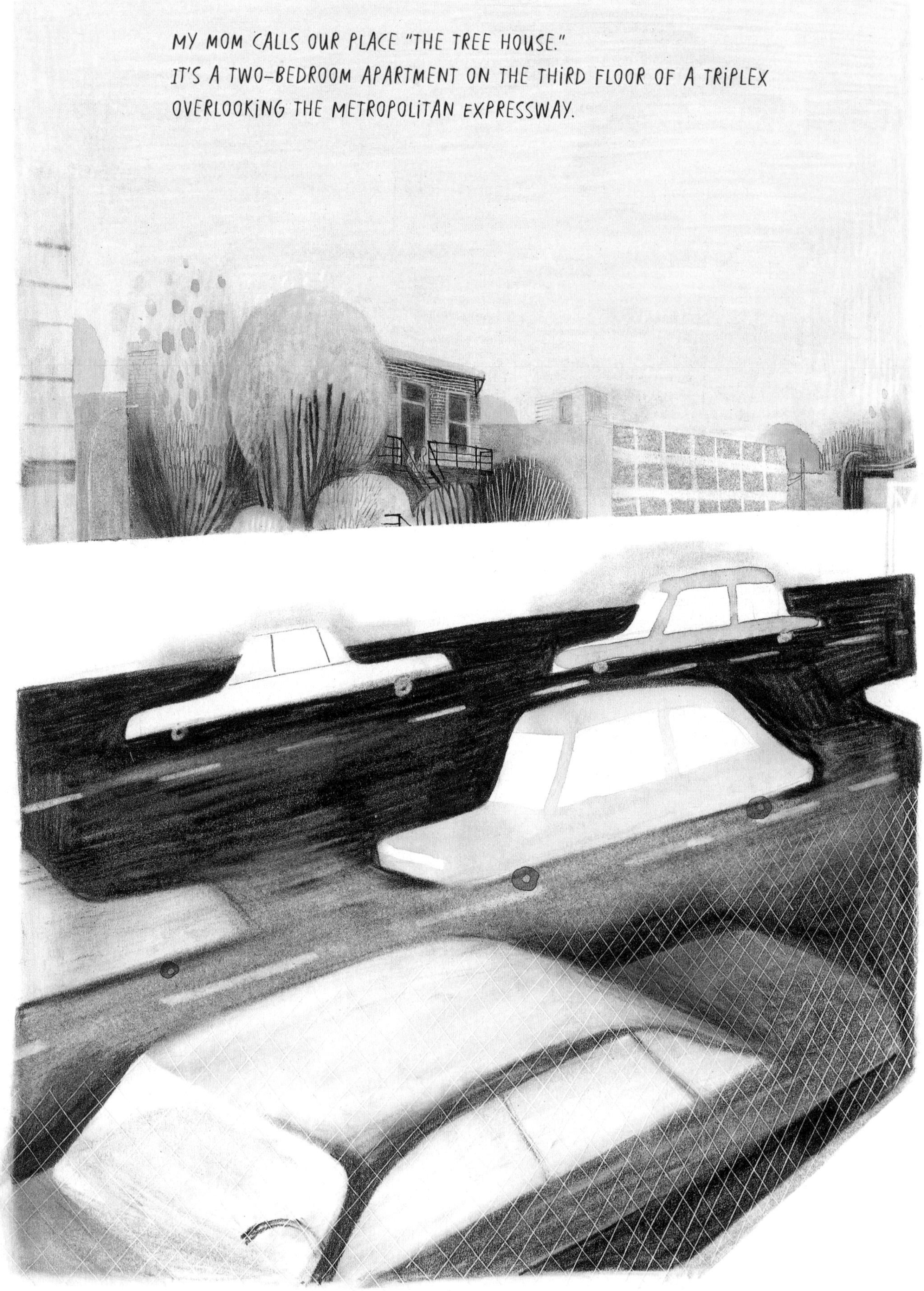
MY MOM CALLS OUR PLACE "THE TREE HOUSE."
IT'S A TWO-BEDROOM APARTMENT ON THE THIRD FLOOR OF A TRIPLEX
OVERLOOKING THE METROPOLITAN EXPRESSWAY.

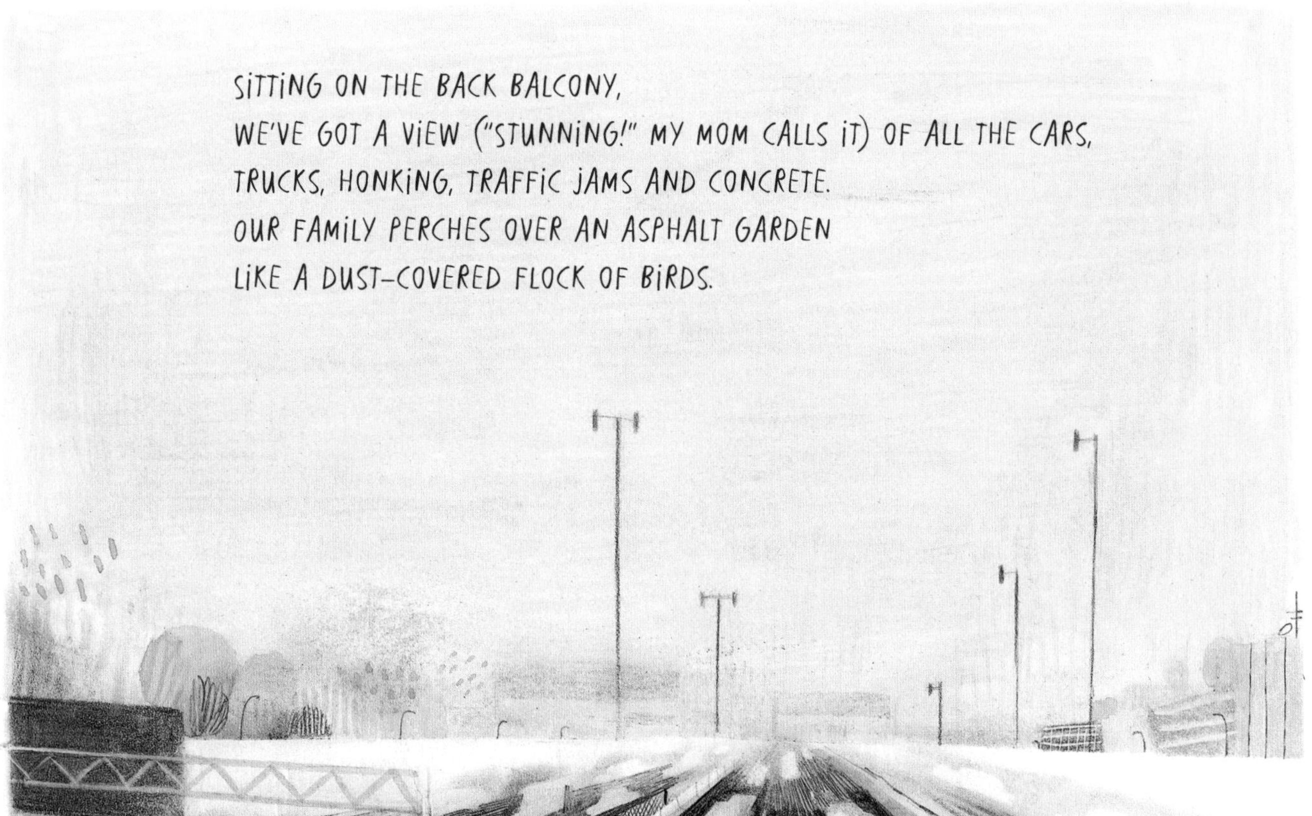
SITTING ON THE BACK BALCONY,
WE'VE GOT A VIEW ("STUNNING!" MY MOM CALLS IT) OF ALL THE CARS,
TRUCKS, HONKING, TRAFFIC JAMS AND CONCRETE.
OUR FAMILY PERCHES OVER AN ASPHALT GARDEN
LIKE A DUST-COVERED FLOCK OF BIRDS.

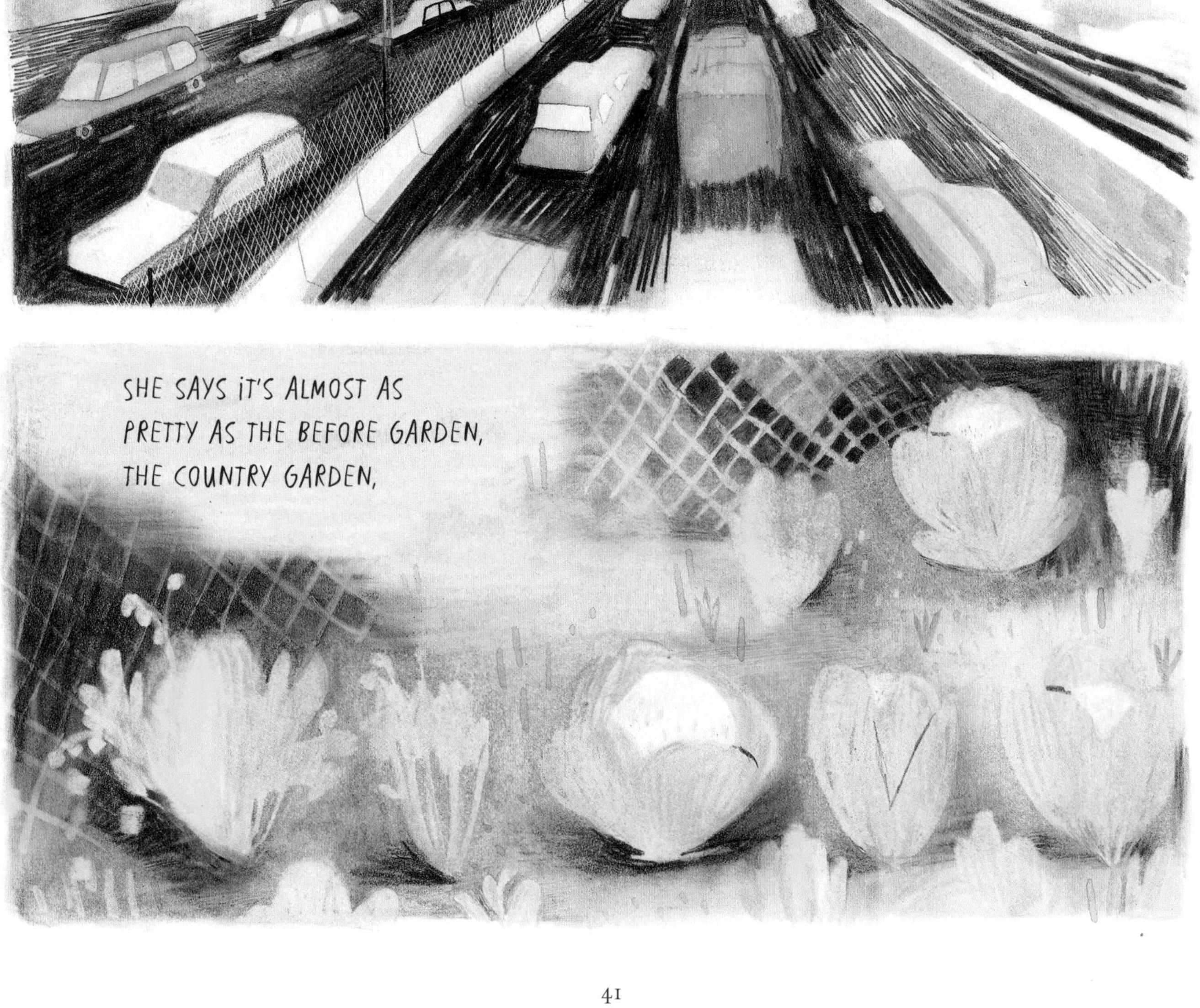
SHE SAYS IT'S ALMOST AS
PRETTY AS THE BEFORE GARDEN,
THE COUNTRY GARDEN,

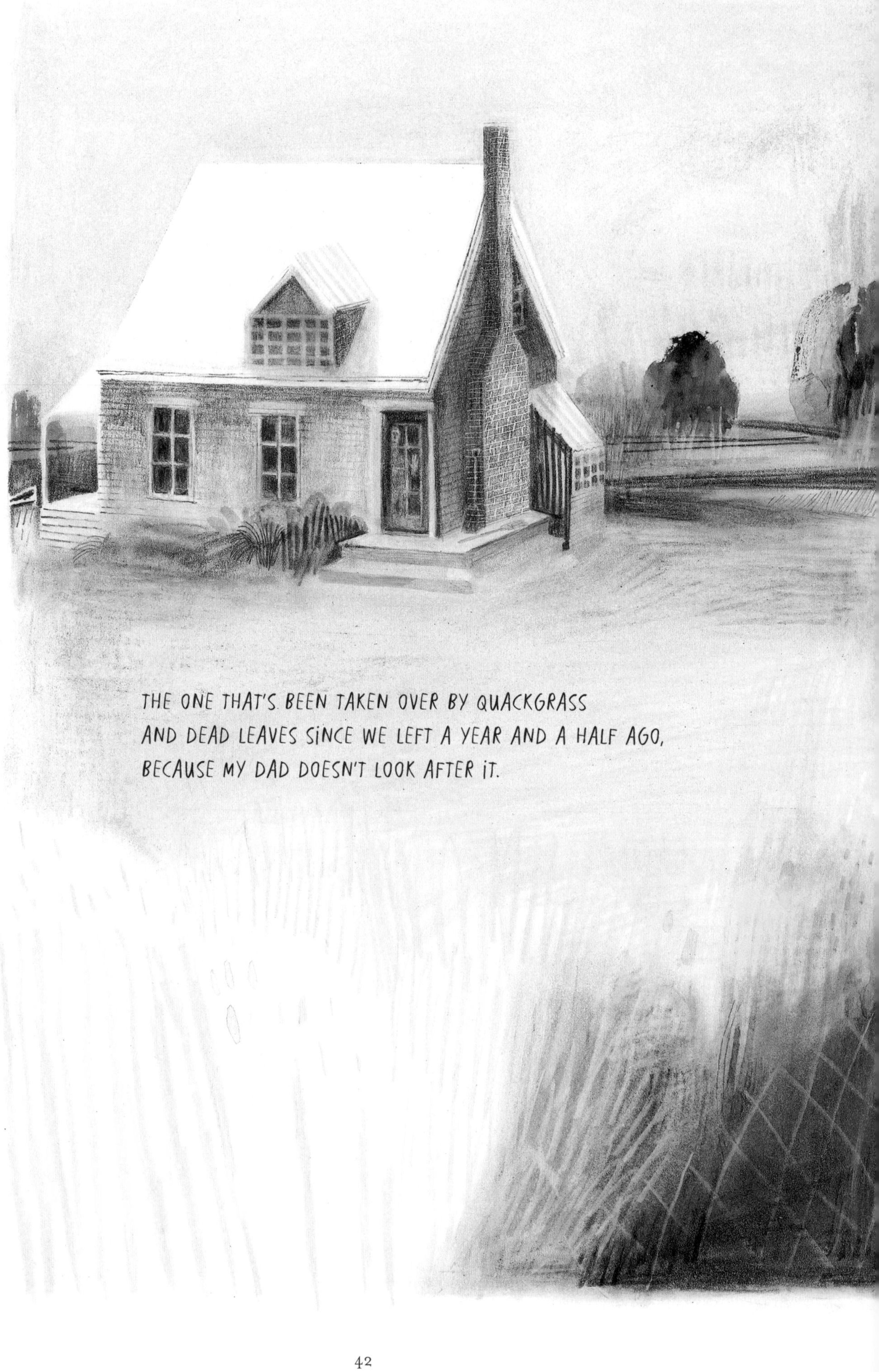
THE ONE THAT'S BEEN TAKEN OVER BY QUACKGRASS
AND DEAD LEAVES SINCE WE LEFT A YEAR AND A HALF AGO,
BECAUSE MY DAD DOESN'T LOOK AFTER IT.

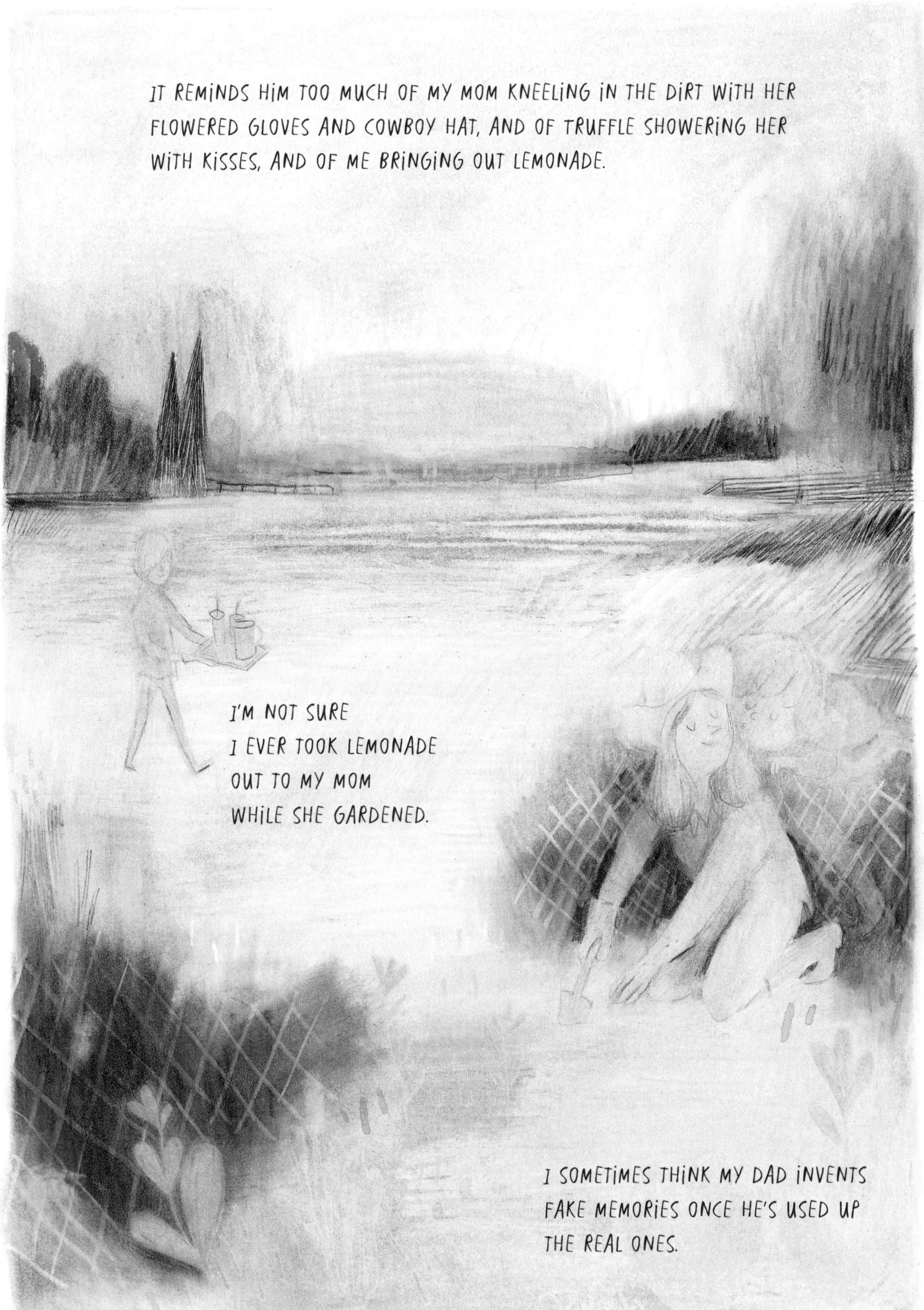
IT REMINDS HIM TOO MUCH OF MY MOM KNEELING IN THE DIRT WITH HER FLOWERED GLOVES AND COWBOY HAT, AND OF TRUFFLE SHOWERING HER WITH KISSES, AND OF ME BRINGING OUT LEMONADE.
I'M NOT SURE I EVER TOOK LEMONADE OUT TO MY MOM WHILE SHE GARDENED.
I SOMETIMES THINK MY DAD INVENTS FAKE MEMORIES ONCE HE'S USED UP THE REAL ONES.

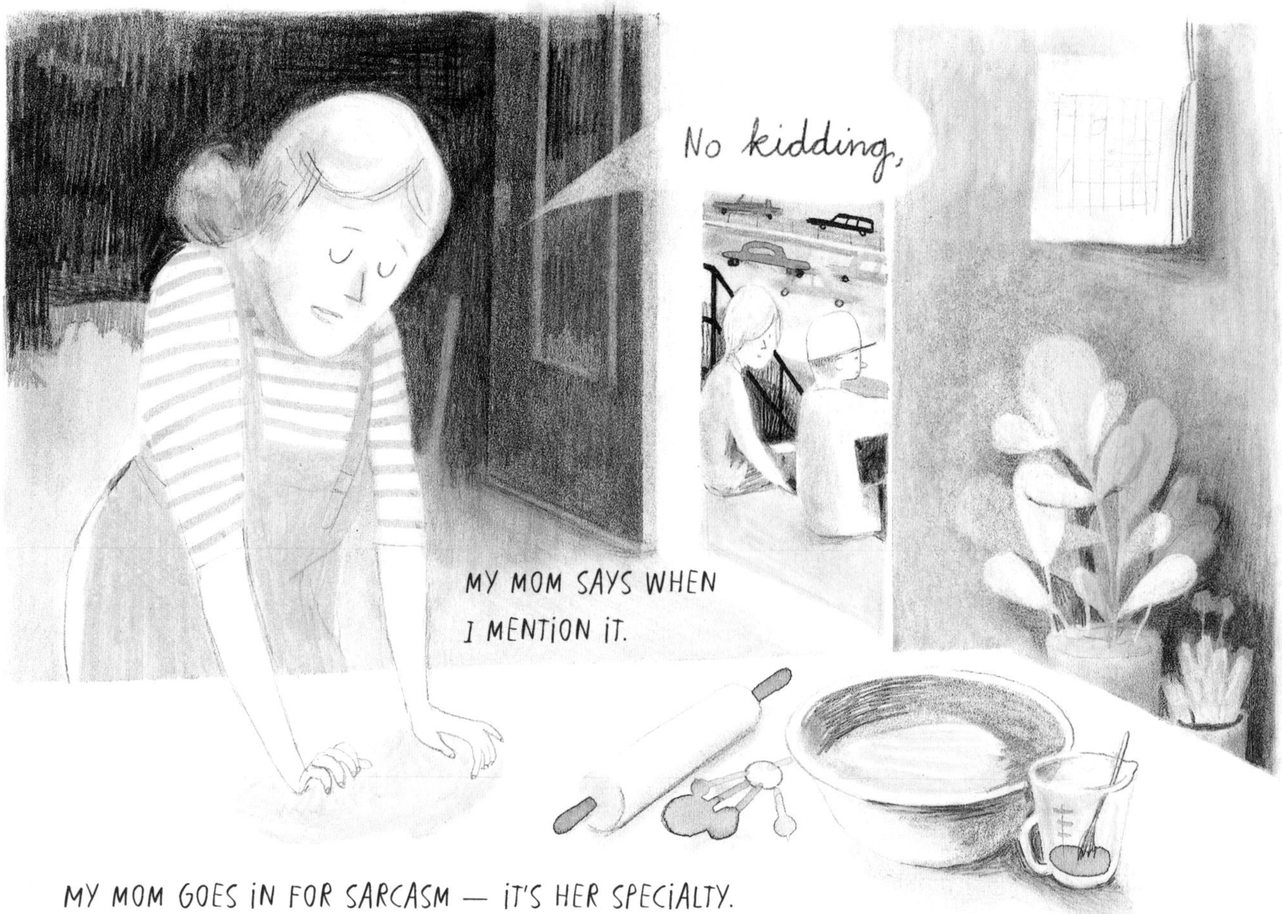
No kidding,
MY MOM SAYS WHEN I MENTION IT.

MY MOM GOES IN FOR SARCASM — IT'S HER SPECIALTY.

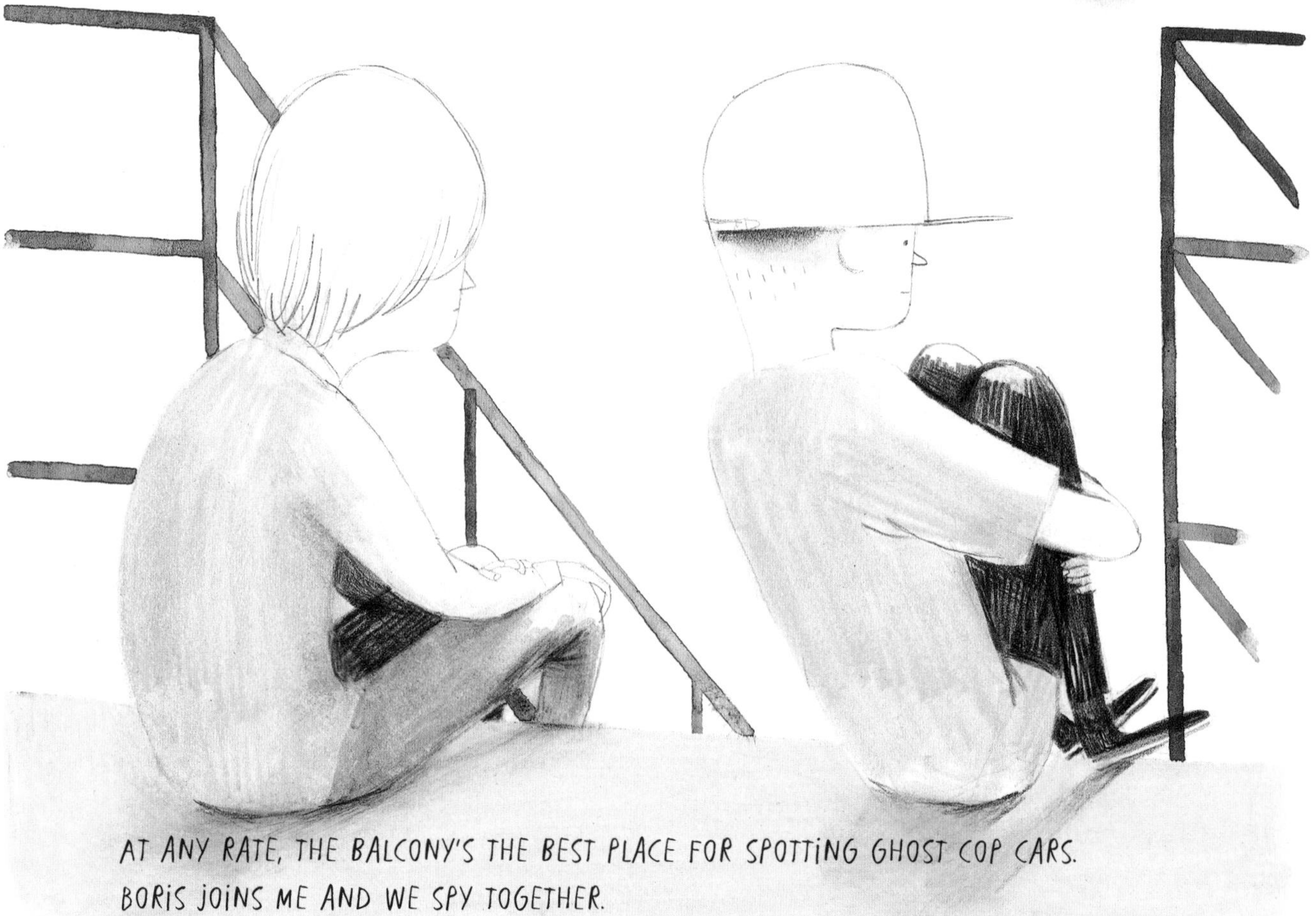

AT ANY RATE, THE BALCONY'S THE BEST PLACE FOR SPOTTING GHOST COP CARS. BORIS JOINS ME AND WE SPY TOGETHER.

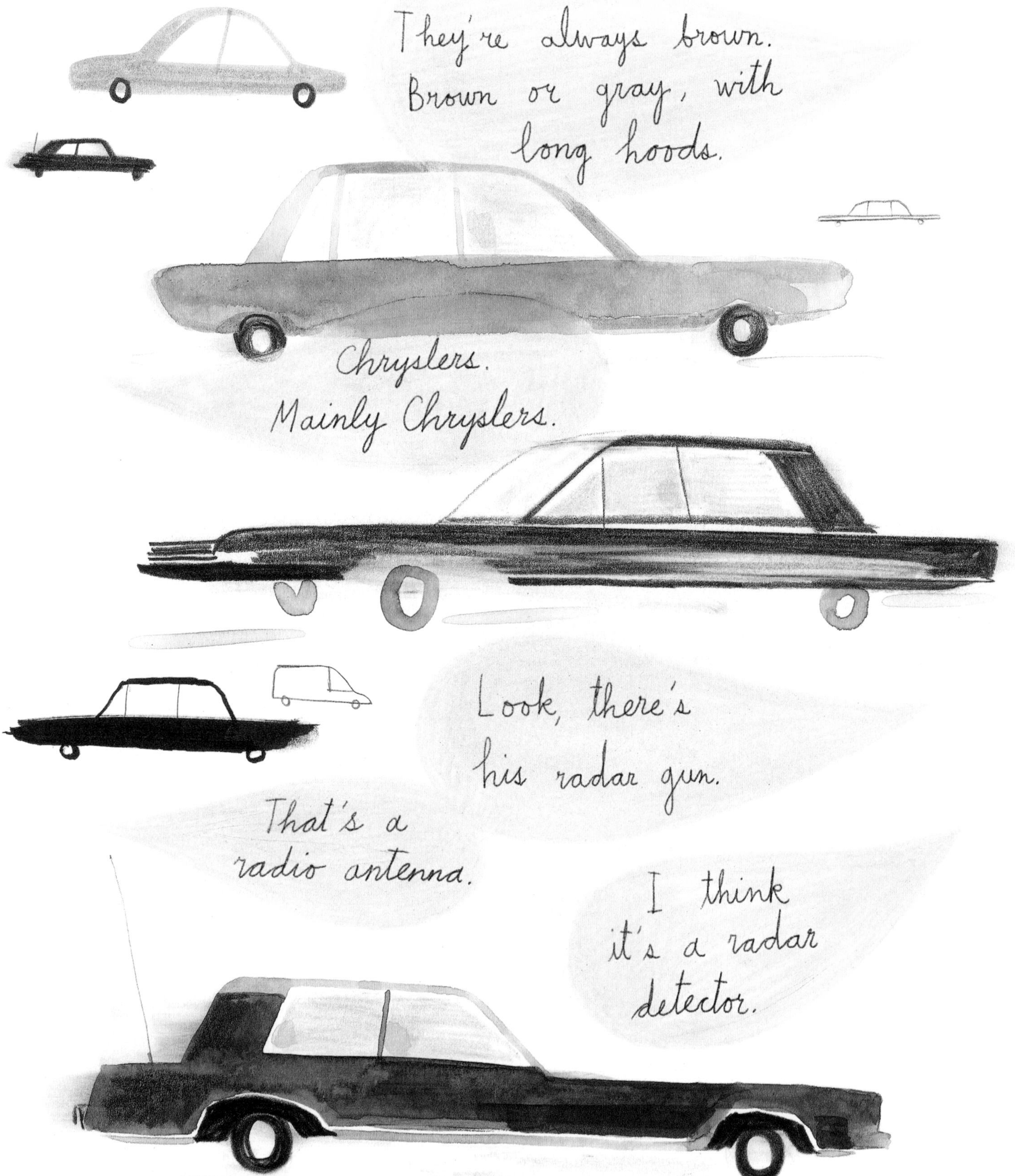
They're always brown. Brown or gray, with long hoods.
Chryslers. Mainly Chryslers.
Look, there's his radar gun.
That's a radio antenna.
I think it's a radar detector.

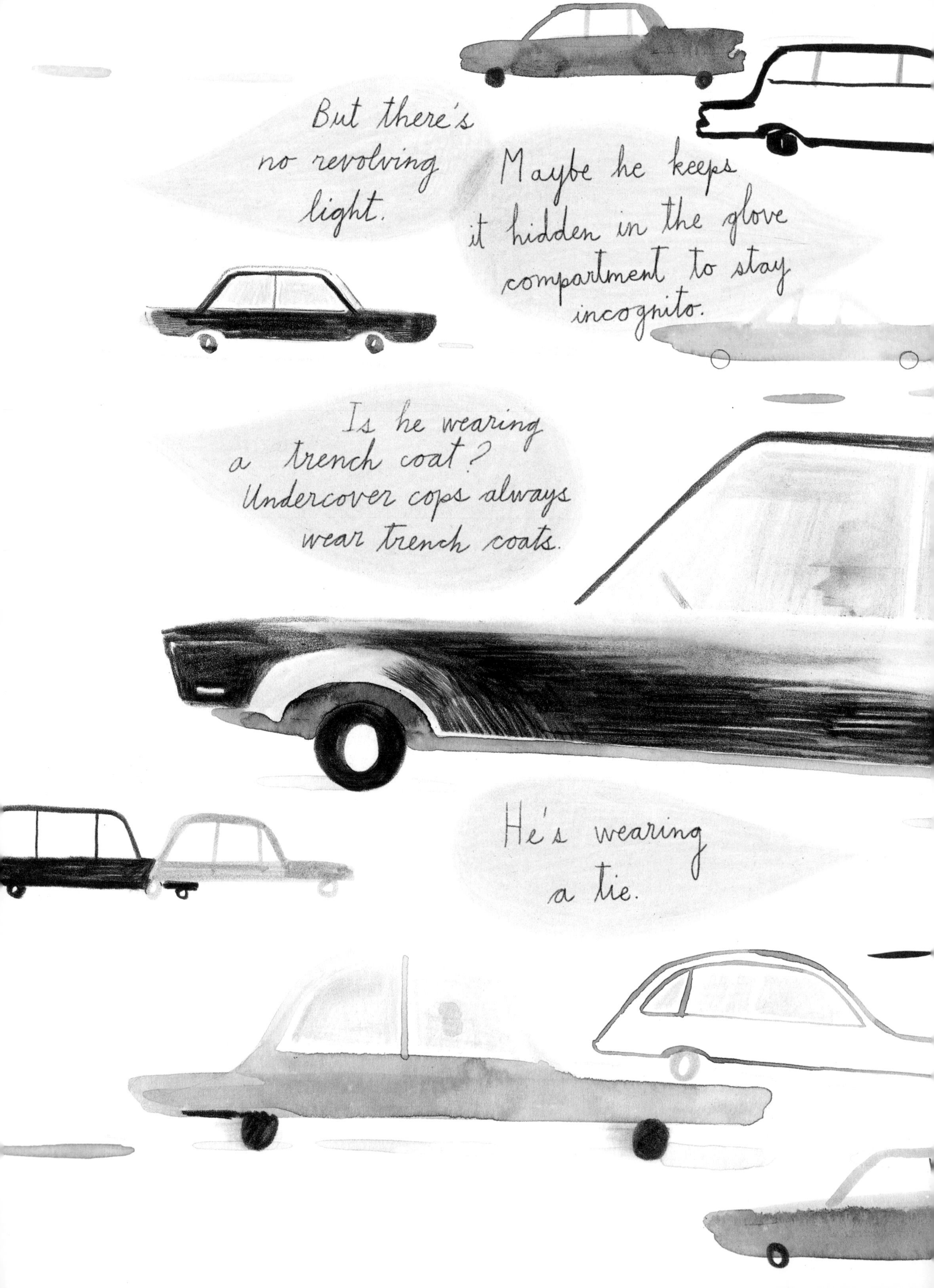
But there's no revolving light.
Maybe he keeps it hidden in the glove compartment to stay incognito.
Is he wearing a trench coat? Undercover cops always wear trench coats.
He's wearing a tie.

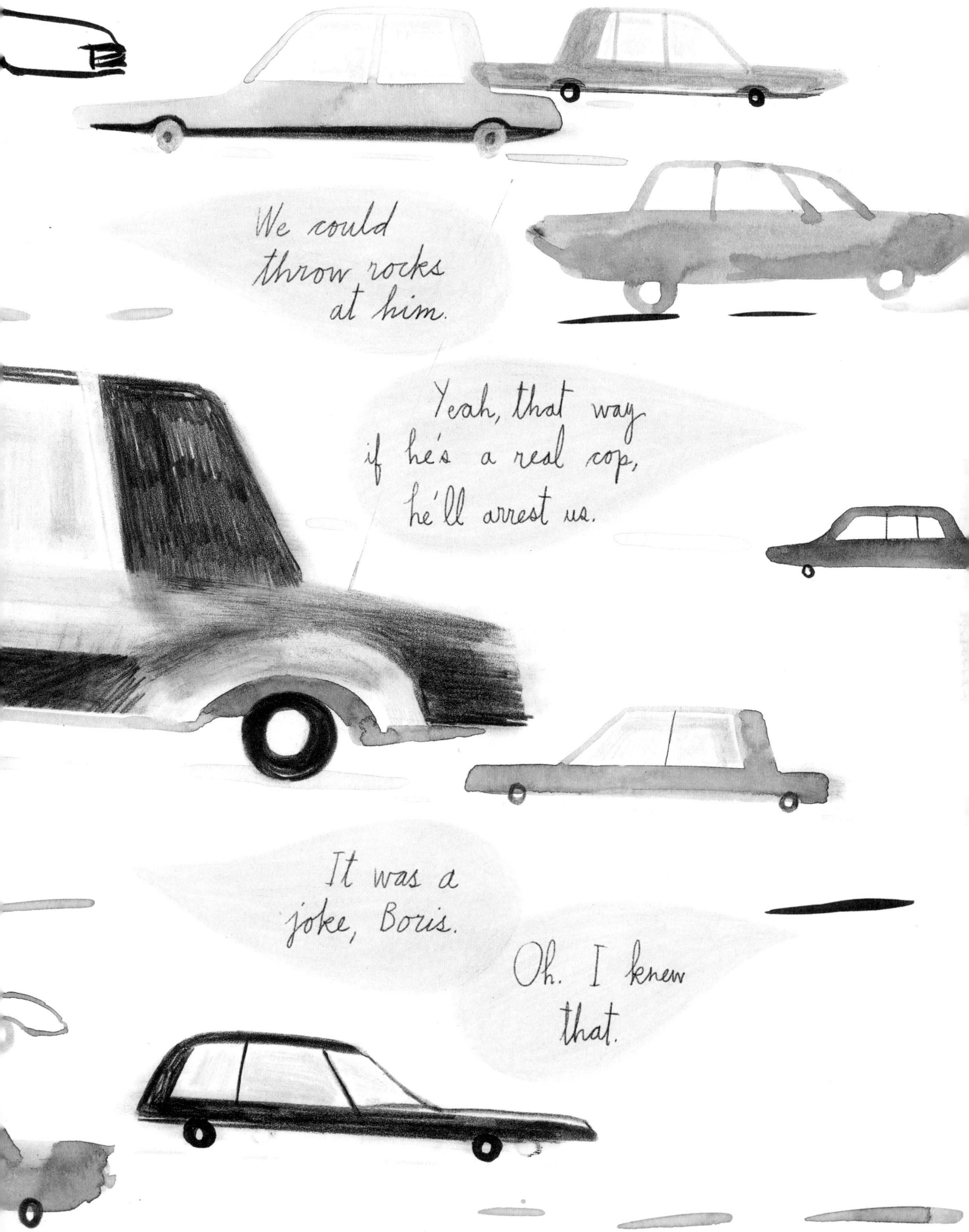
We could throw rocks at him.
Yeah, that way if he's a real cop, he'll arrest us.
It was a joke, Boris.
Oh. I knew that.

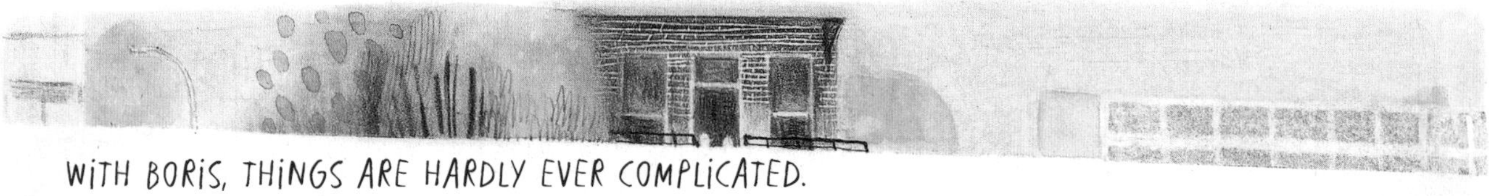

WITH BORIS, THINGS ARE HARDLY EVER COMPLICATED.
OR AT LEAST WHEN WE SPY ON CARS ON THE METROPOLITAN, EVERYTHING'S SIMPLE.
BUT WHEN HE SAYS,

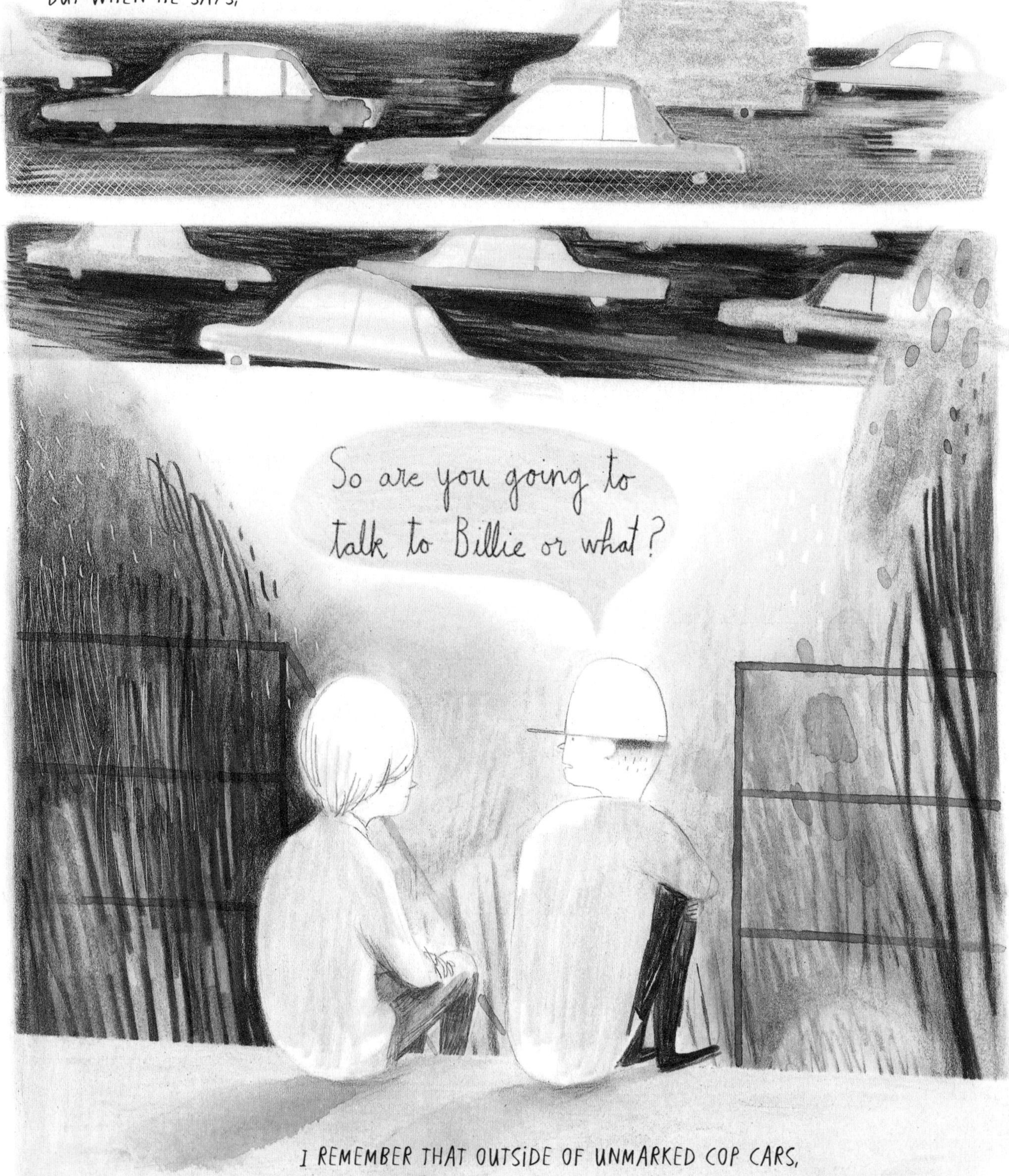
So are you going to talk to Billie or what?
I REMEMBER THAT OUTSIDE OF UNMARKED COP CARS, NOTHING ANYWHERE IN MY LIFE IS SIMPLE.

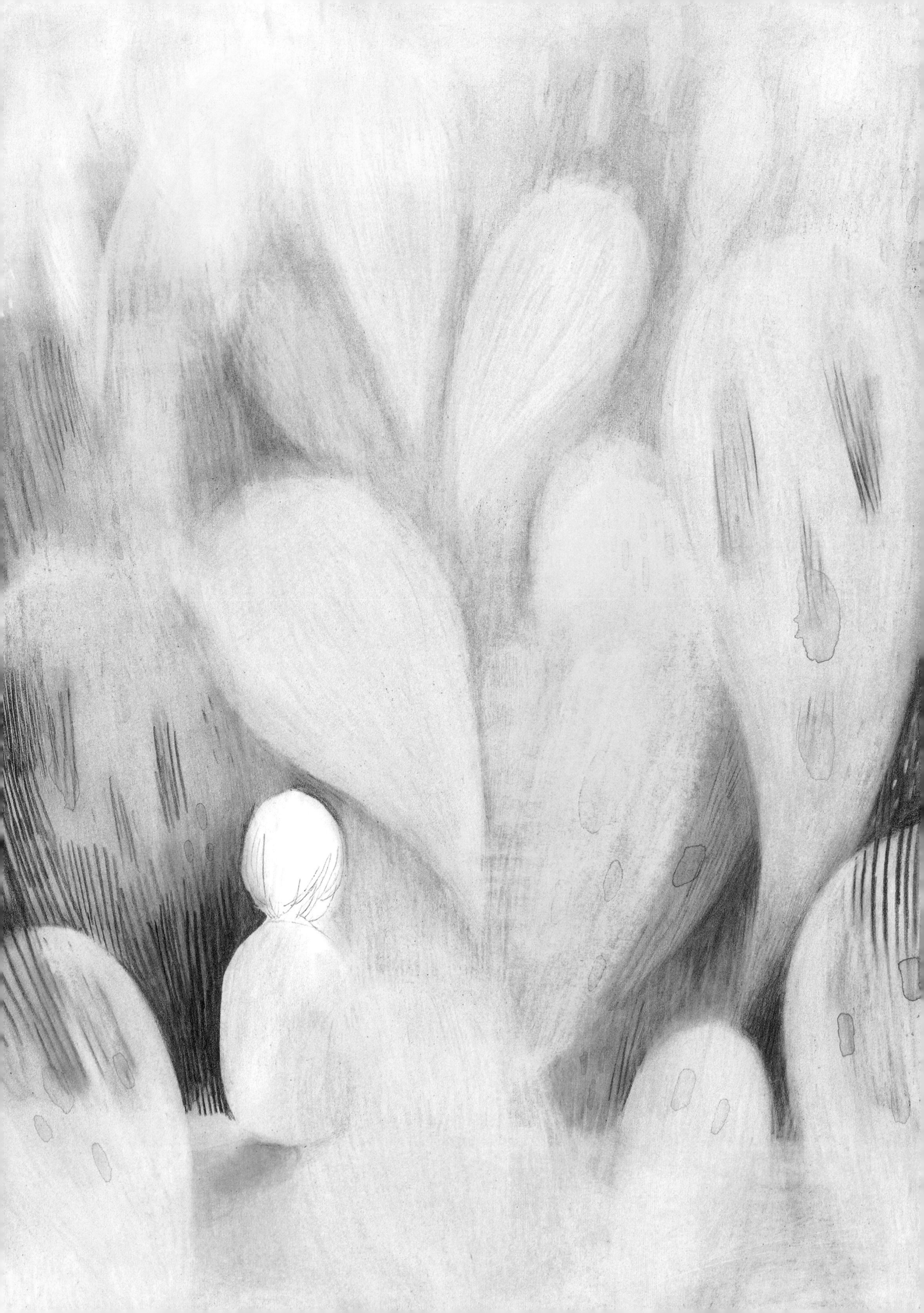

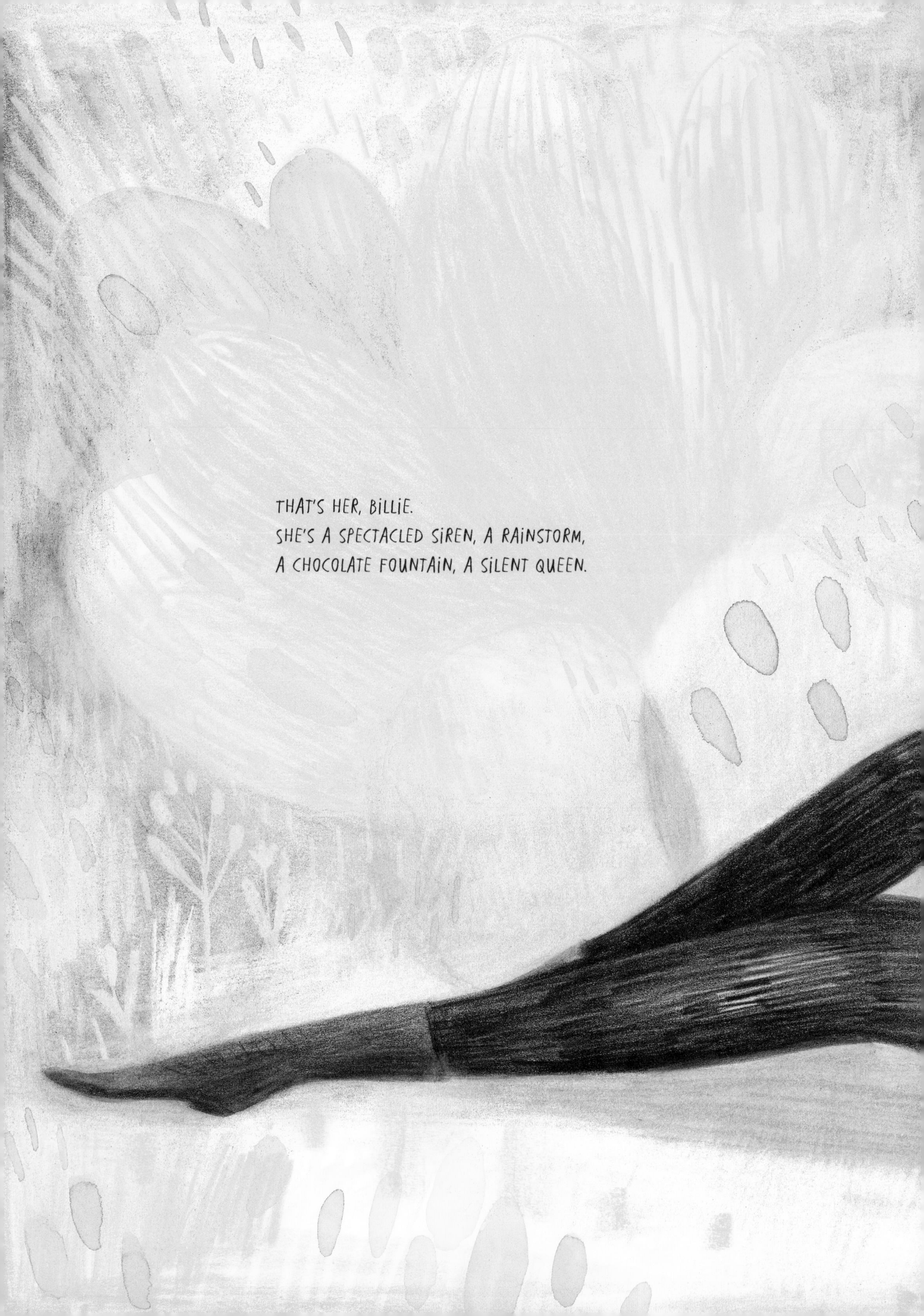

THAT'S HER, BILLIE.
SHE'S A SPECTACLED SIREN, A RAINSTORM,
A CHOCOLATE FOUNTAIN, A SILENT QUEEN.

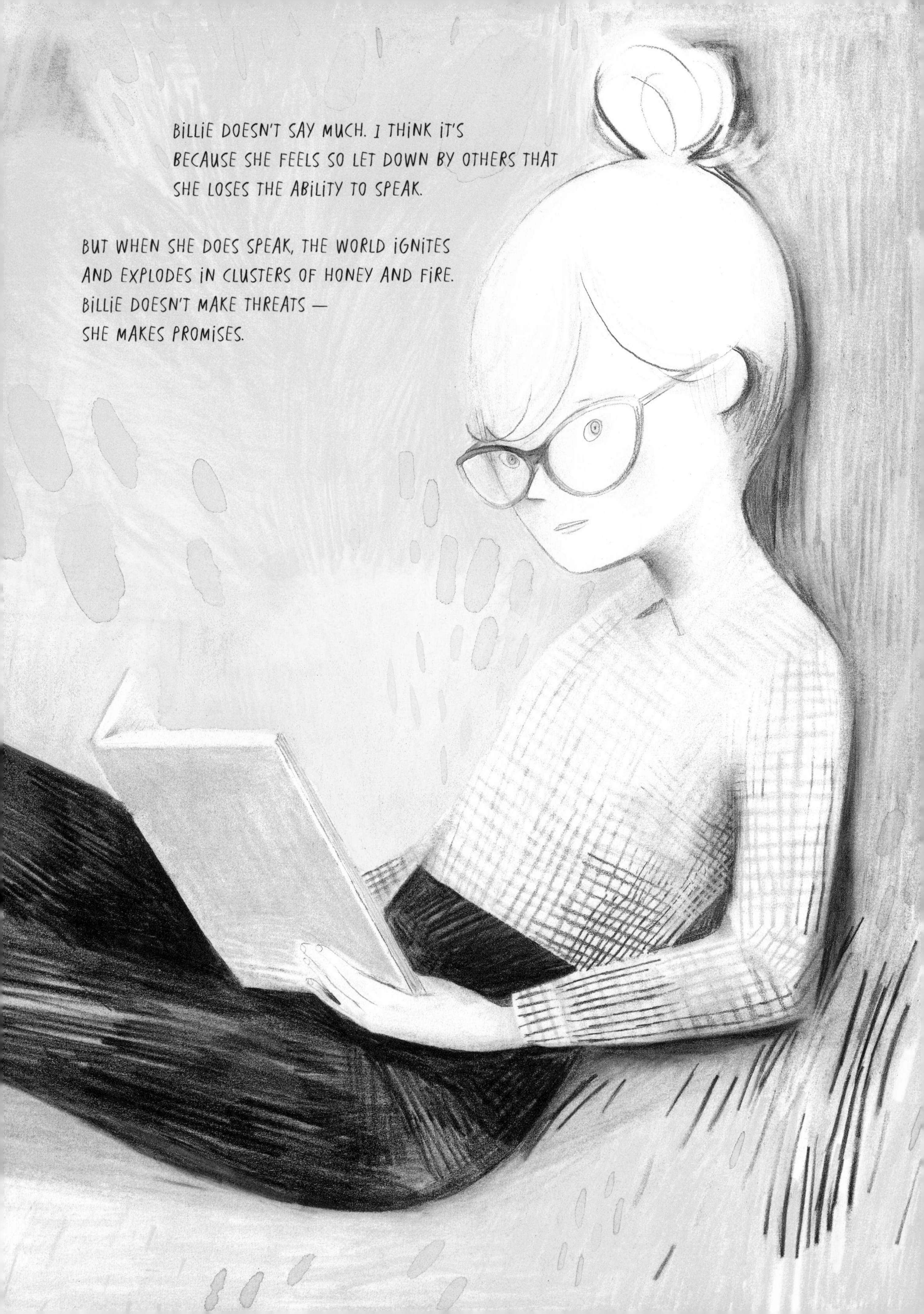
BILLIE DOESN'T SAY MUCH. I THINK IT'S BECAUSE SHE FEELS SO LET DOWN BY OTHERS THAT SHE LOSES THE ABILITY TO SPEAK.
BUT WHEN SHE DOES SPEAK, THE WORLD IGNITES AND EXPLODES IN CLUSTERS OF HONEY AND FIRE. BILLIE DOESN'T MAKE THREATS — SHE MAKES PROMISES.

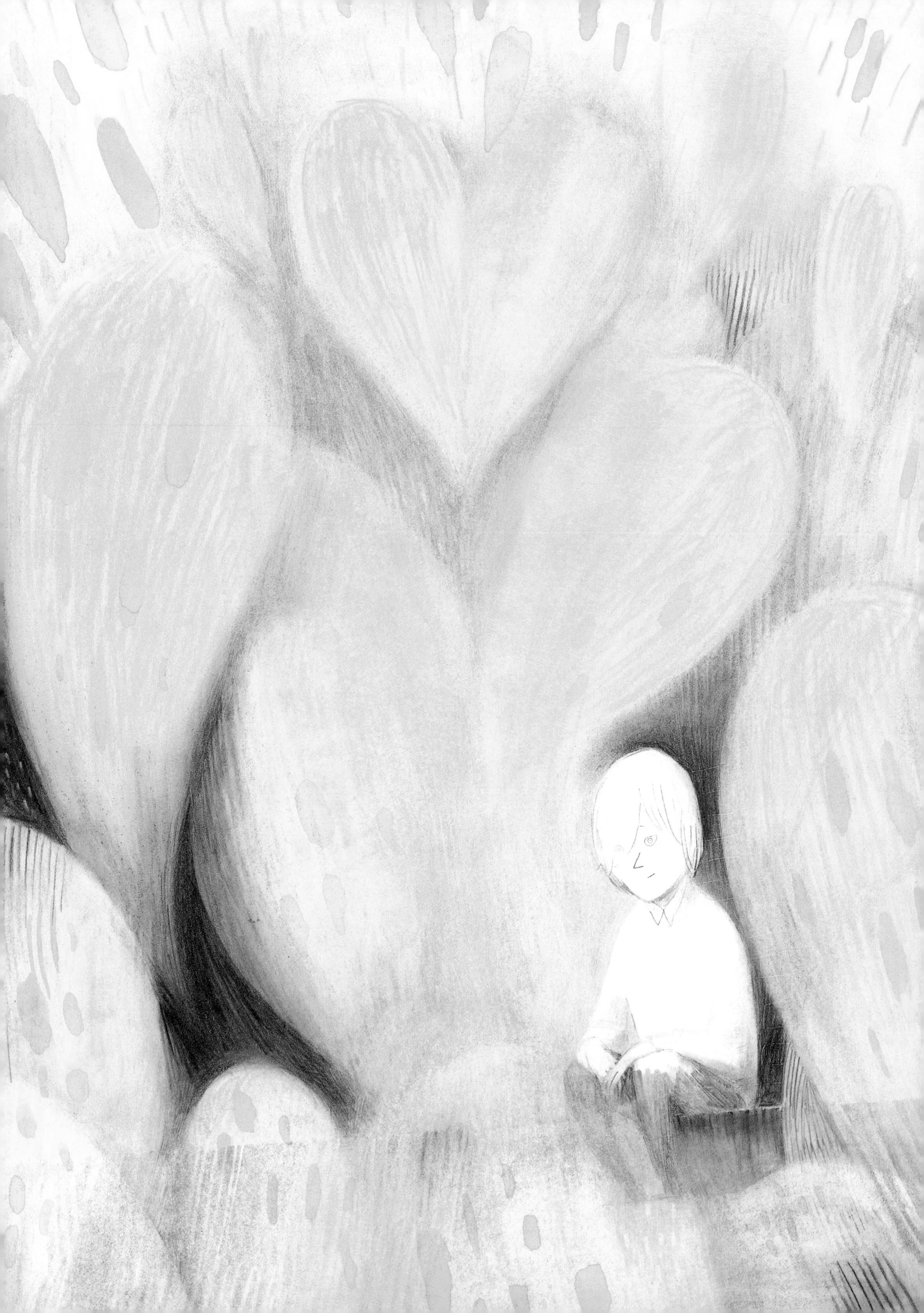

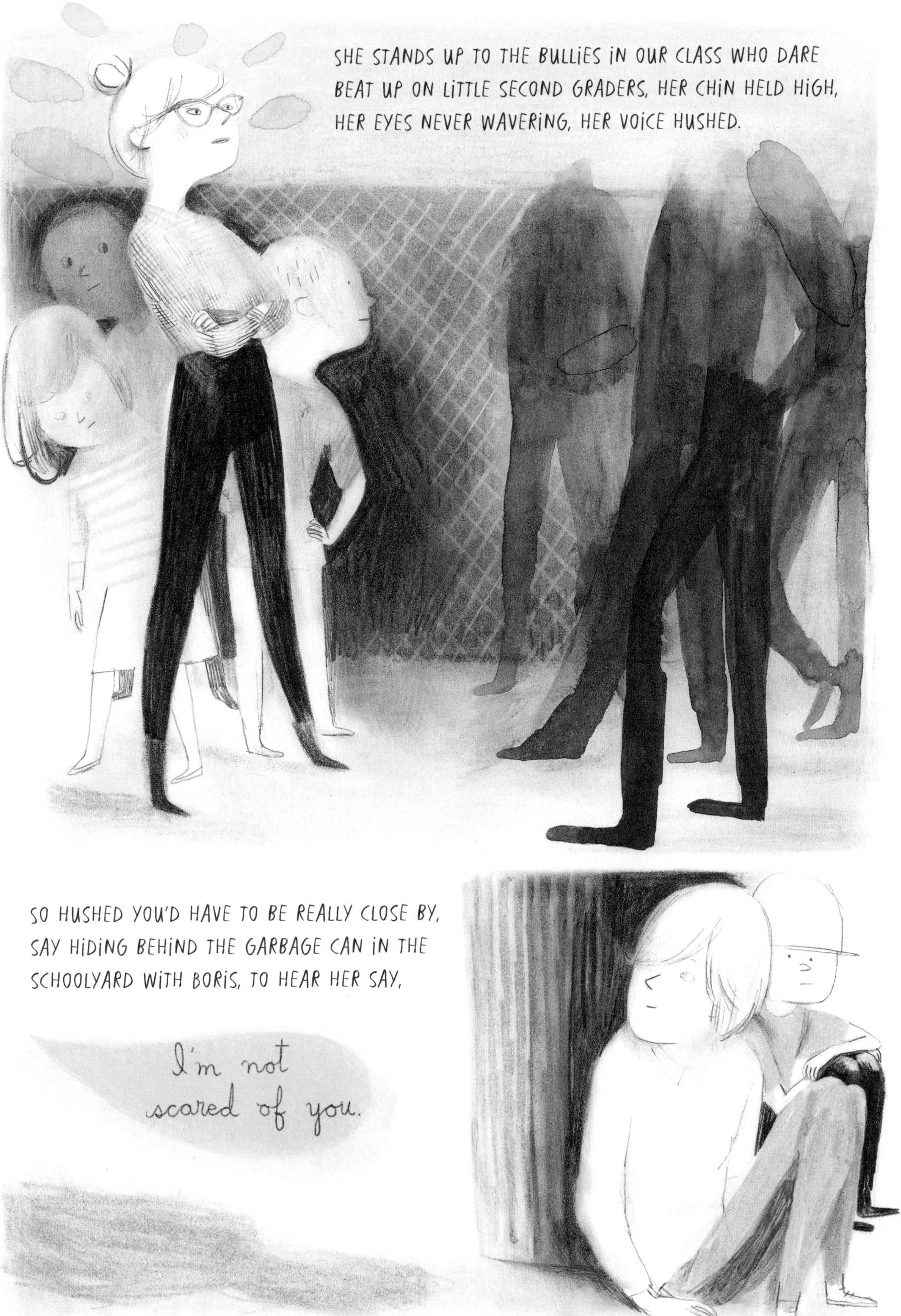
SHE STANDS UP TO THE BULLIES IN OUR CLASS WHO DARE BEAT UP ON LITTLE SECOND GRADERS, HER CHIN HELD HIGH, HER EYES NEVER WAVERING, HER VOICE HUSHED.
SO HUSHED YOU'D HAVE TO BE REALLY CLOSE BY, SAY HIDING BEHIND THE GARBAGE CAN IN THE SCHOOLYARD WITH BORIS, TO HEAR HER SAY,
I'm not scared of you.

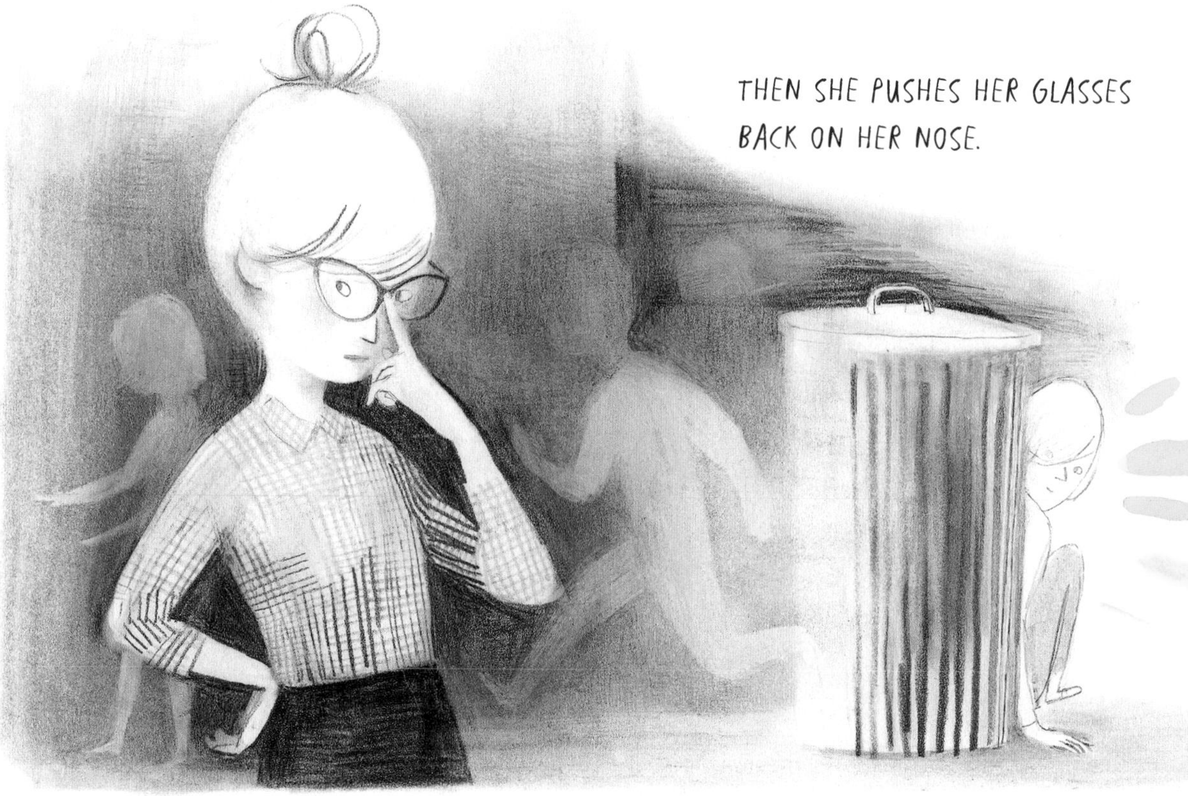
THEN SHE PUSHES HER GLASSES
BACK ON HER NOSE.

WHENEVER SHE'S UPSET, THEY SLIP DOWN JUST A BIT. I BET I'M THE ONLY ONE WHO'S NOTICED — I HOPE SO ANYWAY — BECAUSE BEING THE ONLY ONE TO SEE HER GLASSES SLIP IS ALMOST LIKE BEING ALONE WITH HER.

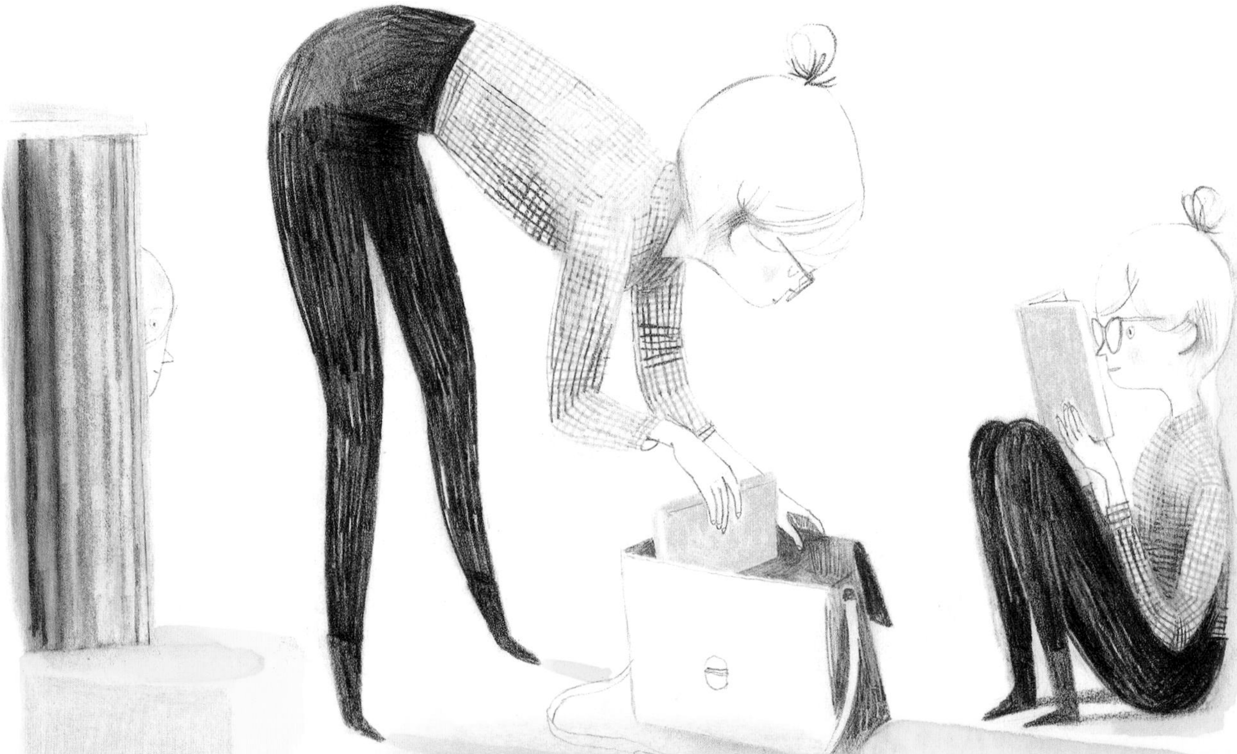

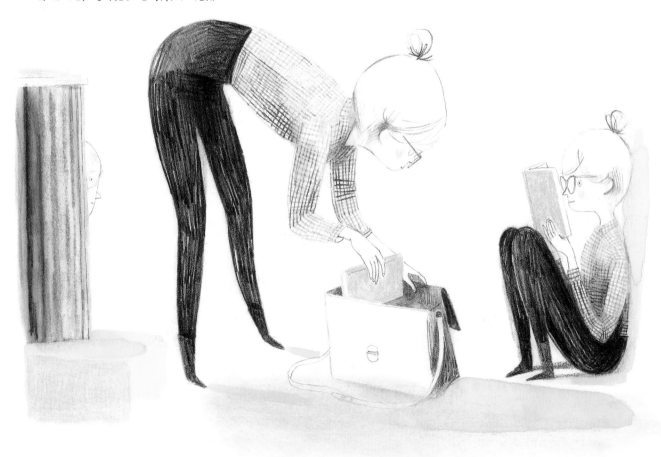

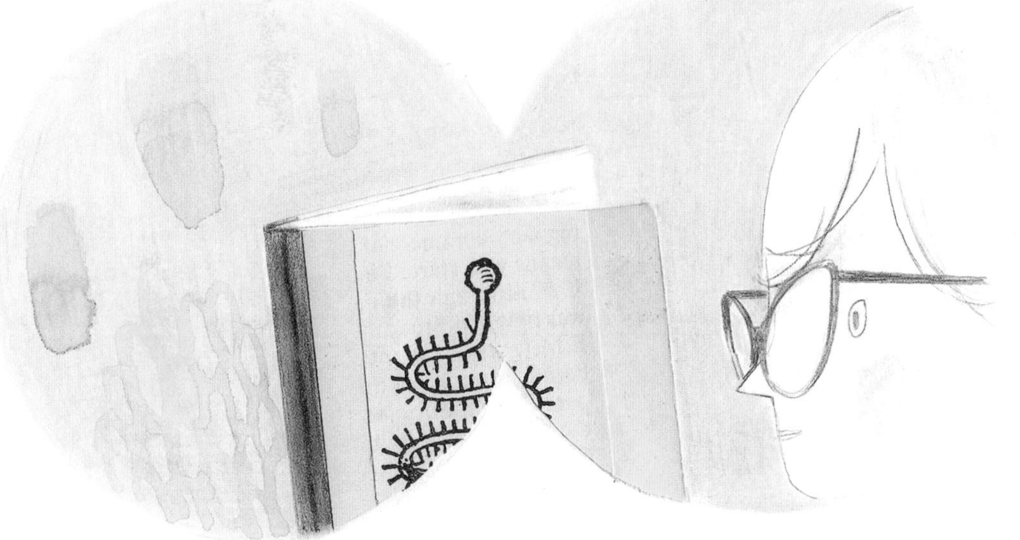

ALL SHE'S INTERESTED IN IS HER BOOKS.
SHE READS SCIENCE FICTION, ADVENTURE STORIES,

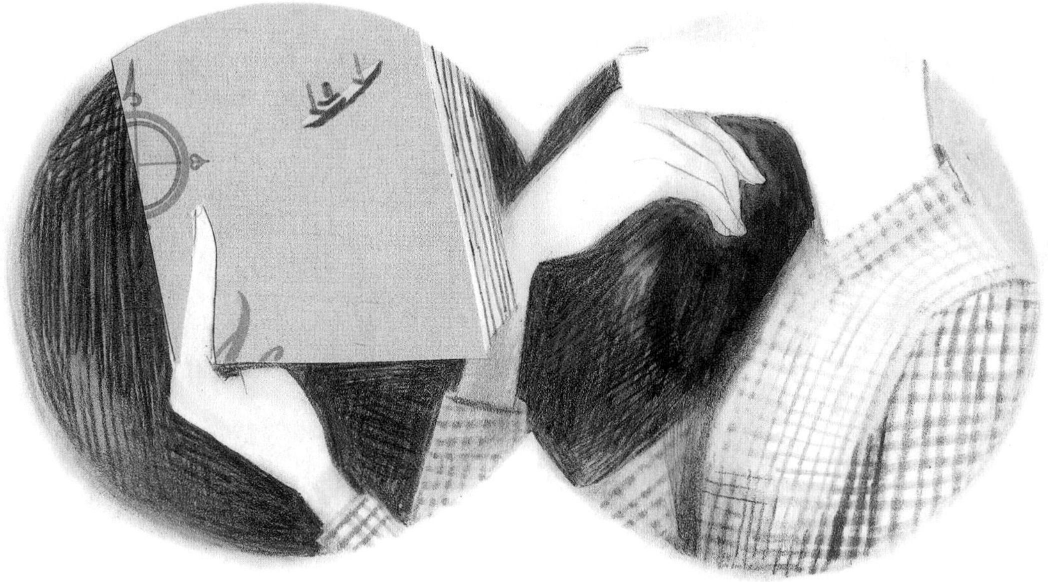

BIOGRAPHIES OF BANDS I ONLY KNOW ABOUT FROM MY DAD'S VINYL COLLECTION.
SHE READS A BOOK A WEEK.

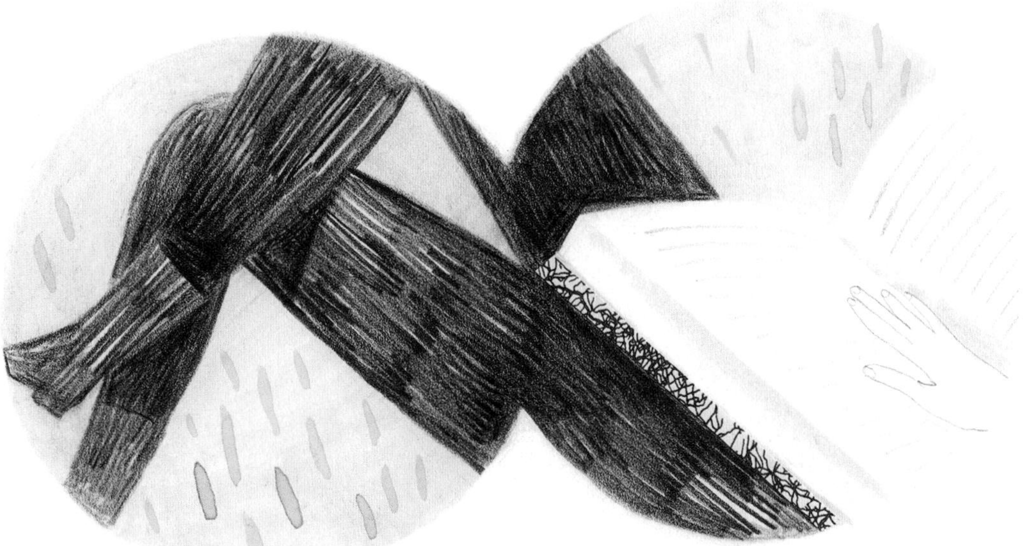

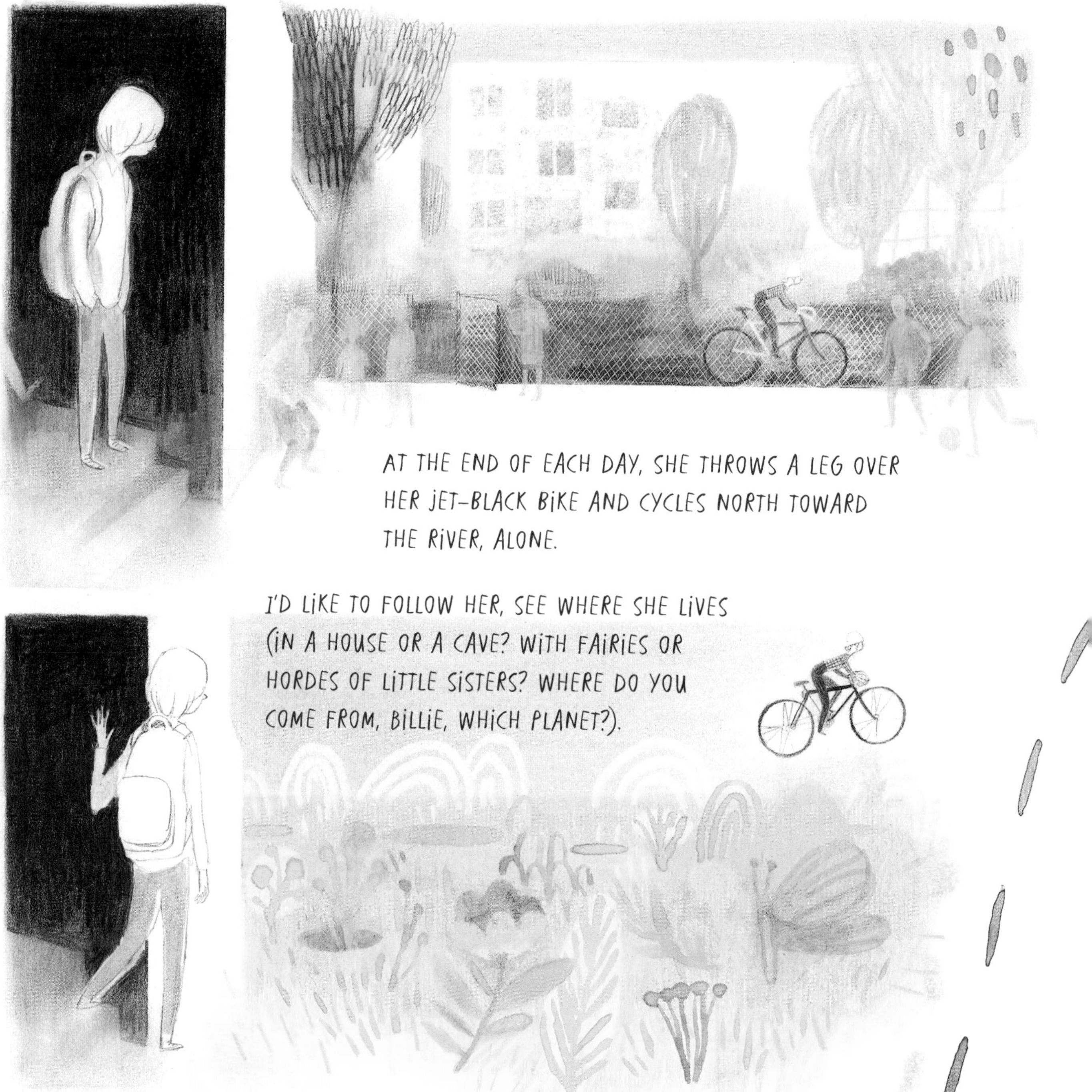
AT THE END OF EACH DAY, SHE THROWS A LEG OVER HER JET-BLACK BIKE AND CYCLES NORTH TOWARD THE RIVER, ALONE.
I'D LIKE TO FOLLOW HER, SEE WHERE SHE LIVES (IN A HOUSE OR A CAVE? WITH FAIRIES OR HORDES OF LITTLE SISTERS? WHERE DO YOU COME FROM, BILLIE, WHICH PLANET?).
BUT MY MOM DOESN'T WANT ME COMING HOME LATE FROM SCHOOL. I'M NOT TO STRAY FROM MY ROUTE. TURN RIGHT OUTSIDE THE SCHOOL, LEFT AT THE END OF THE STREET, LEFT AGAIN TO SKIRT THE BOULEVARD AND ITS DANGERS,

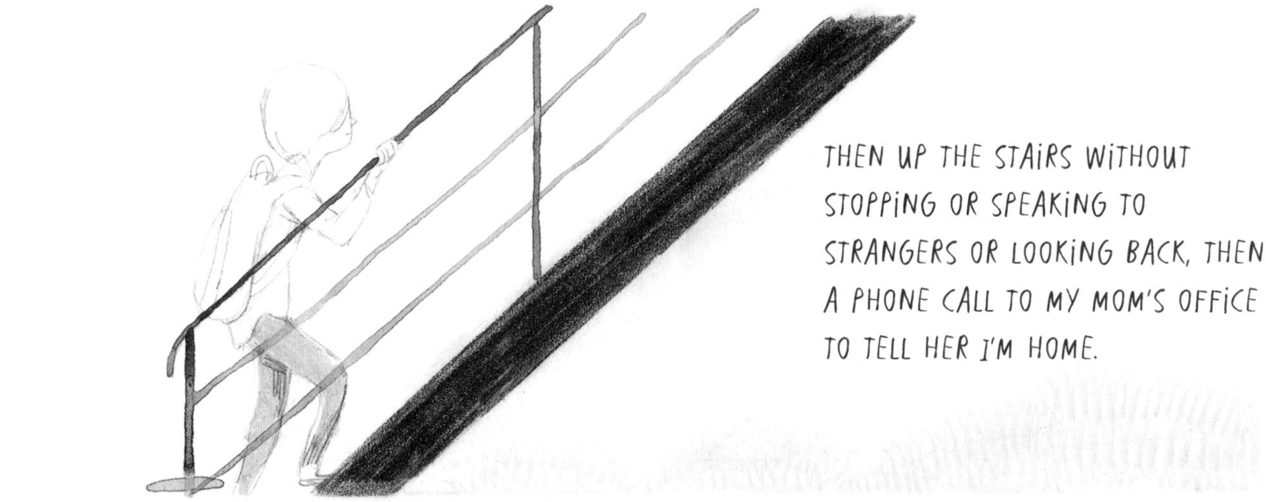
THEN UP THE STAIRS WITHOUT STOPPING OR SPEAKING TO STRANGERS OR LOOKING BACK, THEN A PHONE CALL TO MY MOM'S OFFICE TO TELL HER I'M HOME.

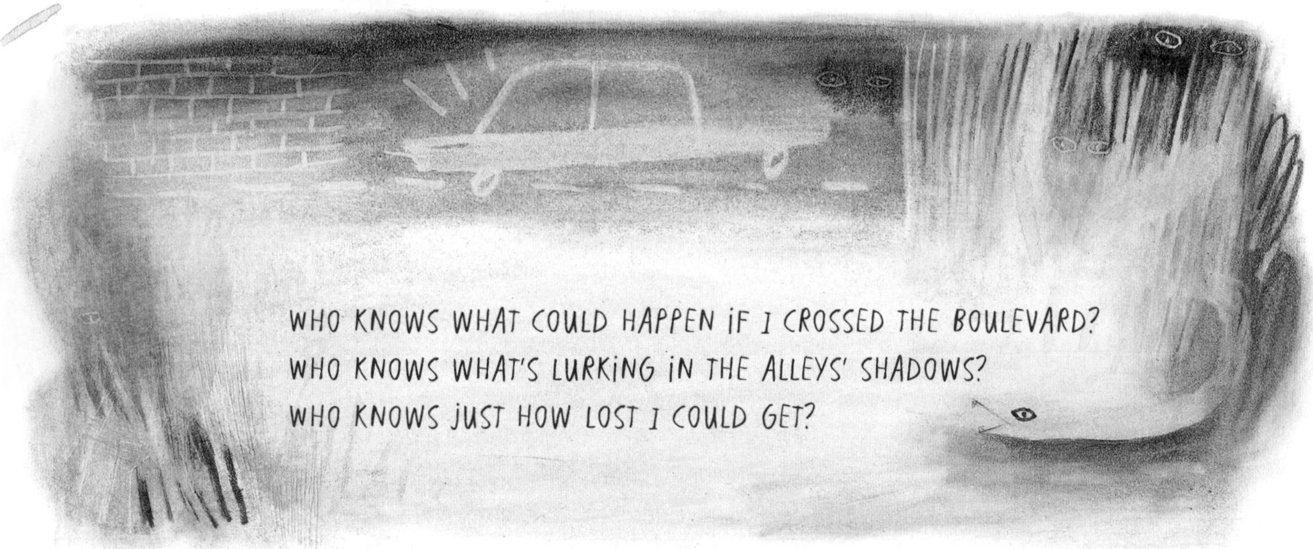
WHO KNOWS WHAT COULD HAPPEN IF I CROSSED THE BOULEVARD?
WHO KNOWS WHAT'S LURKING IN THE ALLEYS' SHADOWS?
WHO KNOWS JUST HOW LOST I COULD GET?

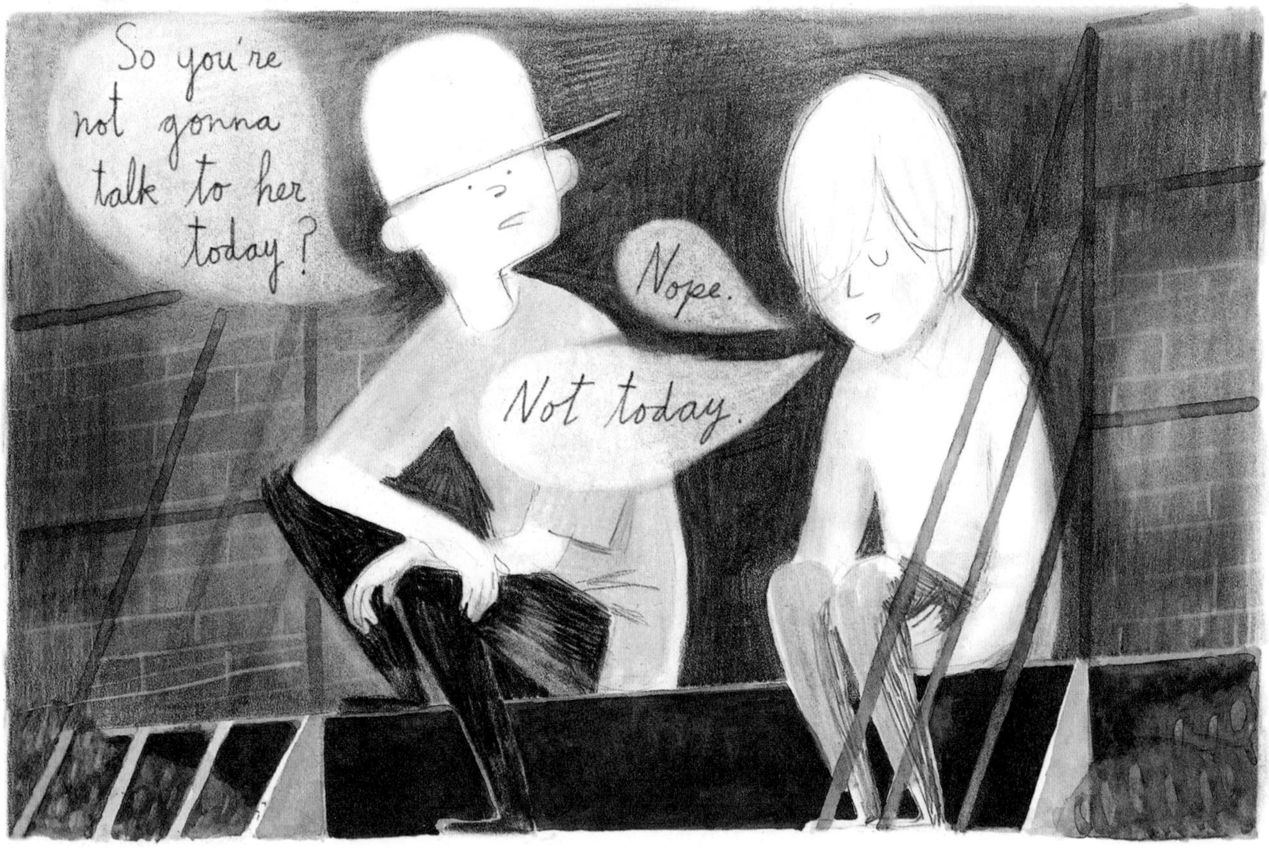
So you're not gonna talk to her today?
Nope.
Not today.

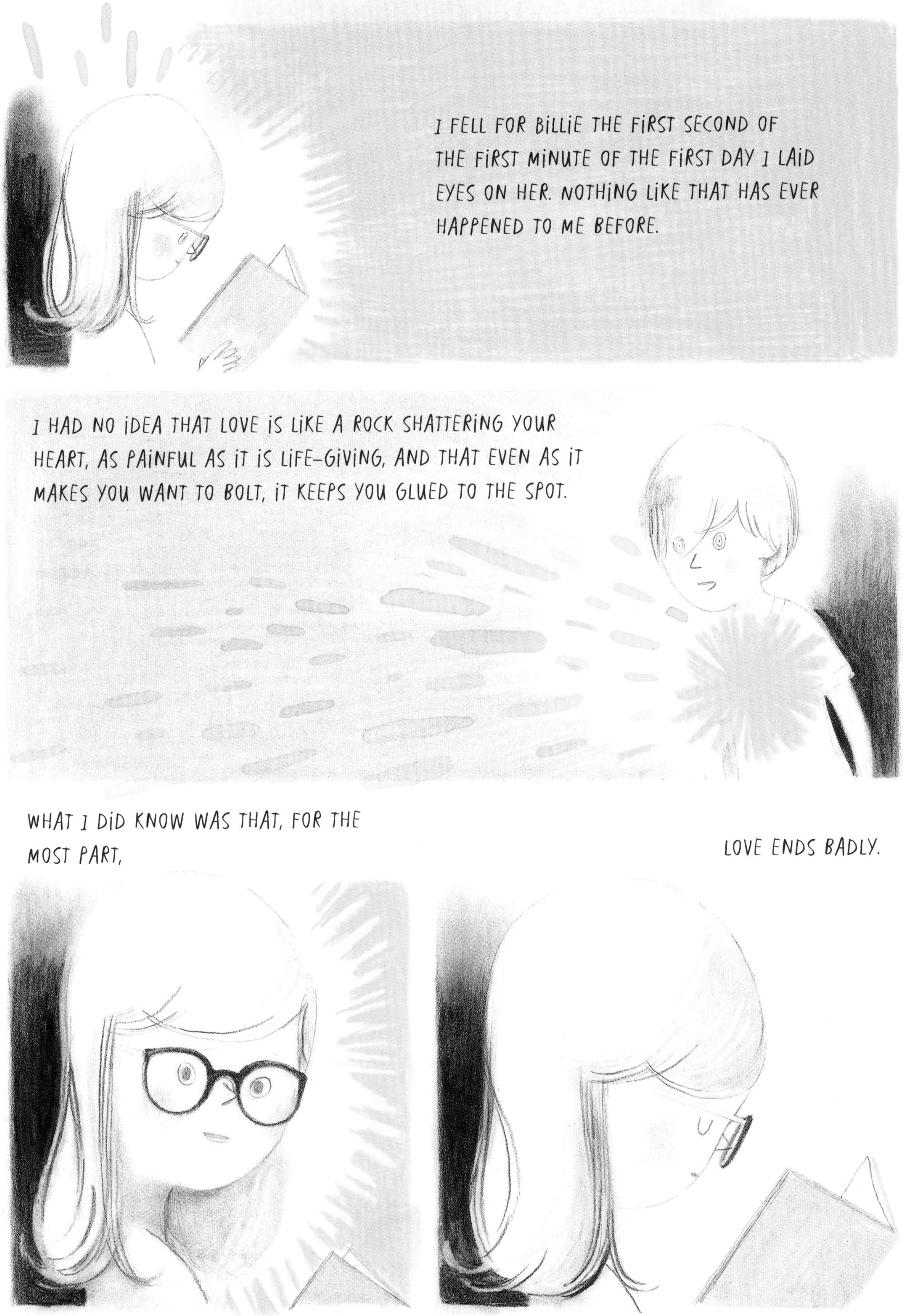
I FELL FOR BILLIE THE FIRST SECOND OF THE FIRST MINUTE OF THE FIRST DAY I LAID EYES ON HER. NOTHING LIKE THAT HAS EVER HAPPENED TO ME BEFORE.
I HAD NO IDEA THAT LOVE IS LIKE A ROCK SHATTERING YOUR HEART, AS PAINFUL AS IT IS LIFE-GIVING, AND THAT EVEN AS IT MAKES YOU WANT TO BOLT, IT KEEPS YOU GLUED TO THE SPOT.
WHAT I DID KNOW WAS THAT, FOR THE MOST PART,
LOVE ENDS BADLY.

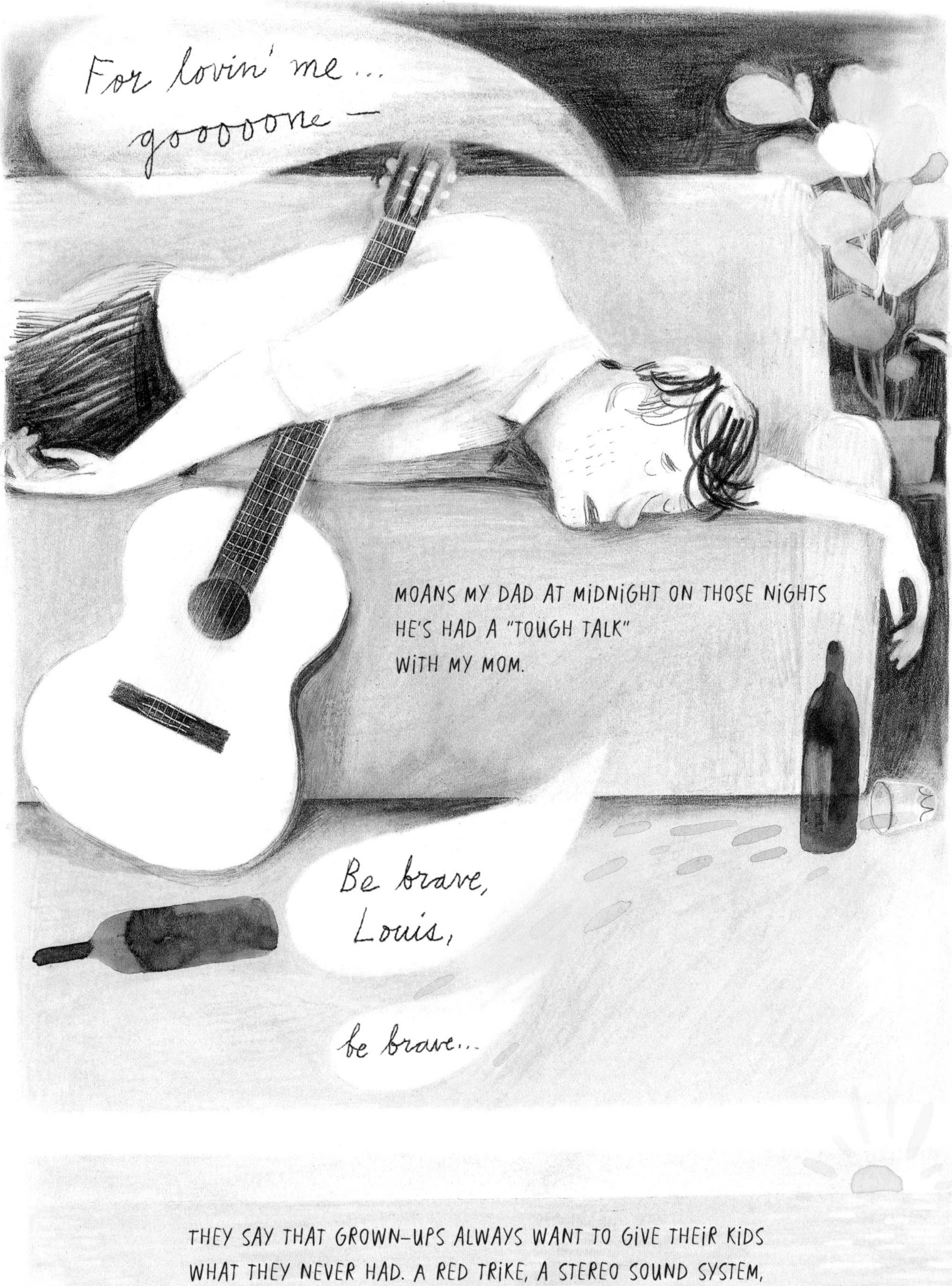
For lovin' me... gooooone—
MOANS MY DAD AT MIDNIGHT ON THOSE NIGHTS HE'S HAD A "TOUGH TALK" WITH MY MOM.
Be brave, Louis,
be brave...
THEY SAY THAT GROWN-UPS ALWAYS WANT TO GIVE THEIR KIDS WHAT THEY NEVER HAD. A RED TRIKE, A STEREO SOUND SYSTEM, A SEASIDE VACATION.

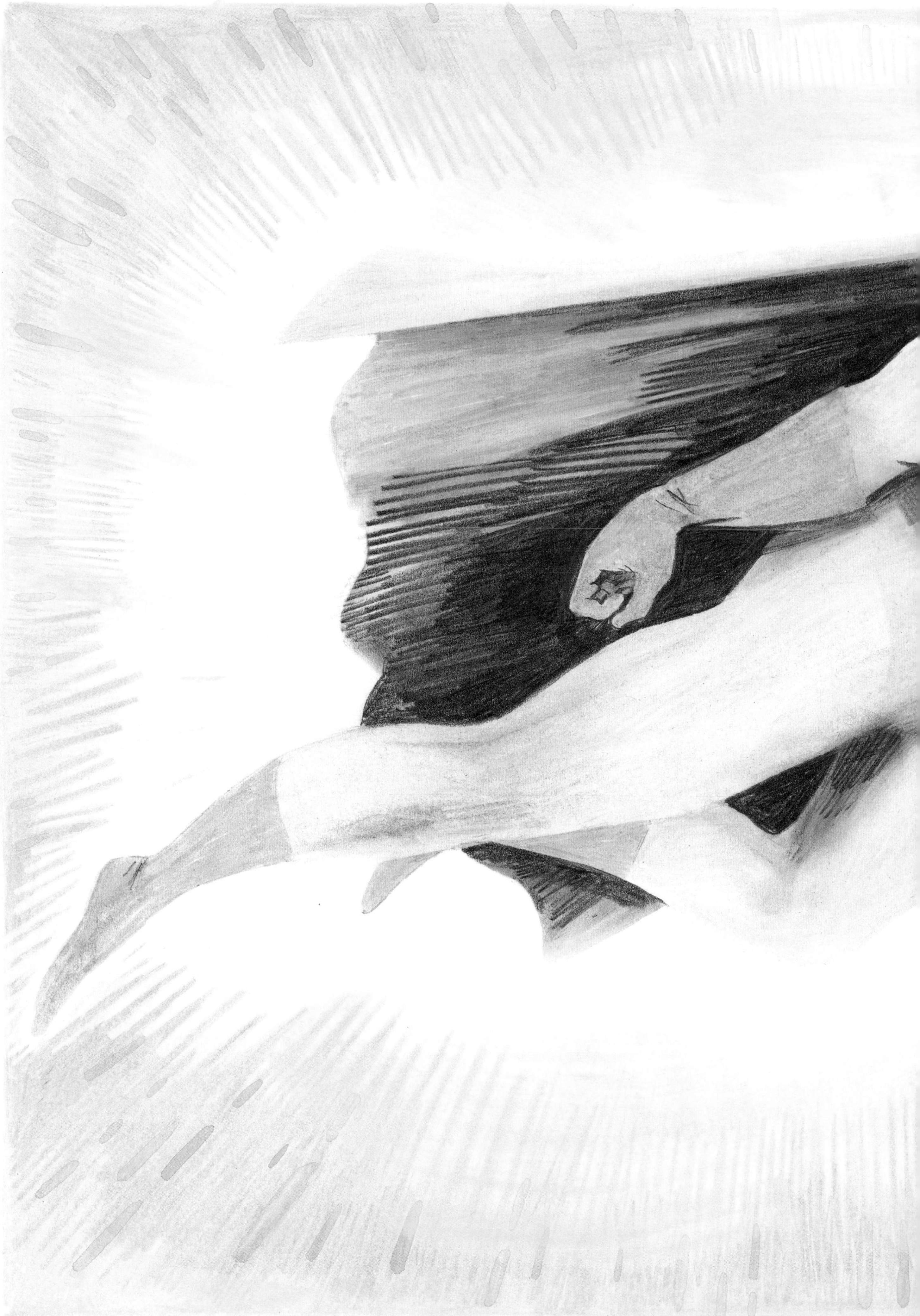

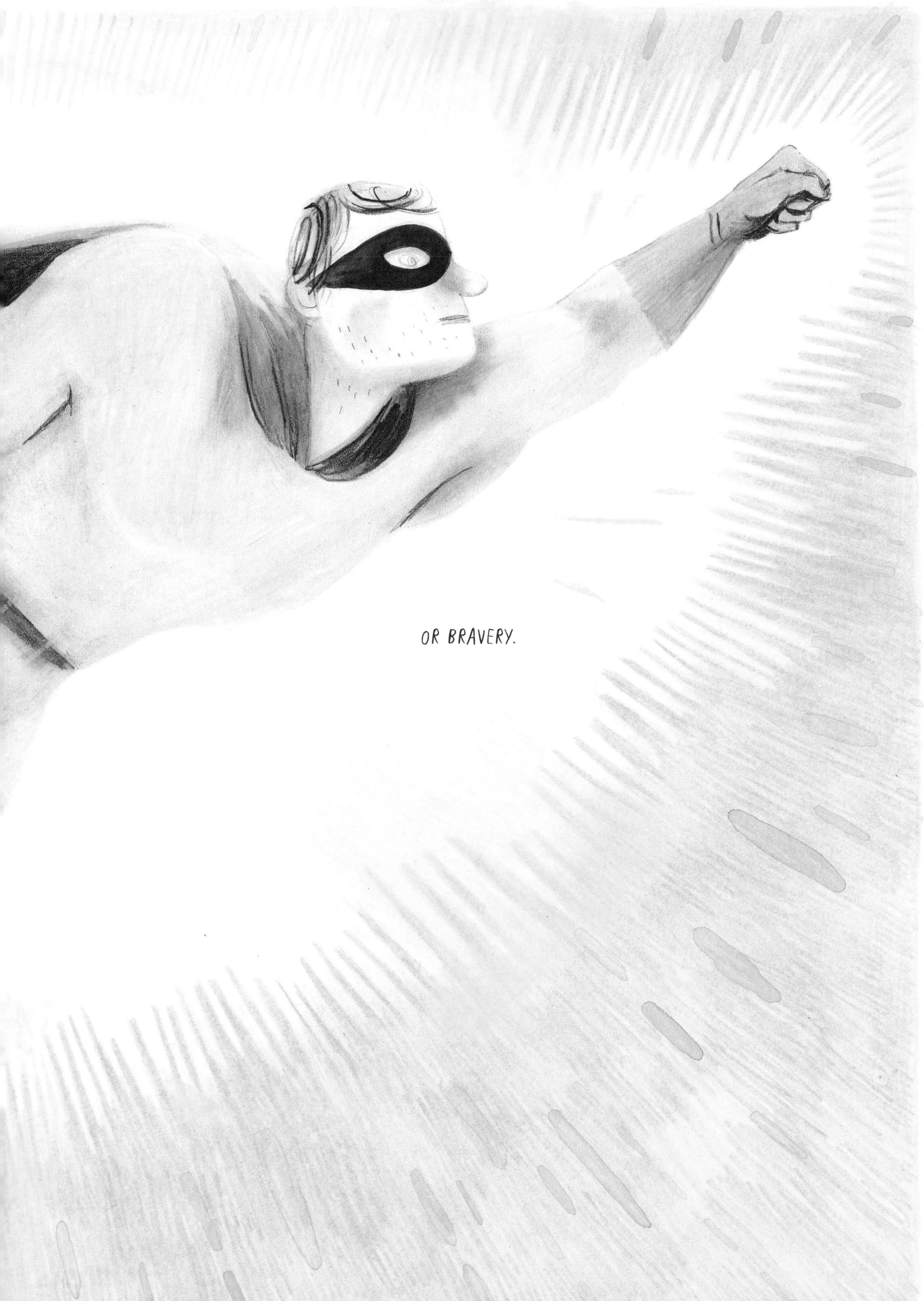
OR BRAVERY.

FOUR DAYS BEFORE SCHOOL'S OUT

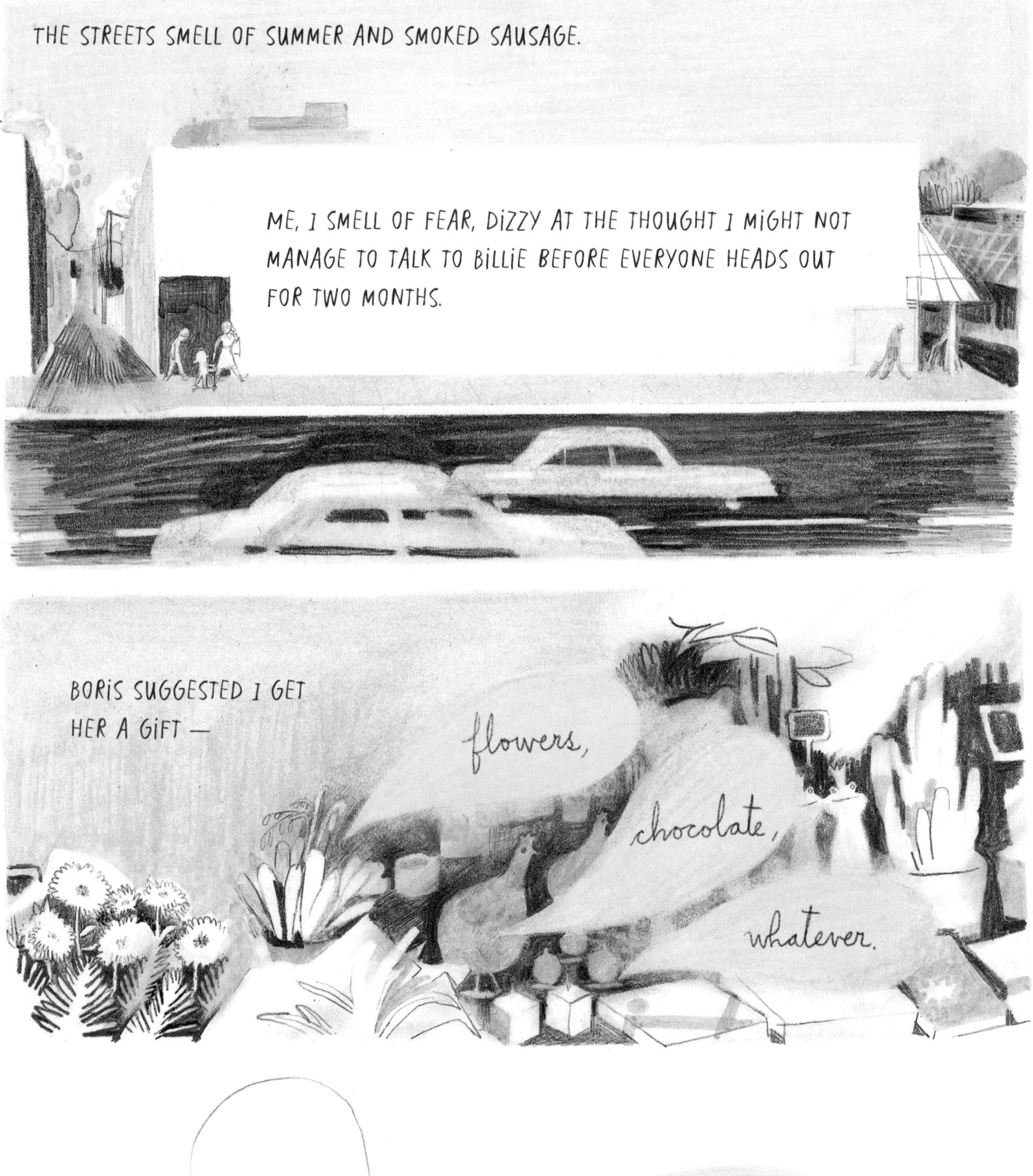
THE STREETS SMELL OF SUMMER AND SMOKED SAUSAGE.
ME, I SMELL OF FEAR, DIZZY AT THE THOUGHT I MIGHT NOT MANAGE TO TALK TO BILLIE BEFORE EVERYONE HEADS OUT FOR TWO MONTHS.
BORIS SUGGESTED I GET HER A GIFT —
flowers,
chocolate,
whatever.
A classic move.
BORIS SPEAKS LIKE AN EXPERT, DESPITE LOOKING ANYTHING BUT.

AT ANY RATE, ONE MORNING I GO SHOPPING WITH MY MOM AND TRUFFLE ON PLAZA ST-HUBERT AND HATCH PLANS TO BUY A PRESENT FOR BILLIE, UNSEEN.

NOT THAT MY MOM WOULD STOP ME, BUT SHE'D WORRY IF SHE KNEW. AFTER ALL, OUR FAMILY'S PRETTY UNLUCKY IN LOVE,

AND SHE WORRIES ENOUGH AS IT IS.

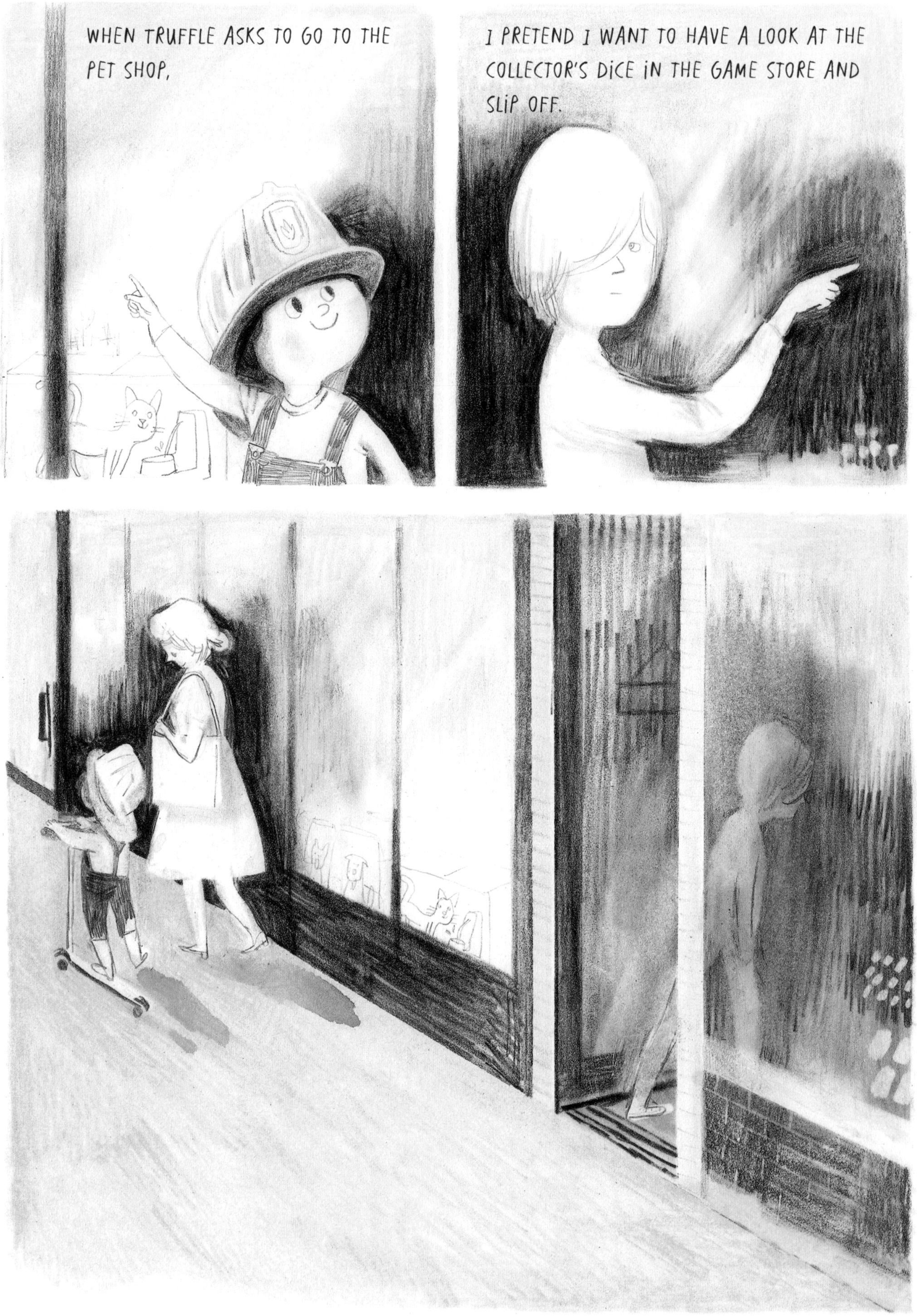
WHEN TRUFFLE ASKS TO GO TO THE PET SHOP,
I PRETEND I WANT TO HAVE A LOOK AT THE COLLECTOR'S DICE IN THE GAME STORE AND SLIP OFF.

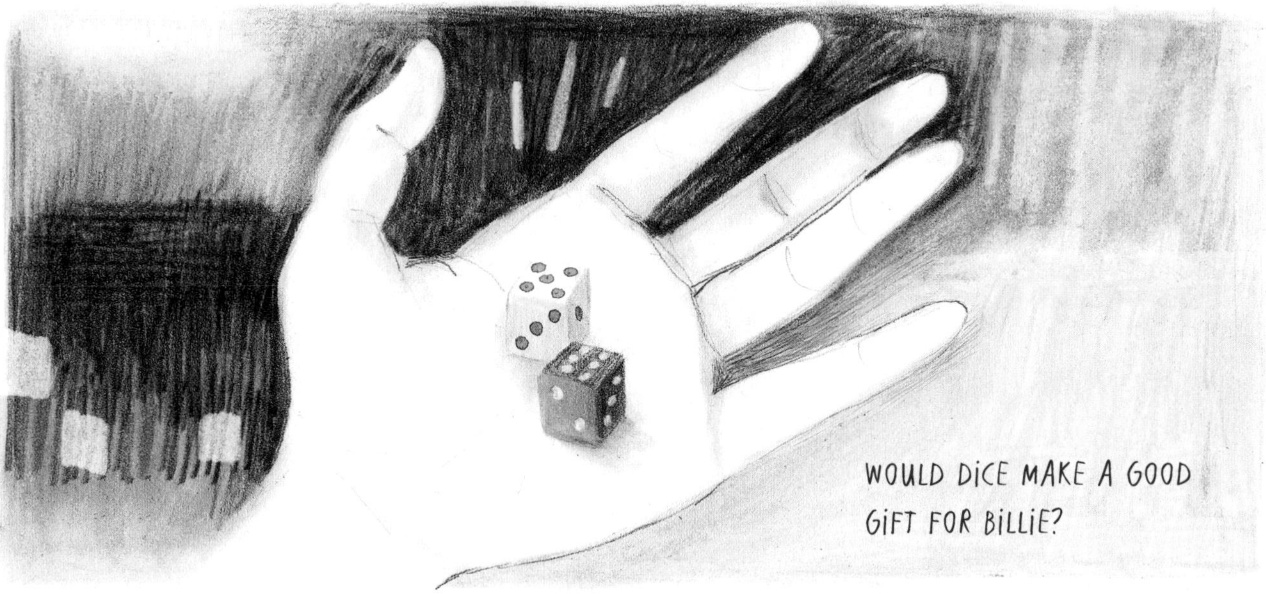
WOULD DICE MAKE A GOOD
GIFT FOR BILLIE?

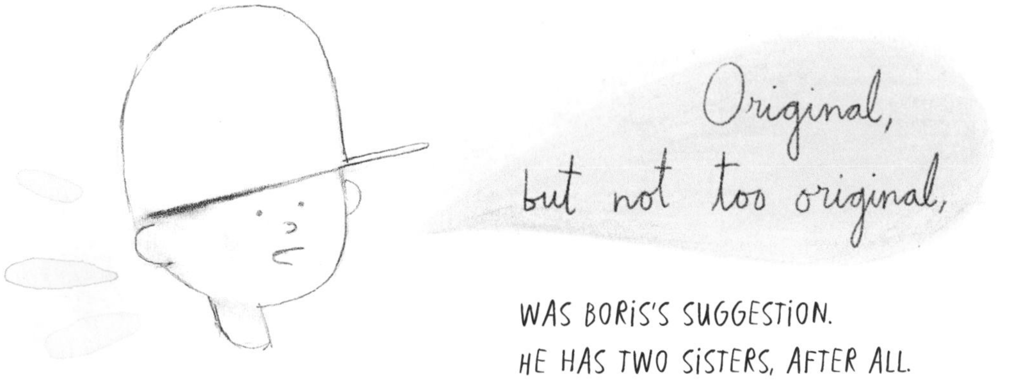
Original,
but not too original,
WAS BORIS'S SUGGESTION.
HE HAS TWO SISTERS, AFTER ALL.

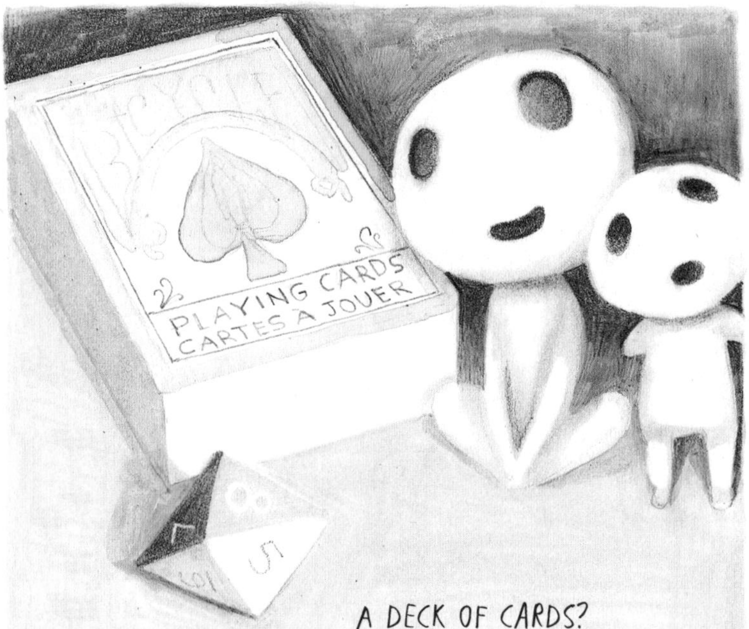
PLAYING CARDS
CARTES A JOUER
A DECK OF CARDS?
A JAPANESE FIGURINE?

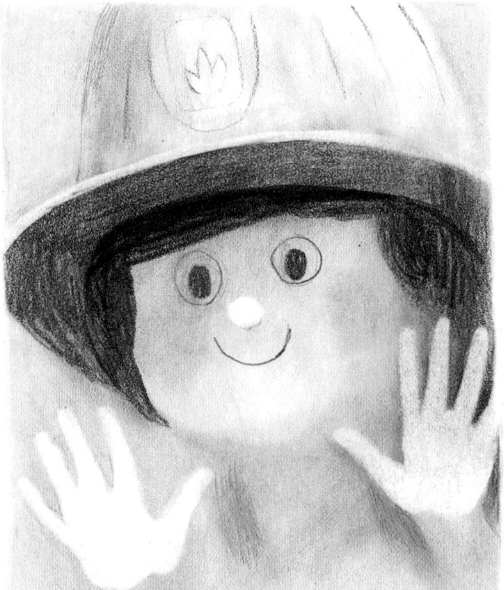
TRUFFLE APPEARS IN THE STORE
WINDOW. TIME'S RUNNING OUT.

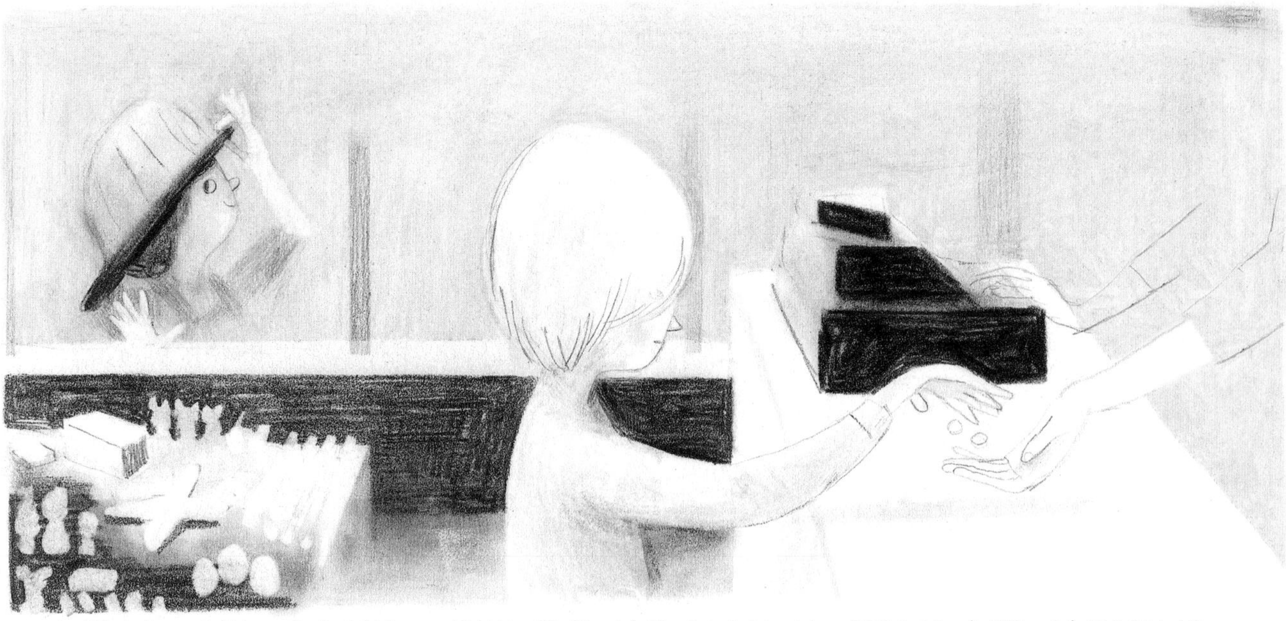

I HURRY AND PAY FOR A PAIR OF EIGHT-SIDED DICE, GOLDEN NUMBERS ON A RED BACKGROUND, AND STUFF THEM INTO MY POCKET.

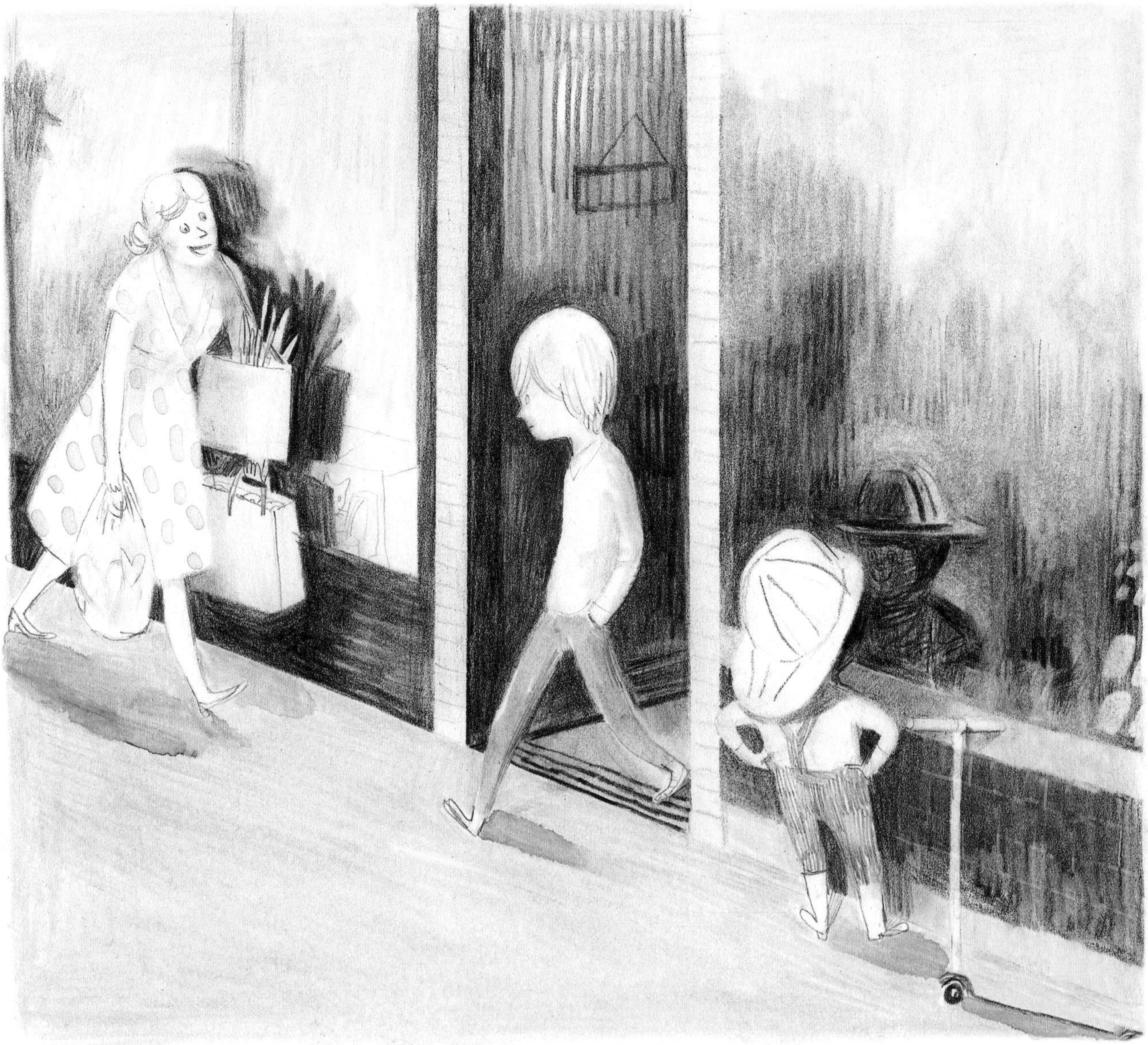

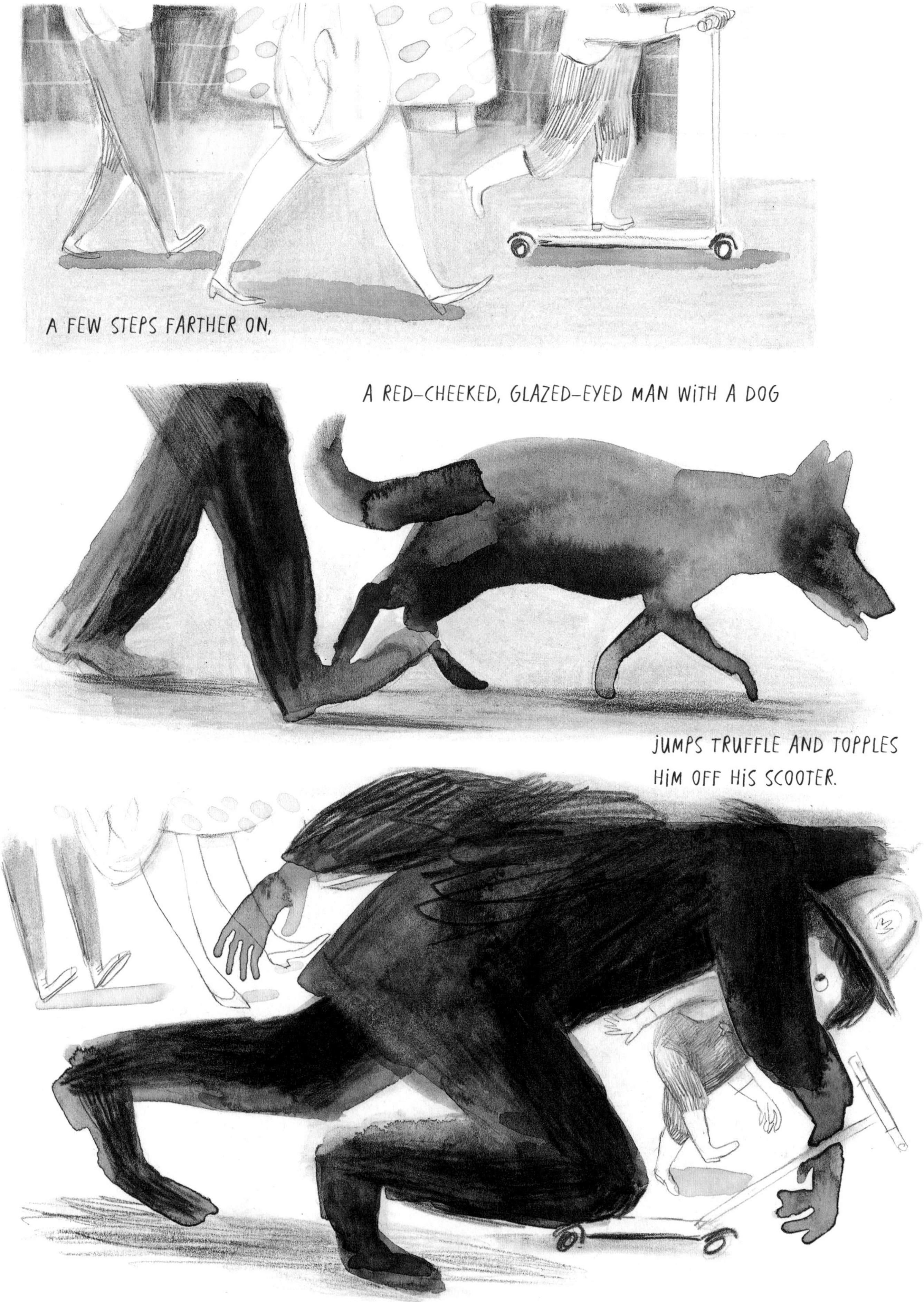
A FEW STEPS FARTHER ON,
A RED-CHEEKED, GLAZED-EYED MAN WITH A DOG
JUMPS TRUFFLE AND TOPPLES
HIM OFF HIS SCOOTER.

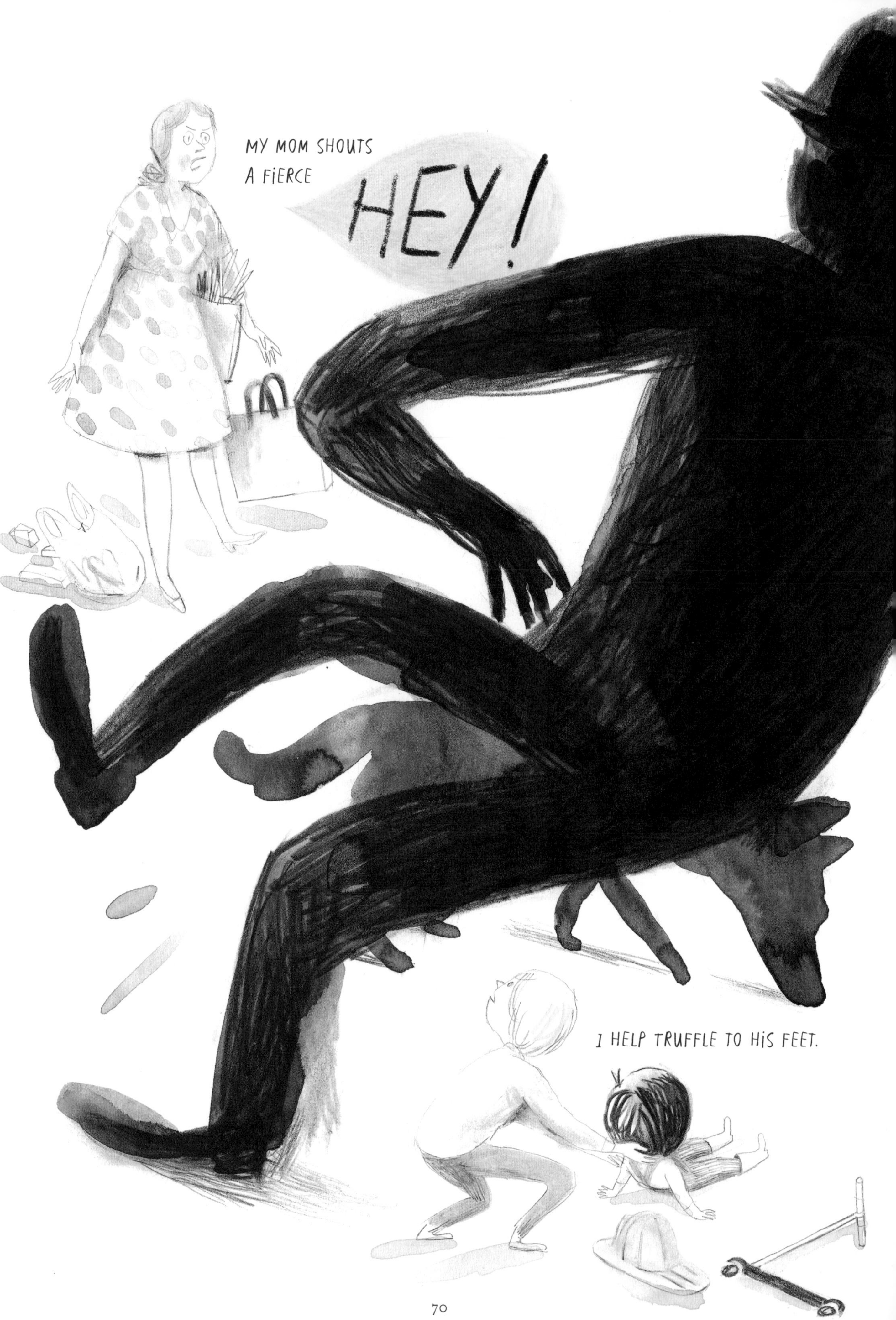
MY MOM SHOUTS
A FIERCE
HEY!
I HELP TRUFFLE TO HIS FEET.

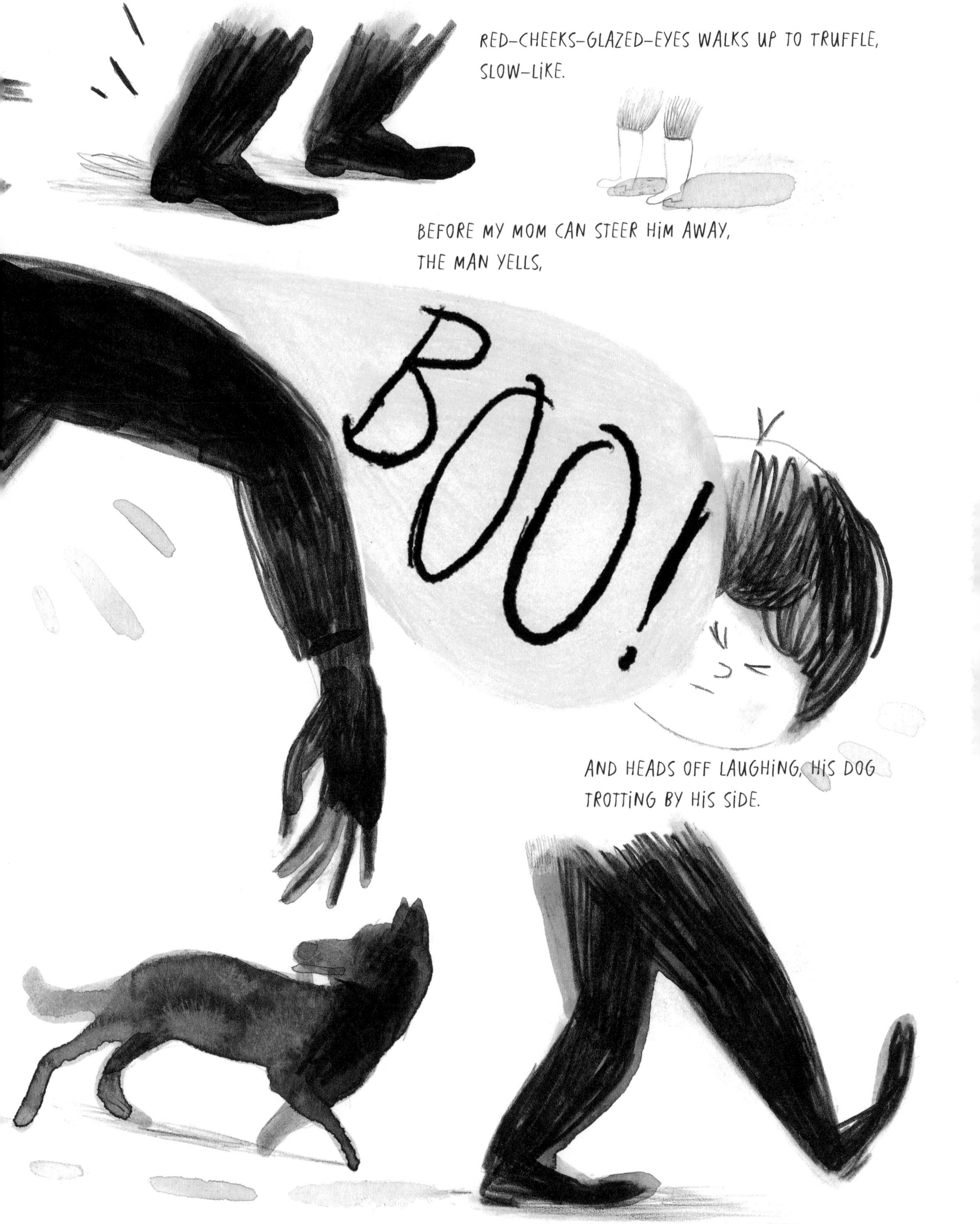
RED-CHEEKS-GLAZED-EYES WALKS UP TO TRUFFLE, SLOW-LIKE.
BEFORE MY MOM CAN STEER HIM AWAY, THE MAN YELLS,
BOO!
AND HEADS OFF LAUGHING, HIS DOG TROTTING BY HIS SIDE.

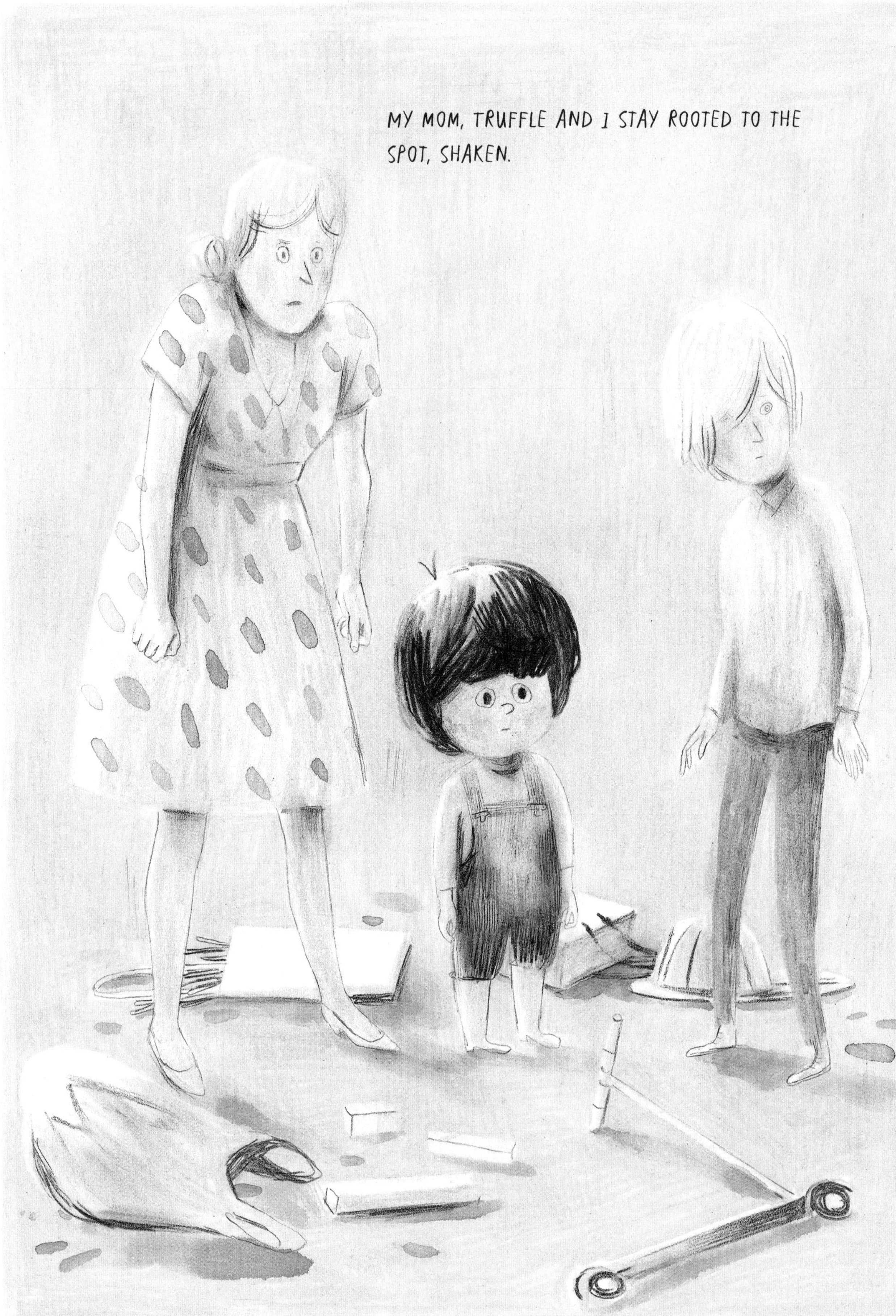
MY MOM, TRUFFLE AND I STAY ROOTED TO THE SPOT, SHAKEN.

TRUFFLE BECAUSE HE CAN'T FIGURE
OUT WHAT JUST HAPPENED.

MY MOM BECAUSE SHE'S SO FURIOUS
SHE CAN'T BUDGE.

ME BECAUSE I FINALLY HAD AN ACTUAL CHANCE TO BE
BRAVE, AND I DID NOTHING.

I'VE GOT TO BE THE BIGGEST BONEHEAD AND THE WORST
LOSER THE EARTH HAS EVER SEEN.

A PAIR OF DICE WON'T CHANGE THAT.

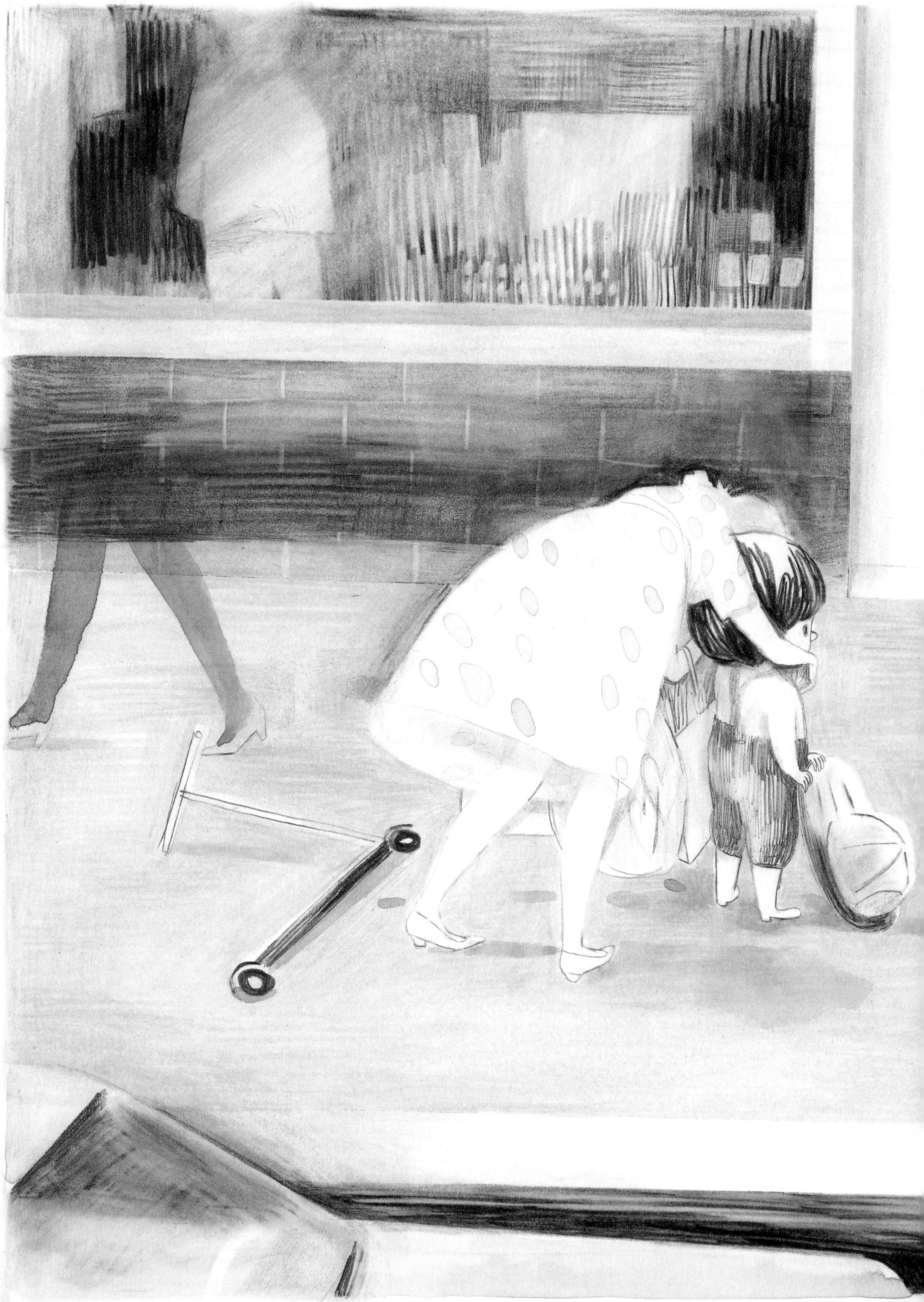

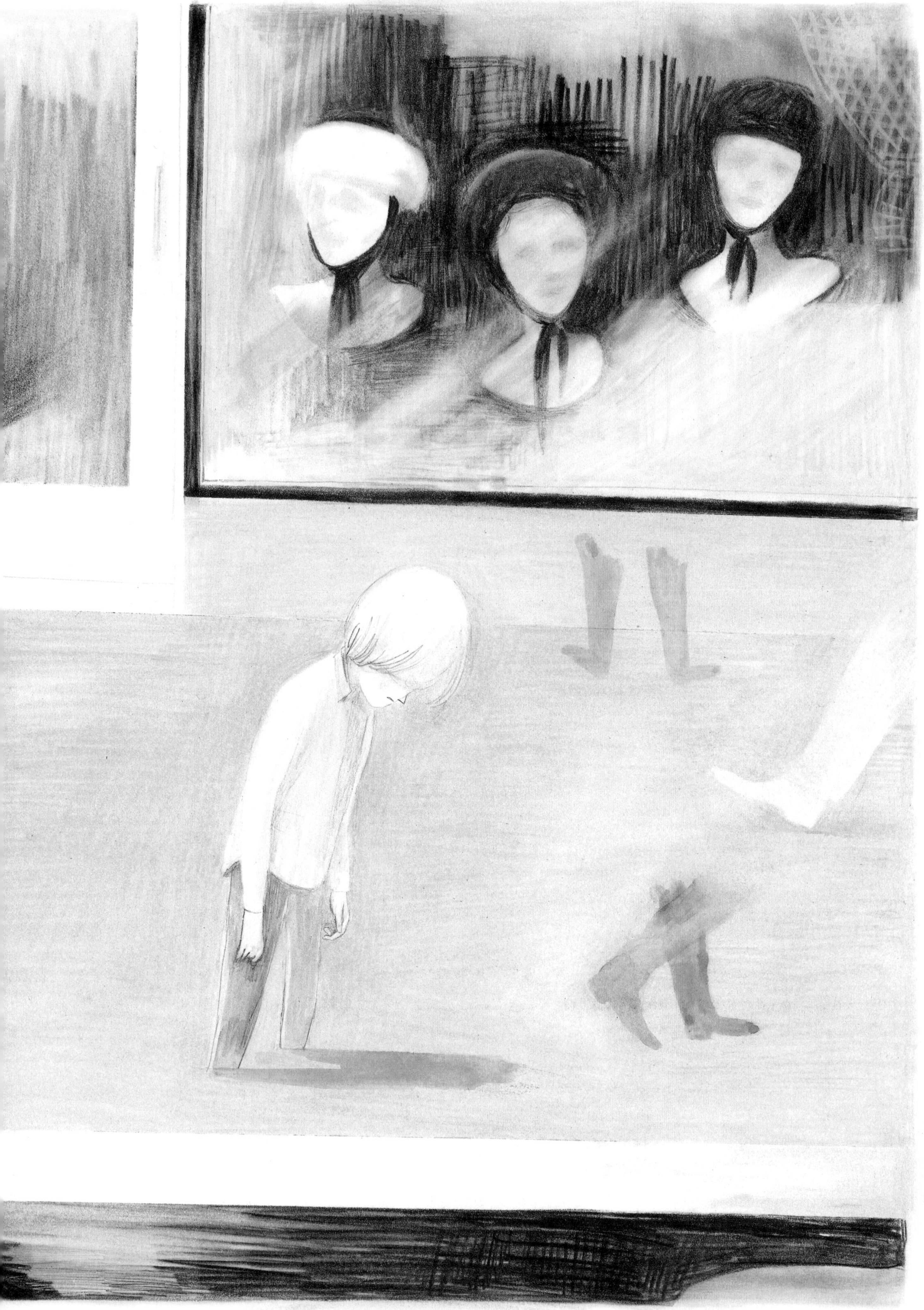

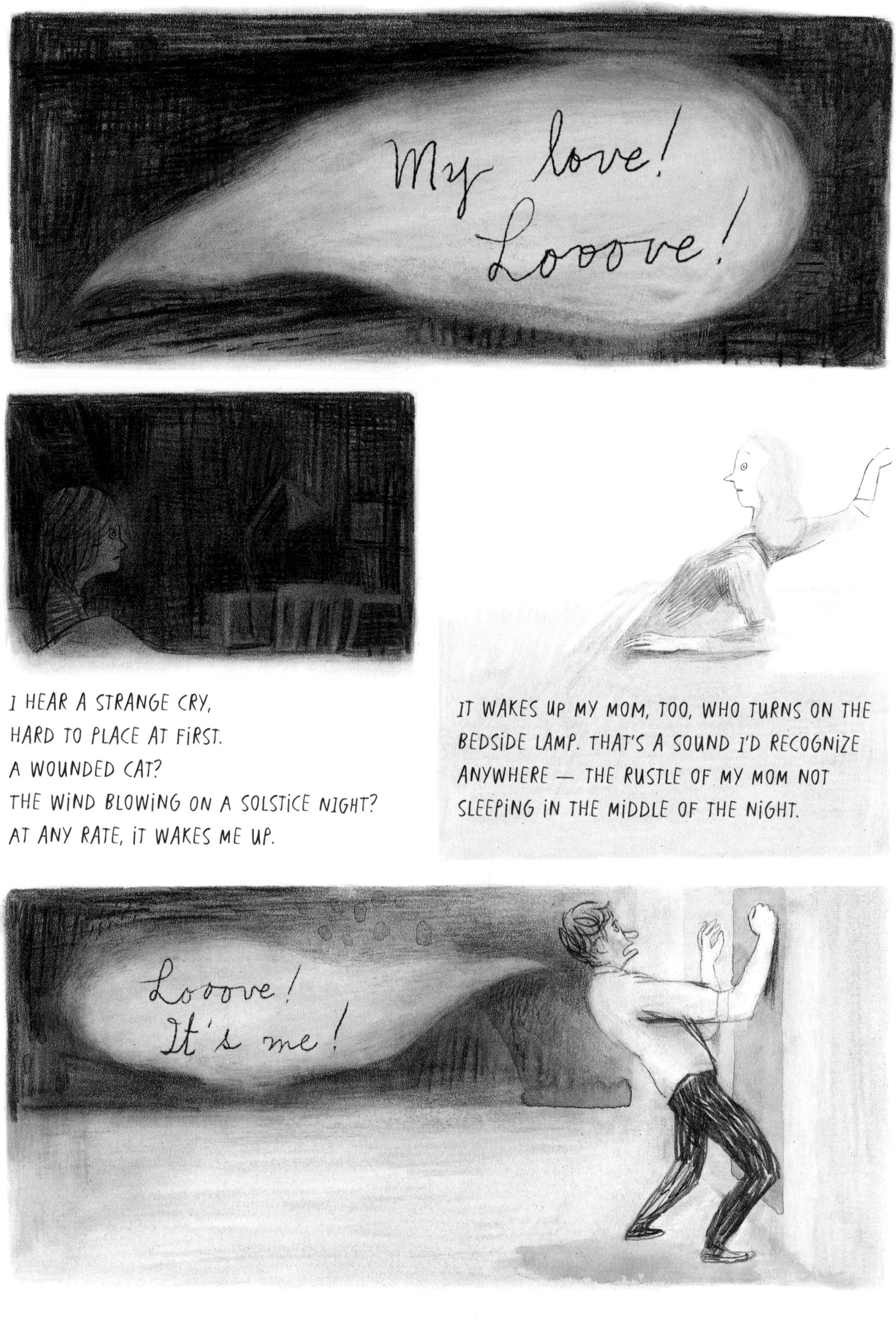
My love! Looove!
I HEAR A STRANGE CRY, HARD TO PLACE AT FIRST. A WOUNDED CAT? THE WIND BLOWING ON A SOLSTICE NIGHT? AT ANY RATE, IT WAKES ME UP.
IT WAKES UP MY MOM, TOO, WHO TURNS ON THE BEDSIDE LAMP. THAT'S A SOUND I'D RECOGNIZE ANYWHERE — THE RUSTLE OF MY MOM NOT SLEEPING IN THE MIDDLE OF THE NIGHT.
Looove! It's me!

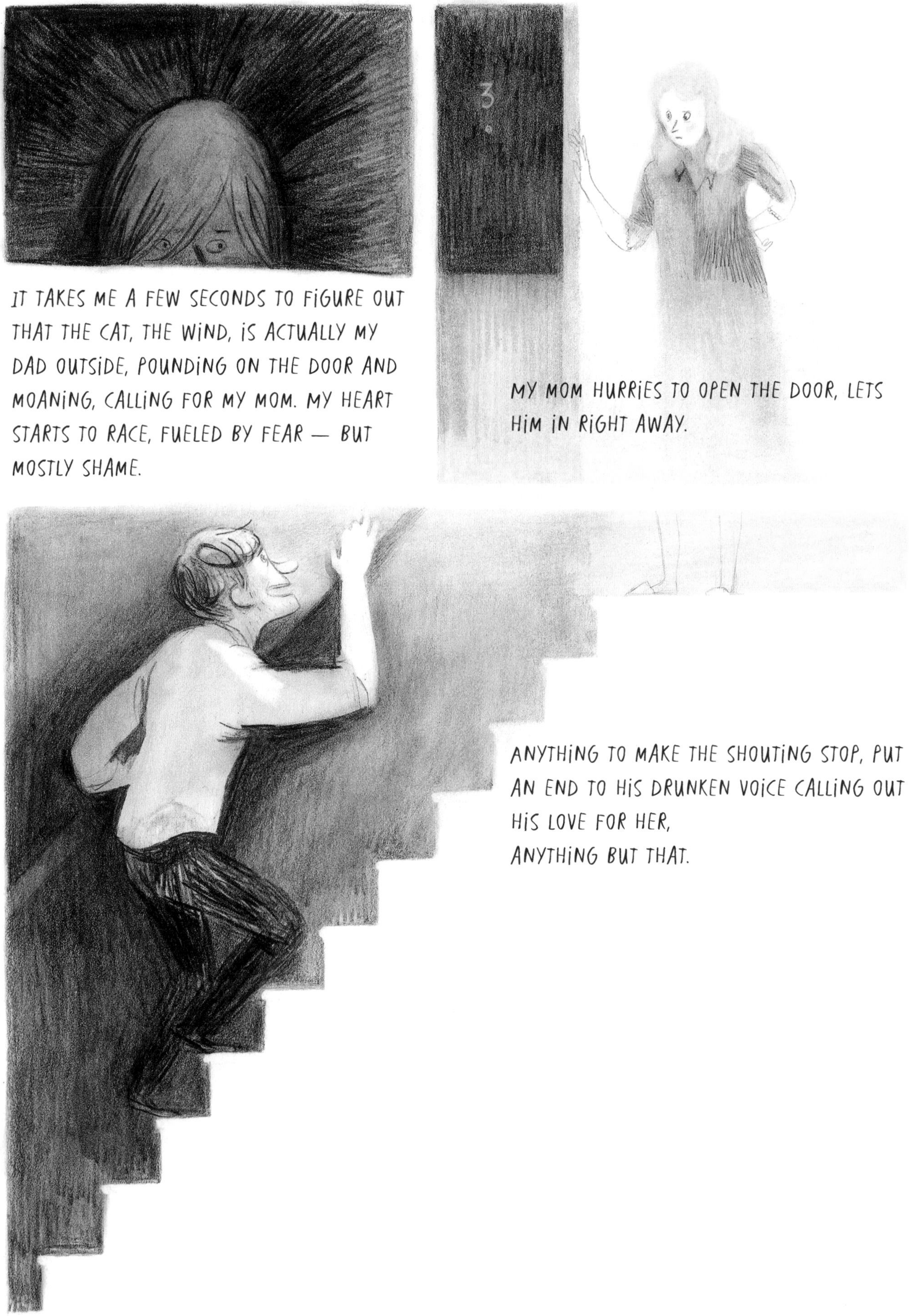
IT TAKES ME A FEW SECONDS TO FIGURE OUT THAT THE CAT, THE WIND, IS ACTUALLY MY DAD OUTSIDE, POUNDING ON THE DOOR AND MOANING, CALLING FOR MY MOM. MY HEART STARTS TO RACE, FUELED BY FEAR — BUT MOSTLY SHAME.
3
MY MOM HURRIES TO OPEN THE DOOR, LETS HIM IN RIGHT AWAY.
ANYTHING TO MAKE THE SHOUTING STOP, PUT AN END TO HIS DRUNKEN VOICE CALLING OUT HIS LOVE FOR HER,
ANYTHING BUT THAT.

I've come for you, my love. I've come for you all.

AT FIRST, HIS VOICE IS SO LOUD I DON'T EVEN HAVE TO STRAIN TO HEAR HIM. BUT MY MOM SWITCHES TO THE GRIM TONE SHE RESERVES FOR LIFE-THREATENING EMERGENCIES OF THE TRUFFLE-ABOUT-TO-SWALLOW-A-DEADLY-MUSHROOM VARIETY.

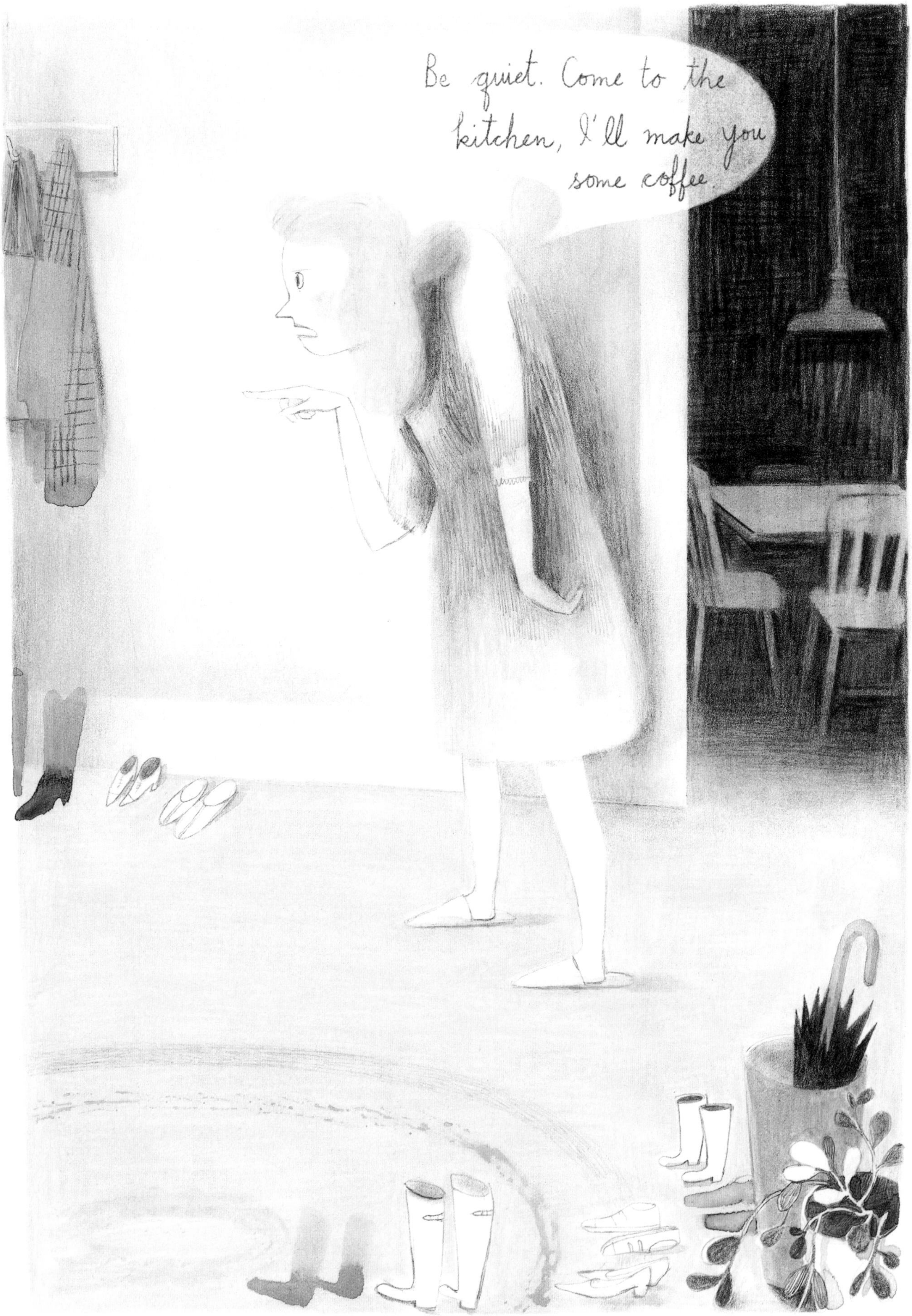
Be quiet. Come to the kitchen, I'll make you some coffee.

THE REST OF THEIR CONVERSATION IS MUFFLED.
ONLY A COUPLE OF OUTBURSTS
REACH MY EARS. FIRST A SENTENCE,

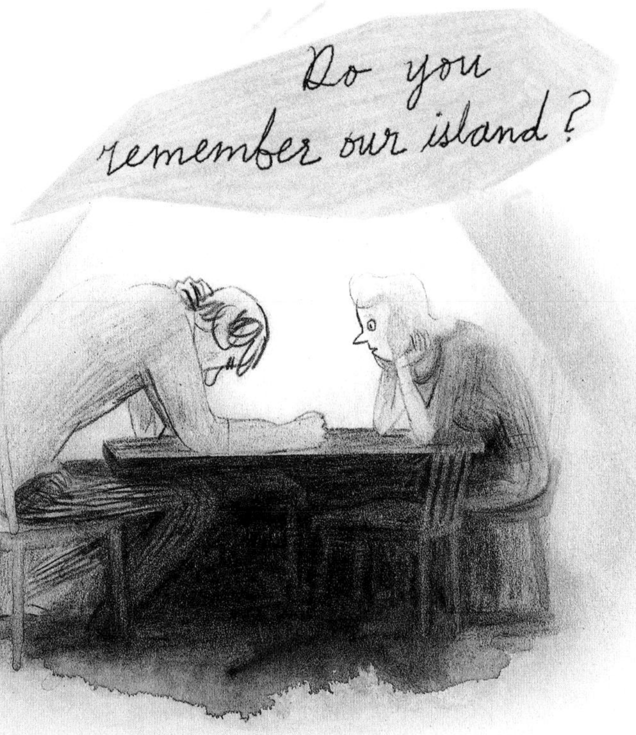
Do you remember our island?

THEN A SHARP, GUT-WRENCHING SOB, LIKE WHEN A POLITICIAN BREAKS
DOWN ANNOUNCING HIS RESIGNATION.
THEN MY MOM'S BROKEN VOICE THAT I WISH I'D NEVER HEARD,

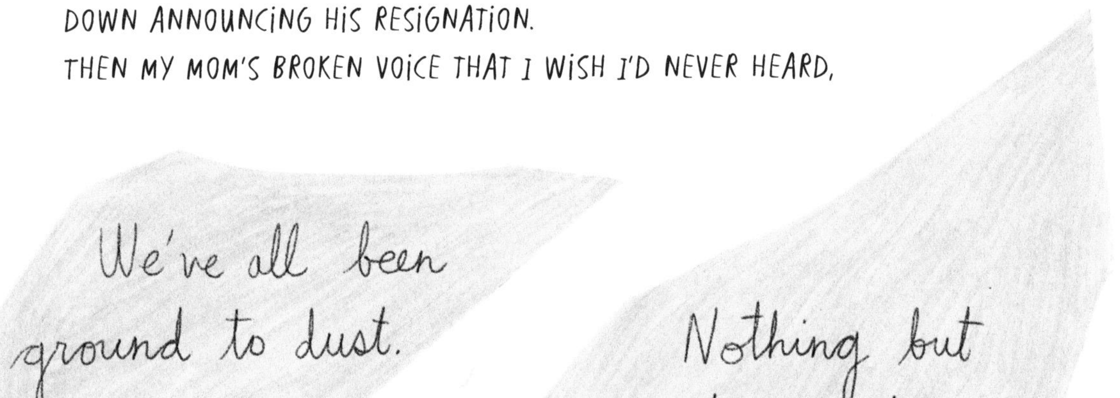
We've all been ground to dust.
Nothing but specks of dust.

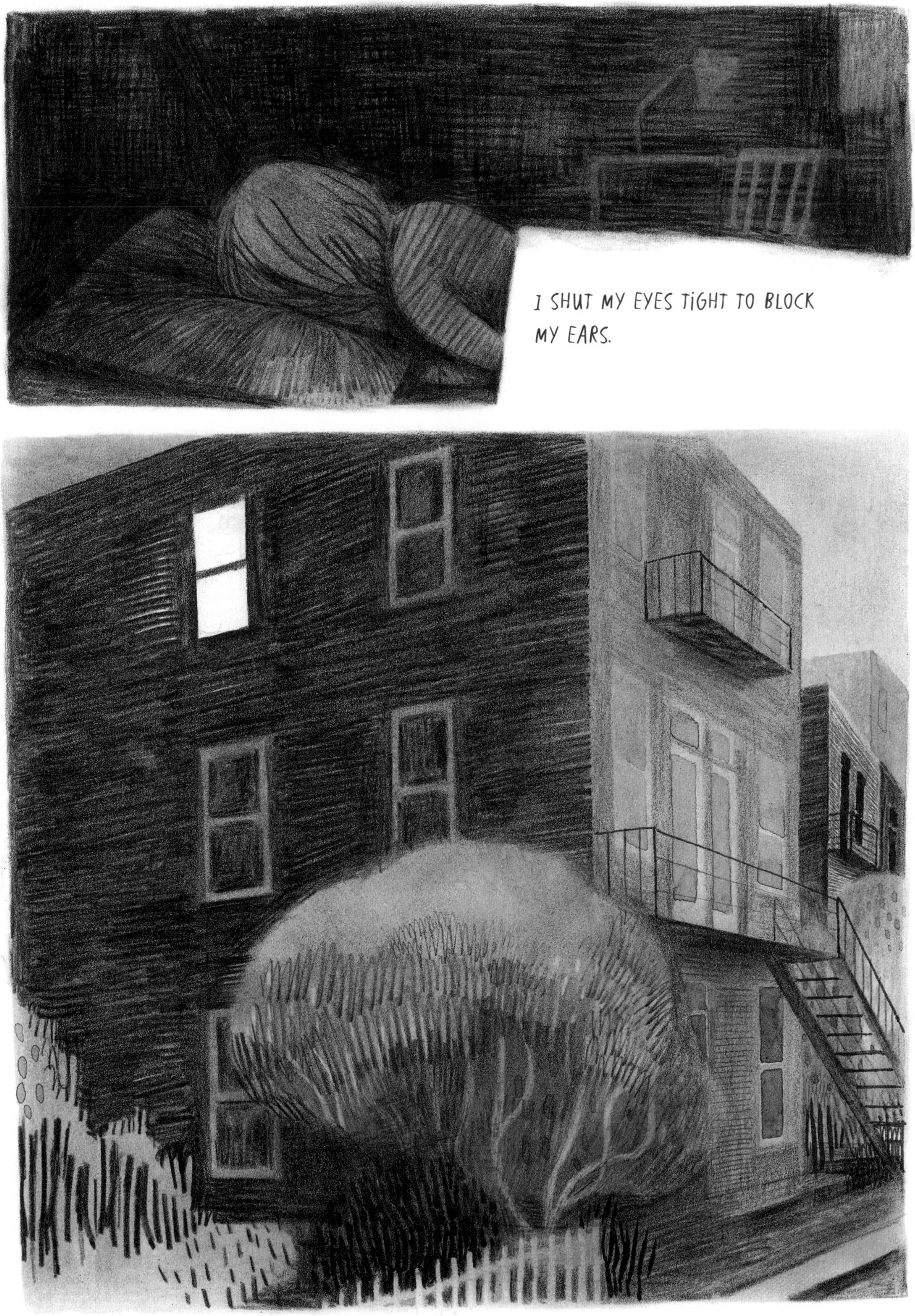
I SHUT MY EYES TIGHT TO BLOCK MY EARS.

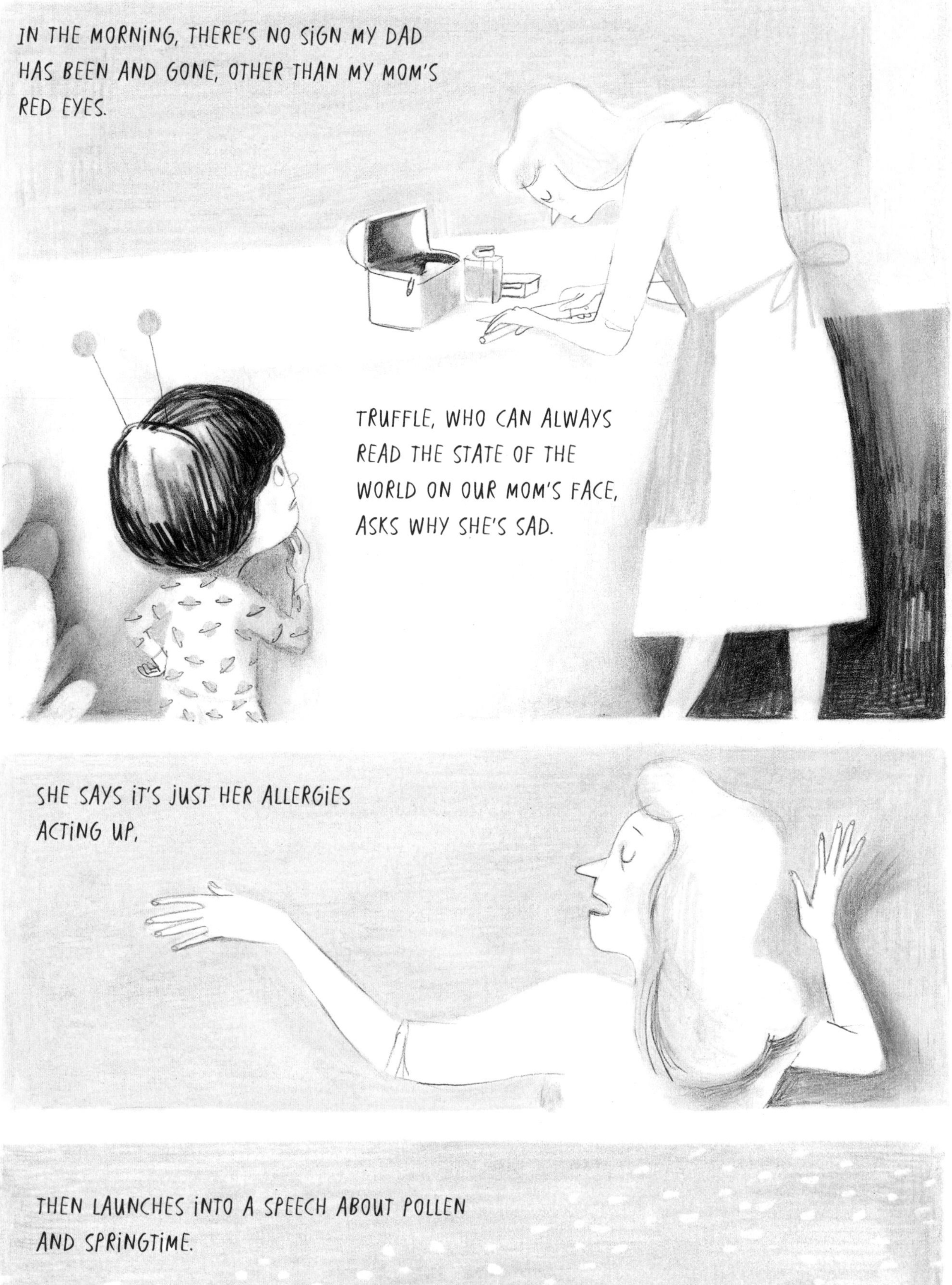
IN THE MORNING, THERE'S NO SIGN MY DAD HAS BEEN AND GONE, OTHER THAN MY MOM'S RED EYES.
TRUFFLE, WHO CAN ALWAYS READ THE STATE OF THE WORLD ON OUR MOM'S FACE, ASKS WHY SHE'S SAD.
SHE SAYS IT'S JUST HER ALLERGIES ACTING UP,
THEN LAUNCHES INTO A SPEECH ABOUT POLLEN AND SPRINGTIME.

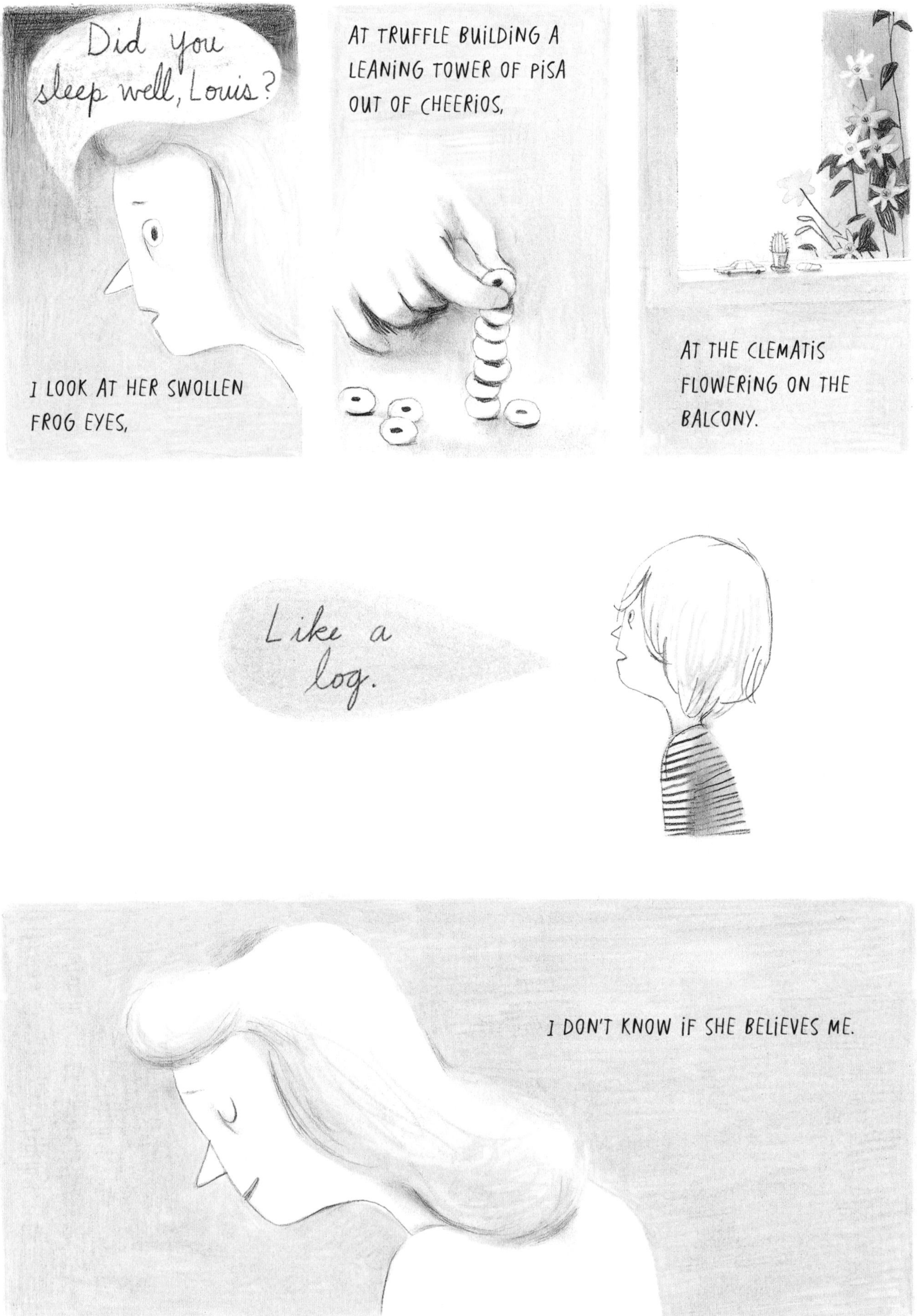
Did you sleep well, Louis?
I LOOK AT HER SWOLLEN FROG EYES,
AT TRUFFLE BUILDING A LEANING TOWER OF PISA OUT OF CHEERIOS,
AT THE CLEMATIS FLOWERING ON THE BALCONY.
Like a log.
I DON'T KNOW IF SHE BELIEVES ME.

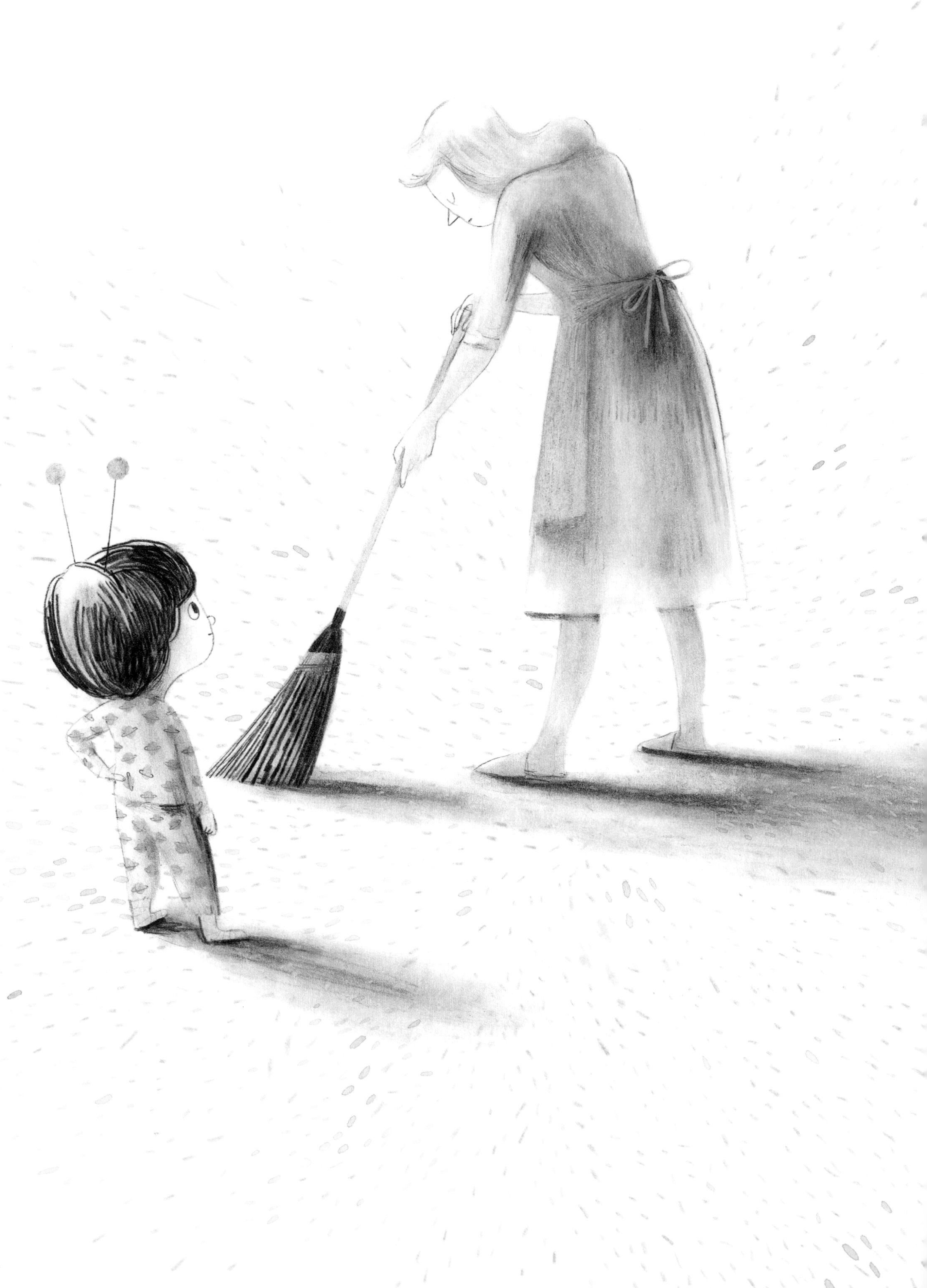

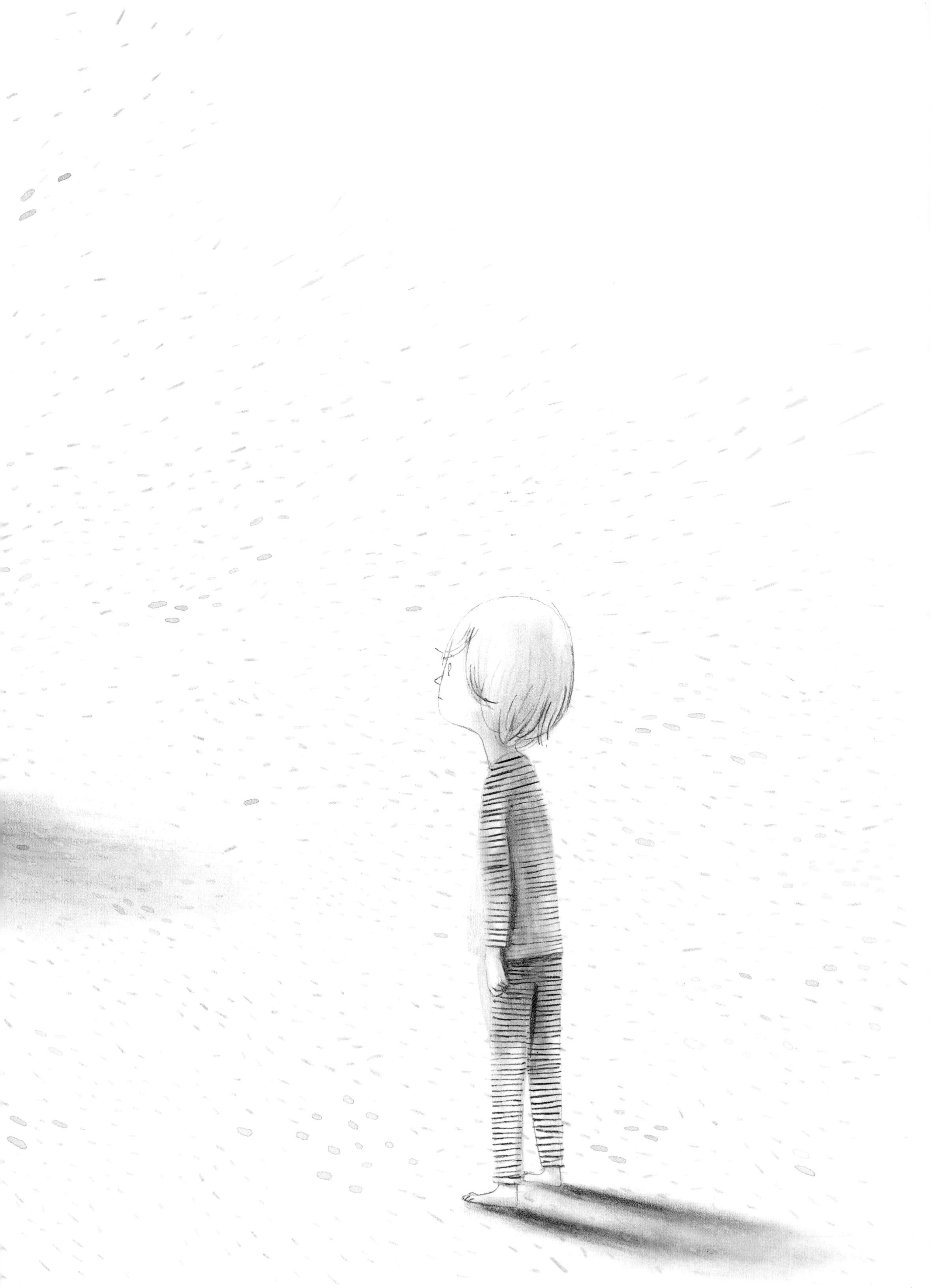

LAST DAY OF SCHOOL

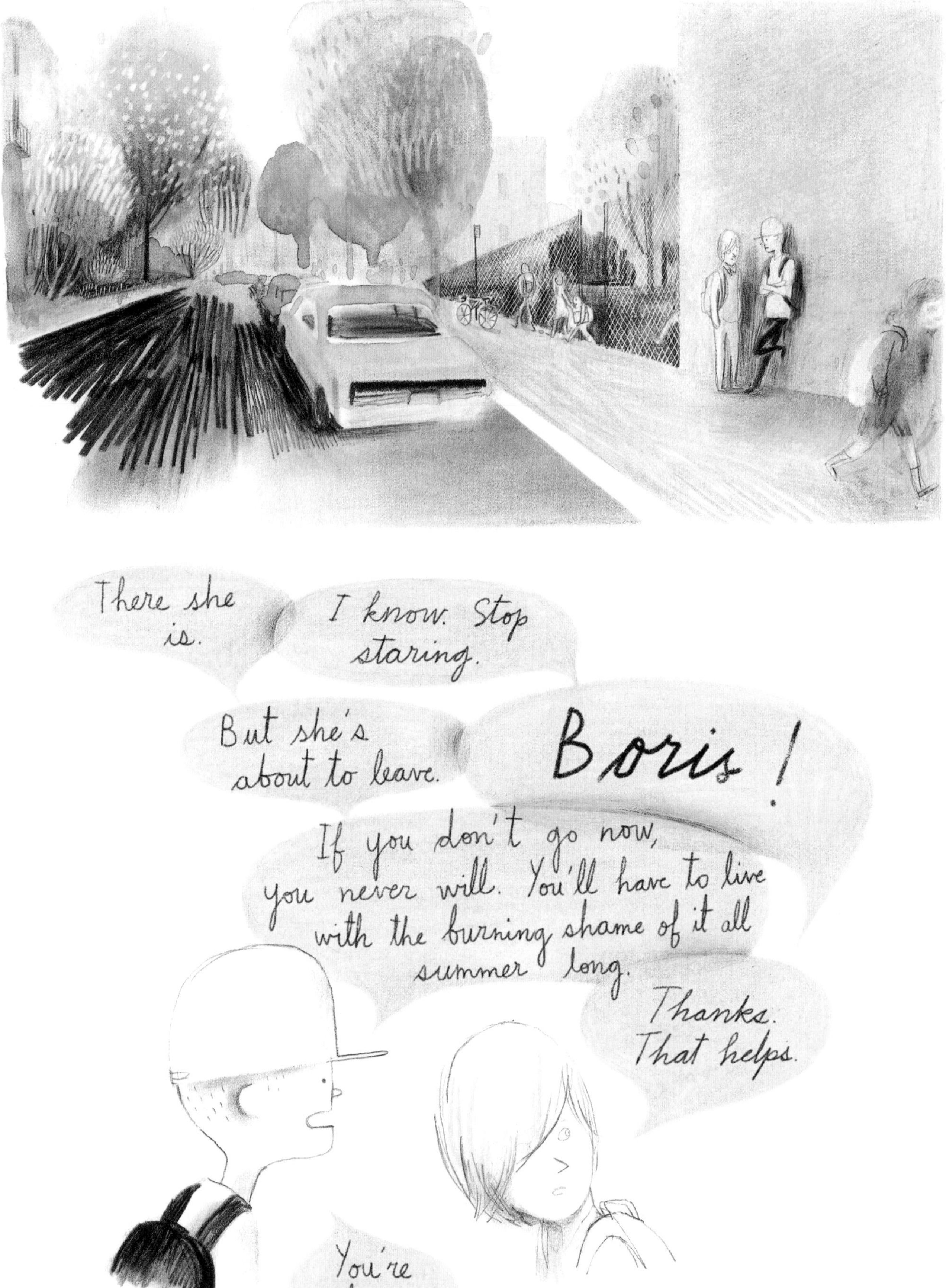
There she is.
I know. Stop staring.
But she's about to leave.
Boris!
If you don't go now, you never will. You'll have to live with the burning shame of it all summer long.
Thanks. That helps.
You're welcome.

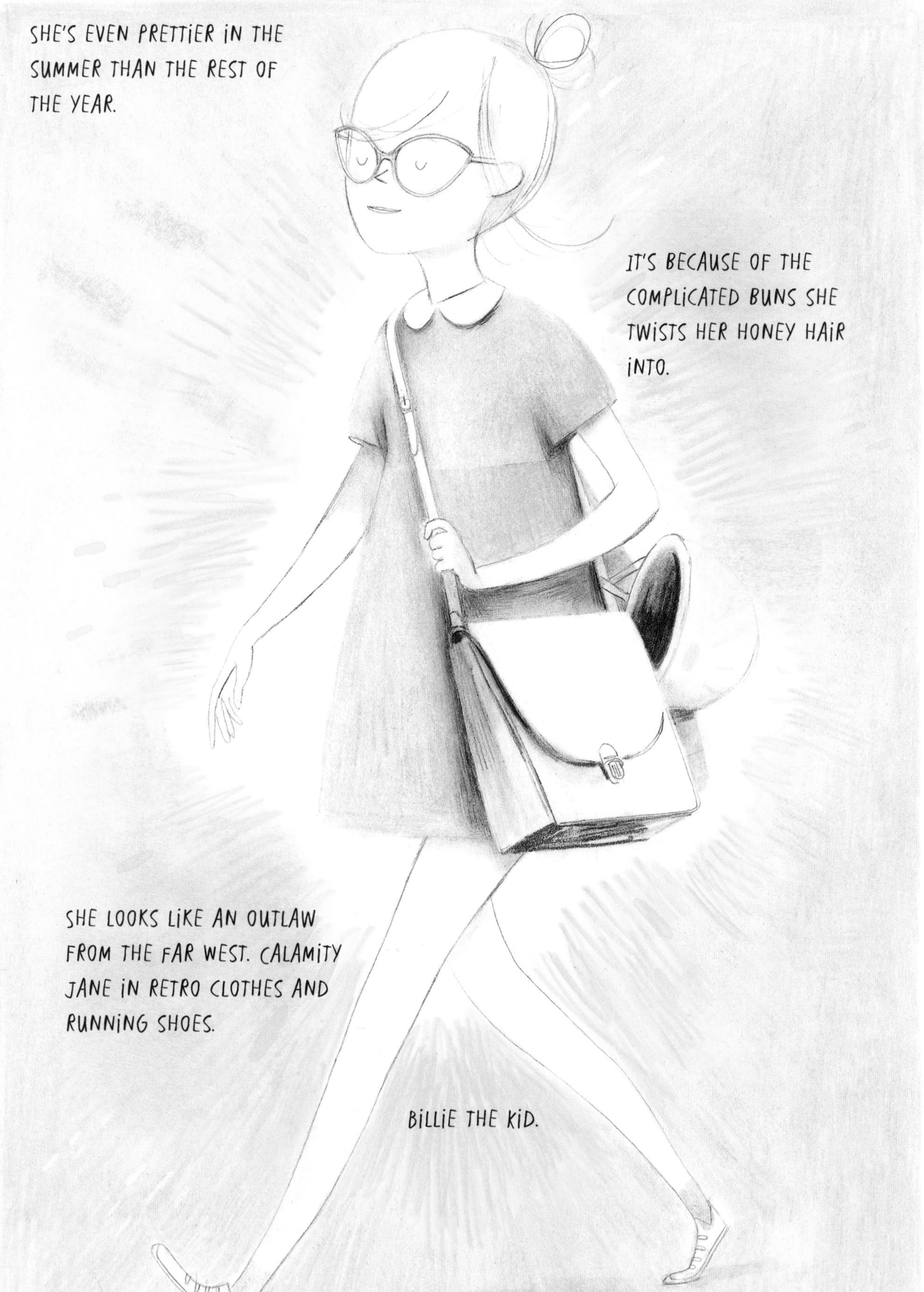
SHE'S EVEN PRETTIER IN THE SUMMER THAN THE REST OF THE YEAR.
IT'S BECAUSE OF THE COMPLICATED BUNS SHE TWISTS HER HONEY HAIR INTO.
SHE LOOKS LIKE AN OUTLAW FROM THE FAR WEST. CALAMITY JANE IN RETRO CLOTHES AND RUNNING SHOES.
BILLIE THE KID.

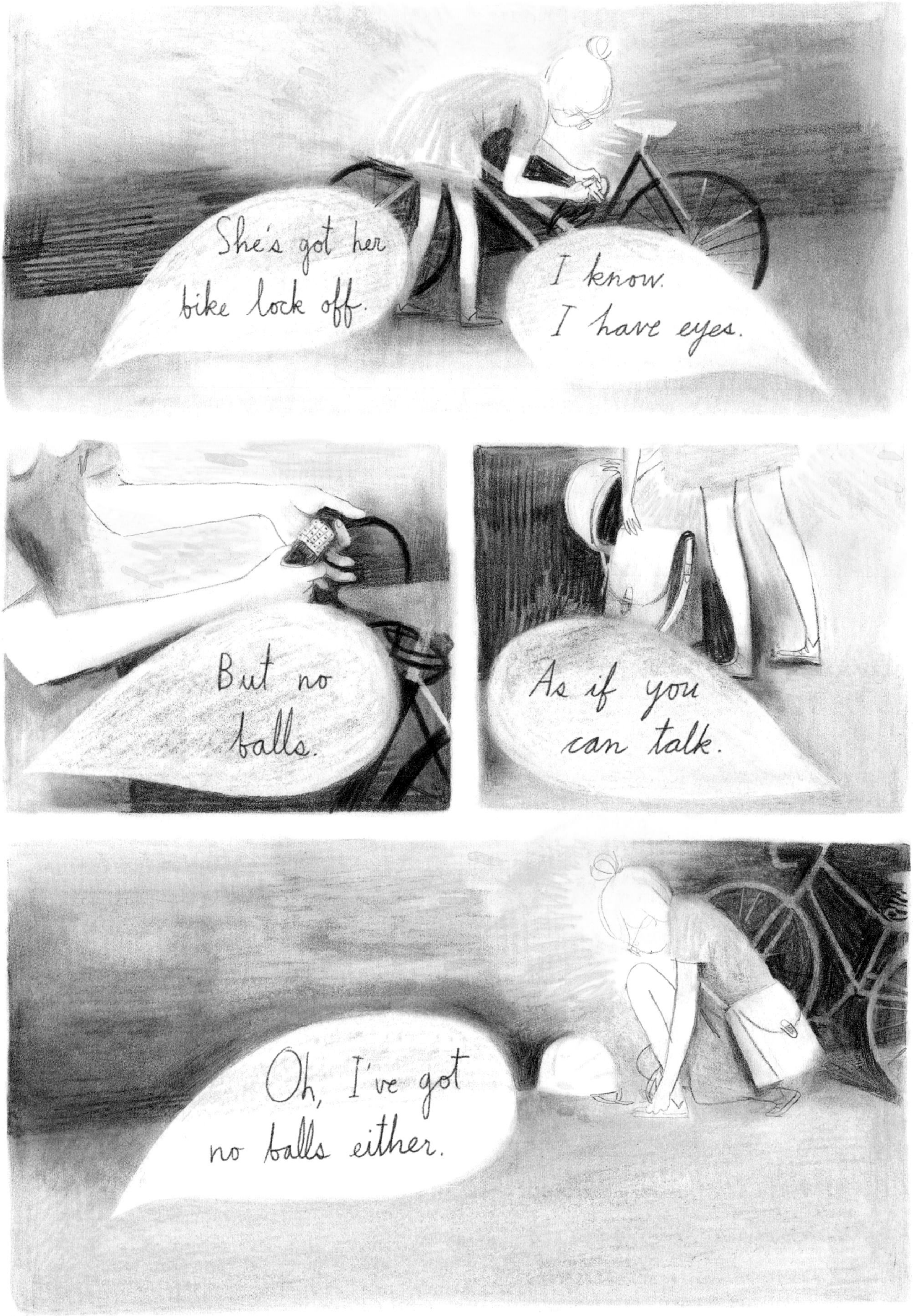
She's got her bike lock off.
I know. I have eyes.
But no balls.
As if you can talk.
Oh, I've got no balls either.

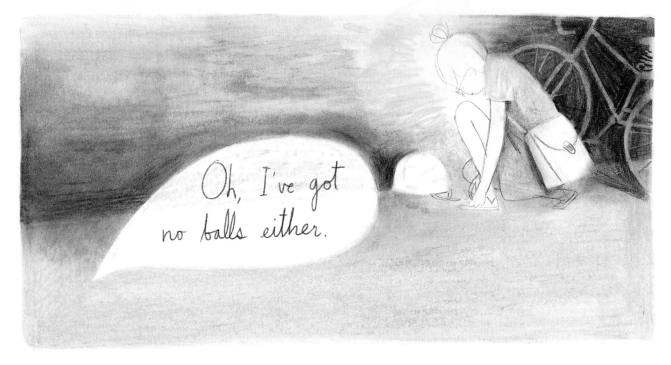

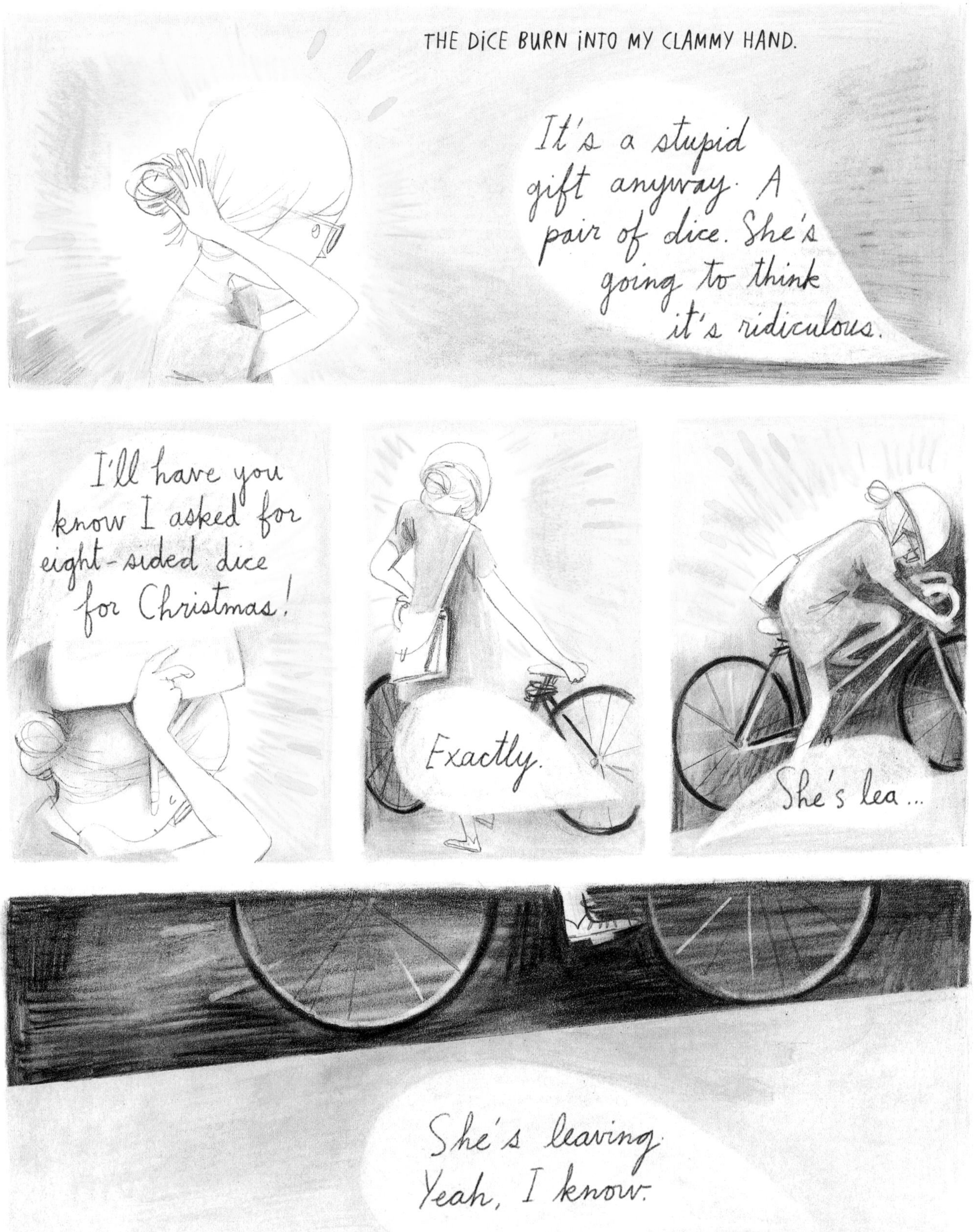
THE DICE BURN INTO MY CLAMMY HAND.
It's a stupid gift anyway. A pair of dice. She's going to think it's ridiculous.
I'll have you know I asked for eight-sided dice for Christmas!
Exactly.
She's lea...
She's leaving.
Yeah, I know.

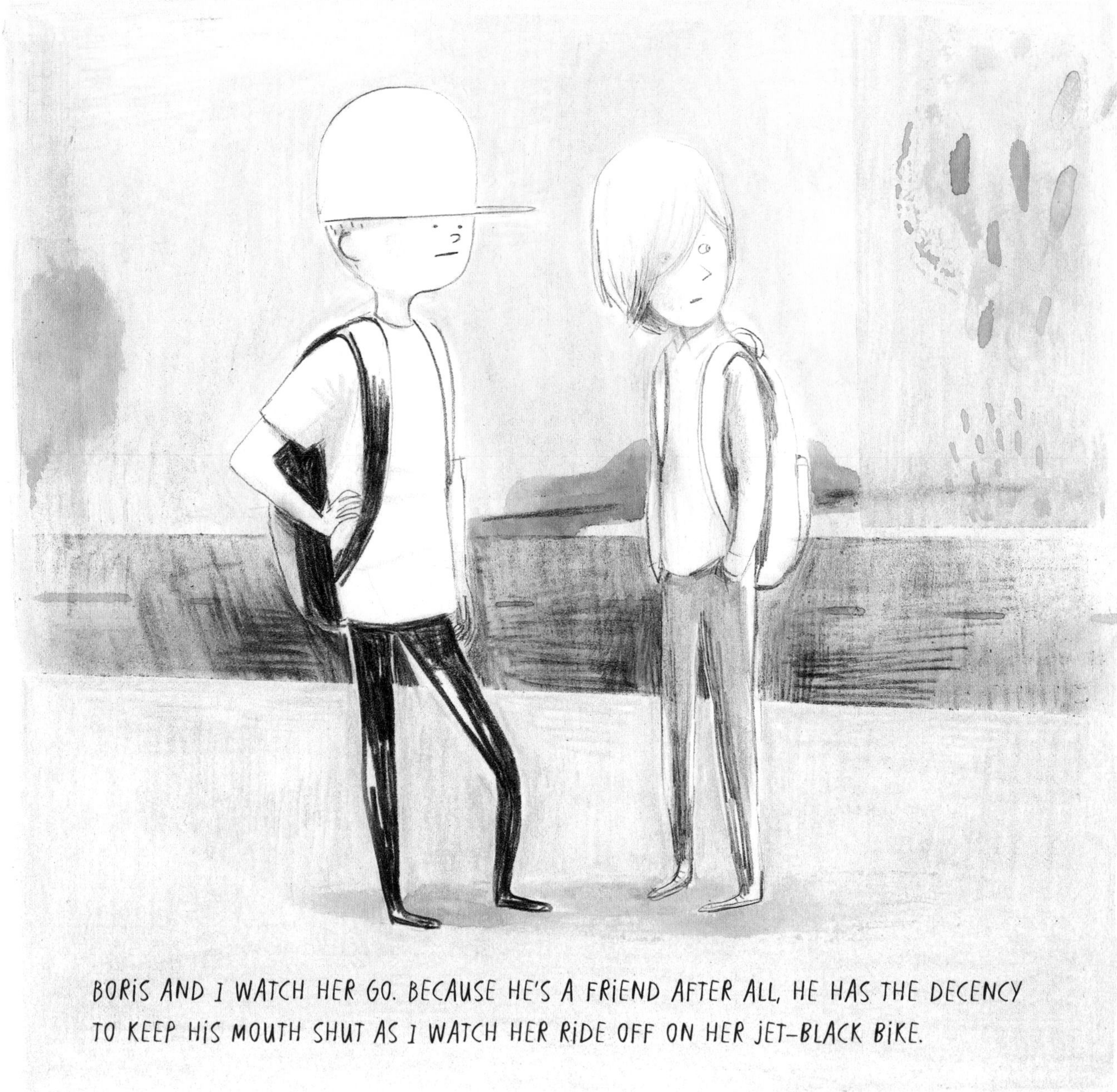
BORIS AND I WATCH HER GO. BECAUSE HE'S A FRIEND AFTER ALL, HE HAS THE DECENCY TO KEEP HIS MOUTH SHUT AS I WATCH HER RIDE OFF ON HER JET-BLACK BIKE.

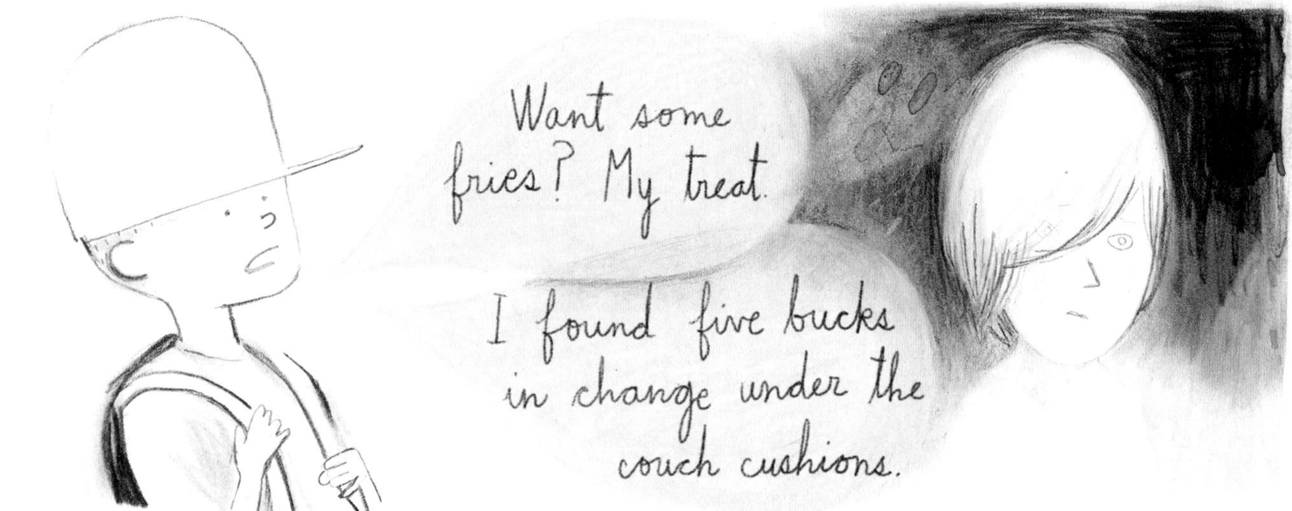
Want some fries? My treat.
I found five bucks in change under the couch cushions.

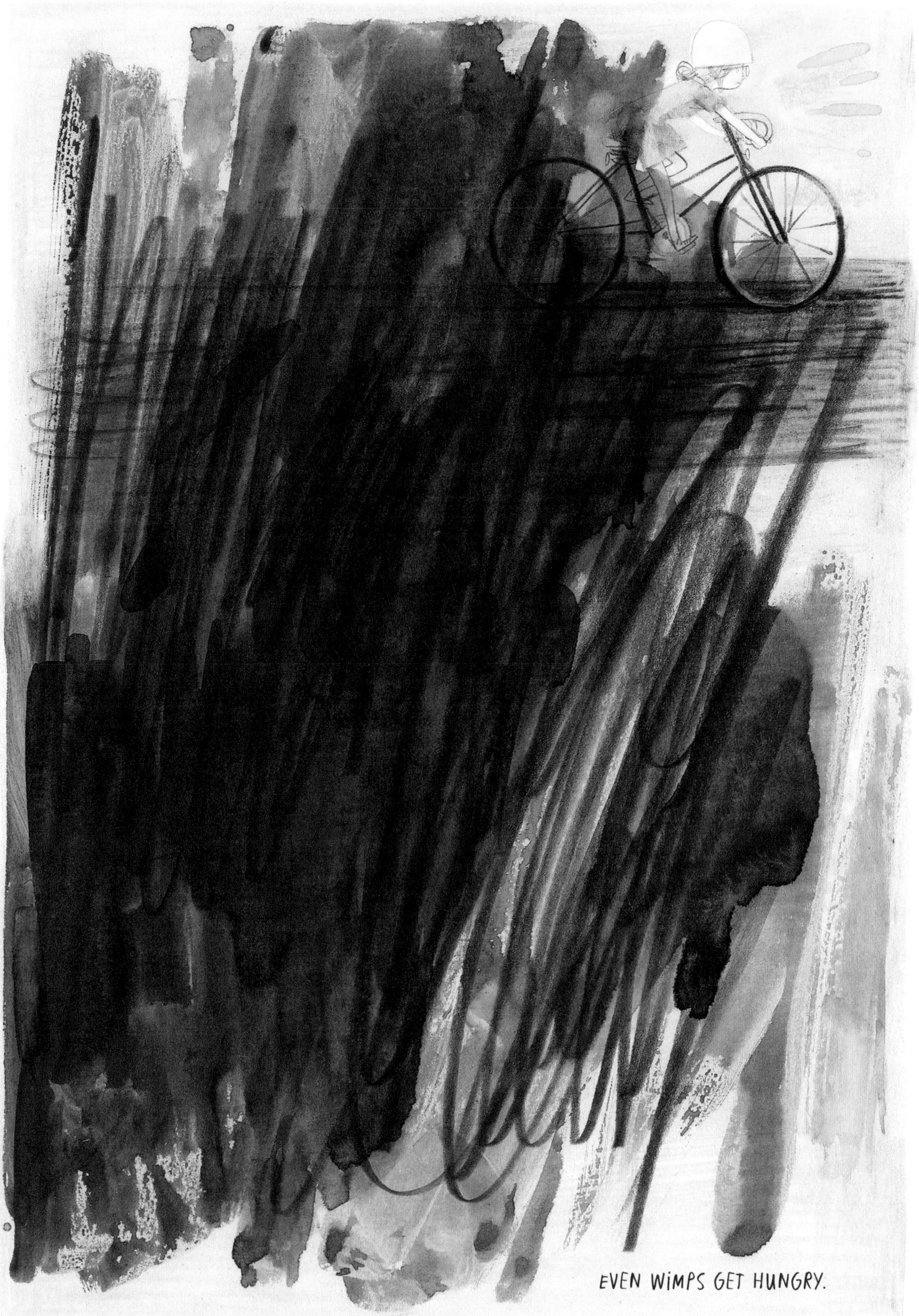
EVEN WIMPS GET HUNGRY.

BORIS AND I EAT FRENCH FRIES FOR A WEEK, THEN HE HEADS OFF TO HIS GRANDMA'S PLACE UP NORTH.

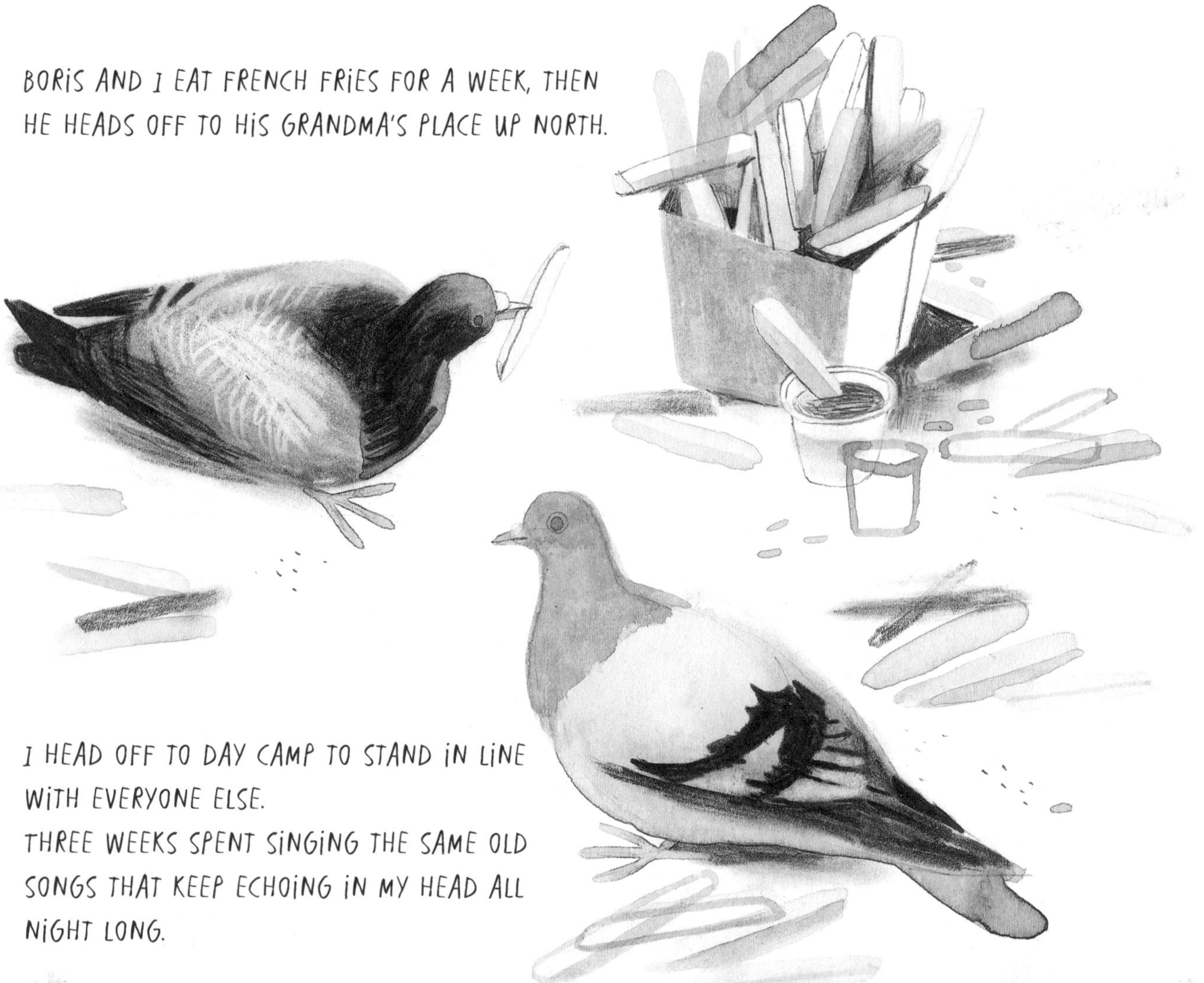

I HEAD OFF TO DAY CAMP TO STAND IN LINE WITH EVERYONE ELSE.
THREE WEEKS SPENT SINGING THE SAME OLD SONGS THAT KEEP ECHOING IN MY HEAD ALL NIGHT LONG.

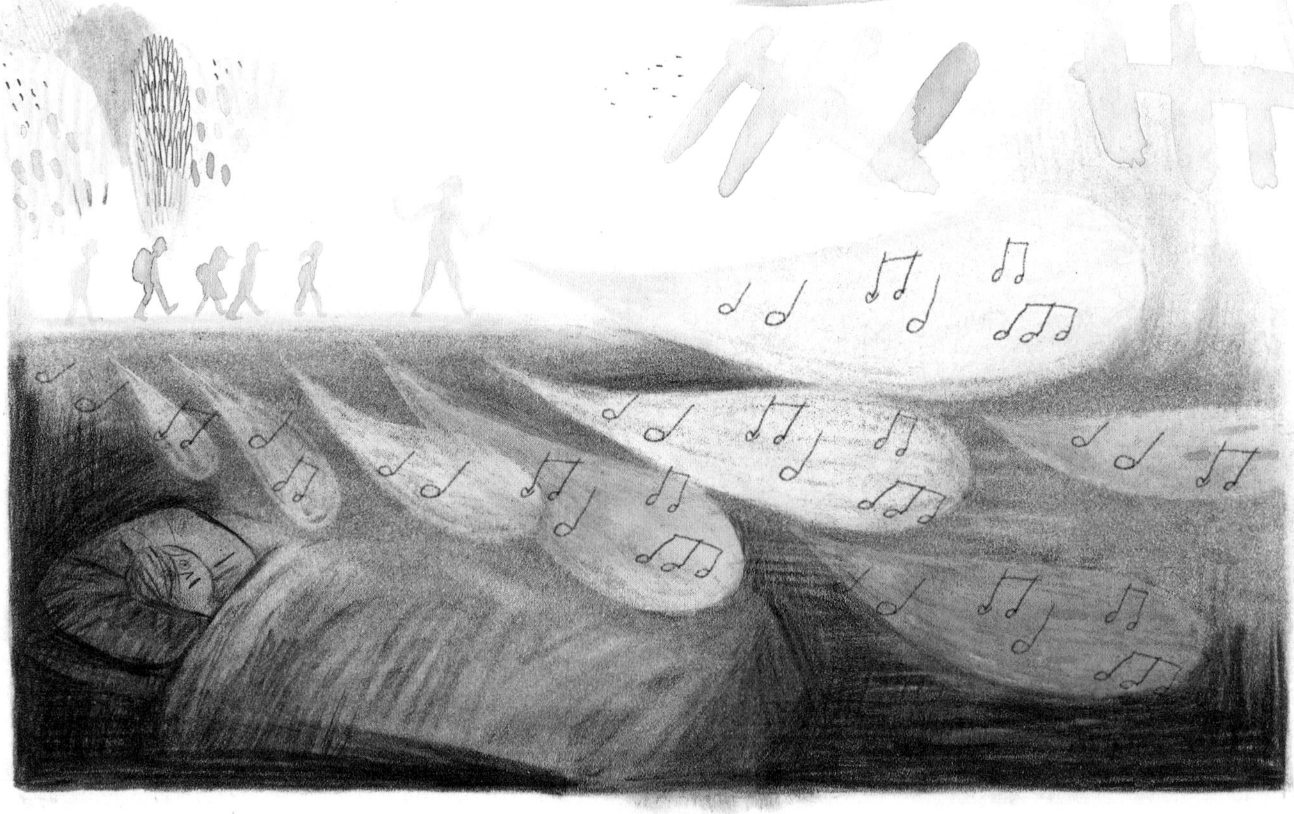

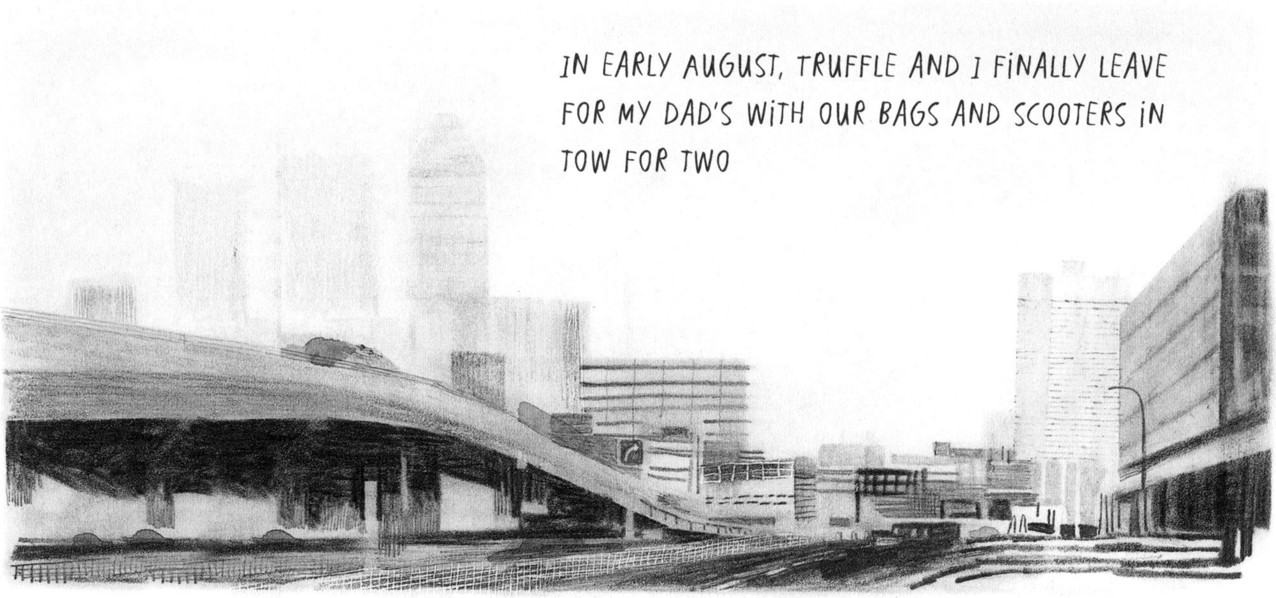
IN EARLY AUGUST, TRUFFLE AND I FINALLY LEAVE FOR MY DAD'S WITH OUR BAGS AND SCOOTERS IN TOW FOR TWO

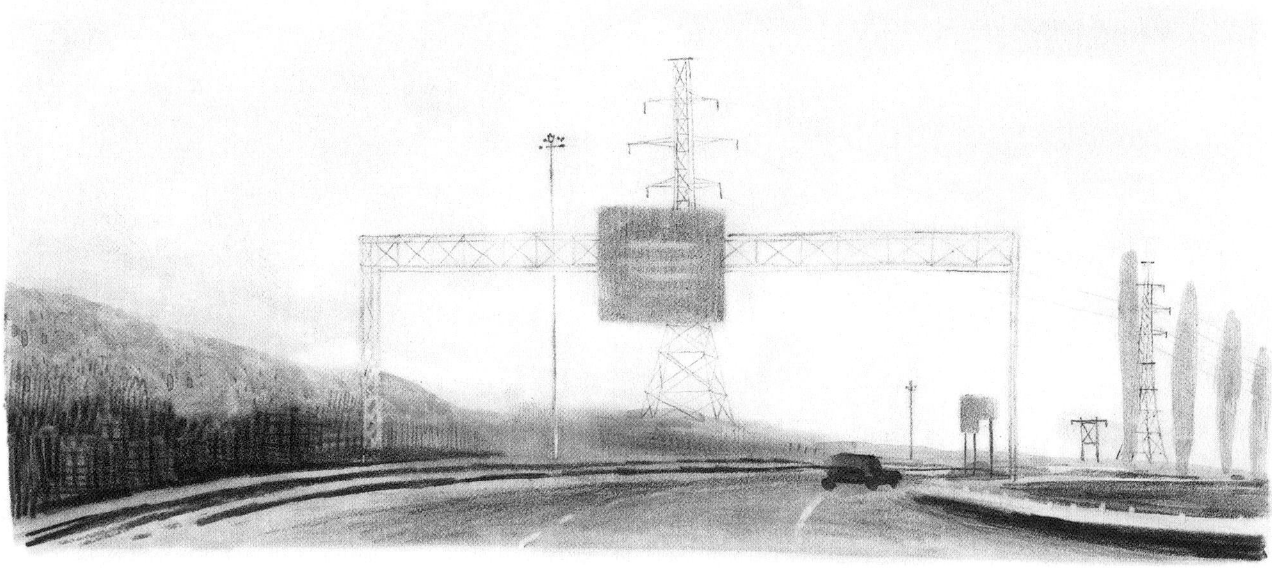

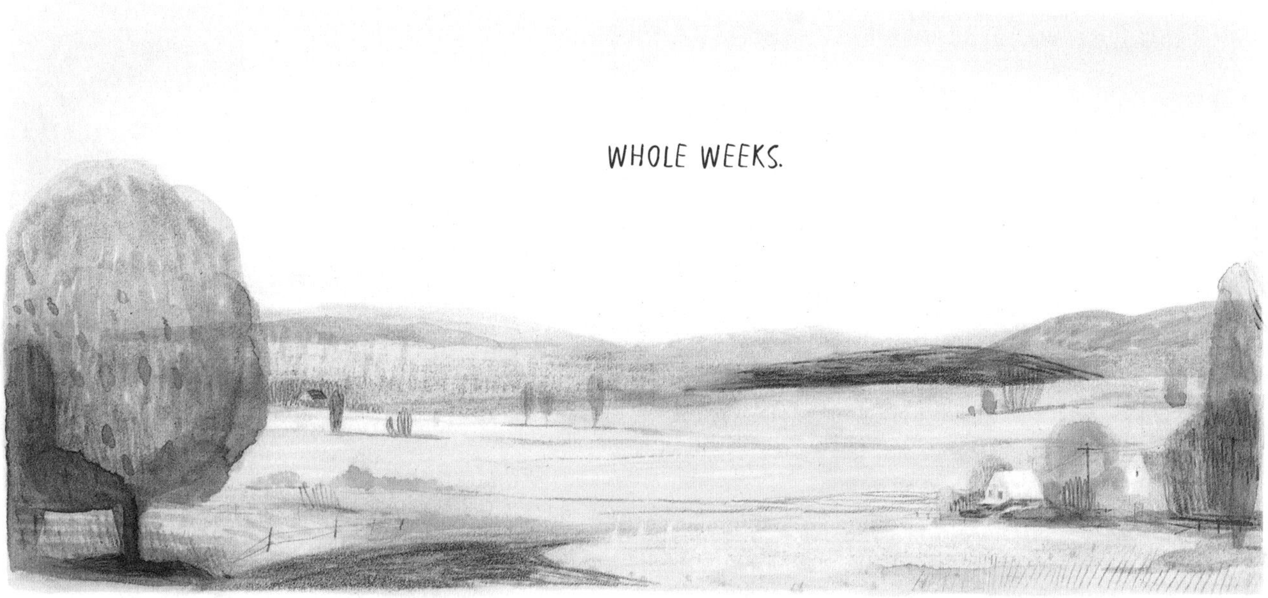
WHOLE WEEKS.

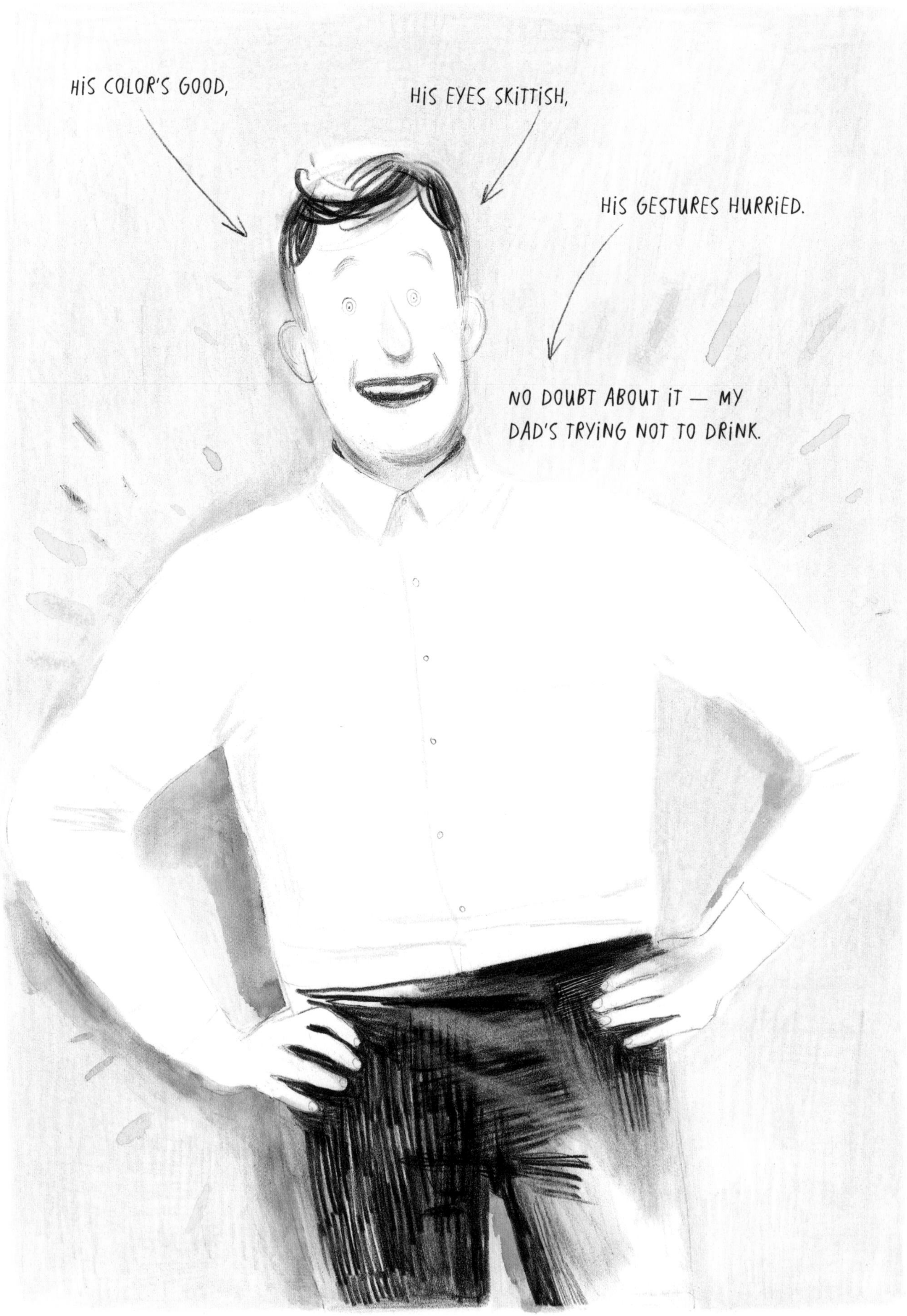
HIS COLOR'S GOOD,
HIS EYES SKITTISH,
HIS GESTURES HURRIED.
NO DOUBT ABOUT IT — MY DAD'S TRYING NOT TO DRINK.

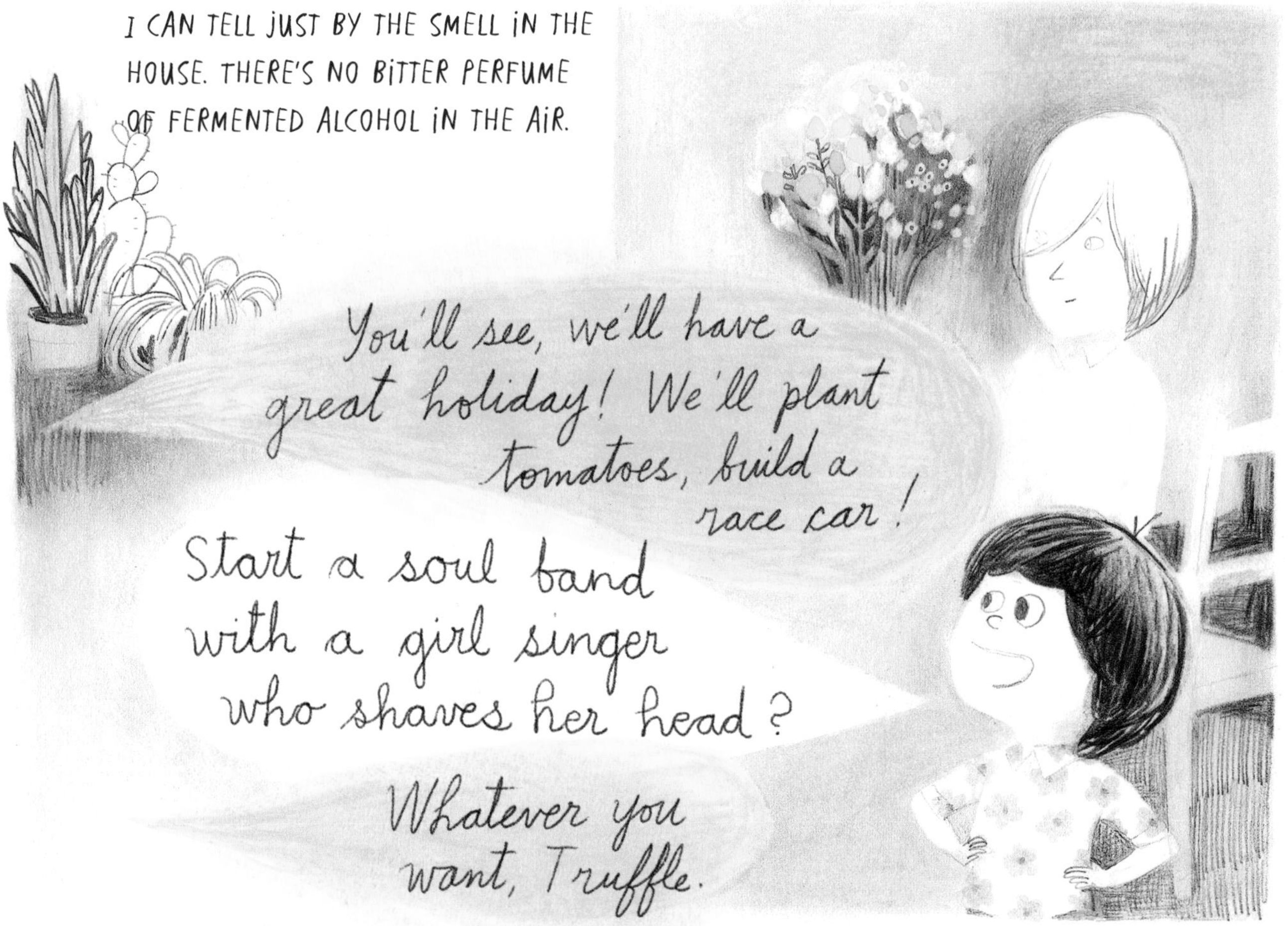
I CAN TELL JUST BY THE SMELL IN THE HOUSE. THERE'S NO BITTER PERFUME OF FERMENTED ALCOHOL IN THE AIR.
You'll see, we'll have a great holiday! We'll plant tomatoes, build a race car!
Start a soul band with a girl singer who shaves her head?
Whatever you want, Truffle.

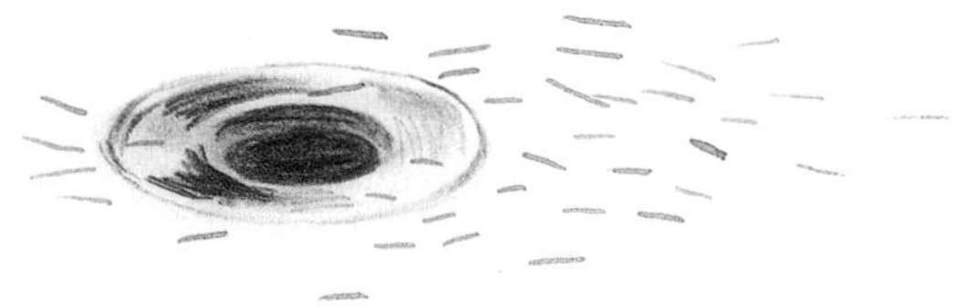
I CONSIDER CALLING MY MOM TO REASSURE HER. IT'S NOT LIKE SHE SAID ANYTHING, BUT I SAW THE WAY SHE CUT HERSELF SOME BANGS ON IMPULSE IN THE BATHROOM THE MORNING WE LEFT.

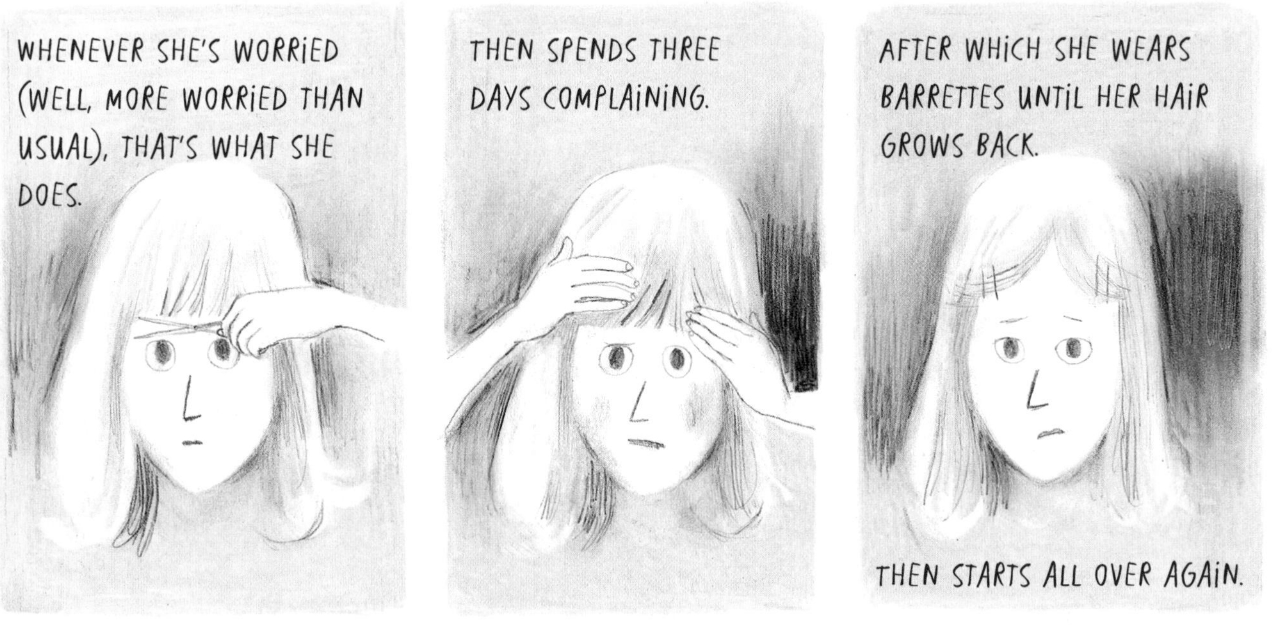
WHENEVER SHE'S WORRIED (WELL, MORE WORRIED THAN USUAL), THAT'S WHAT SHE DOES.
THEN SPENDS THREE DAYS COMPLAINING.
AFTER WHICH SHE WEARS BARRETTES UNTIL HER HAIR GROWS BACK.
THEN STARTS ALL OVER AGAIN.

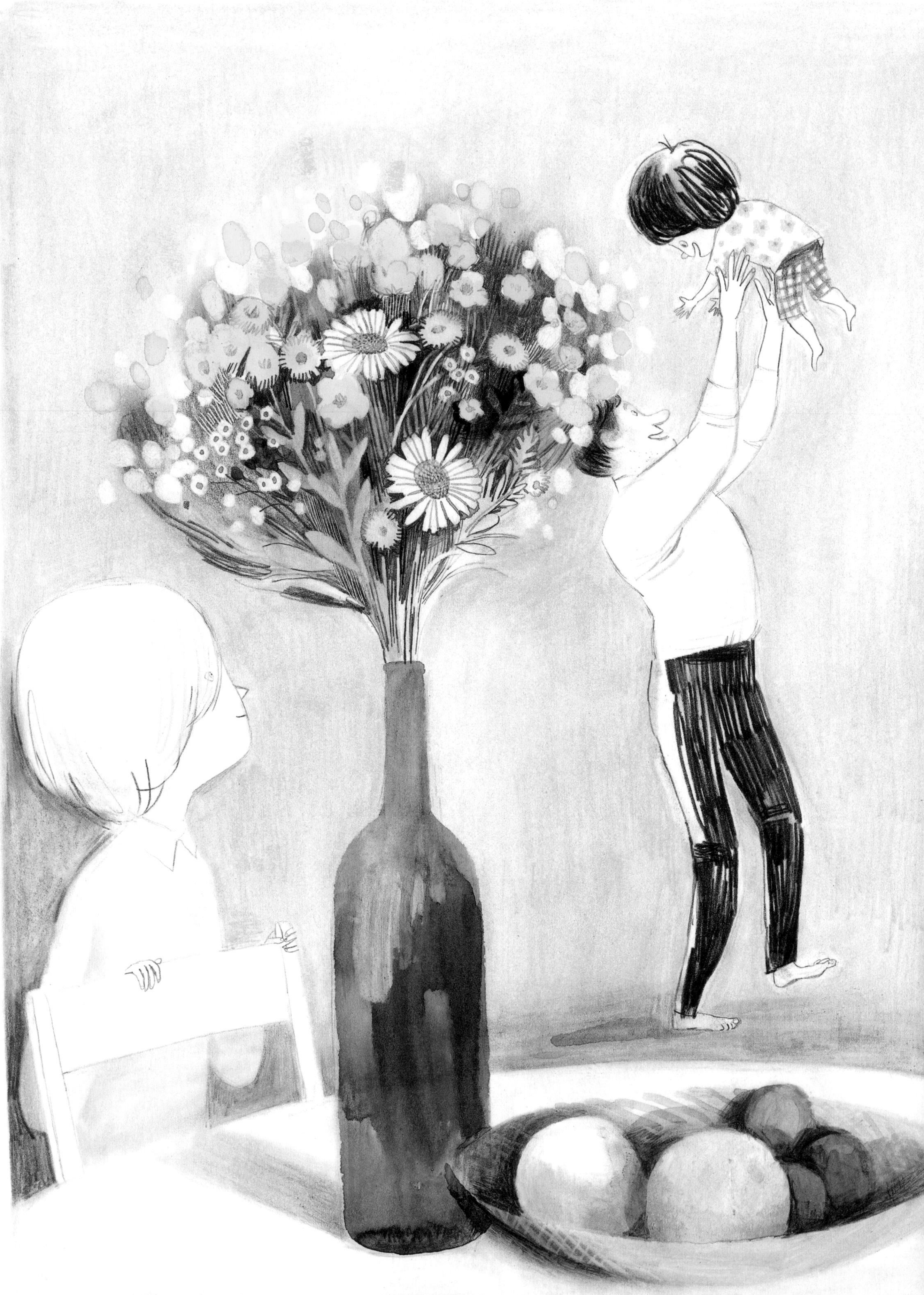

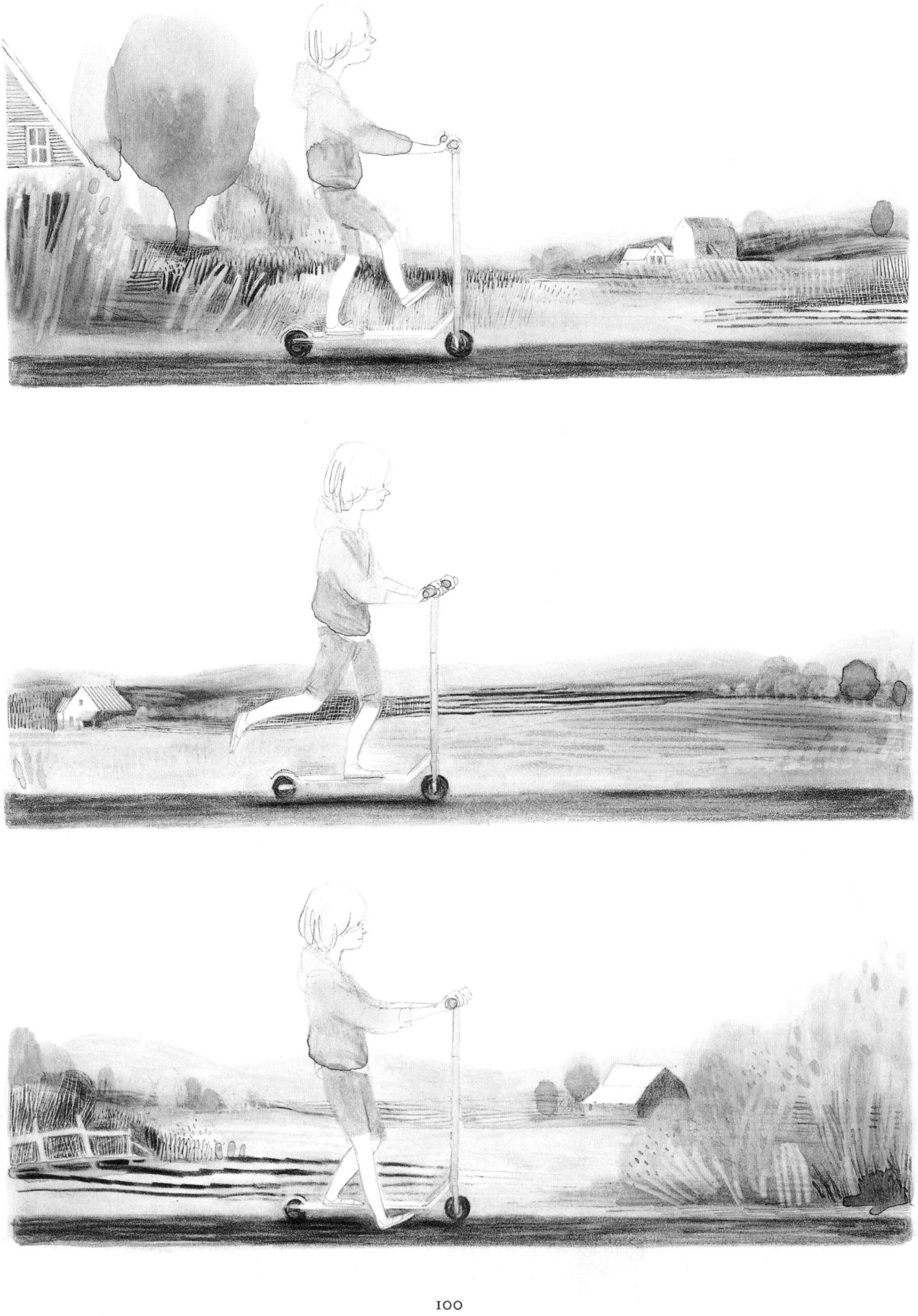

AT FIRST, I THINK IT'S A BAG OR A PILE OF BRANCHES.

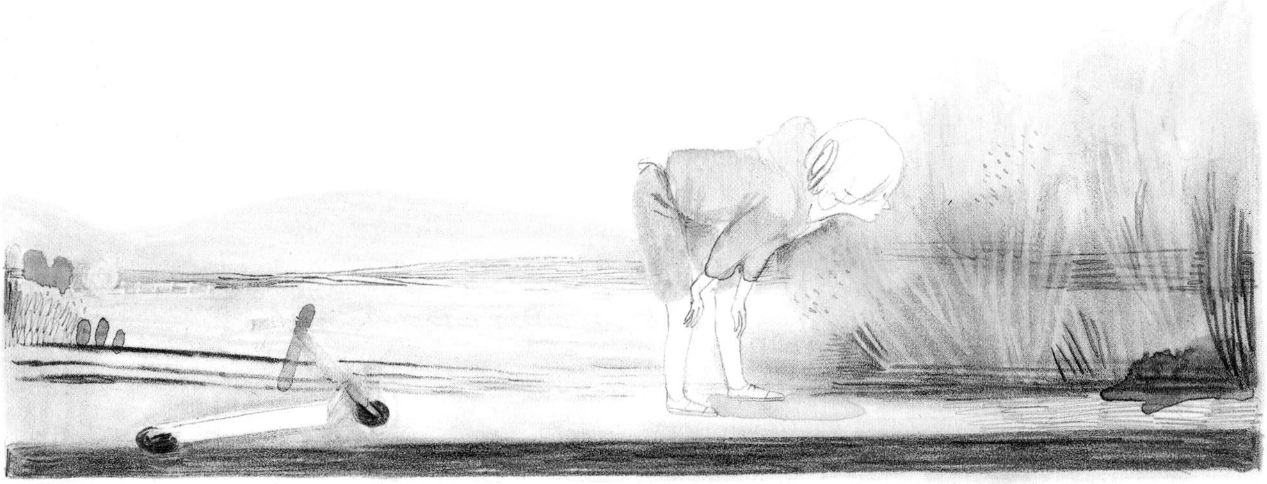

THEN I SEE IT'S AN ANIMAL.

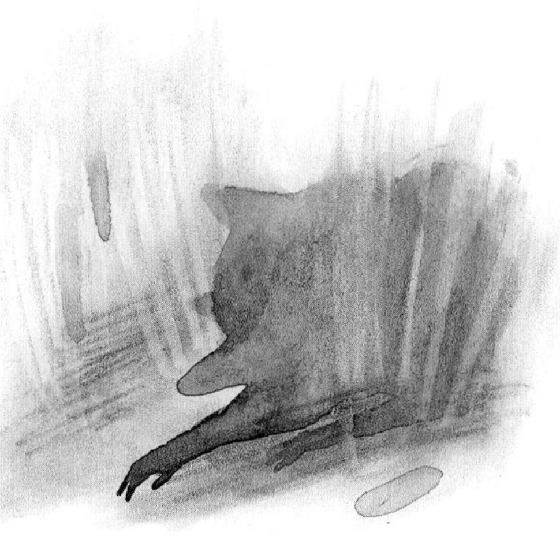

A GOPHER?

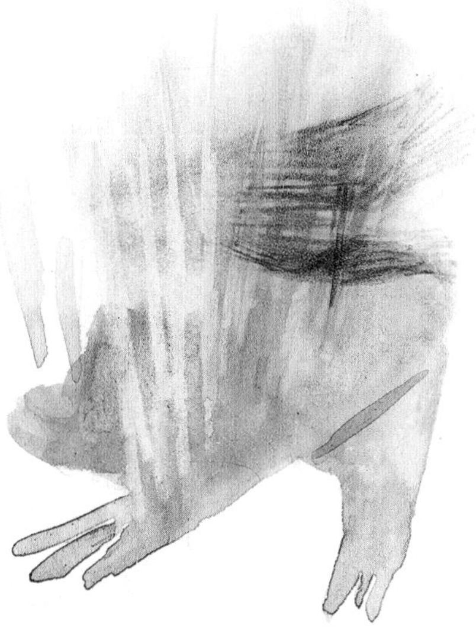

A BEAVER?

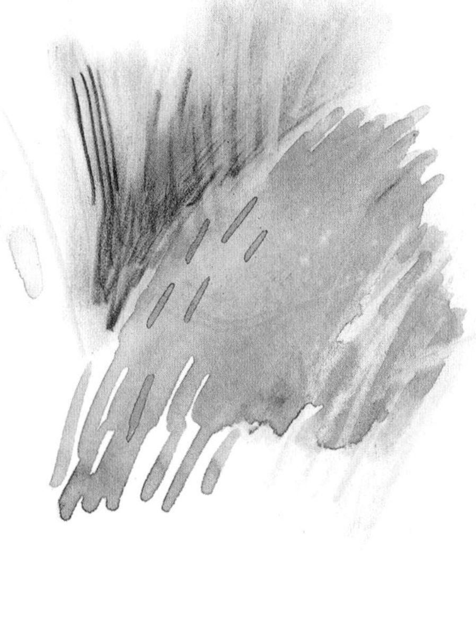

A RACCOON?

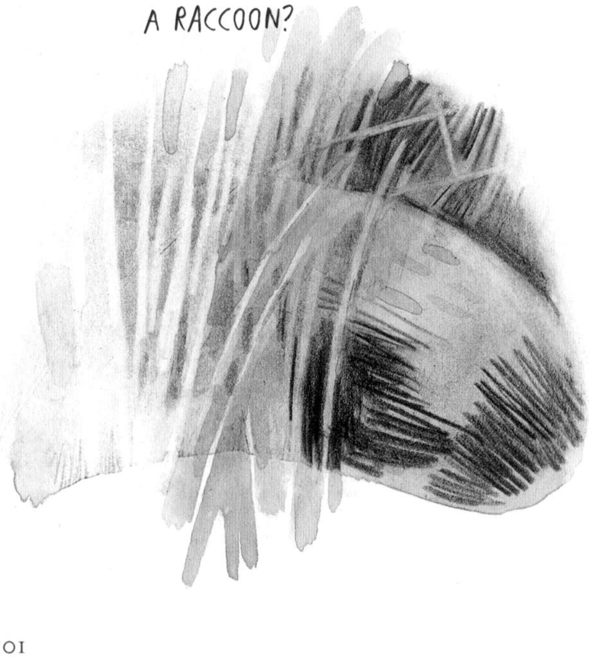

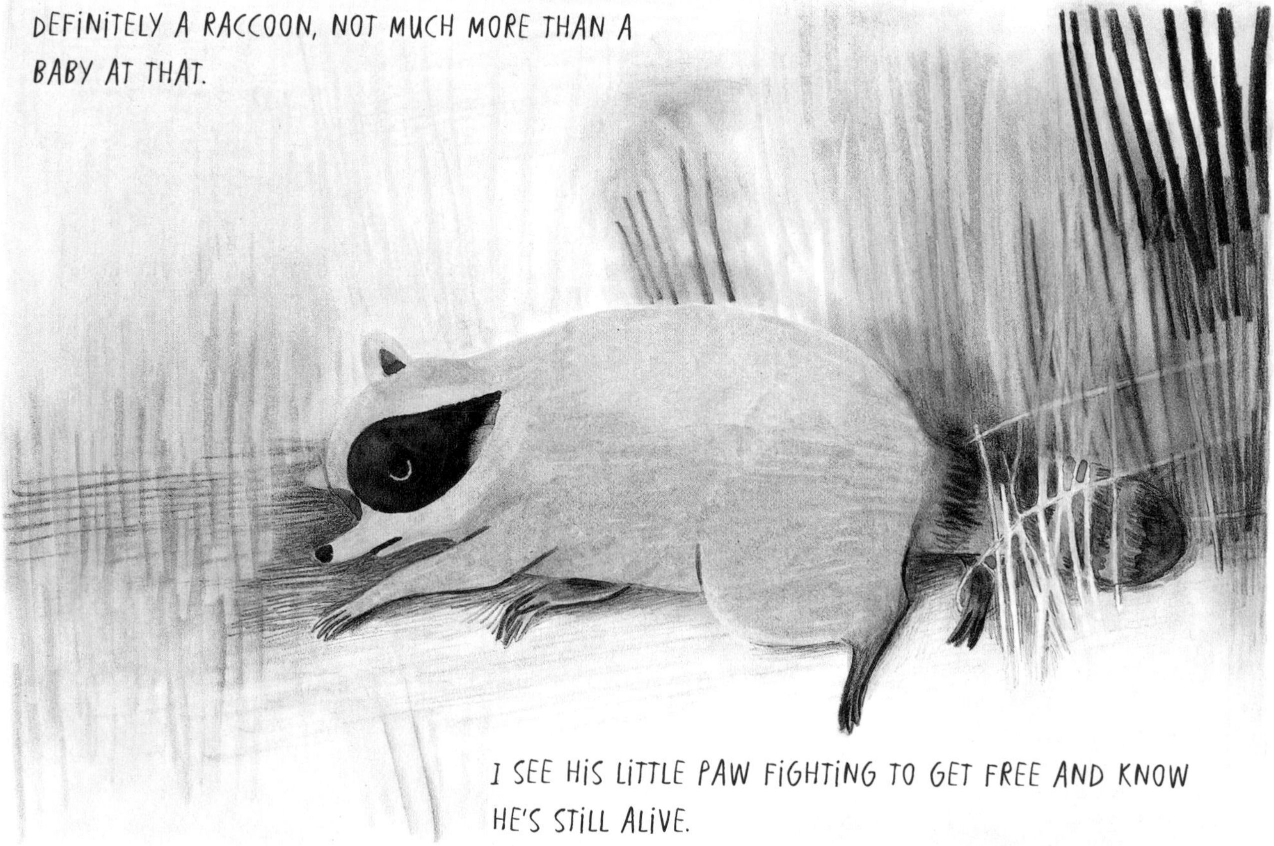
DEFINITELY A RACCOON, NOT MUCH MORE THAN A BABY AT THAT.
I SEE HIS LITTLE PAW FIGHTING TO GET FREE AND KNOW HE'S STILL ALIVE.

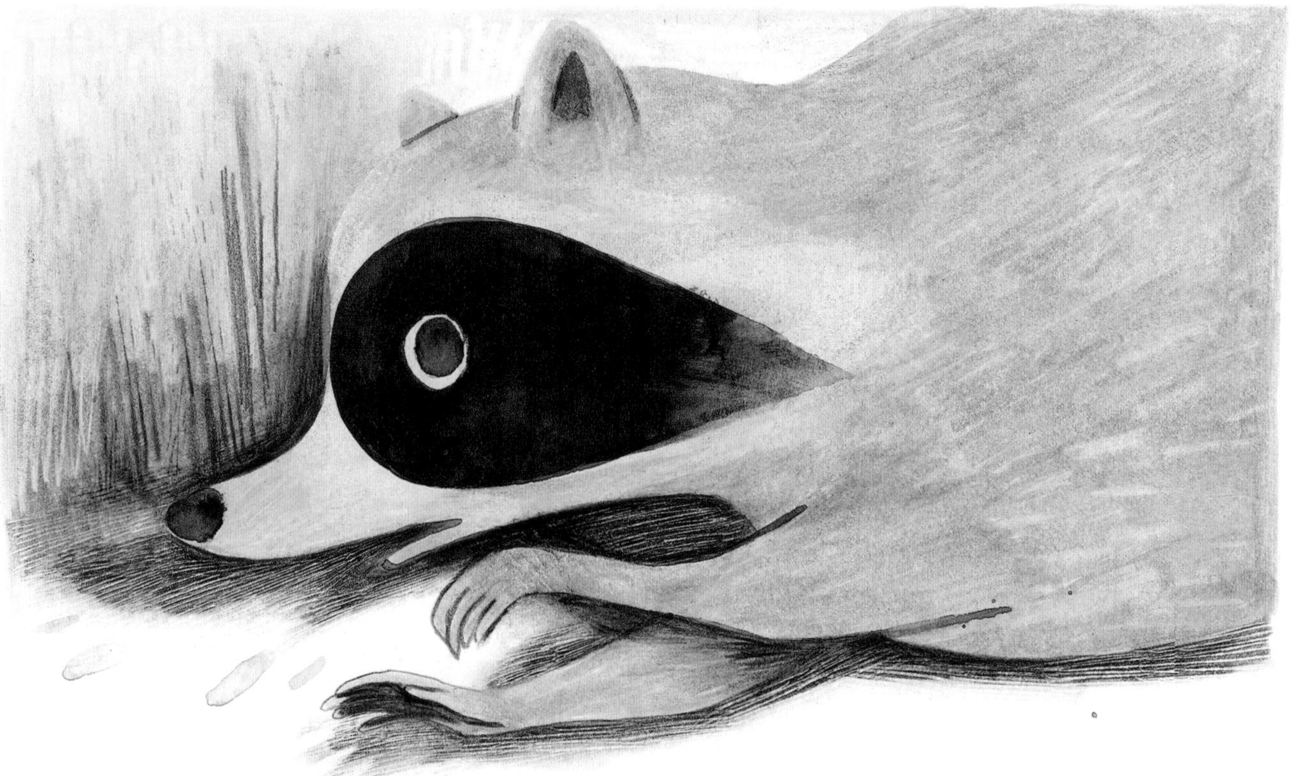

SHORT, JAGGED BREATHS. WARY EYES ASSAULTED BY THE LIGHT. I REMEMBER THAT RACCOONS DON'T LIKE FULL SUN.

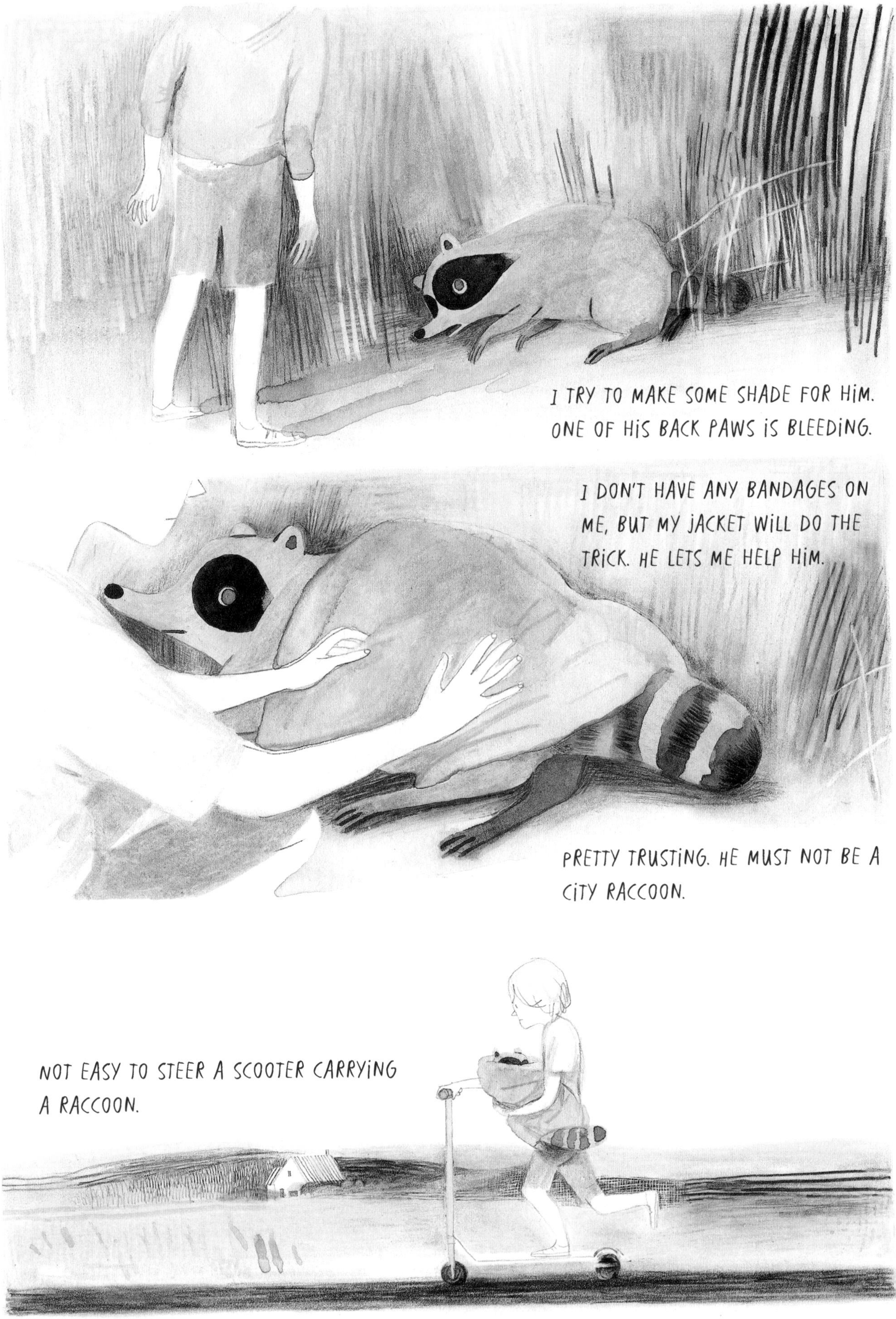
I TRY TO MAKE SOME SHADE FOR HIM. ONE OF HIS BACK PAWS IS BLEEDING.
I DON'T HAVE ANY BANDAGES ON ME, BUT MY JACKET WILL DO THE TRICK. HE LETS ME HELP HIM.
PRETTY TRUSTING. HE MUST NOT BE A CITY RACCOON.
NOT EASY TO STEER A SCOOTER CARRYING A RACCOON.

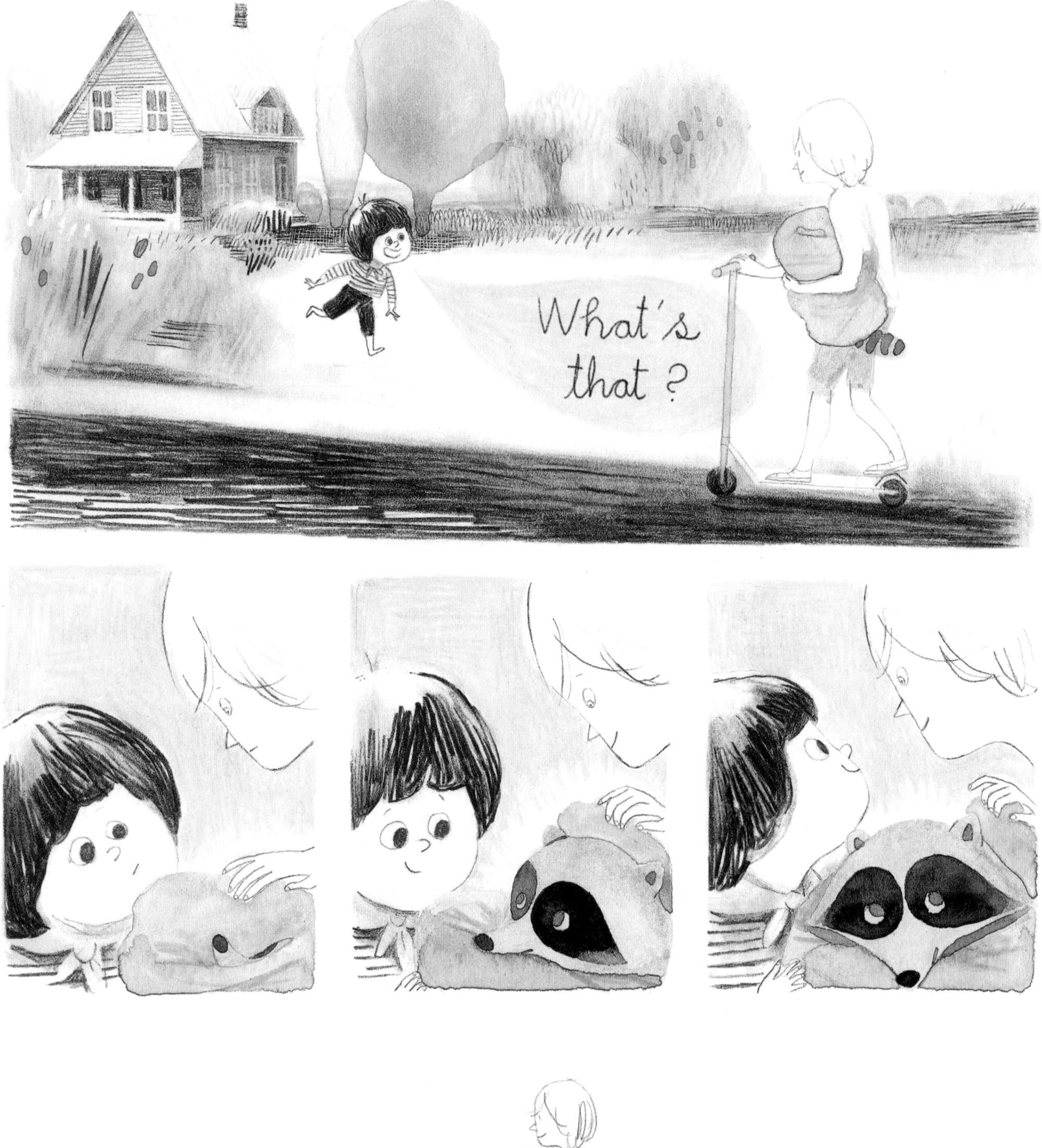
What's that ?

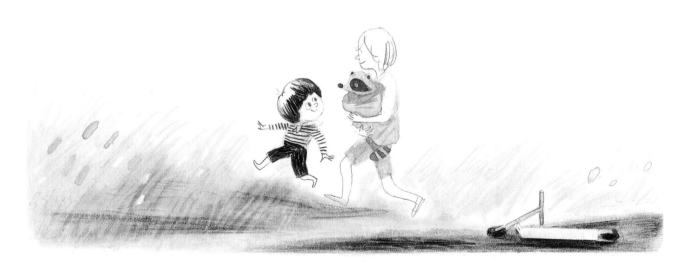

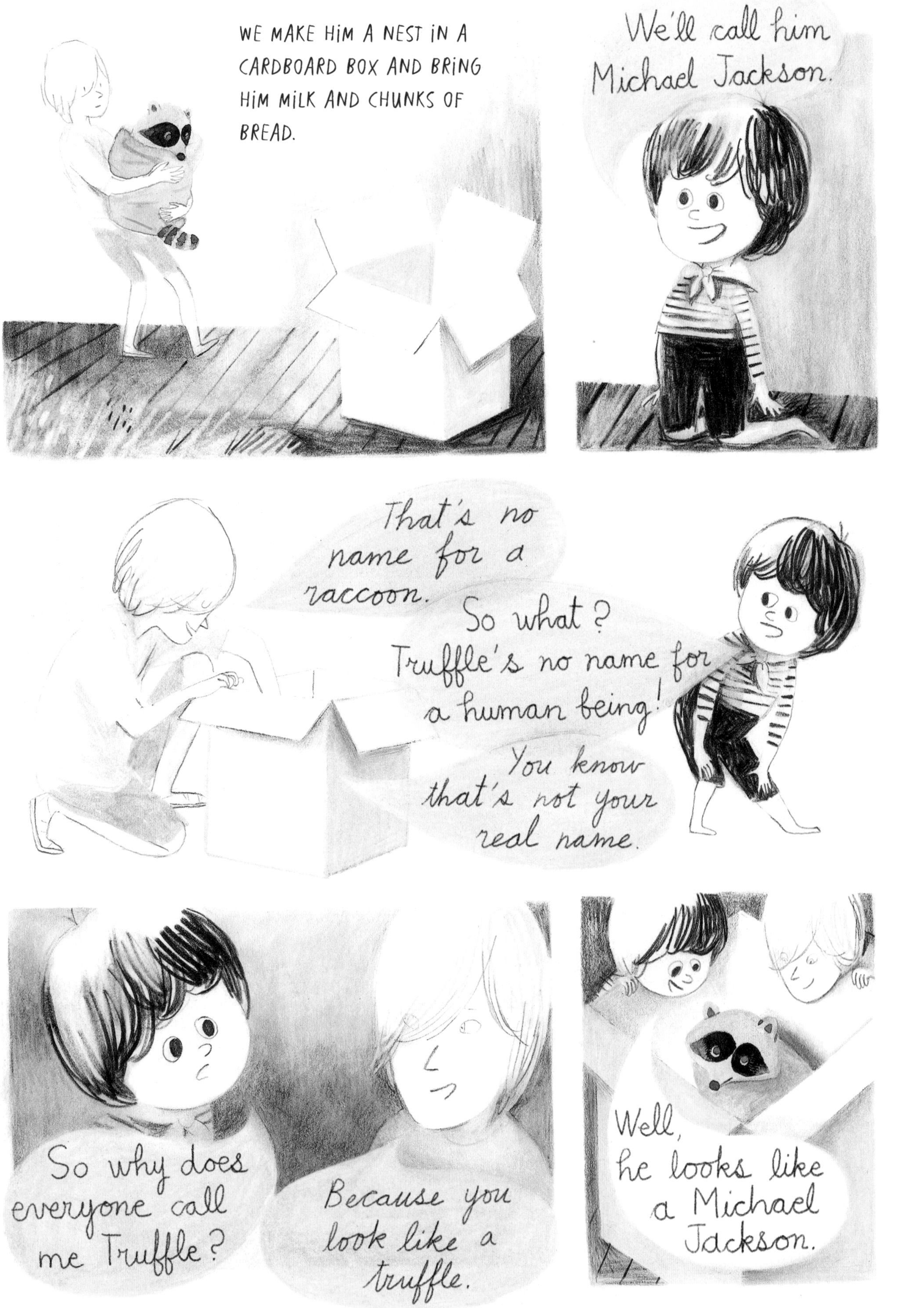
WE MAKE HIM A NEST IN A CARDBOARD BOX AND BRING HIM MILK AND CHUNKS OF BREAD.
We'll call him Michael Jackson.
That's no name for a raccoon.
So what? Truffle's no name for a human being!
You know that's not your real name.
So why does everyone call me Truffle?
Because you look like a truffle.
Well, he looks like a Michael Jackson.

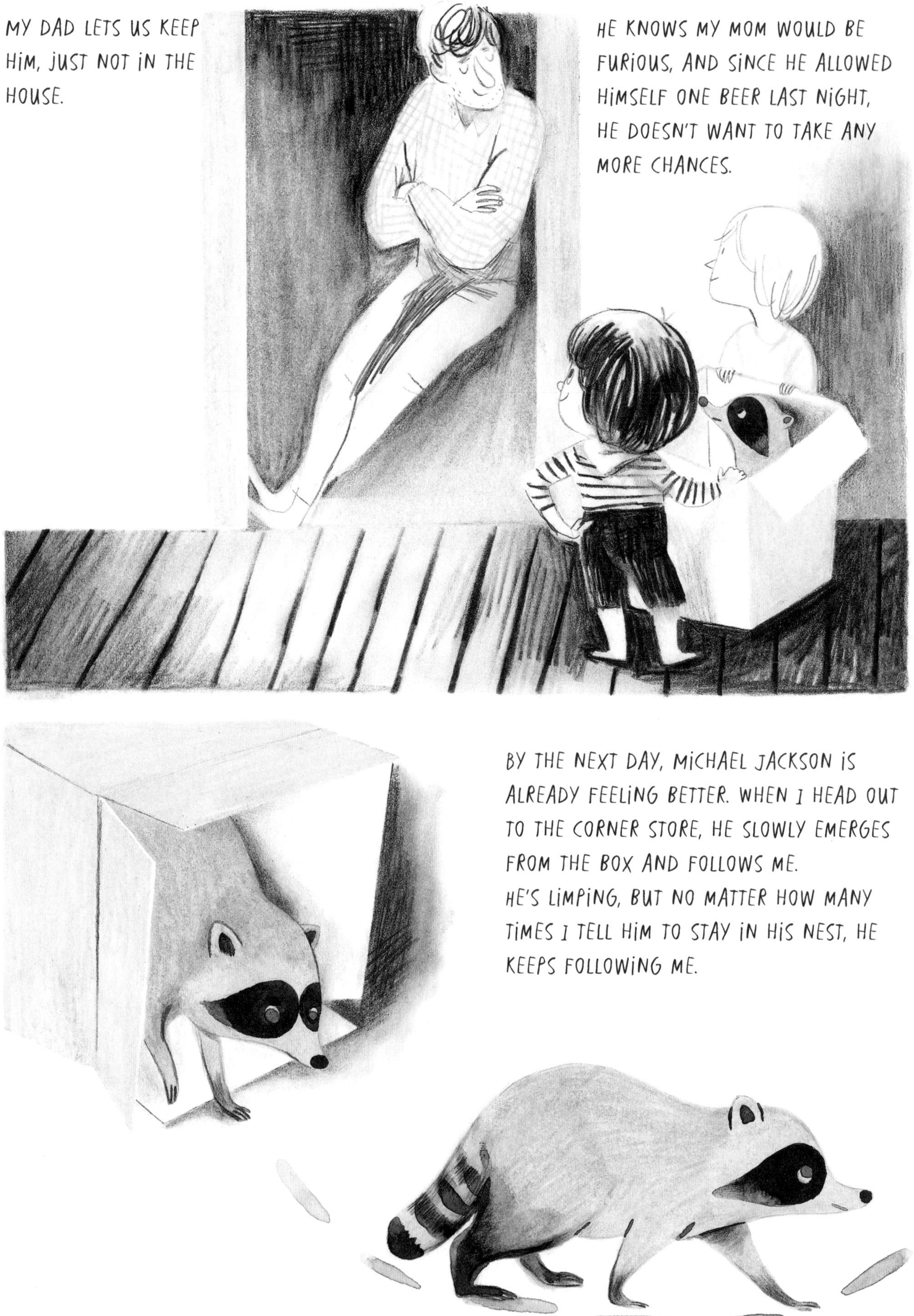
MY DAD LETS US KEEP HIM, JUST NOT IN THE HOUSE.
HE KNOWS MY MOM WOULD BE FURIOUS, AND SINCE HE ALLOWED HIMSELF ONE BEER LAST NIGHT, HE DOESN'T WANT TO TAKE ANY MORE CHANCES.
BY THE NEXT DAY, MICHAEL JACKSON IS ALREADY FEELING BETTER. WHEN I HEAD OUT TO THE CORNER STORE, HE SLOWLY EMERGES FROM THE BOX AND FOLLOWS ME.
HE'S LIMPING, BUT NO MATTER HOW MANY TIMES I TELL HIM TO STAY IN HIS NEST, HE KEEPS FOLLOWING ME.

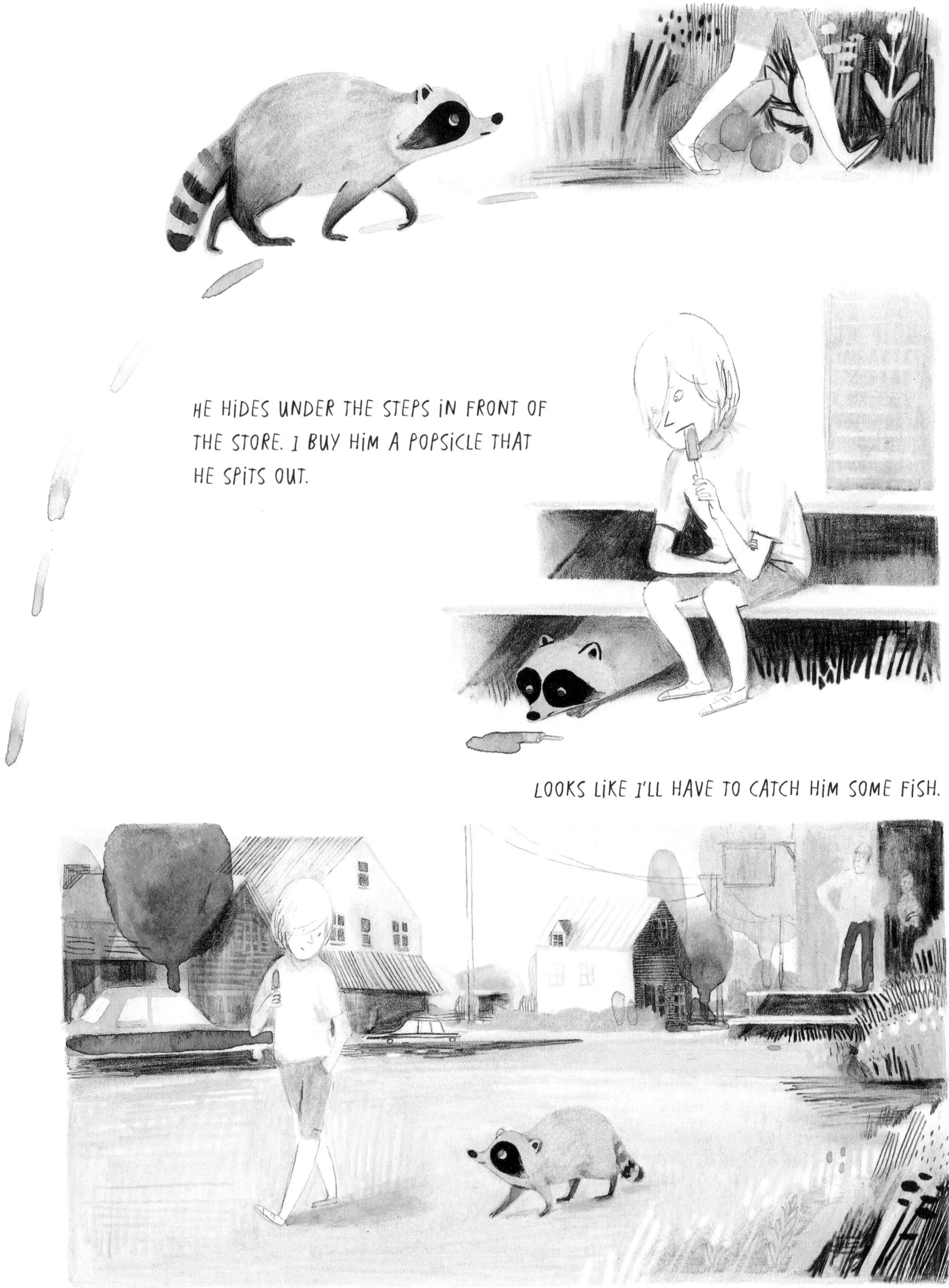
HE HIDES UNDER THE STEPS IN FRONT OF THE STORE. I BUY HIM A POPSICLE THAT HE SPITS OUT.
LOOKS LIKE I'LL HAVE TO CATCH HIM SOME FISH.

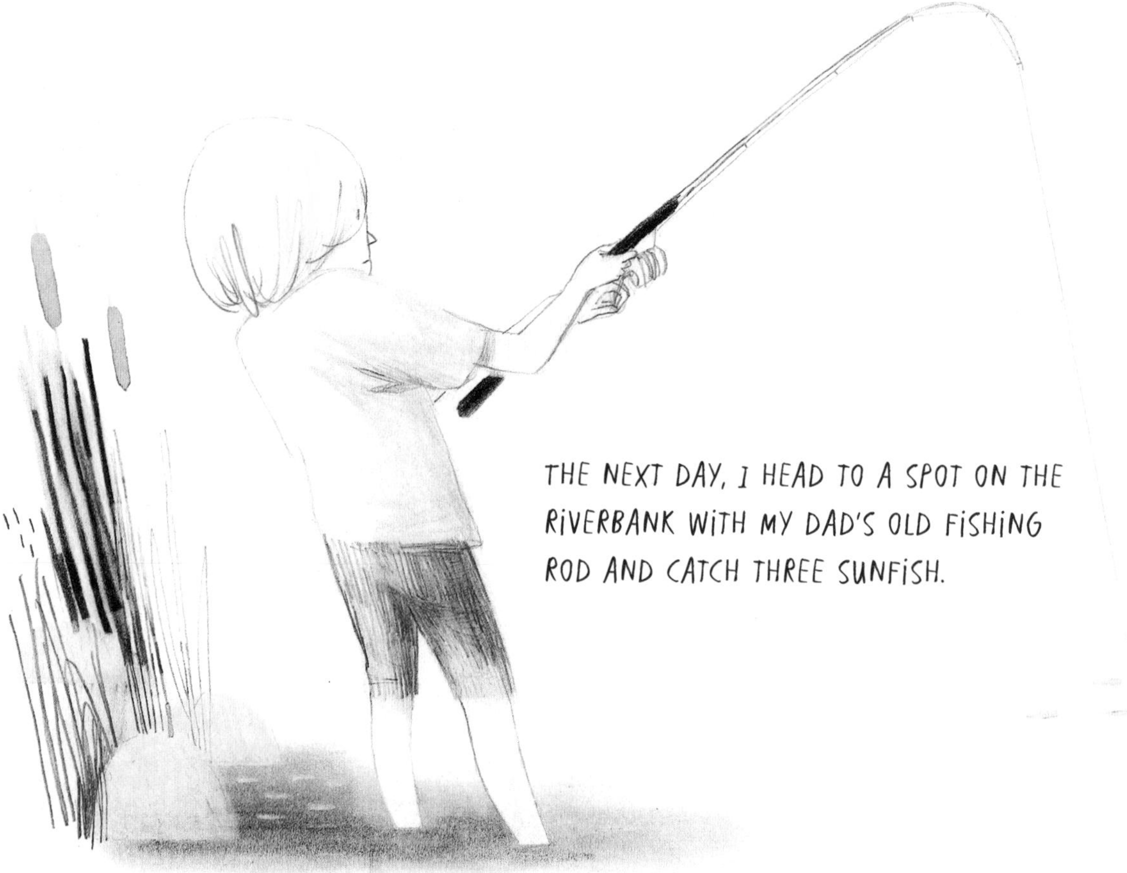

THE NEXT DAY, I HEAD TO A SPOT ON THE RIVERBANK WITH MY DAD'S OLD FISHING ROD AND CATCH THREE SUNFISH.

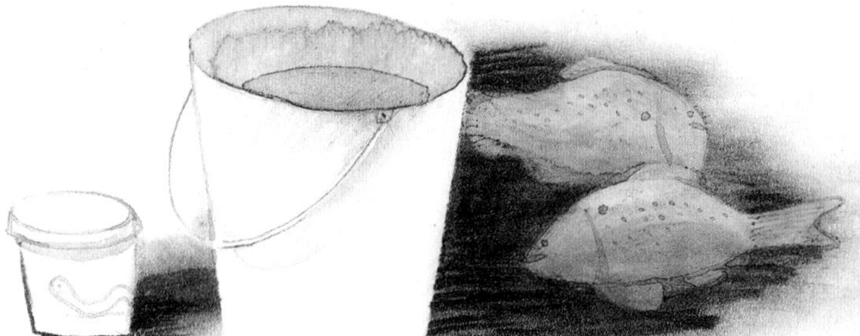

HE DEVOURS THEM ALL.

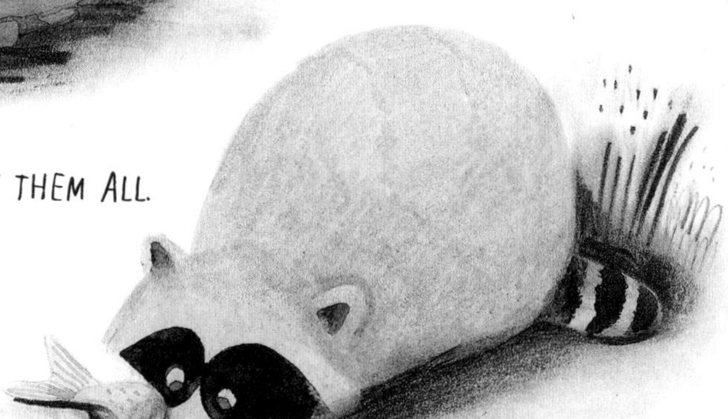

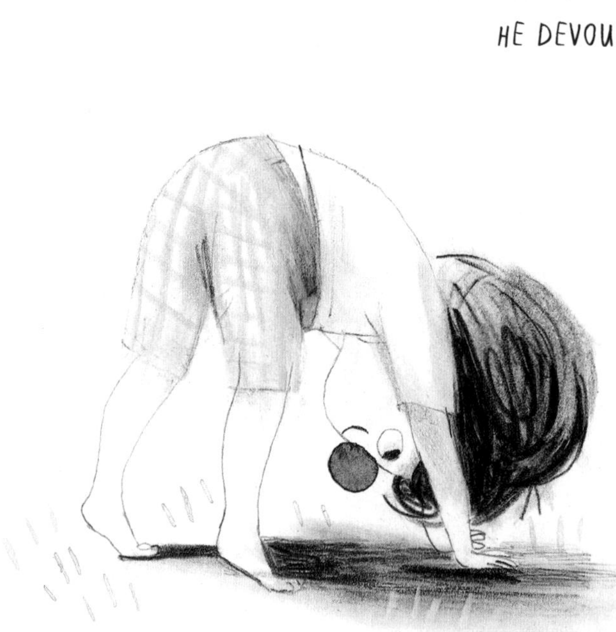

TRUFFLE DECIDES TO TEACH HIM SOME CIRCUS TRICKS.

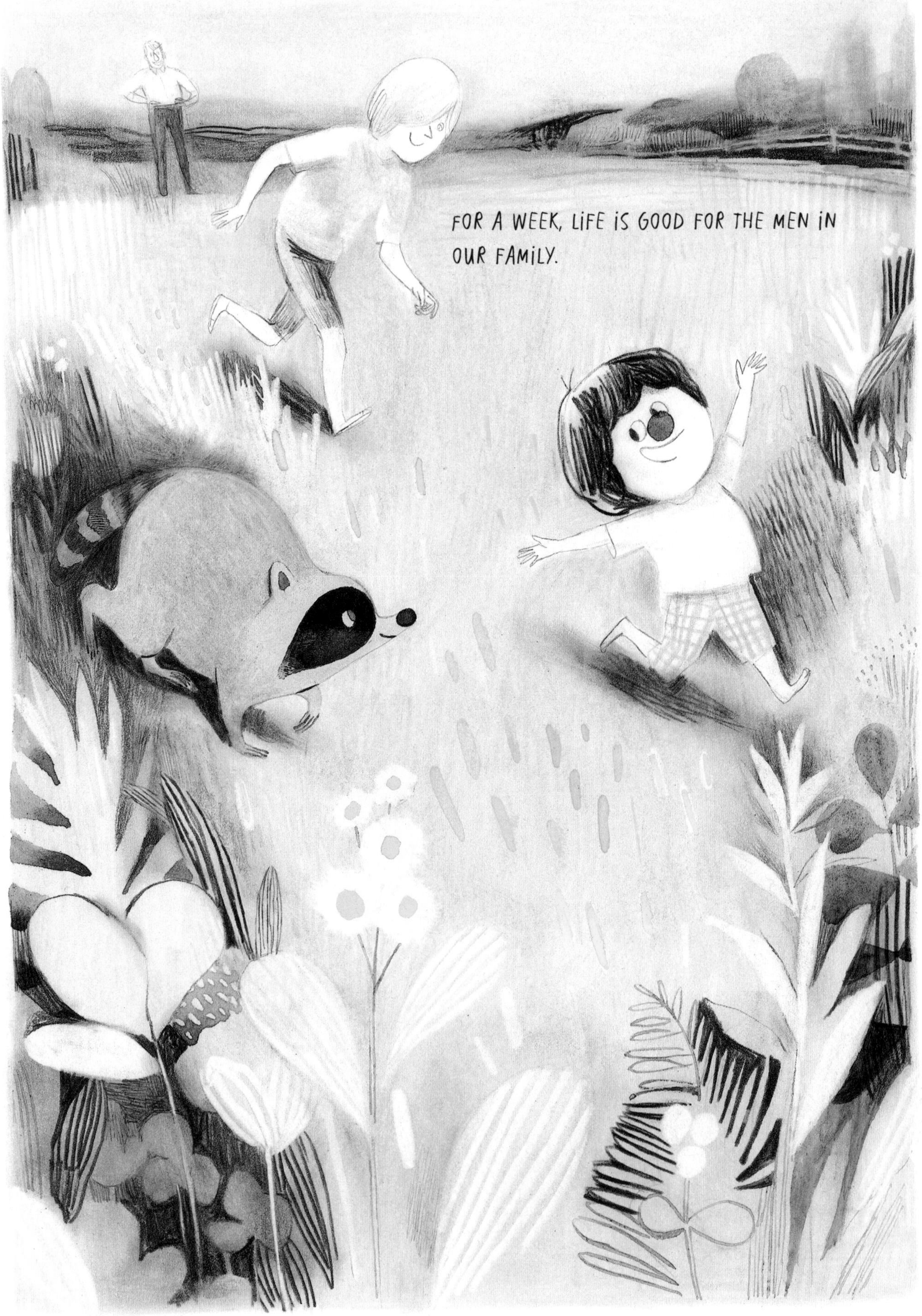
FOR A WEEK, LIFE IS GOOD FOR THE MEN IN OUR FAMILY.

# TRUFFLE'S ACCIDENT

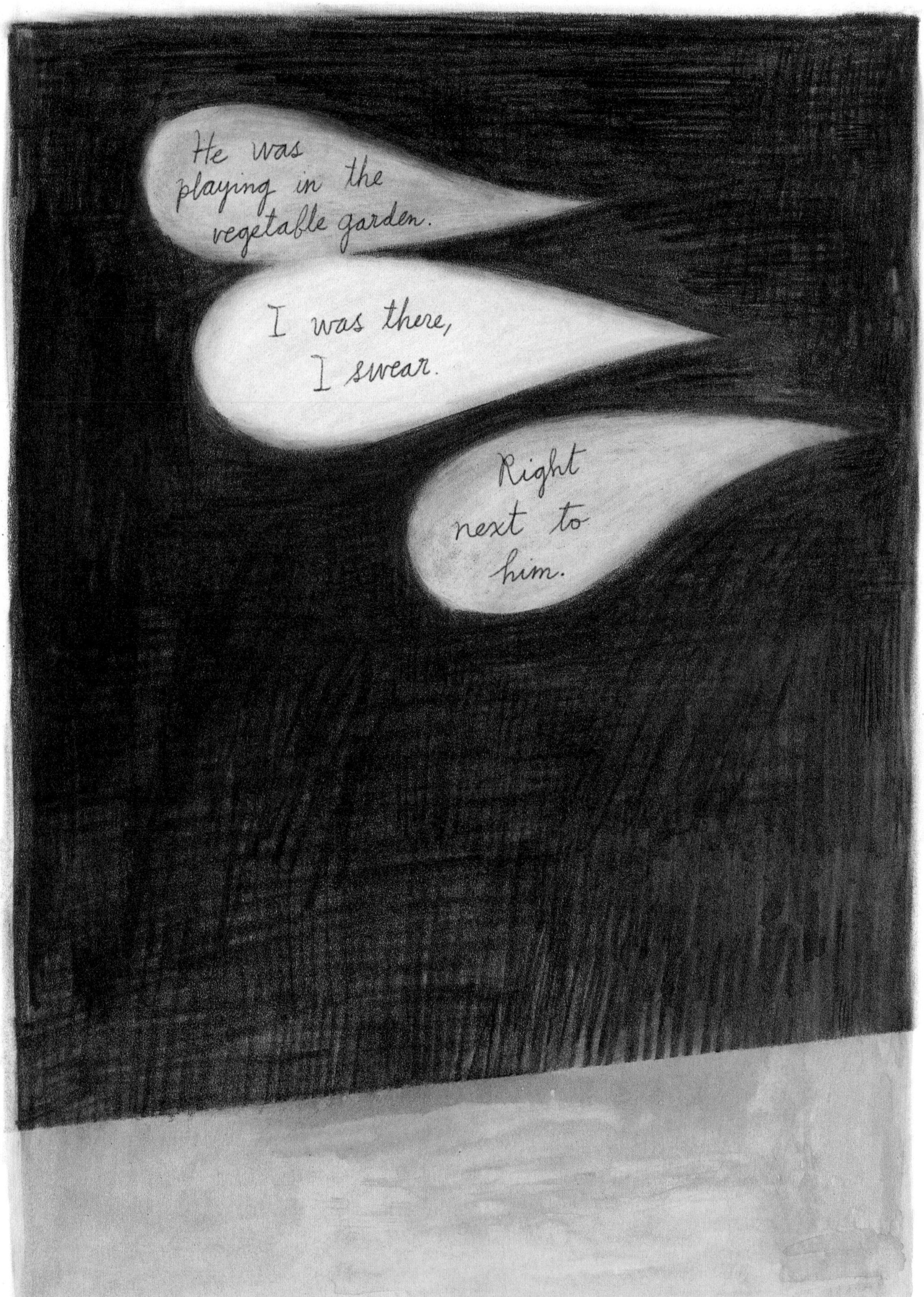
He was playing in the vegetable garden.
I was there, I swear.
Right next to him.

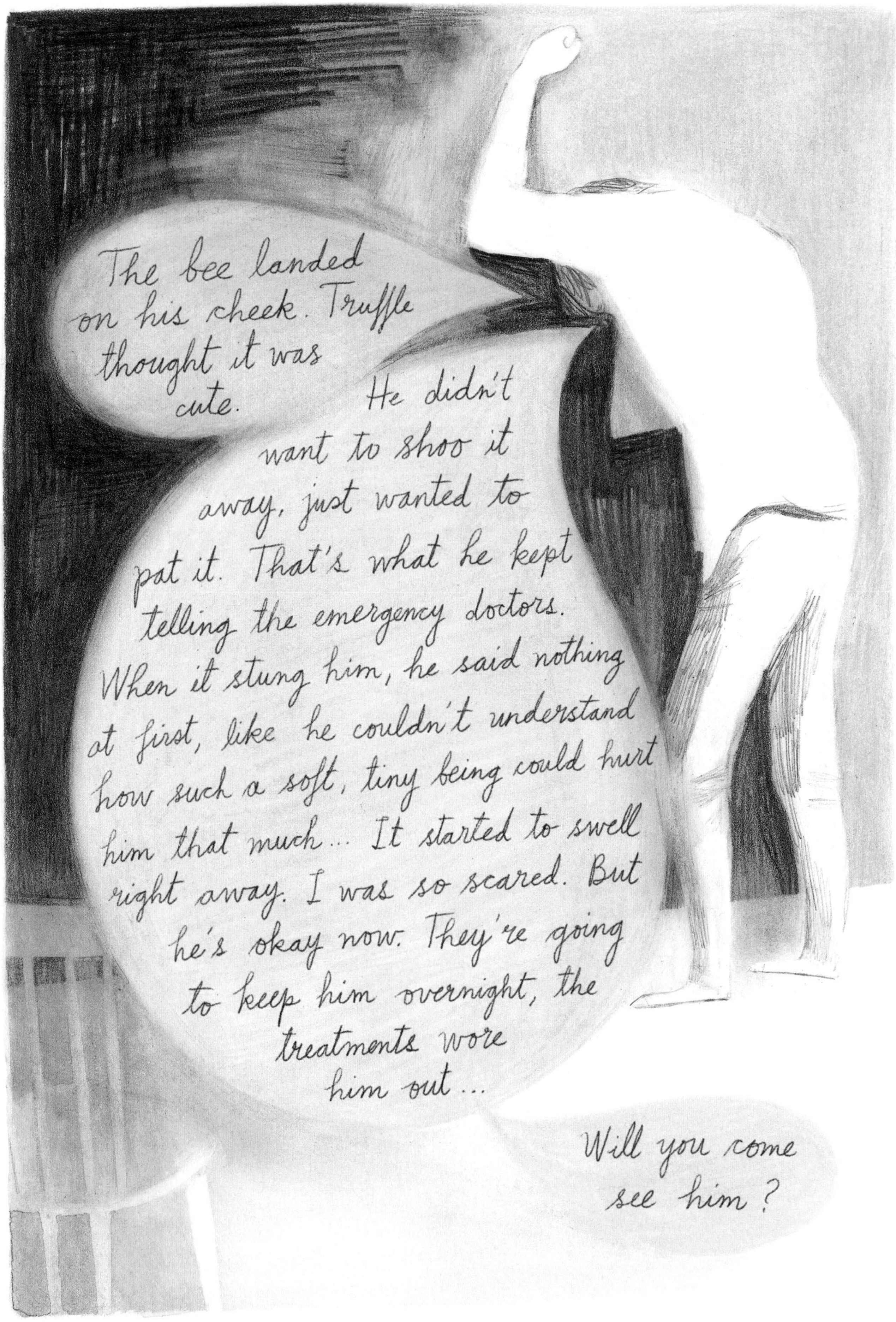
The bee landed on his cheek. Truffle thought it was cute.
He didn't want to shoo it away, just wanted to pat it. That's what he kept telling the emergency doctors. When it stung him, he said nothing at first, like he couldn't understand how such a soft, tiny being could hurt him that much... It started to swell right away. I was so scared. But he's okay now. They're going to keep him overnight, the treatments wore him out...
Will you come see him?

THE FIRST SURPRISE IS WHEN MY MOM SHOWS UP TWO HOURS AFTER TRUFFLE'S BEE STING AND DOESN'T EVEN YELL AT MY DAD. SHE JUST HUGS US EXTRA-LONG, ESPECIALLY TRUFFLE, ALL SWOLLEN IN HIS HOSPITAL BED.

THE SECOND SURPRISE IS WHEN MY MOM MAKES US PANCAKES THE NEXT MORNING IN THE KITCHEN IN THE WOODEN HOUSE, AND HOW IT SEEMS SO NORMAL THAT IT'S SUPER WEIRD.

THE THIRD SURPRISE IS WHEN MY MOM AND MY DAD SIT DOWN UNDER THE WILLOW TREE IN THE GOLDEN LIGHT OF DAY'S END AND I HEAR, LIKE A CHORUS, LIKE A SPOONFUL OF MAPLE SYRUP, MY MOM'S LAUGH.

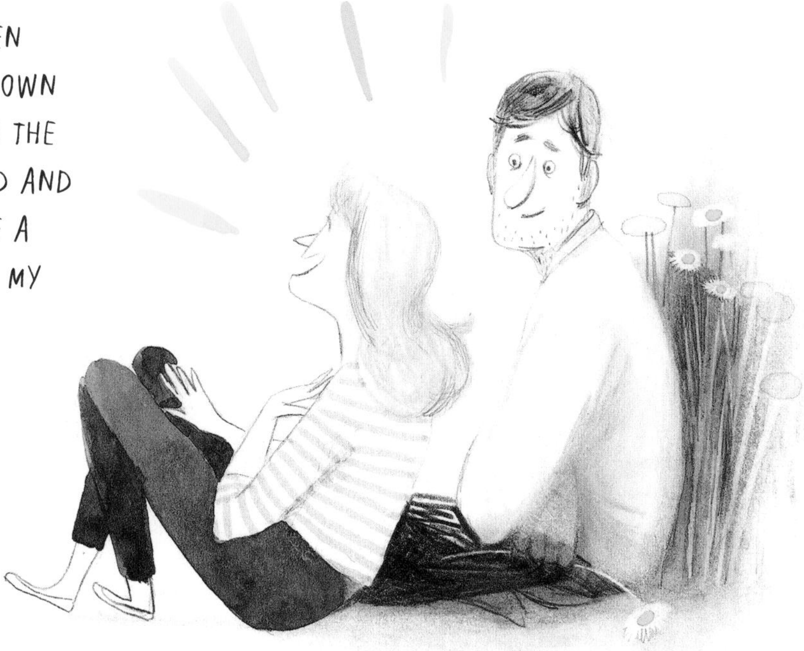

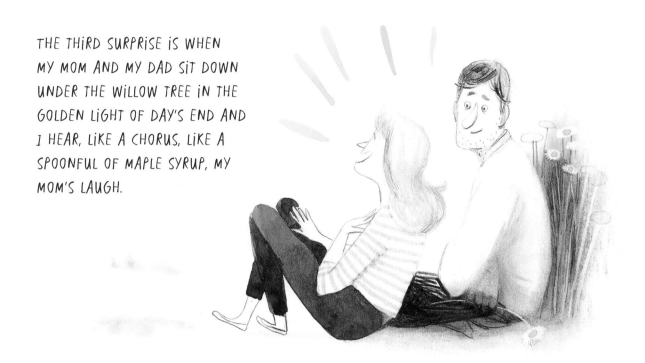

THE FOURTH THING, SO SURPRISING THAT YOU'D NEED TO COME UP WITH ANOTHER WORD FOR IT, "SUPERPRISING" MAYBE, IS WHEN MY MOM WALKS OUT OF MY DAD'S BEDROOM THE NEXT MORNING, HER HAIR A RAT'S NEST, A SILLY GRIN ON HER FACE.

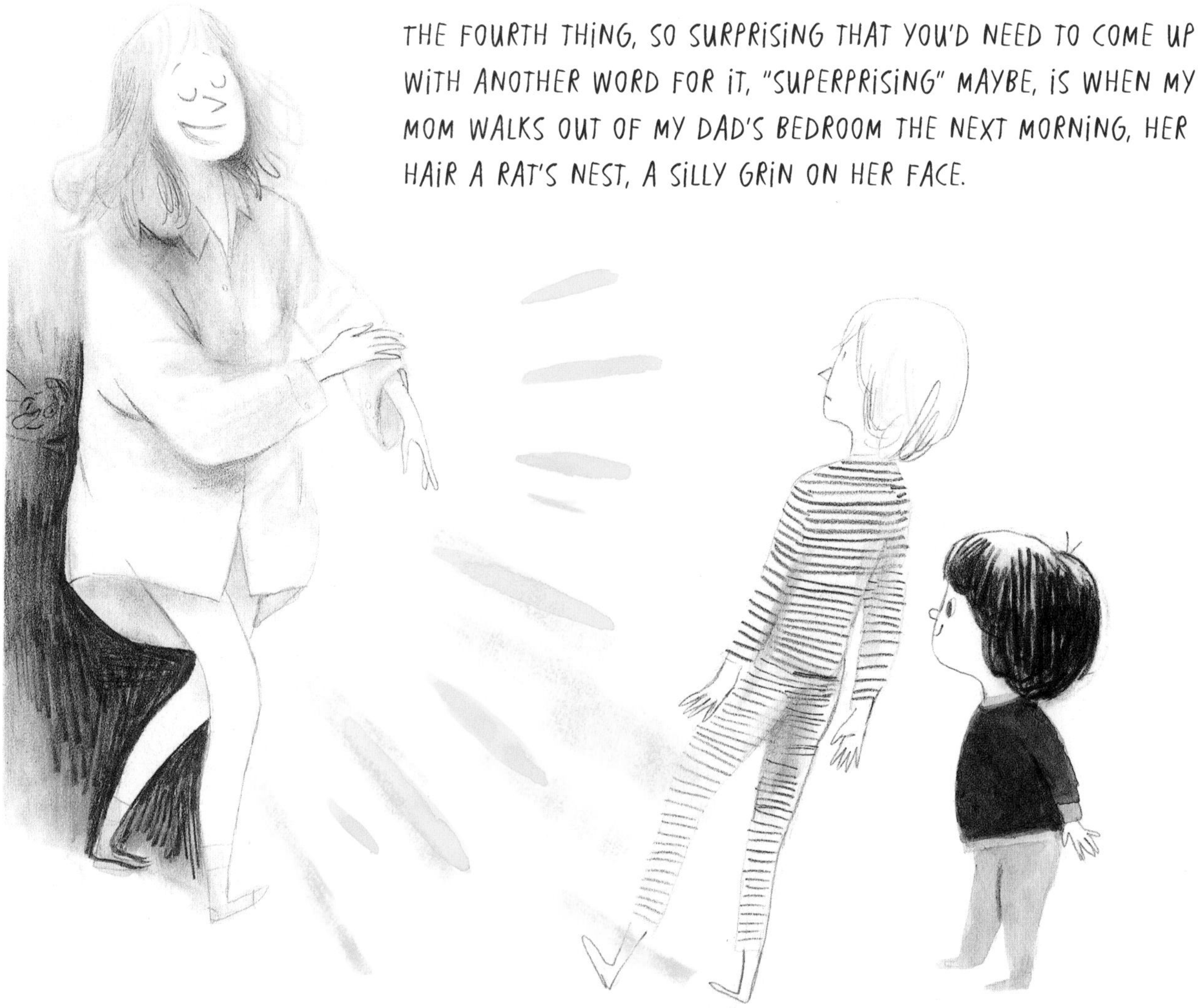

THEY DON'T EVEN WAIT FOR BREAKFAST TO BE OVER. TRUFFLE STILL HAS A MOUTHFUL OF CEREAL WHEN MY DAD TELLS US TO PACK OUR BAGS. ALL FOUR OF US ARE OFF TO NEW YORK.

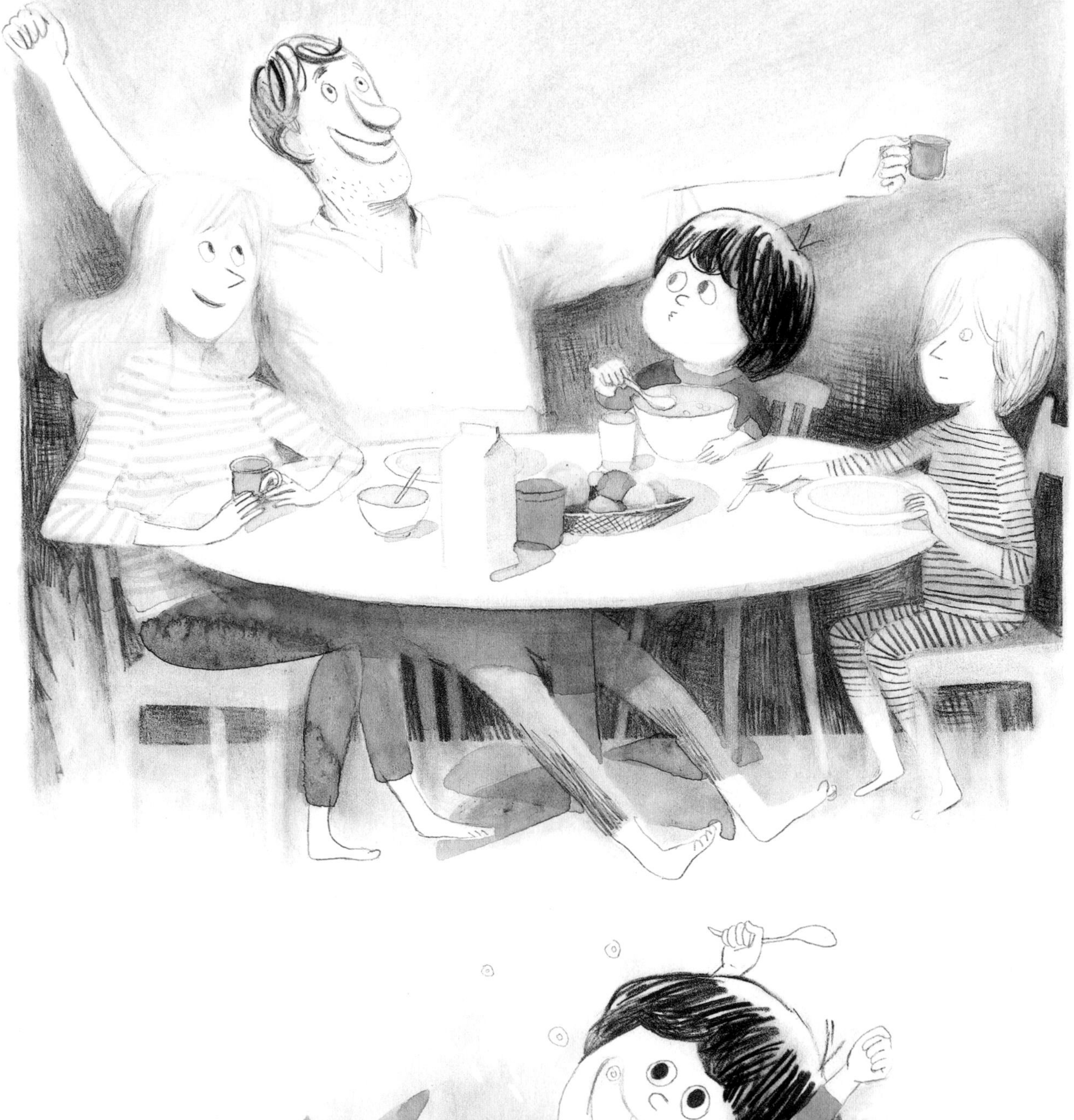

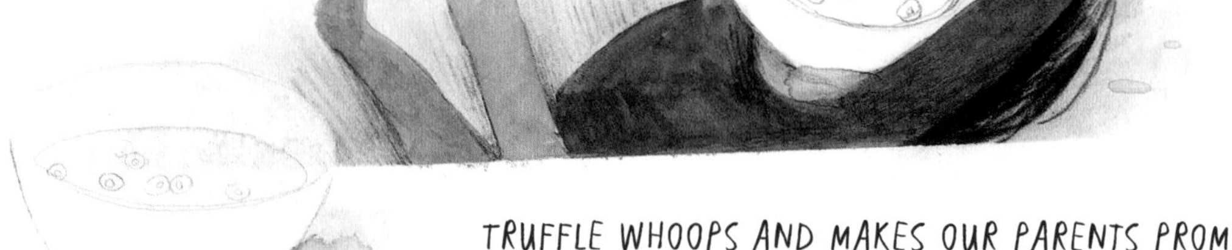

TRUFFLE WHOOPS AND MAKES OUR PARENTS PROMISE TO TAKE HIM TO THE APOLLO THEATER TO SEE THE PICTURES OF JAMES BROWN.

I CAN BARELY HEAR
MY MOM, WHOSE VOICE
TAPERS OFF WHENEVER
SHE'S GOT SOMETHING
TO HIDE,

*What would you like to visit, Louis?*

I PASTE ON MY BEST SMILE, THE
ONE I USE THE WAY SHE USES
HER SHRUNKEN VOICE,

*Whatever you guys want.*

I STOCKPILE APPLES AND
FISH FOR MICHAEL JACKSON,
WHO'S BEEN FOLLOWING THE
CONVERSATION FROM THE
WINDOWSILL.

WHEN I SHOW HIM HIS MEALS FOR THE NEXT FEW DAYS
AND CAUTION HIM NOT TO EAT EVERYTHING AT ONCE,

HE LOOKS AT ME WITH SOMETHING SO
LIKE A SMILE THAT I ALMOST EXPECT HIM
TO ANSWER BACK.

Be brave, my raccoon,
be brave. I'll be back
before you know it.

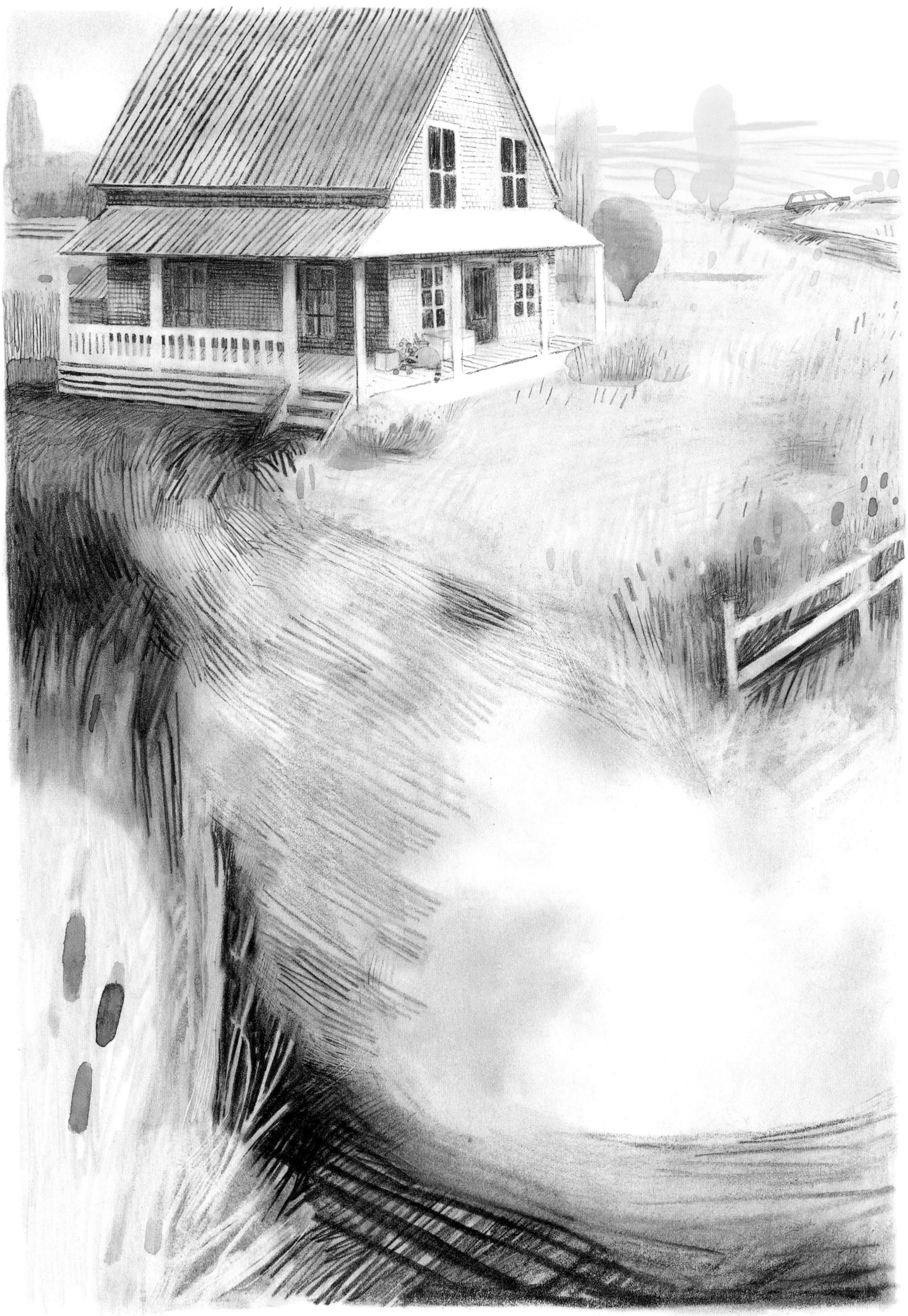

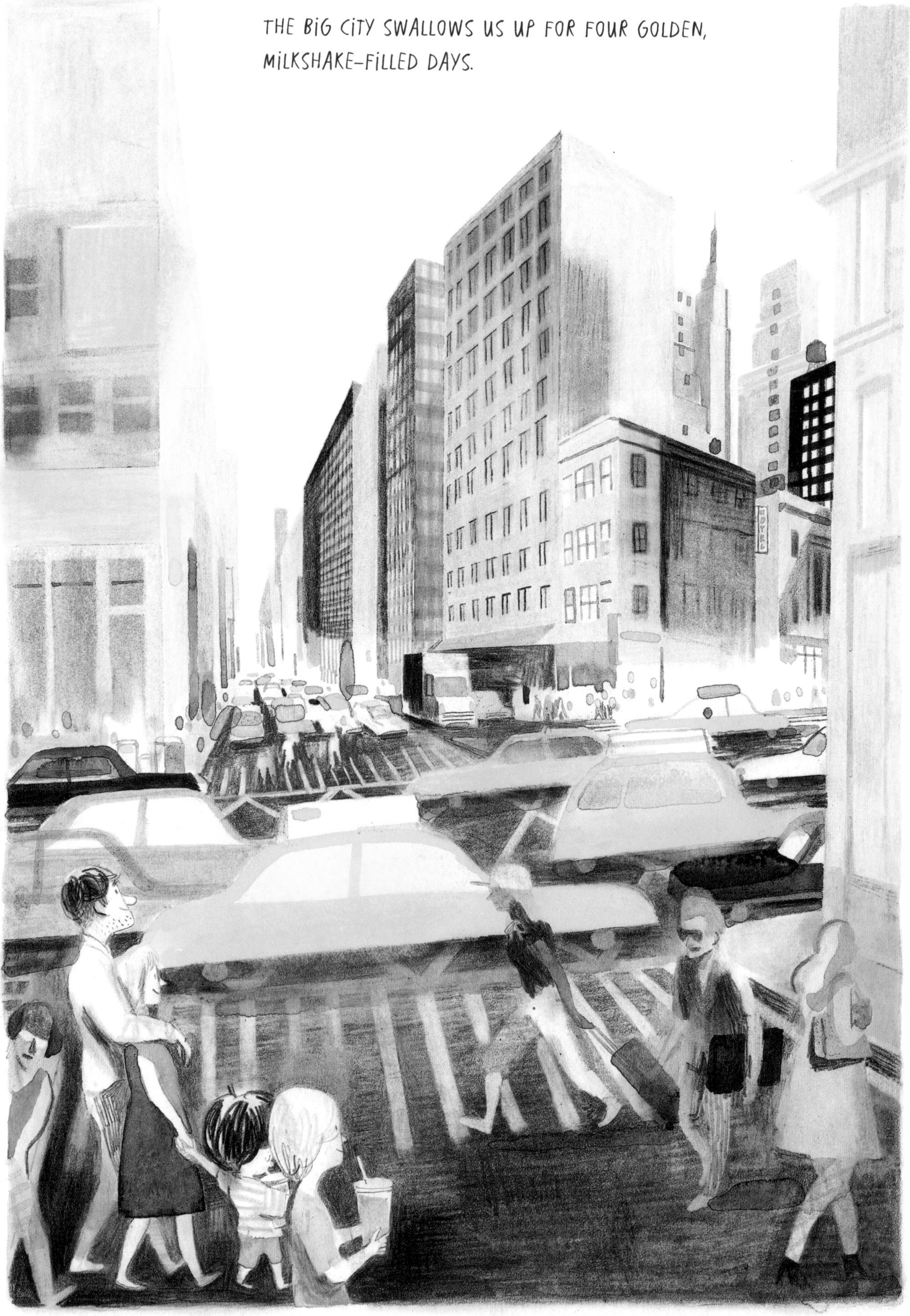
THE BIG CITY SWALLOWS US UP FOR FOUR GOLDEN, MILKSHAKE-FILLED DAYS.

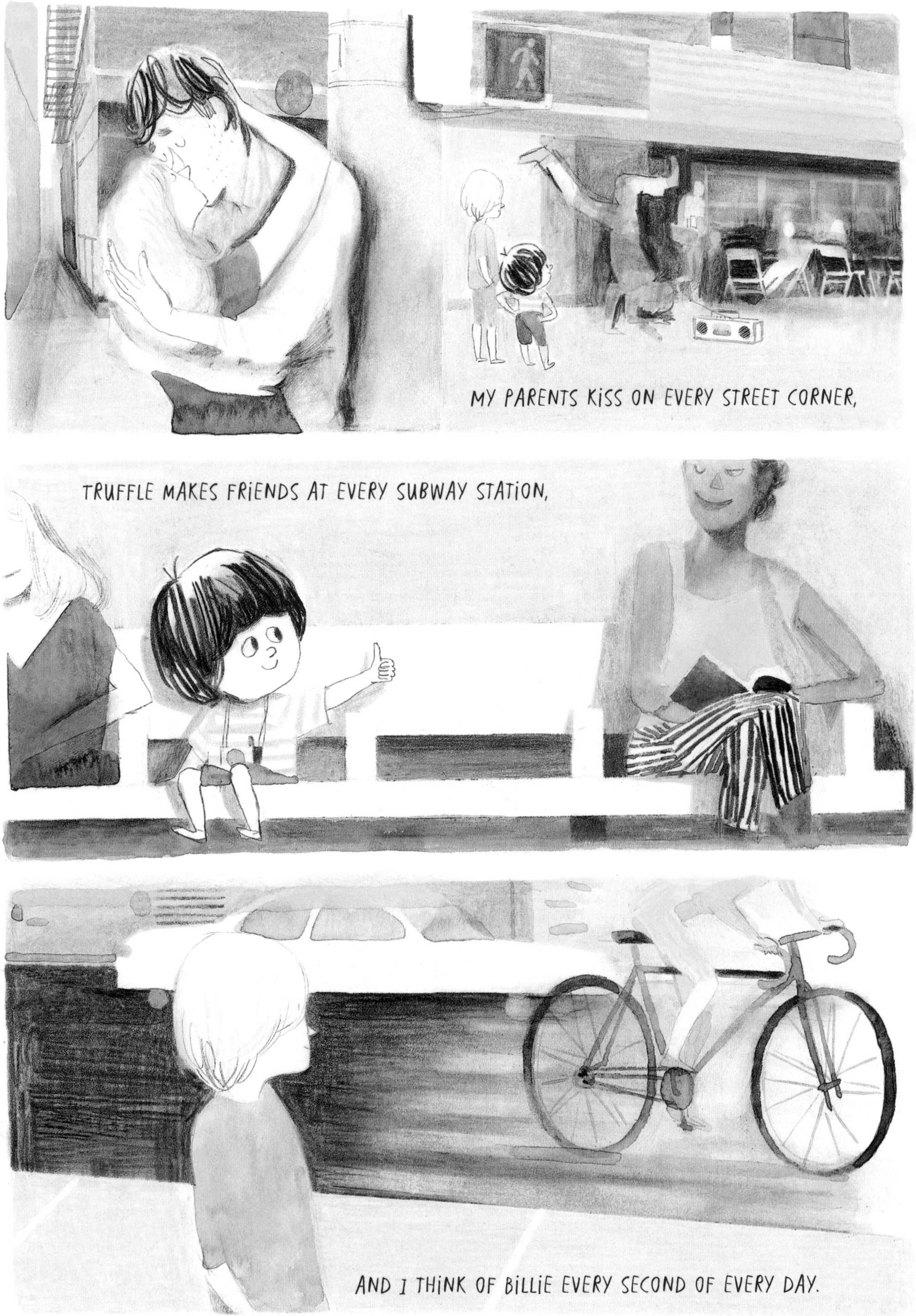
MY PARENTS KISS ON EVERY STREET CORNER,
TRUFFLE MAKES FRIENDS AT EVERY SUBWAY STATION,
AND I THINK OF BILLIE EVERY SECOND OF EVERY DAY.

I IMAGINE BEING HERE WITH HER, CROSSING THE SPANGLED STREETS, LOOKING THROUGH STORE DISPLAYS FOR RECORDS.

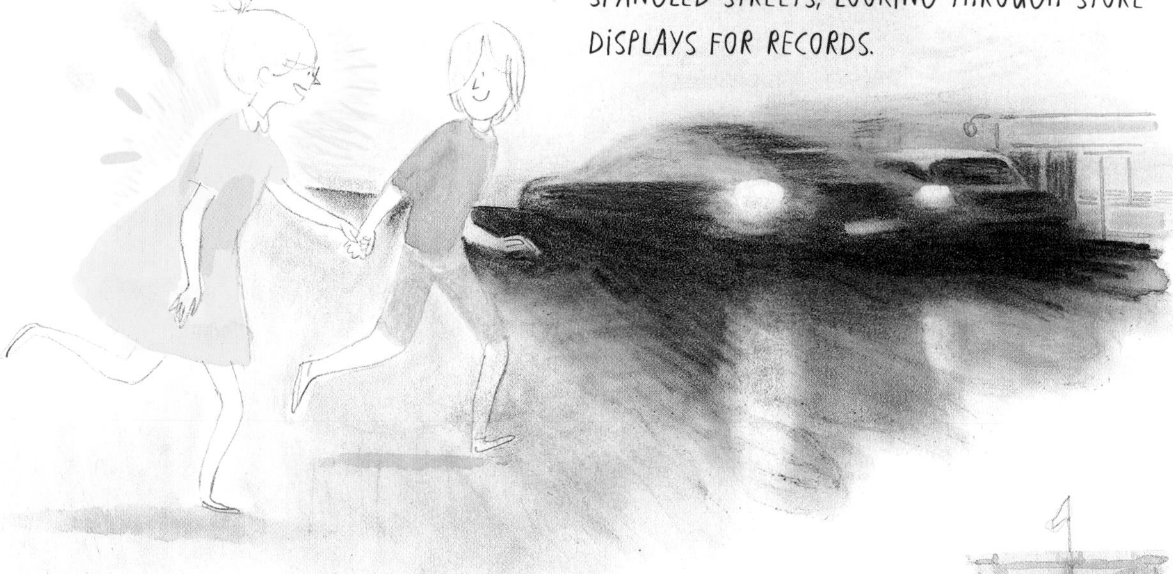

I SEE US ON THE BROOKLYN BRIDGE AND UNDER THE FLASHING LIGHTS OF CONEY ISLAND.

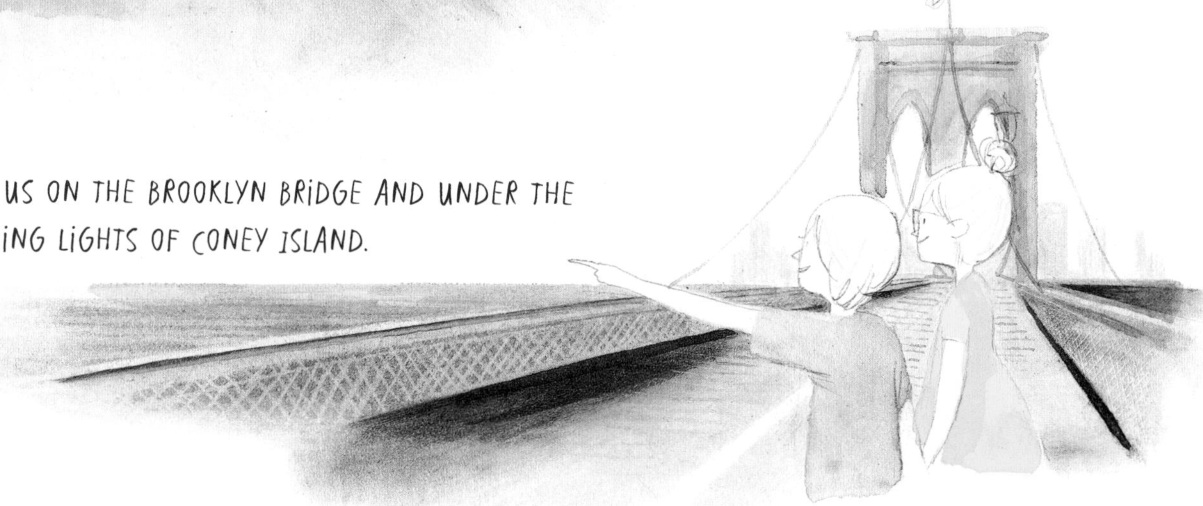

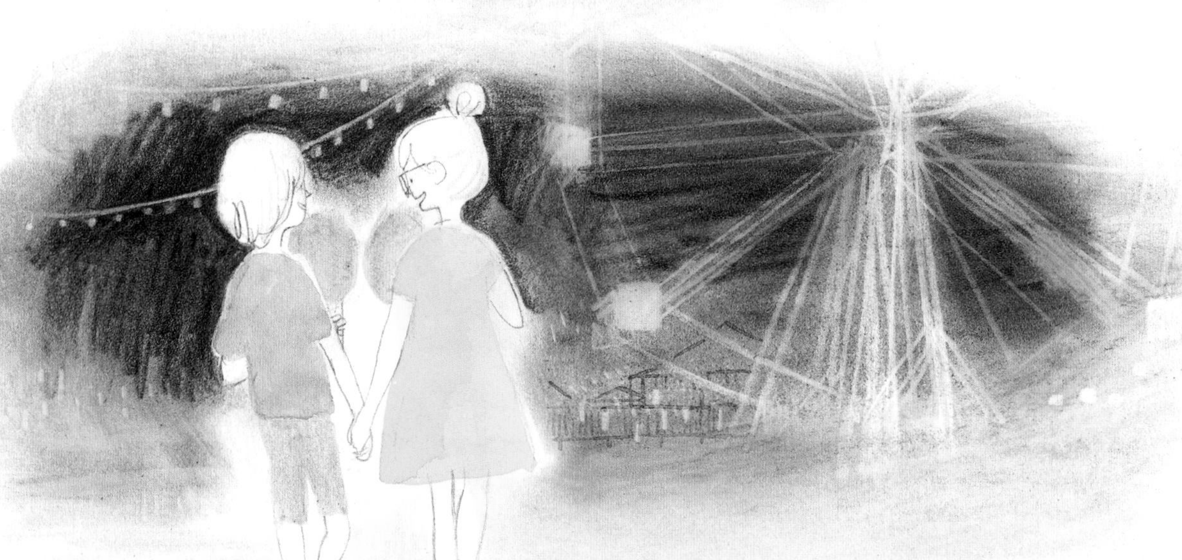

I HOLD HER HAND WHEREVER WE GO, AND I'M AS COURAGEOUS AS CAN BE.

MY DAD'S FEELING COURAGEOUS, TOO.

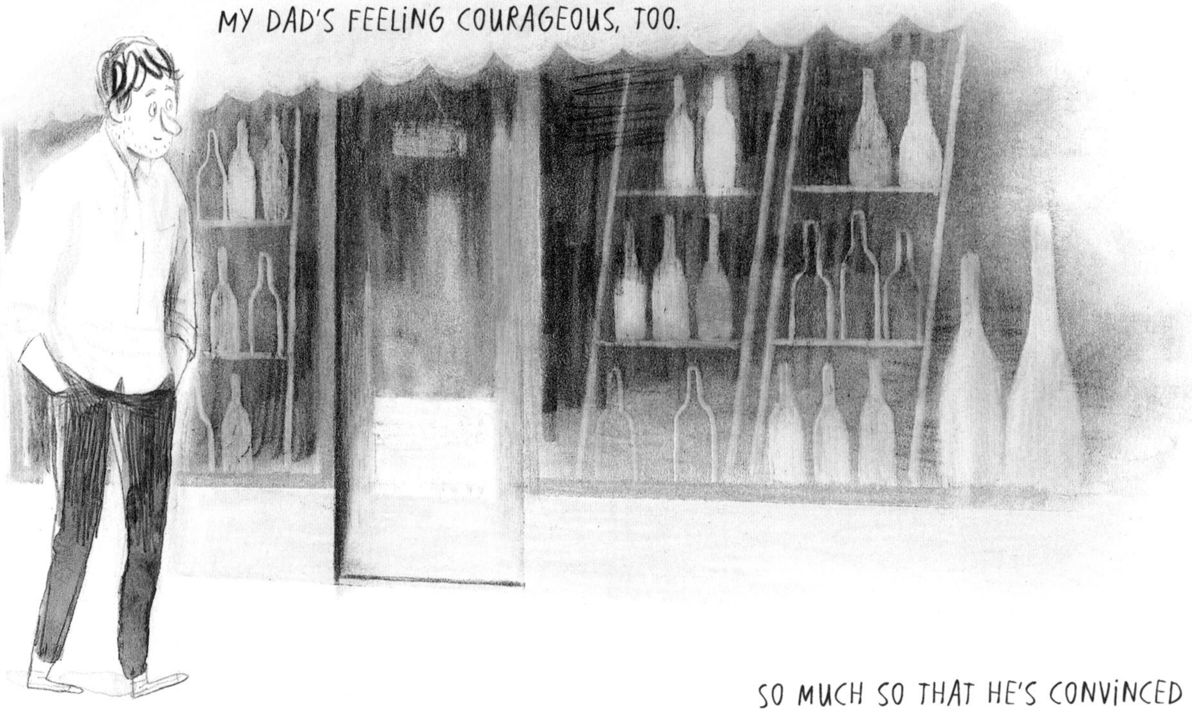

SO MUCH SO THAT HE'S CONVINCED THAT ONE LITTLE GLASS OF WINE WITH DINNER WON'T HURT A SOUL.

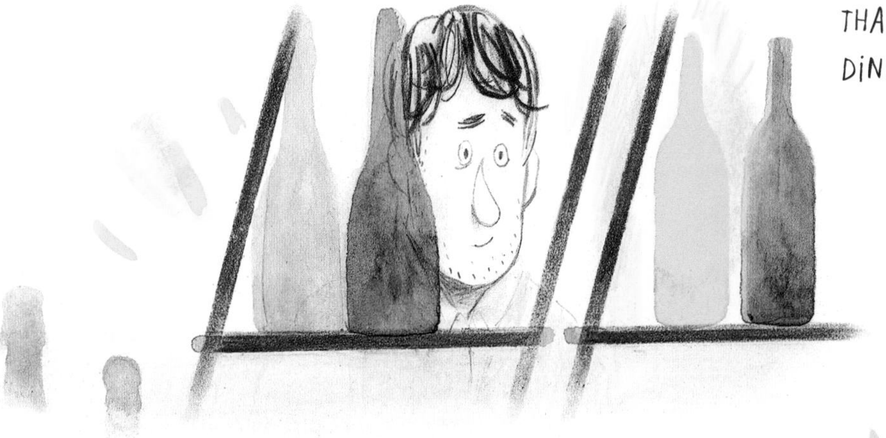

IT'S SUCH A BEAUTIFUL SUMMER EVENING IN THE PARK, AND MY MOM WILL SOON JOIN US WITH TRUFFLE AND FRIES AND SMOKED MEAT. SHE'LL BE GLAD TO HAVE A GLASS, TOO.

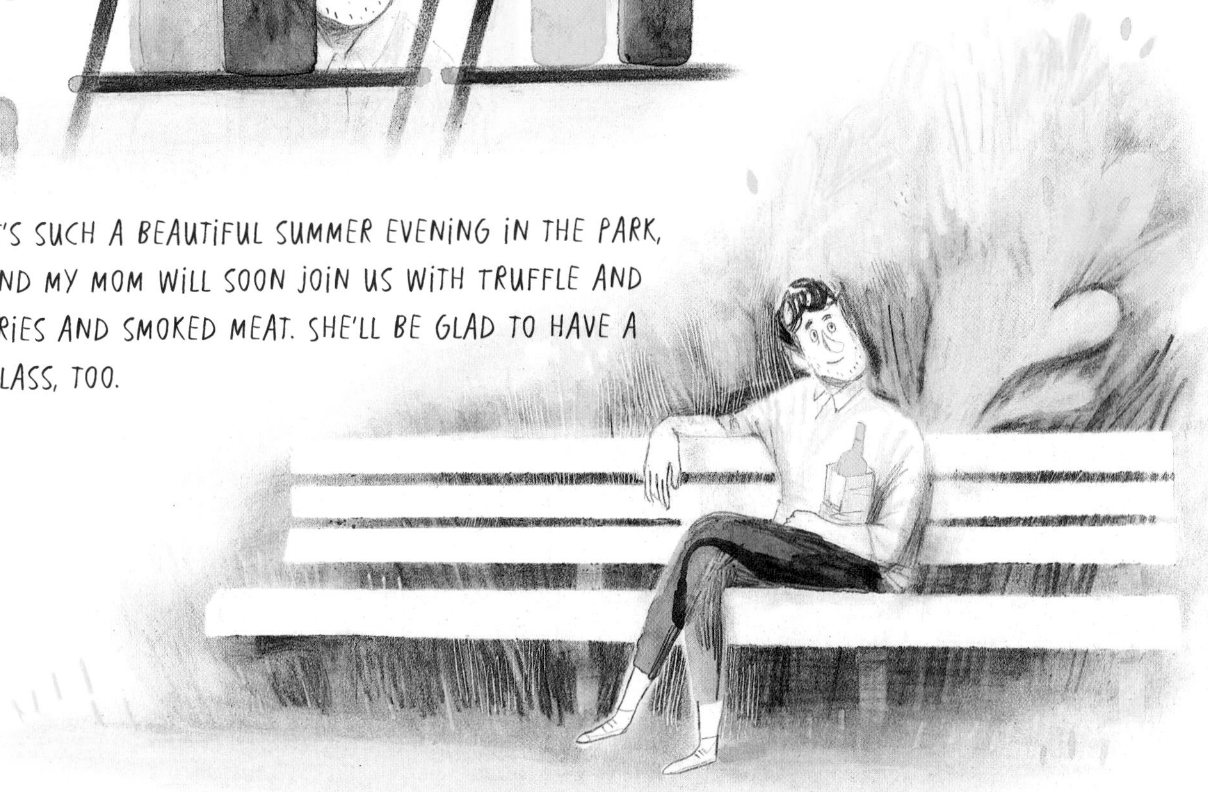

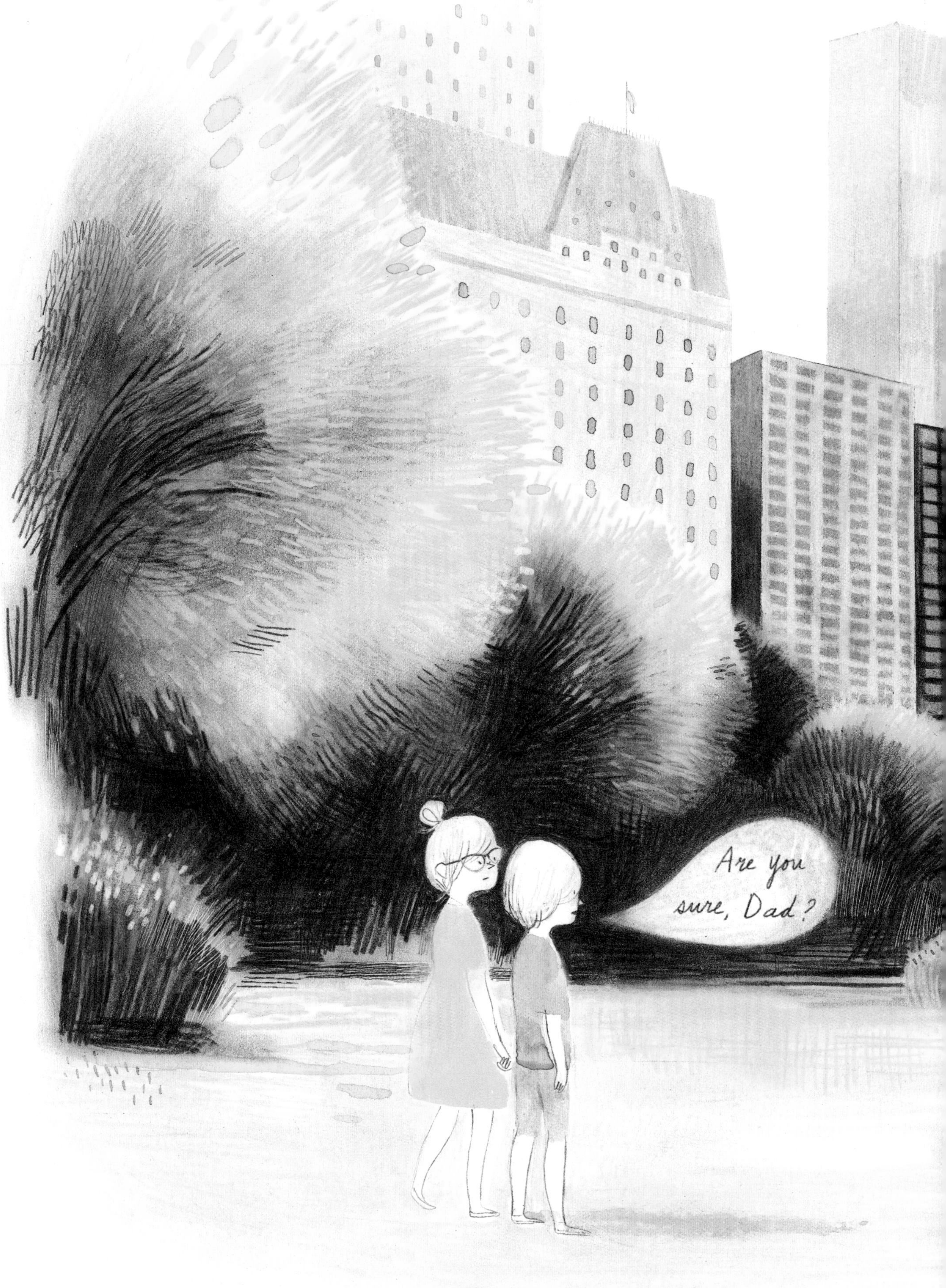
Are you sure, Dad?

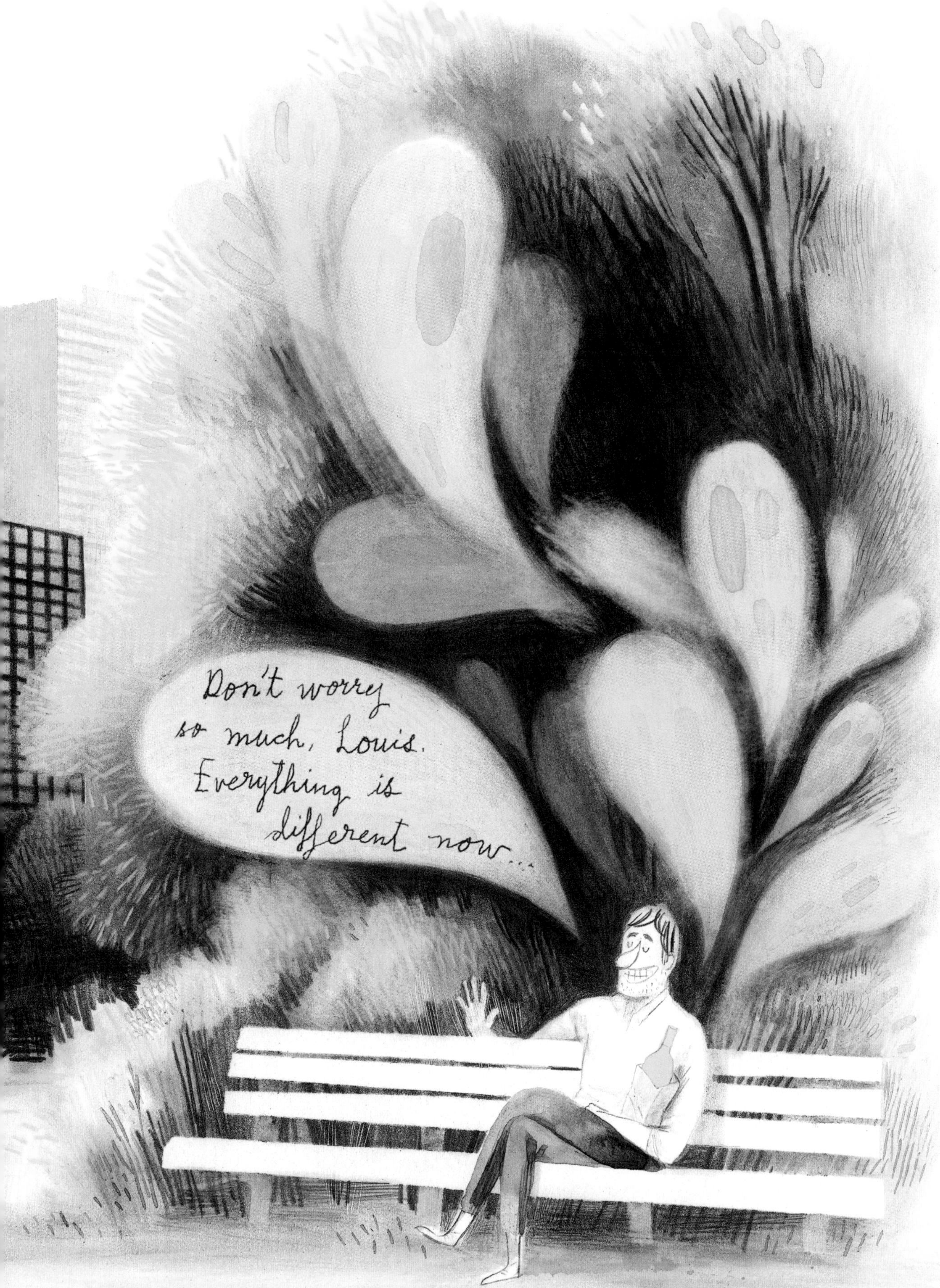
Don't worry so much, Louis. Everything is different now...

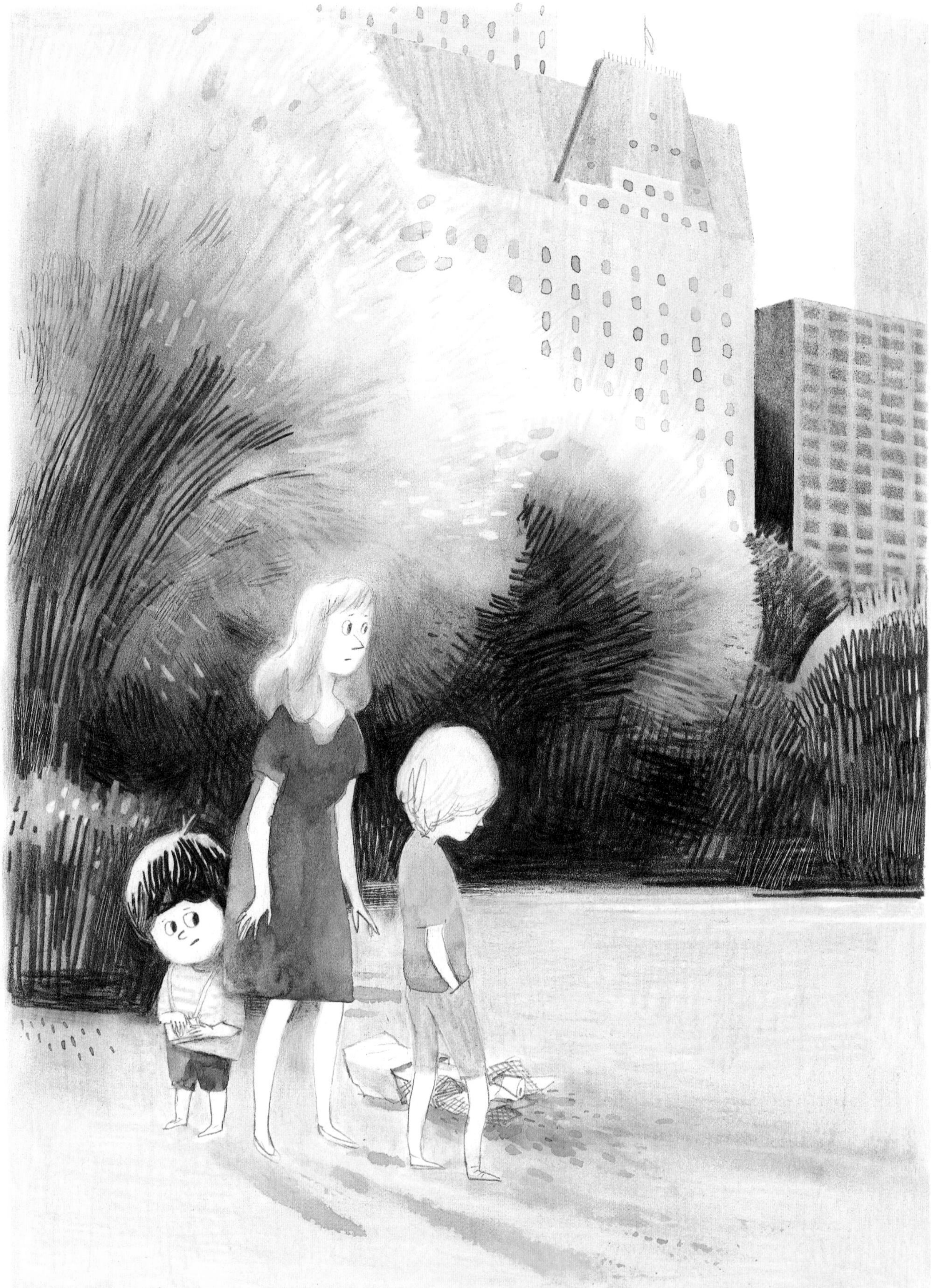

END OF THE ROAD

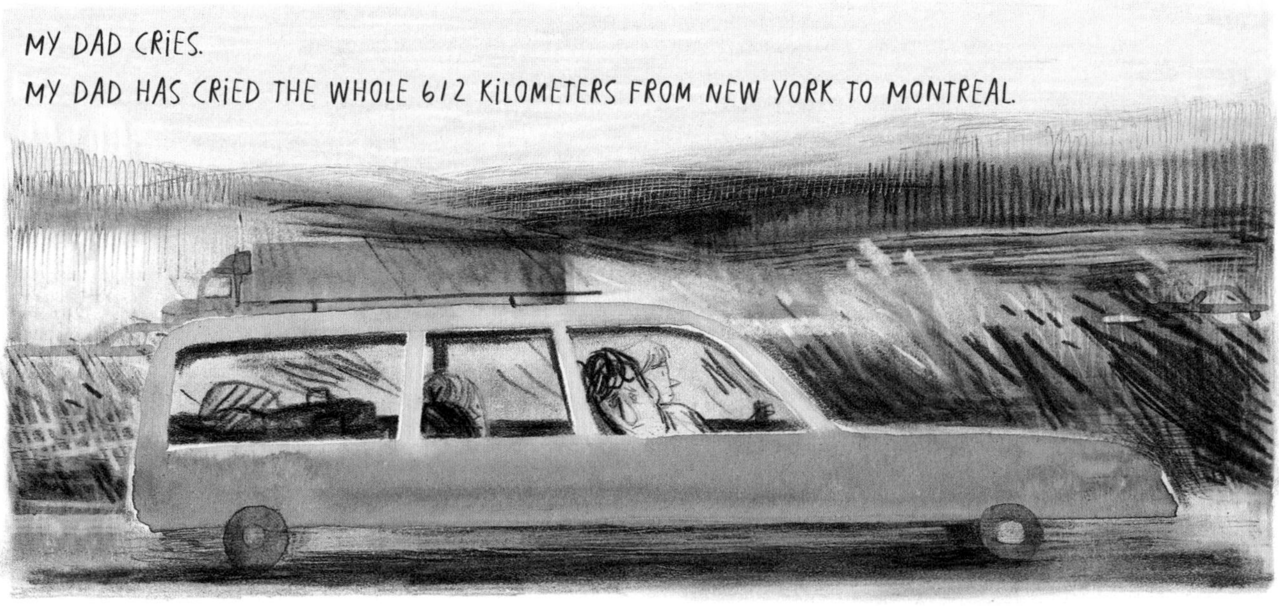
MY DAD CRIES.
MY DAD HAS CRIED THE WHOLE 612 KILOMETERS FROM NEW YORK TO MONTREAL.

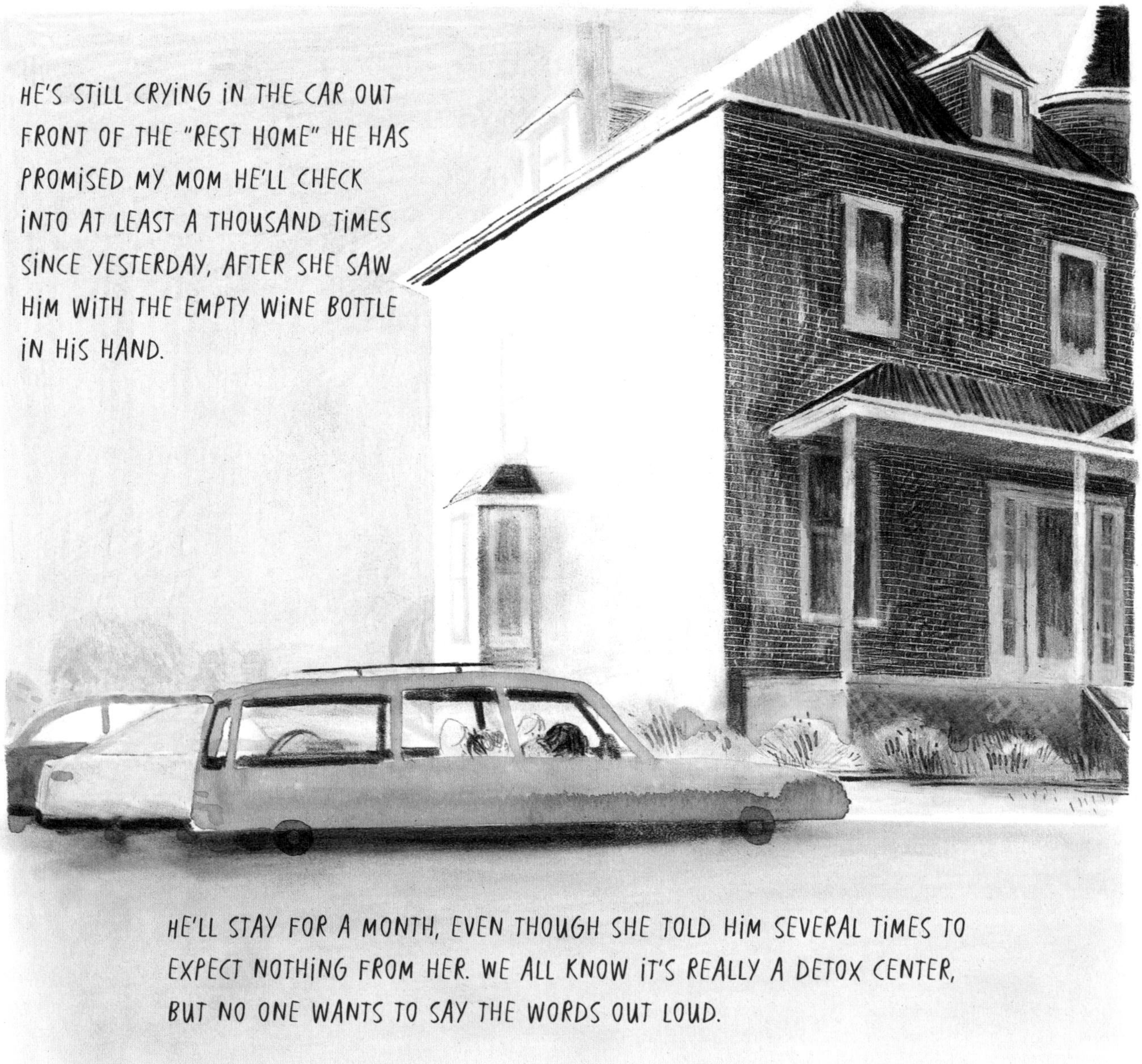
HE'S STILL CRYING IN THE CAR OUT FRONT OF THE "REST HOME" HE HAS PROMISED MY MOM HE'LL CHECK INTO AT LEAST A THOUSAND TIMES SINCE YESTERDAY, AFTER SHE SAW HIM WITH THE EMPTY WINE BOTTLE IN HIS HAND.
HE'LL STAY FOR A MONTH, EVEN THOUGH SHE TOLD HIM SEVERAL TIMES TO EXPECT NOTHING FROM HER. WE ALL KNOW IT'S REALLY A DETOX CENTER, BUT NO ONE WANTS TO SAY THE WORDS OUT LOUD.

MY DAD CRIES MOST OF ALL WHEN WE SAY GOOD-BYE, AND EVEN THOUGH HE SAYS HE ISN'T SCARED, THAT EVERYTHING WILL BE OKAY, IT'S CLEAR THE OPPOSITE IS TRUE, THAT HE'S SCARED AND THAT NOTHING WILL BE OKAY. HE CAN'T HAVE ANY VISITORS — THEY'RE SUPPOSED TO BE BAD FOR TREATMENT.

AND YET,
HE STEPS INSIDE,
TURNING ONE LAST TIME TO TRUFFLE AND ME.

WHAT I SEE IN HIS EYES RIGHT THEN,

SOMETHING LIKE AN EARTHQUAKE OR A DROWNING,

MAKES ME THINK THAT I MIGHT HAVE TO BE LIKE HIM AND DRINK ALL KINDS OF WINE TO FORGET.

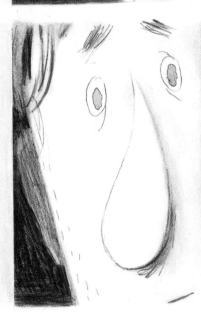

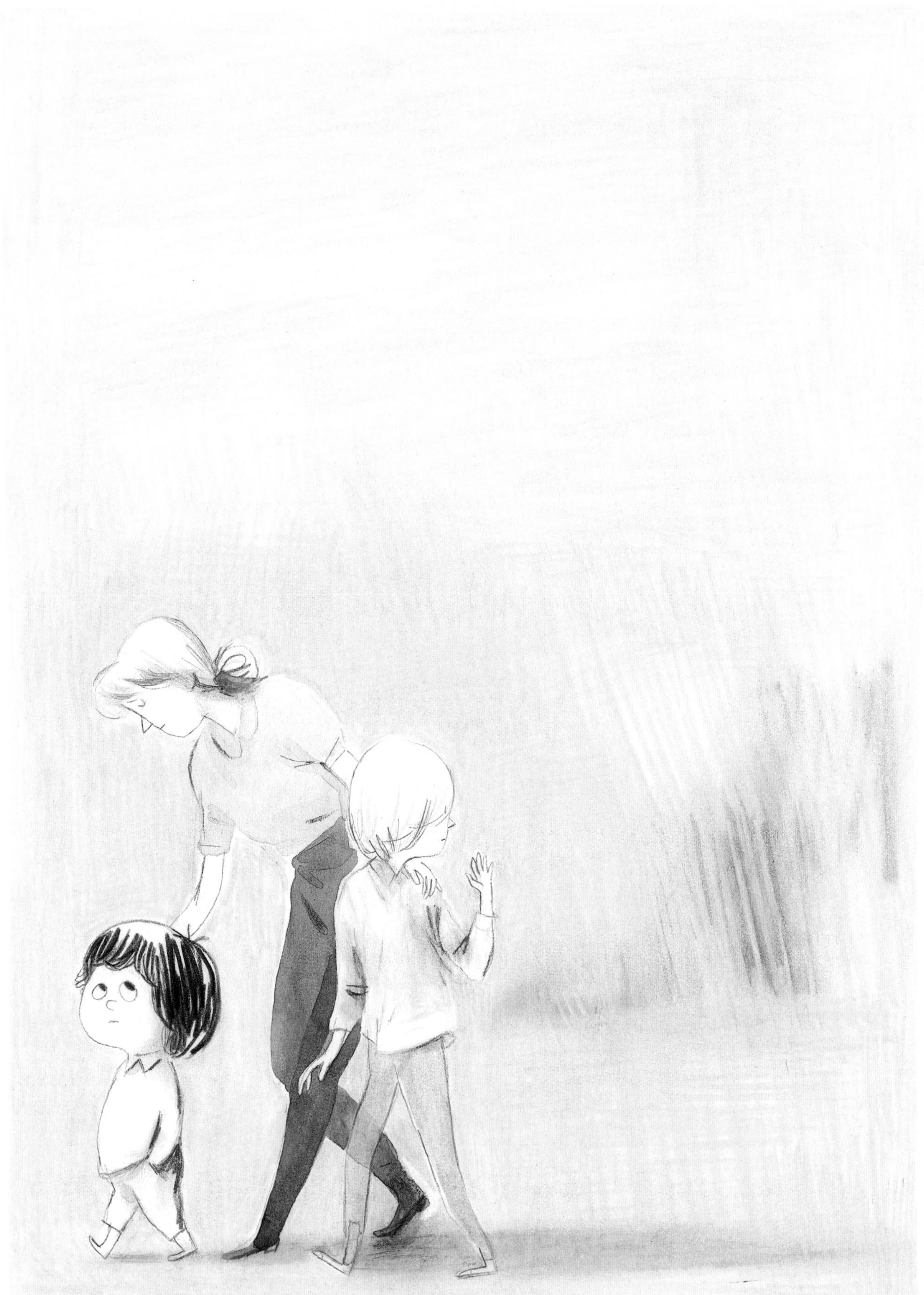

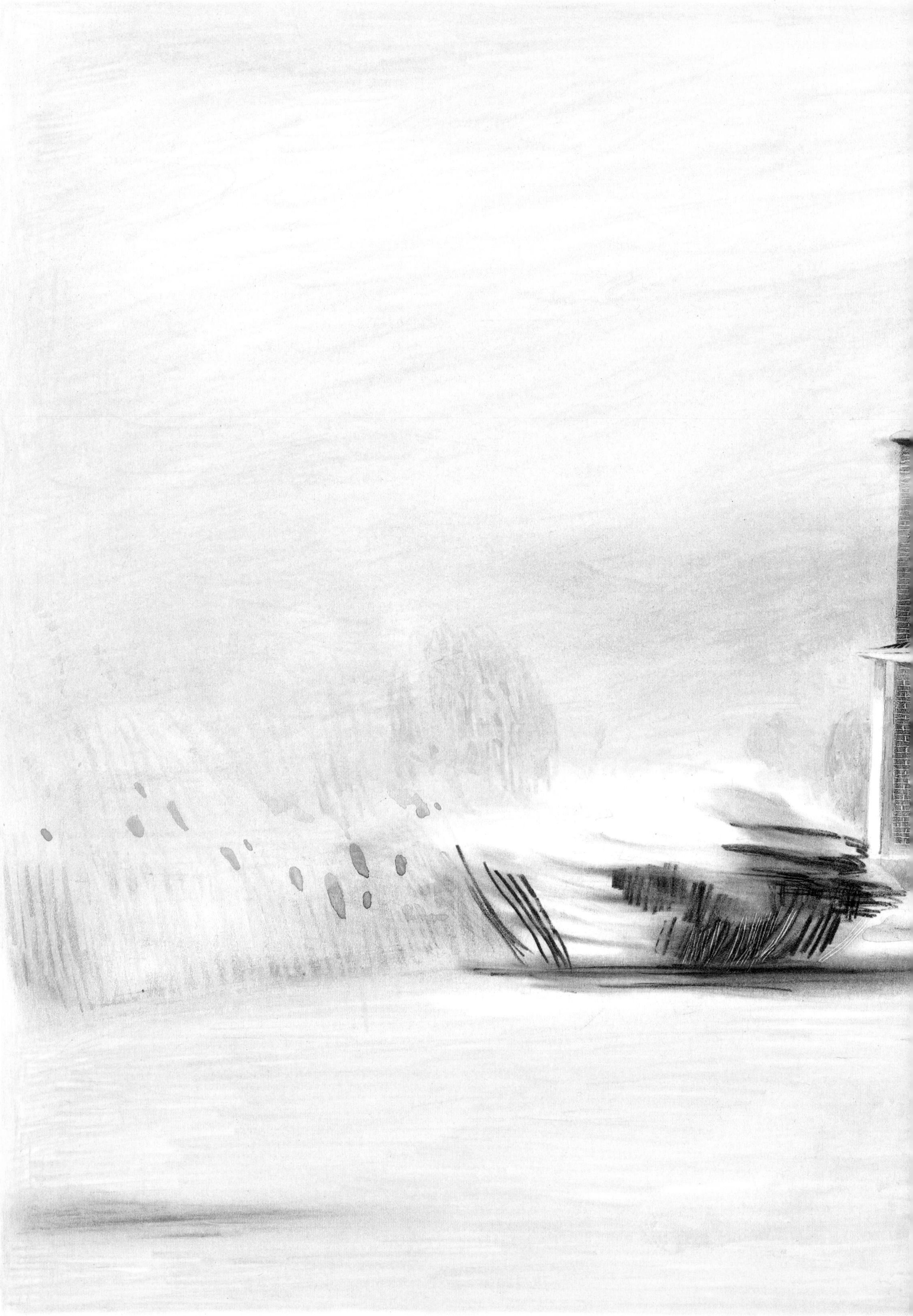

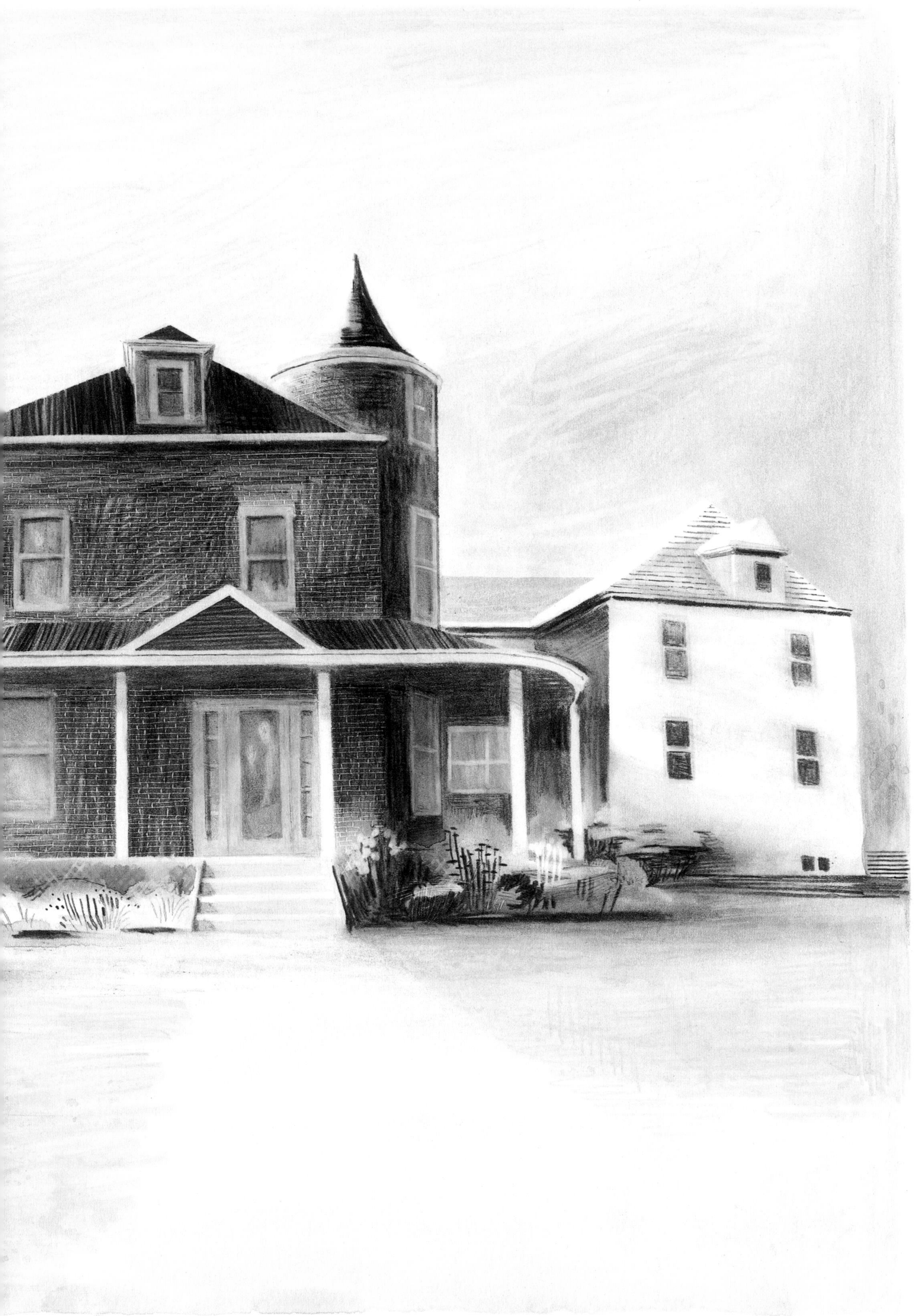

BACK HOME, BORIS DOESN'T ASK ANY
QUESTIONS.

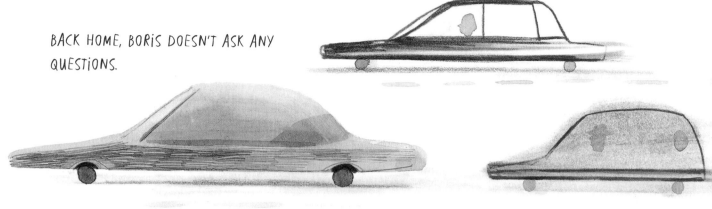

ABOUT NEW YORK OR ANYTHING ELSE.

HE DOESN'T EVEN ASK ME FOR NEWS
OF MICHAEL JACKSON —

LIKE ME, HE KNOWS THE RACCOON RETURNED
TO THE FOREST FAR FROM HUMAN BEINGS A
LONG TIME AGO, AND RIGHTLY SO.

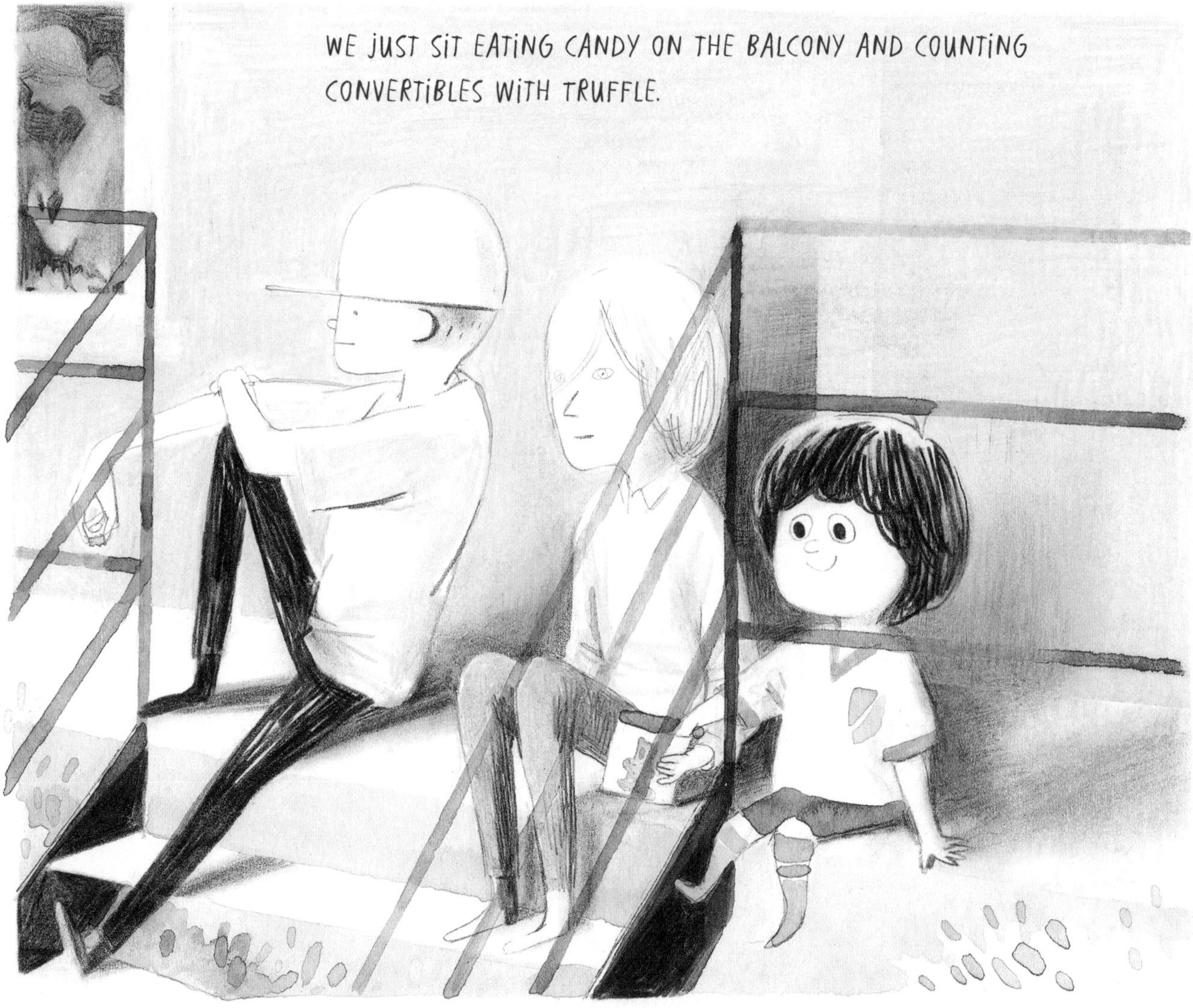
WE JUST SIT EATING CANDY ON THE BALCONY AND COUNTING CONVERTIBLES WITH TRUFFLE.

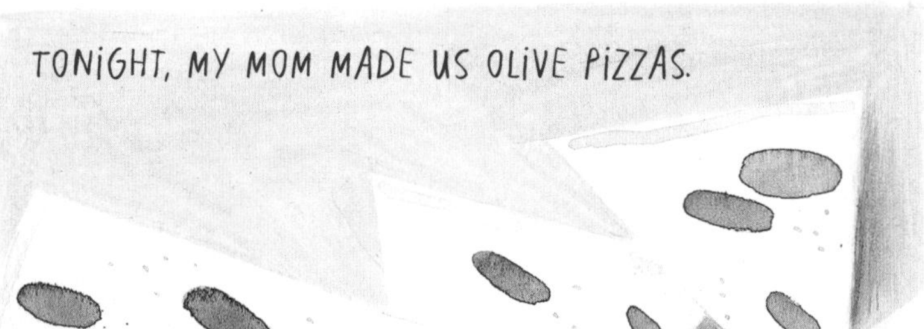
TONIGHT, MY MOM MADE US OLIVE PIZZAS.

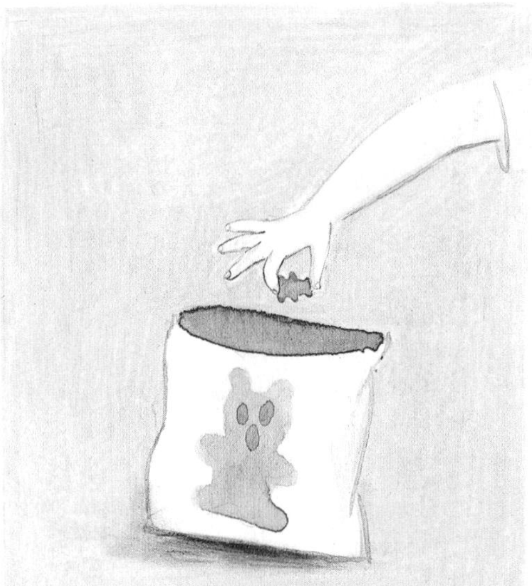
SINCE MY DAD ENTERED TREATMENT, IT'S LIKE WE'VE BEEN LIVING IN A CHINA SHOP. DON'T TOUCH ANYTHING, DON'T BREAK ANYTHING.

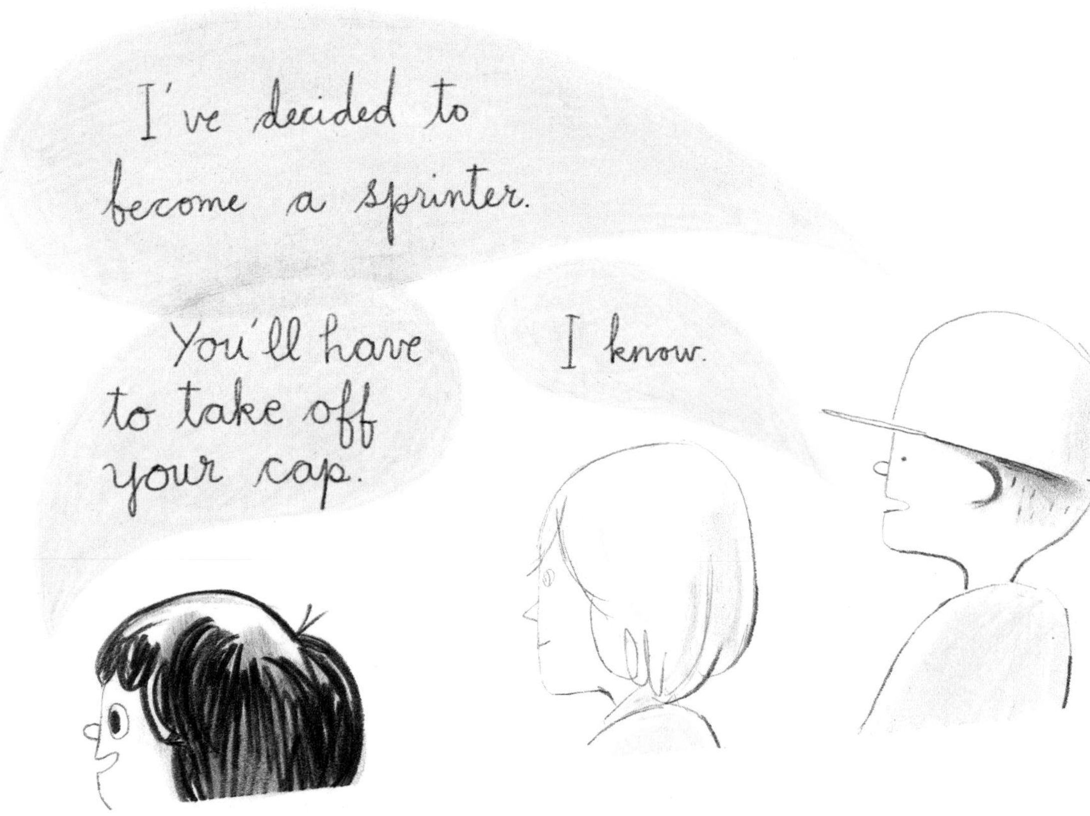
I've decided to become a sprinter.
You'll have to take off your cap.
I know.

BORIS ONLY TAKES OFF HIS BASEBALL CAP WHEN ABSOLUTELY NECESSARY.
HE MUST REALLY LOVE TO RUN.

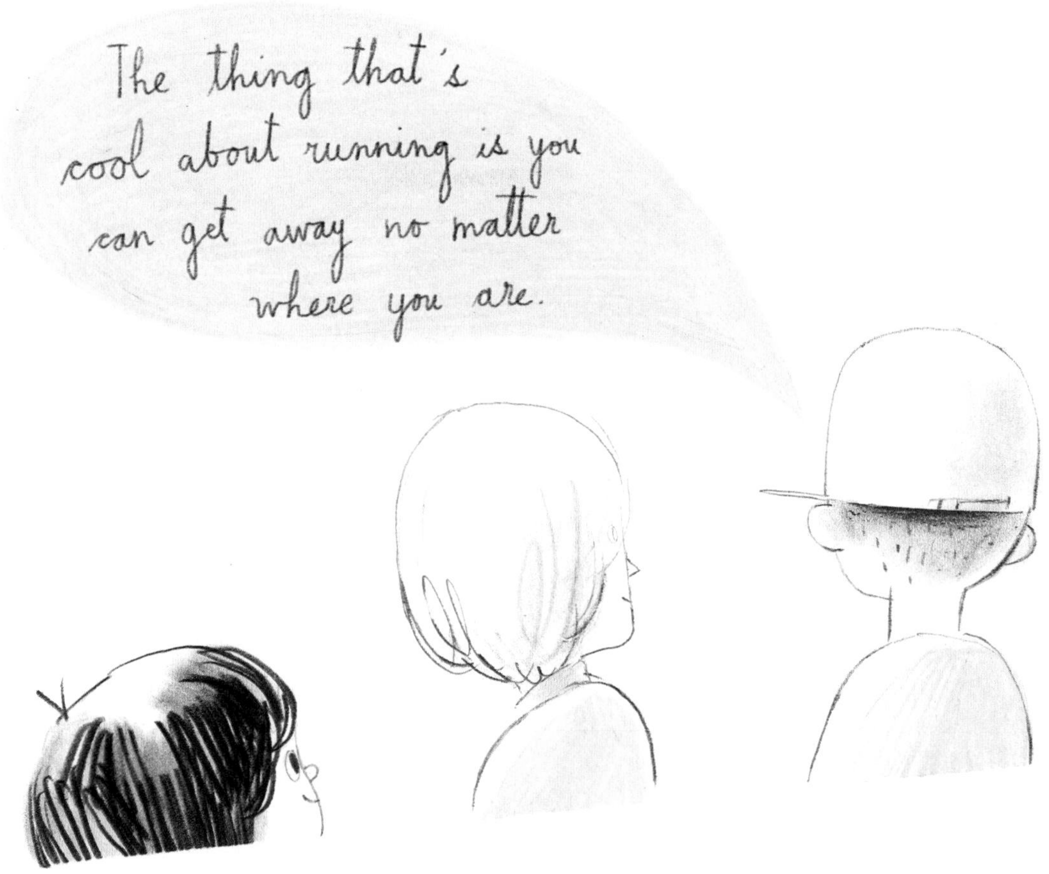
The thing that's cool about running is you can get away no matter where you are.

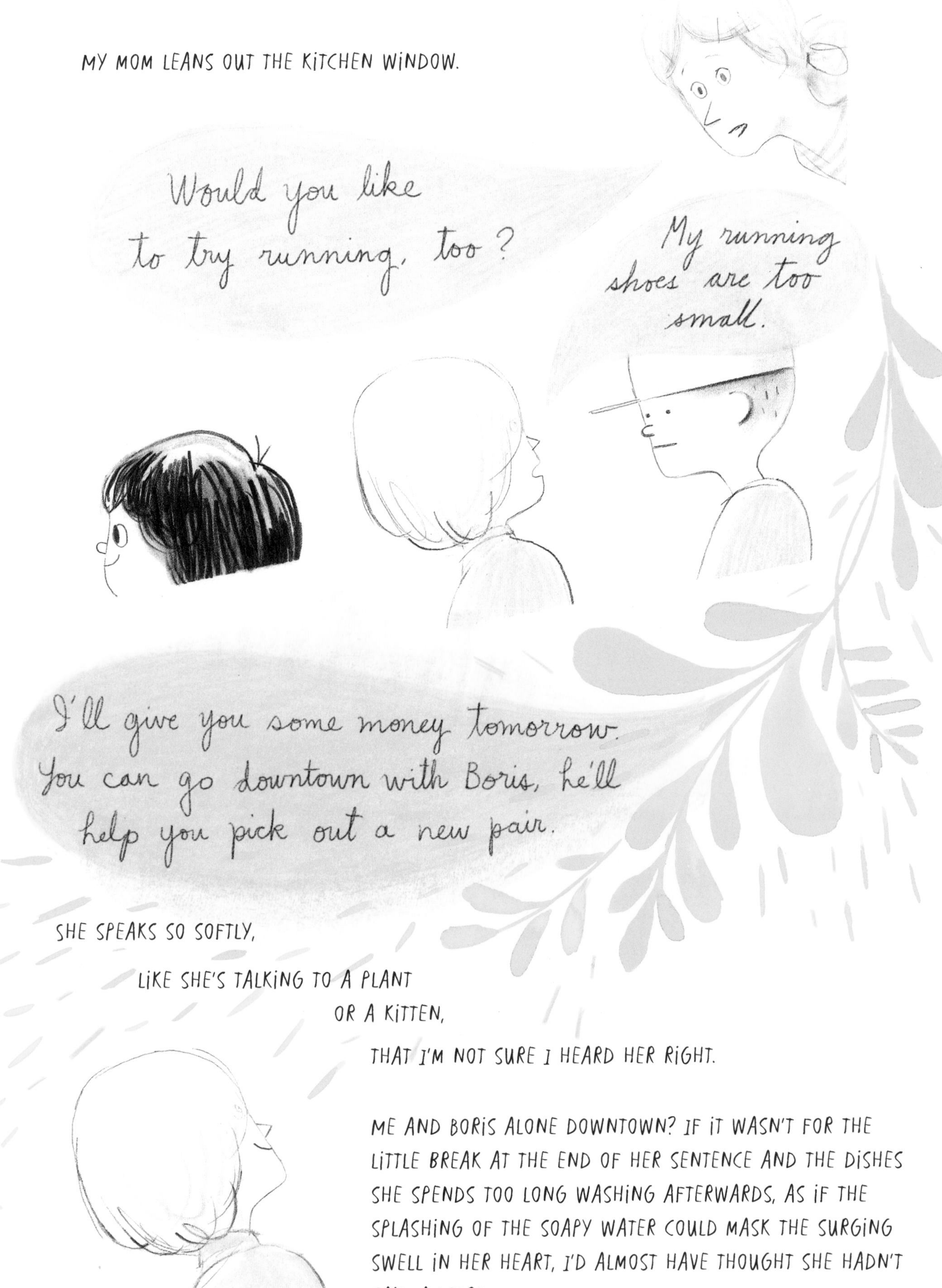
MY MOM LEANS OUT THE KITCHEN WINDOW.
Would you like to try running, too?
My running shoes are too small.
I'll give you some money tomorrow. You can go downtown with Boris, he'll help you pick out a new pair.
SHE SPEAKS SO SOFTLY,
LIKE SHE'S TALKING TO A PLANT
OR A KITTEN,
THAT I'M NOT SURE I HEARD HER RIGHT.
ME AND BORIS ALONE DOWNTOWN? IF IT WASN'T FOR THE LITTLE BREAK AT THE END OF HER SENTENCE AND THE DISHES SHE SPENDS TOO LONG WASHING AFTERWARDS, AS IF THE SPLASHING OF THE SOAPY WATER COULD MASK THE SURGING SWELL IN HER HEART, I'D ALMOST HAVE THOUGHT SHE HADN'T SAID A WORD.

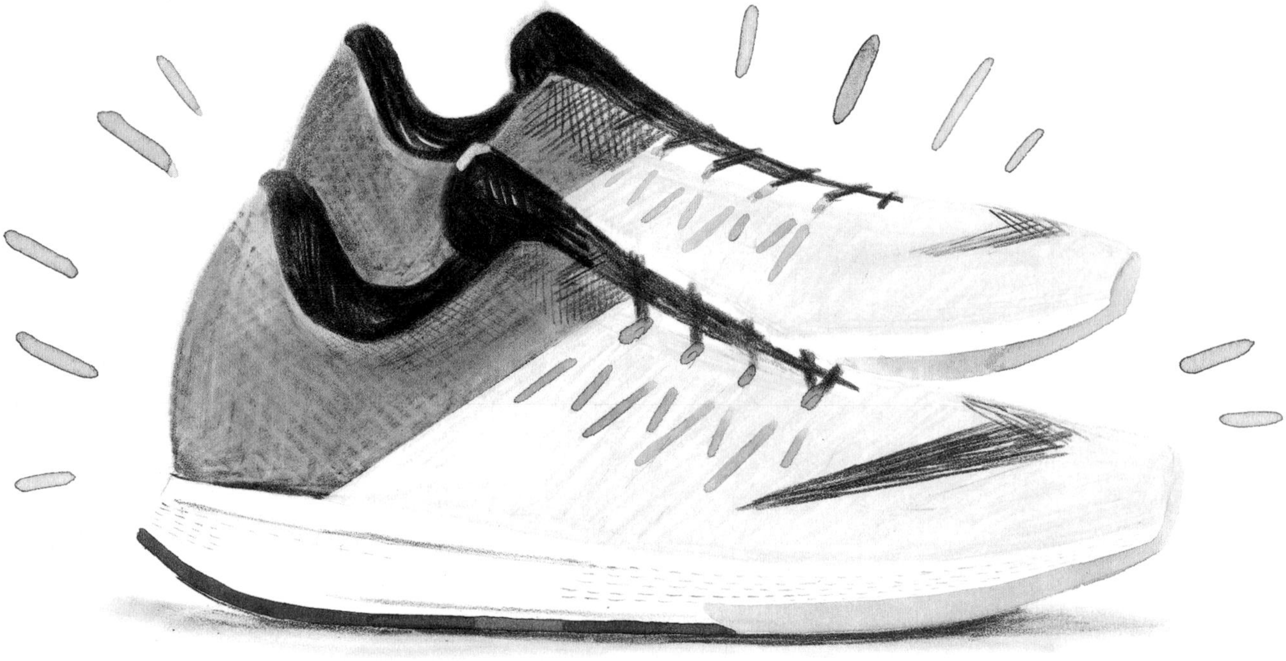

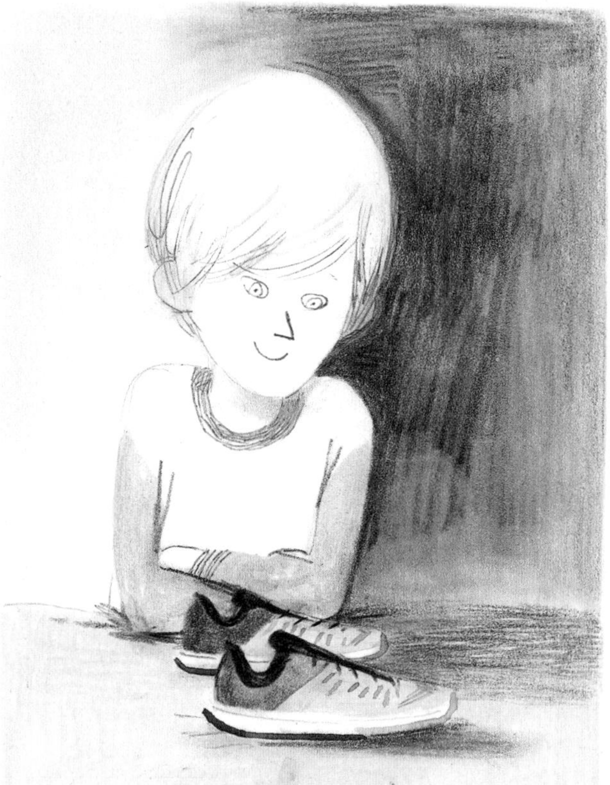

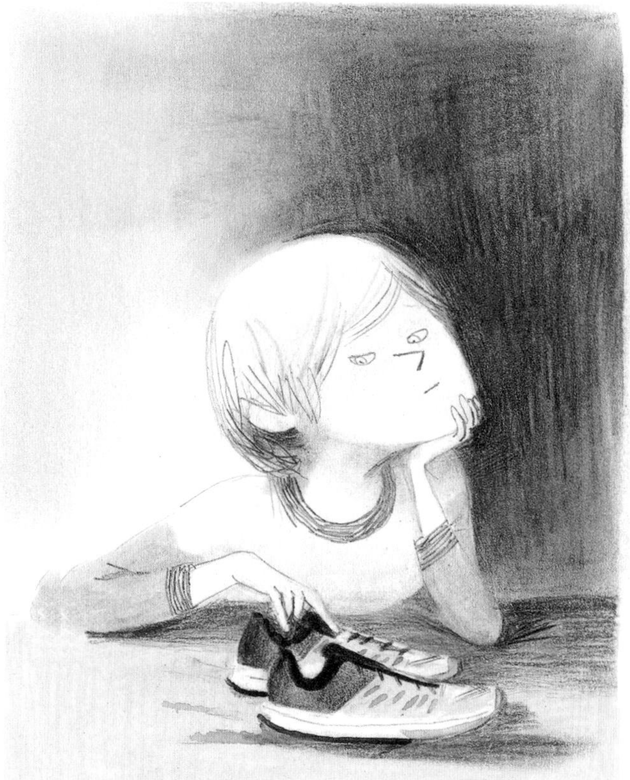

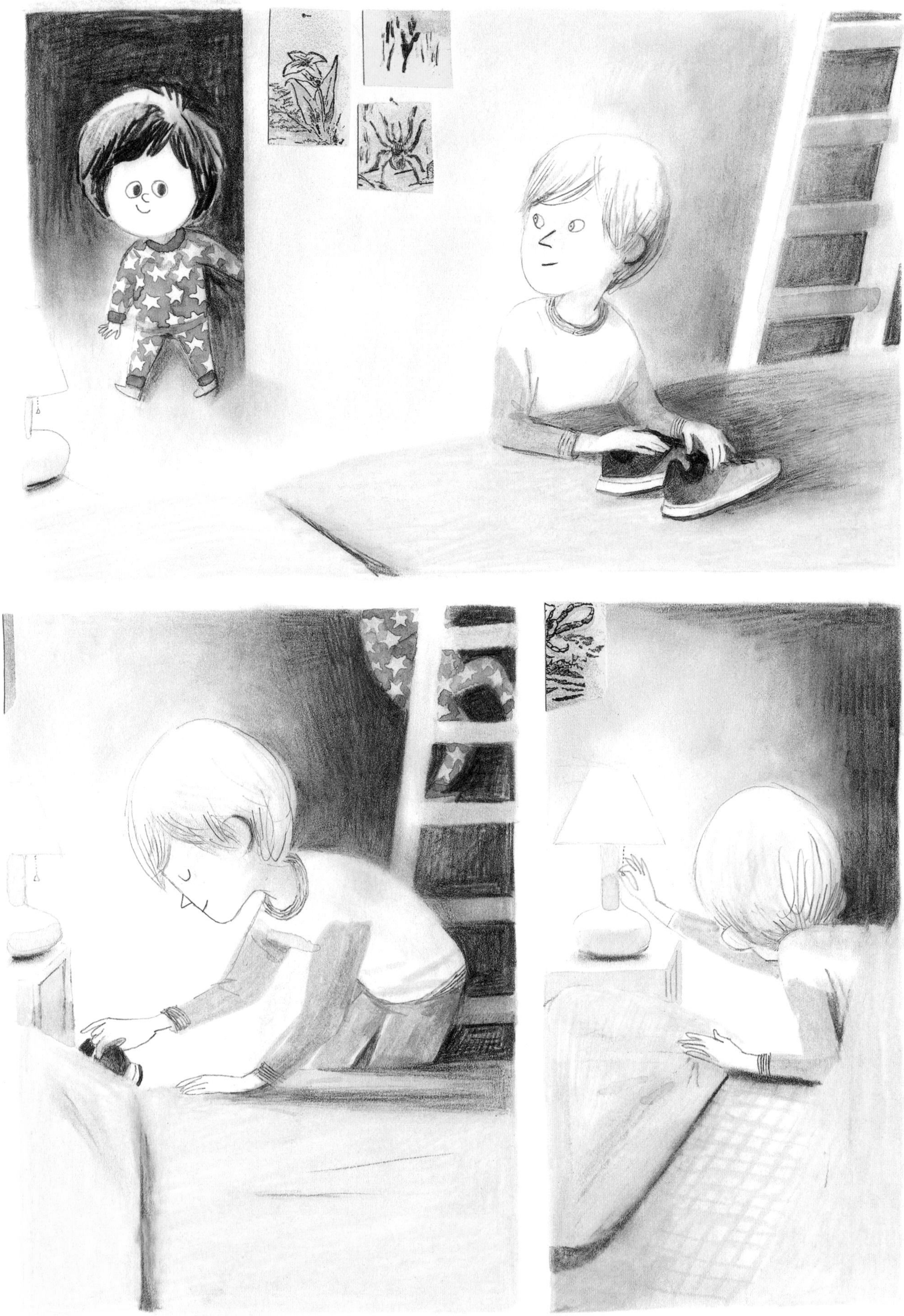

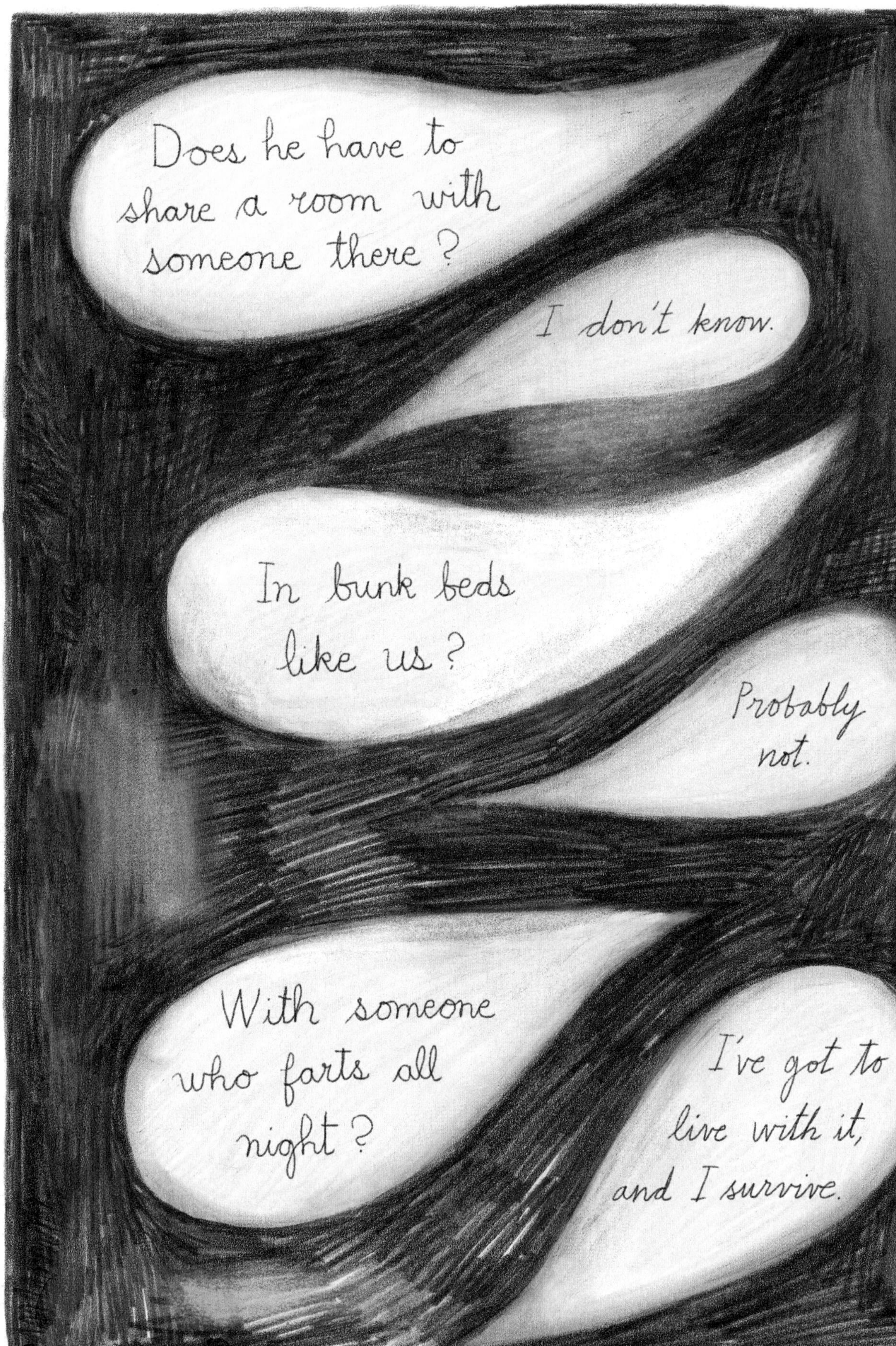
Does he have to share a room with someone there?
I don't know.
In bunk beds like us?
Probably not.
With someone who farts all night?
I've got to live with it, and I survive.

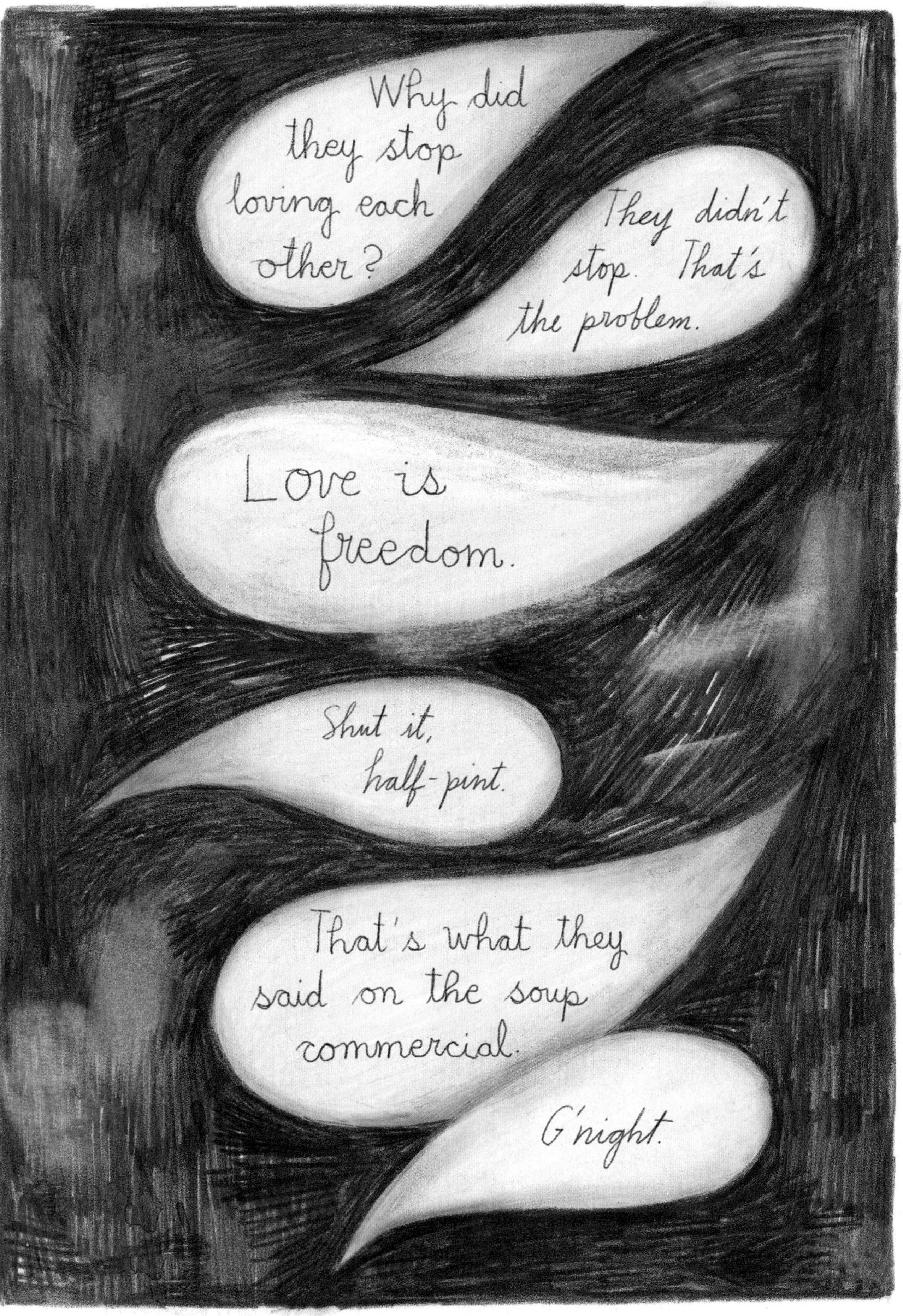
Why did they stop loving each other?
They didn't stop. That's the problem.
Love is freedom.
Shut it, half-pint.
That's what they said on the soup commercial.
G'night.

SLEEP, ALMOST.

FIRST DAY OF SCHOOL

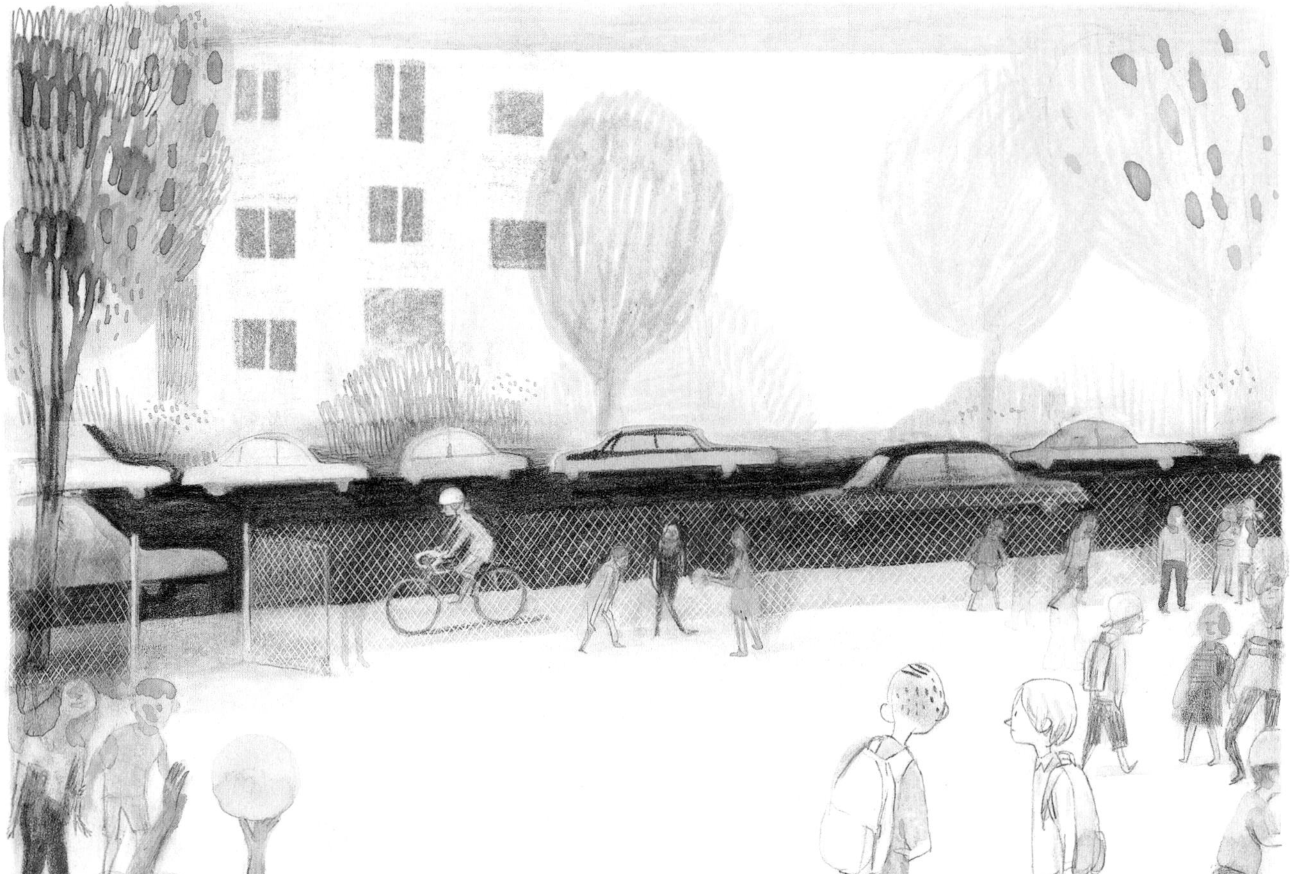

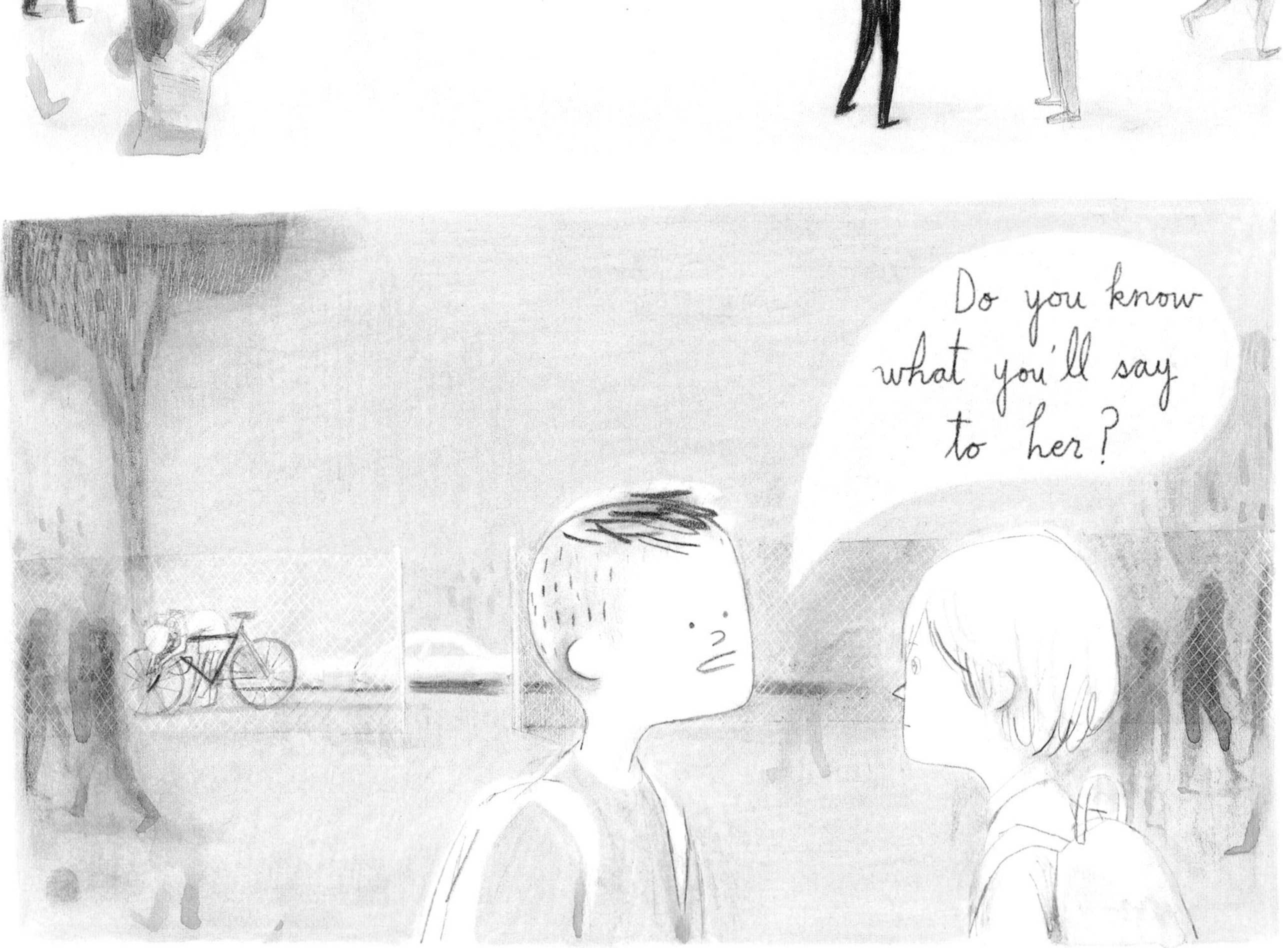
Do you know what you'll say to her?

I'll tell her how long
I've been waiting. My whole life
and more. My past lives, too, when I was
a shining knight and a caveman. I'll say she's
like a gorgeous cactus. I'll say I may look like a
zero on the manliness scale, but that I learned this
summer that bravery has not much to do with
manliness and lots to do with danger and that absolutely
nothing — other than war and the hockey finals maybe —
is as dangerous as standing in front of a gorgeous
cactus to declare your love. I'll tell her that putting
myself in danger's way with her is more awesome than
anything, and that if I start crying I hope she'll
understand that they're tears of bravery, and that I bet
if those tears, with my dad's and my brother's and the
tears of the undercover cops after an amazing takedown,
were collected together in a jar, they'd spill over the
side and flow onto the ground between the cracks
in the concrete, through channels and underground,
and the next day a flower would sprout, nothing
particularly spectacular or exotic, just a small
dandelion, no big deal, but something real,
and I'd offer it to her and I'd say,
"This is the flower of bravery,
it's for you, I love you."

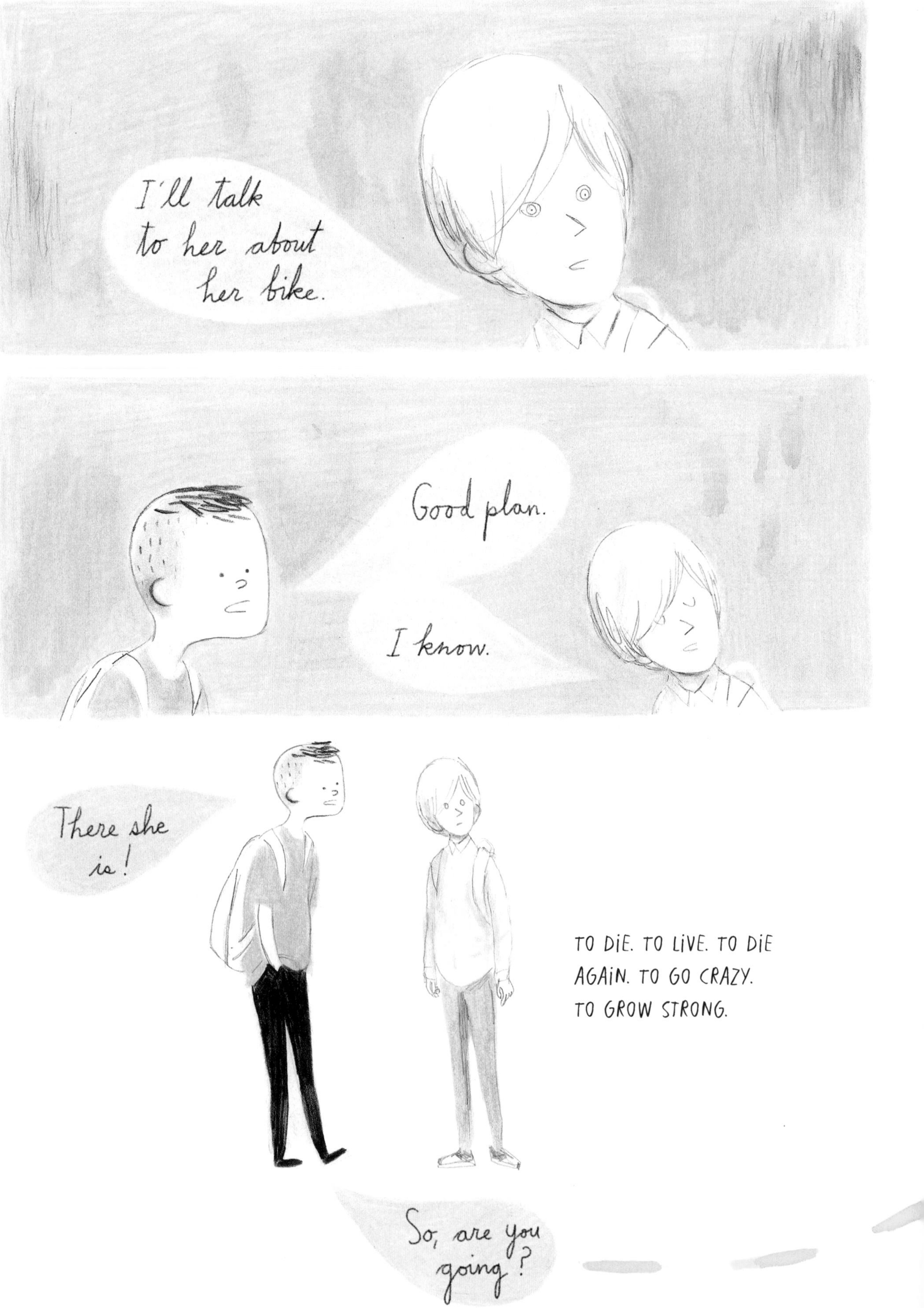
I'll talk to her about her bike.
Good plan.
I know.
There she is!
TO DIE. TO LIVE. TO DIE AGAIN. TO GO CRAZY. TO GROW STRONG.
So, are you going?

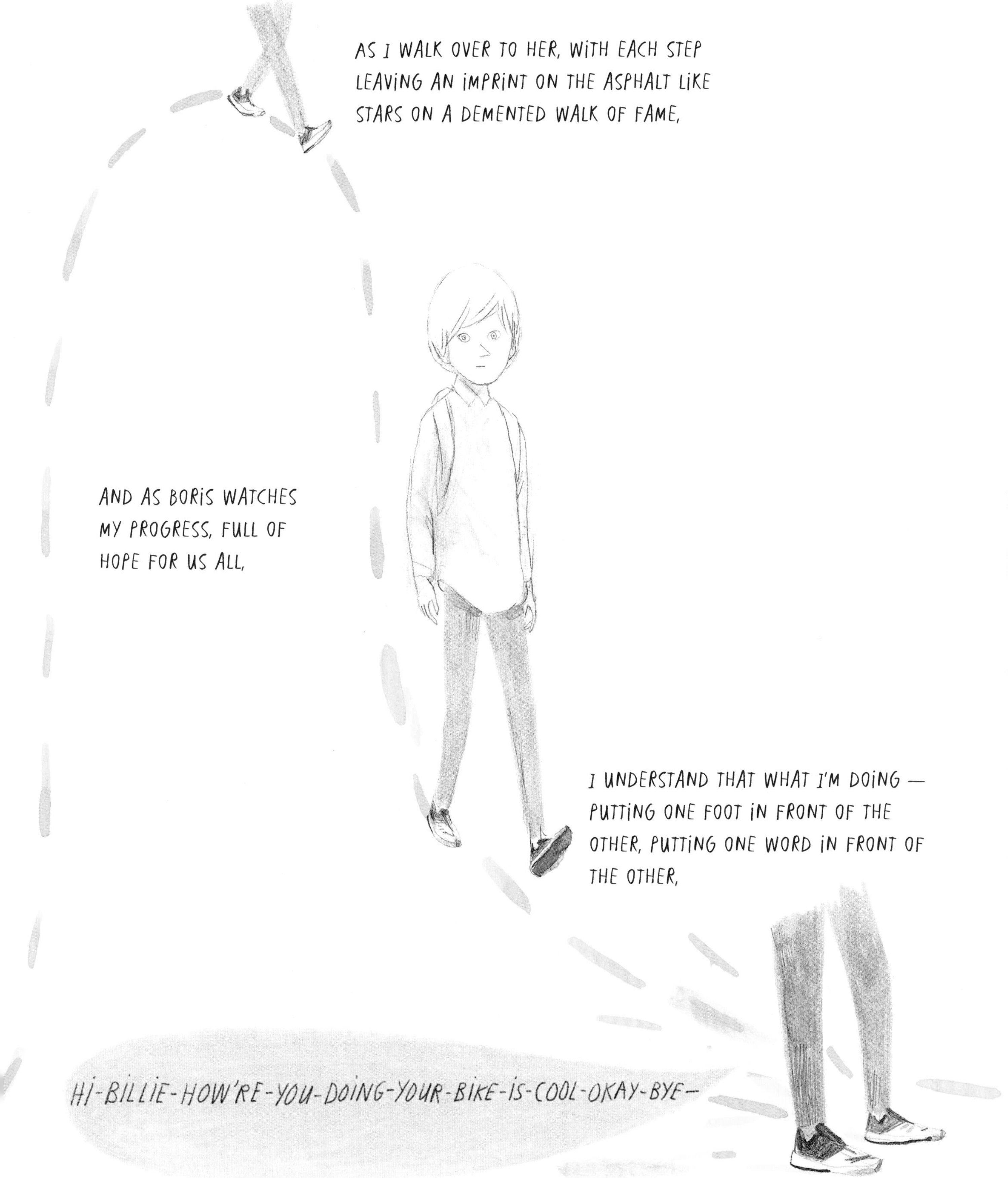
AS I WALK OVER TO HER, WITH EACH STEP LEAVING AN IMPRINT ON THE ASPHALT LIKE STARS ON A DEMENTED WALK OF FAME,
AND AS BORIS WATCHES MY PROGRESS, FULL OF HOPE FOR US ALL,
I UNDERSTAND THAT WHAT I'M DOING — PUTTING ONE FOOT IN FRONT OF THE OTHER, PUTTING ONE WORD IN FRONT OF THE OTHER,
HI-BILLIE-HOW'RE-YOU-DOING-YOUR-BIKE-IS-COOL-OKAY-BYE—

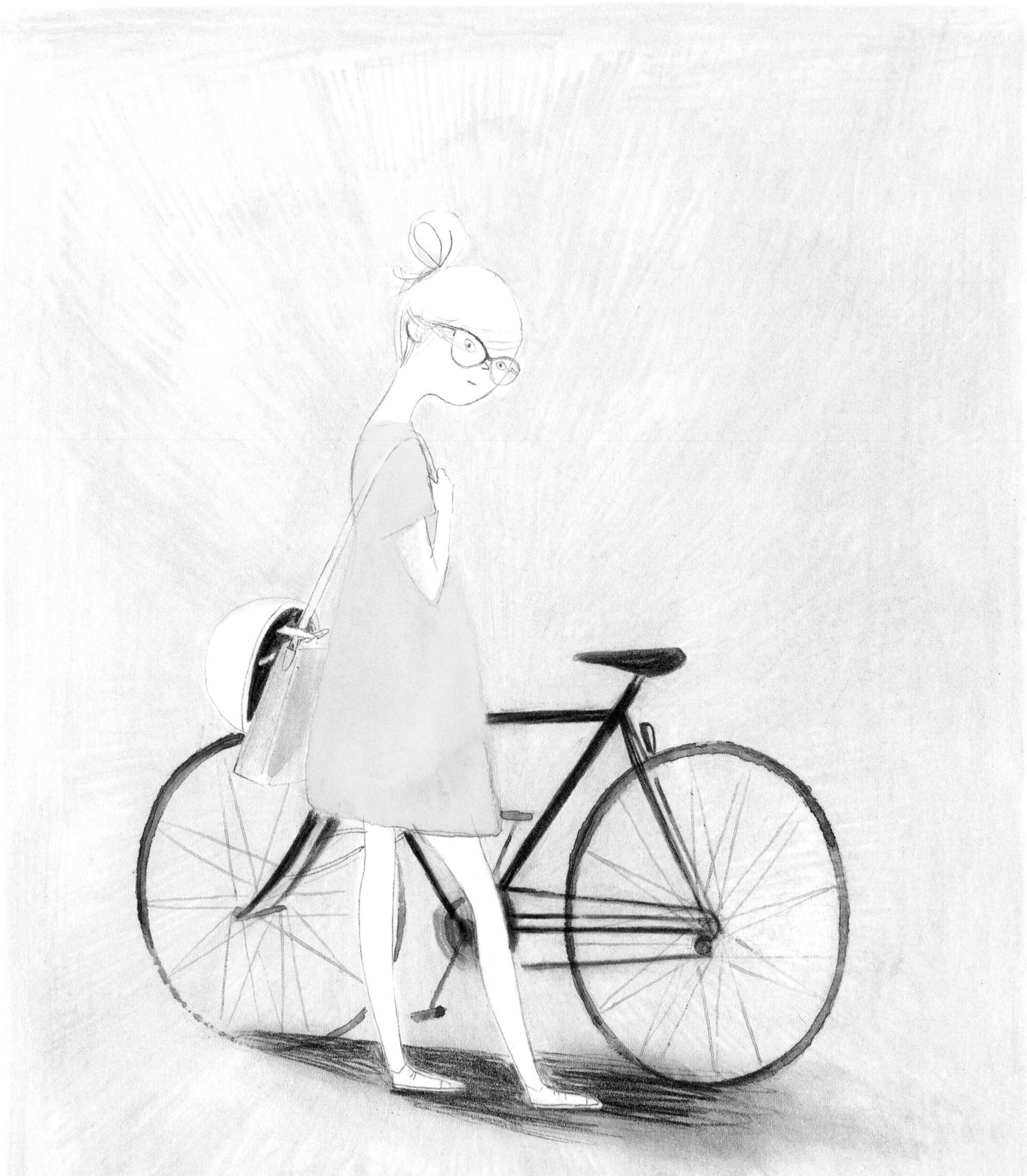
IS NOTHING SHORT OF A MIRACLE.

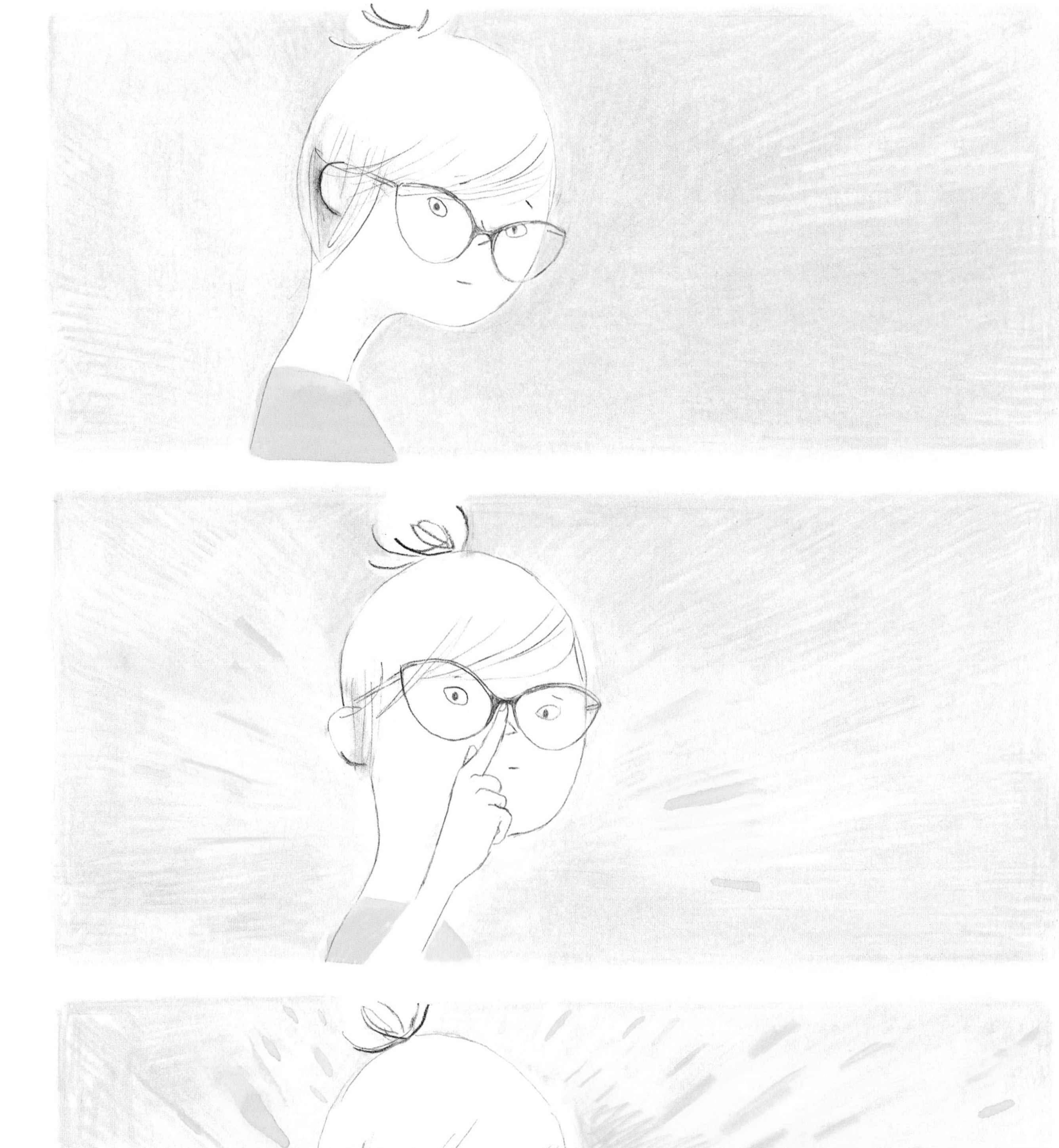

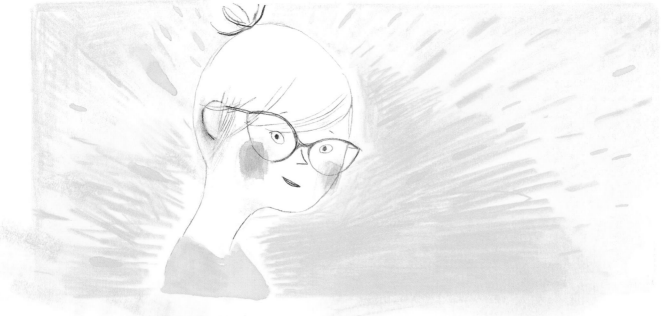

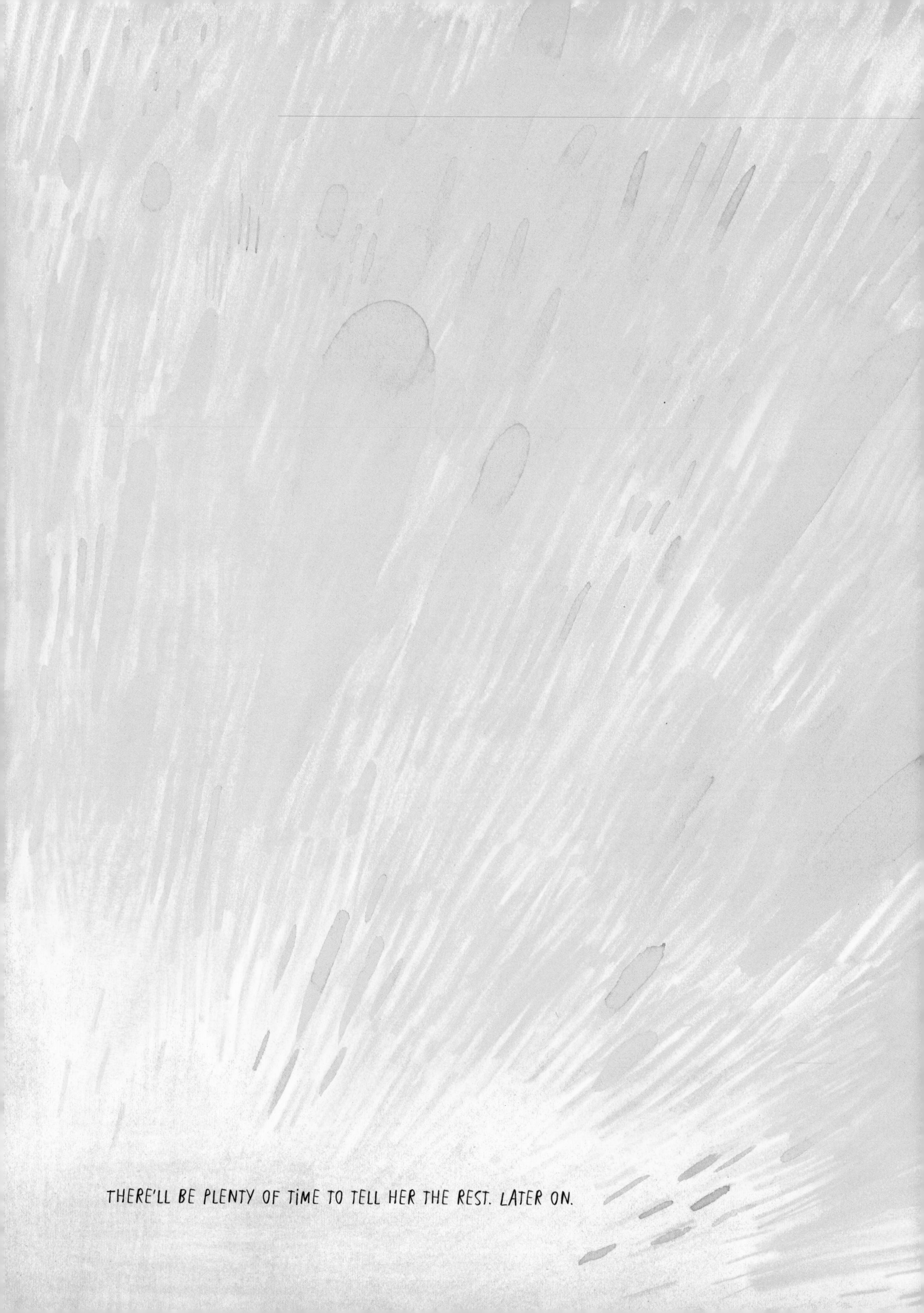
THERE'LL BE PLENTY OF TIME TO TELL HER THE REST. LATER ON.